Pr

The L

"It's as sweet as it sounds—a lite [illegible] s us that there's value in the 'failures' in life—missed connections, broken relationships, unattained college degrees. They may, inadvertently, set us on the right path. Same for small daily interactions like a conversation on public transport. . . . If you're looking for a little hope, or a reminder of how chance encounters can change life for the better, this is the ticket."

—*USA Today*

"A heartfelt story about chance, loss, and aging, populated by messy characters you will root for in this delightful ride."

—*Montecito Journal*

"Freya Sampson's writing is like a feel-good magical potion made of everything that's beautiful in life: a hug, a cup of tea, a warm blanket, a puppy. *The Lost Ticket* is the perfect sophomore novel: the descriptions of London are whimsical and immersive; the characters are relatable and lovable; the story is uplifting and romantic, full of emotions and heart, celebrating the importance of making human connections and embracing our dreams. This book is my happy place! Whatever Freya writes next, I'm on board."

—Ali Hazelwood, #1 *New York Times* bestselling author of *Bride*

"It's hard to think of another book quite as delightful as this one. *The Lost Ticket* is basically the best hug in the world in book form. It's a story about love and second chances and the best kind of unlikely friendships. Pick up this book if you're yearning for some joy in your life!"

—Jesse Q. Sutanto, national bestselling author of *The Good, the Bad, and the Aunties*

"*The Lost Ticket* is one of the loveliest novels I've read. Gorgeously written, it's brimming over with hope, inspiration, and endearing humor. I completely adored this wonderful, warm hug of a book."

—India Holton, national bestselling author of *The Secret Service of Tea and Treason*

"Freya Sampson's *The Lost Ticket* is an unputdownable masterpiece of heart, hope, and humanity. I cheered, swooned, and gasped with each turn of the plot, staying up well past my bedtime because I needed to know what would happen next. Sampson's lovable cast of characters will steal your heart, lift your spirit, and make you wish you were a passenger on the 88 bus. Do yourself a favor and buy this book; you won't regret coming along for the ride."

—Sarah Grunder Ruiz, author of *Last Call at the Local*

"A gorgeous story that's equal parts heartbreaking and heartwarming. A reminder that love is unwavering and ageless and will always carry us through. Freya Sampson is a brilliant writer."

—Lia Louis, author of *Better Left Unsent*

"In these chaotic times, this is a much-needed story about kindness, the importance of friendship, and the wonder of hope. *The Lost Ticket* is a delight, a beautiful example of how the ripples from one chance encounter can change many lives for the better. I loved it. Everyone should read this book!"

—Jenny Bayliss, author of *A December to Remember*

"Sampson's true gift is bringing to life an improvised family of three-dimensional characters with real struggles and real humanity. In a way, *The Lost Ticket* is the ultimate literary British Invasion, uniting the Beatles' 'With a Little Help from My Friends' with the Rolling Stones' 'You Can't Always Get What You Want.'"

—*BookPage*

"Sampson has done a masterful job of misdirection, offering tidbits of information that seem to lead one way but then are shown to have been leading somewhere else altogether. This is an engaging read that touches on aging and the physical incapacities it brings, lost and misplaced love, the power of accepting people as they truly are, finding the reliance to build a life on one's own, and the family that can be forged in friendships. A warming story of love and happiness found despite hardships, difficulties, and the passage of time."

—*Kirkus Reviews*

Praise for
The Last Chance Library

"A wonderfully warm and uplifting story of kindness, community, and love that made me laugh, cry, and cheer."

—Clare Pooley, *New York Times* bestselling author of *Iona Iverson's Rules for Commuting*

"*The Last Chance Library* is a heart-squeezing and charming story about grief, love, and the power of community. An absolute delight."

—Colleen Oakley, *USA Today* bestselling author of *The Mostly True Story of Tanner & Louise*

"Both spellbinding and tender, *The Last Chance Library* is a gorgeous love letter to books, a celebration of the characters that make a community, and an inspiring call to muster our courage and fight for the things that matter. Simply put, this book is sublime."

—Libby Hubscher, author of *Play for Me*

"A sweet testament to the power of reading, community, and the library."

—*Booklist*

"*The Last Chance Library* is absolutely irresistible! Curl up and indulge in Freya Sampson's charming novel about a shy librarian in a small town with a great cause. You'll have such a good time, and you'll love the unexpected twist at the end!"

—Nancy Thayer, *New York Times* bestselling author of *All the Days of Summer*

"Sampson has created a gem of a book populated by vivid personalities and a story that weaves together heroes and villains, love and loss, mourning and growth, as it follows June and the Chalcot community as they seek to save their library—which offers so much more than books. A delightful exploration of personal growth, inner strength, and the importance of family, friends, and love."

—*Kirkus Reviews* (starred review)

"Fans of libraries and heartfelt, humorous women's fiction with a powerful message and a hint of romance won't want to miss this one! It's so good that readers may very well devour it in one sitting."

—*Library Journal* (starred review)

"With *The Last Chance Library*, British author Freya Sampson delivers a refreshingly feel-good first novel about the sustaining power of books and how libraries unite communities and forge lasting relationships that improve lives. . . . *The Last Chance Library* unravels with great wit and tenderness. Sampson assembles clever, funny scenes where June transforms from a wallflower into a take-charge, crafty young woman who is forced to handle difficult people and navigate situations that enlarge her ingenuity. Readers will eagerly invest in the cause to save the library and be greatly amused by plot twists that play out with pleasant surprises and heart-tugging twists."

—Shelf Awareness

TITLES BY FREYA SAMPSON

The Last Chance Library
The Lost Ticket
Nosy Neighbors

Nosy Neighbors

FREYA SAMPSON

BERKLEY
NEW YORK

BERKLEY
An imprint of Penguin Random House LLC
penguinrandomhouse.com

Library of Congress Cataloging-in-Publication Data

Names: Sampson, Freya, author.
Title: Nosy neighbors / Freya Sampson.
Description: New York : Berkley, 2024.
Identifiers: LCCN 2023031118 (print) | LCCN 2023031119 (ebook) |
ISBN 9780593550526 (trade paperback) |
ISBN 9780593550519 (hardcover) | ISBN 9780593550533 (ebook)
Subjects: LCGFT: Novels.
Classification: LCC PR6119.A475 N67 2024 (print) | LCC PR6119.A475 (ebook) |
DDC 823/.92—dc23/eng/20230714
LC record available at https://lccn.loc.gov/2023031118
LC ebook record available at https://lccn.loc.gov/2023031119

First Edition: April 2024

Printed in the United States of America
1st Printing

For Bethany, my favorite person

Nosy Neighbors

One

DOROTHY

Years later, when the residents of Shelley House looked back on the extraordinary events of that long, turbulent summer, they would disagree on how it all began. Tomasz in flat five said it started the day the letters arrived: six innocuous-looking brown envelopes that fell through the communal letterbox one Wednesday morning in May. Omar in flat three claimed the problems came a few weeks later when an ambulance pulled up in front of the building, its siren wailing, and the body was loaded into the back. And Gloria from flat six said her astrologer had told her way back in January there would be drama and destruction in her near future (and, more importantly, that she'd be engaged by Christmas).

But for Dorothy Darling, flat two, there was never any question of when the trouble began. She could pinpoint the exact moment when everything changed: the single flap of a butterfly's wing that would eventually lead to the tornado that engulfed them all.

It was the day the girl with pink hair arrived at Shelley House.

That morning had started out like any other. Dorothy was woken at six thirty by thumping from the flat overhead. She lay in bed for several minutes, her eyes squeezed shut as she chased the last shadows of her dream. When she could put it off no longer, she rose, her knees clicking obstinately as she moved through to the bathroom to perform her morning ablutions. In the kitchen, Dorothy lit the stove with a match and did her morning stretches while she waited for an egg to boil and her pot of English breakfast tea to steep. Once they were ready, she carried a tray through to the drawing room, where she consumed breakfast sitting at a card table in the bay window. So far, so normal.

As she ate, Dorothy observed her neighbors depart the building. There was the tall, ferocious man from flat five, accompanied by his equally ferocious, pavement-fouling dog. Next came the pretty-if-only-she'd-stop-scowling teenager from flat three, staring at her phone and pointedly ignoring her father, who followed her carrying a battered briefcase under one arm and an overflowing box of recycling under the other. As he emptied the contents into the communal bins, a tin can missed the deposit and rolled onto the pavement. The man hurried off after his daughter, oblivious. Dorothy reached for the diary and pencil she kept near at all times.

7:48 a.m. O.S. (3) Erroneous rubbish disposal.

Once the morning rush hour had passed, Dorothy washed up her crockery, dressed, brushed her long silver hair, and put on her string of pearls. She was back at the window by eight fifty, just in time to see the redheaded woman from flat six departing hand-in-hand with her current paramour, a tall, bovine man in a cheap leather jacket. After that there was a lull and Dorothy changed the beds and dusted the picture frames and objets on the mantelpiece, accompanied by Wagner's *Götterdämmerung* to block out the din from the flat above.

And then, a little after ten, she was brewing her second pot of tea when she heard a tremendous bang from outside. Dorothy abandoned the kettle and rushed to the front window, where she watched an old, ramshackle blue car pull up in front of the building, its rear wheel mounting the curb. A great cloud of black smoke burped from the exhaust pipe as the engine puttered out, and a moment later the door opened and the driver emerged. It was a young person who looked to be somewhere in their twenties, although at first glance, Dorothy was unsure if it was a man or a woman. They had short, unkempt hair dyed a lurid neon pink and were dressed in a pair of dungarees of the sort one might expect a laborer on a building site to wear. The youth did not seem to have any kind of coat or knitwear, despite it being unseasonably cool for early May, and Dorothy could see tattoos snaking up their arms like graffiti. The person reached into the back seat of the car and heaved out a large, well-worn backpack, then kicked the door shut, causing the vehicle to shake precariously. It was only when they turned to face Shelley House that Dorothy realized she was looking at a young woman.

The girl's face gave nothing away as she surveyed the building, but Dorothy could imagine her taking it in with a mixture of apprehension and awe. After all, one did not come across dwellings like Shelley House every day. Built during the reign of Queen Victoria and named after the English Romantic poet, its broad façade was a mixture of precise red brickwork and embossed white masonry, topped by an ornate balustrade. Wide stone steps led up to the imposing front door, over which the words SHELLEY HOUSE, 1891 were engraved in Gothic script. Impressive bay windows framed the door on the first two floors, while the highest floor—once the servants' quarters before the building was converted into flats—had smaller, rectangular dormer windows. Dorothy could still remember the first time she had seen the building herself; how she had stopped in the middle of the pavement and stared, mouth agape, marveling at its grandeur and history. It was the most beautiful house she had ever seen, and Dorothy had pledged there and then that it would become her home. Thirty-four years later, it still was.

The pink-haired girl continued regarding the building, and as her eyes swept along the ground floor they seemed to pause for a moment on Dorothy's window. Dorothy instinctively drew back, even though she knew nobody could see her through the net curtain. Still, she found her heart beating a little faster as she watched the young woman climb the steps and disappear from view at the front door. Who was she coming to visit in the middle of the working day? Perhaps the uncouth new tenant in flat four? Dorothy waited to hear the sound of a distant bell ringing and was therefore utterly confounded when she heard the unfamiliar chime of her own. Good gracious, it was for her! Should she answer it? It had been a long time since Dorothy had had a caller, and the girl hardly looked trustworthy. Perhaps she was one of those scoundrels who preyed on vulnerable elderly people, tricking her way into their homes, robbing them, and then leaving them for dead? Of course, Dorothy was neither vulnerable nor stupid enough to fall for such a trick, but this young rapscallion was not to know that. Should she fetch a knife from the kitchen drawer, just in case?

The bell sounded again, jolting Dorothy. She reached for her pencil—the nib was sharp enough to be used as a weapon, if circumstances required—and moved to her front door. Some years earlier, a previous landlord had installed an overly elaborate entry system whereby when someone rang her bell, a video appeared on a little screen by her door, showing Dorothy who was there and even allowing her to speak to them before she "buzzed" them in. Dorothy had been horrified by it, even when the engineer insisted that the video was one-way and the person outside could not see her. Now she lowered her face so that her nose was almost touching the screen. It showed a grainy black-and-white image of the woman, who was chewing a fingernail as she waited for an answer. What could she possibly want?

The bell sounded a third time, a longer, more persistent ring. Dorothy cleared her throat before she pressed the button labeled INTERCOM.

"Who are you and what do you want from me?" She had to shout to be heard above the third act of *Götterdämmerung*, which was still playing in the background.

"I've come about the room."

Dorothy frowned. "You must be mistaken. There is no room here, I assure you."

She heard an audible sigh through the intercom. "Has it gone already? You could have let me know; I've driven all the way here especially."

Dorothy bristled at the girl's impertinent tone. "Then you can go back whence you came. And take that menace of a car with you."

Even on the tiny monitor, Dorothy could see a flash of anger in the girl's face.

"It is parked illegally," Dorothy clarified.

The visitor did not even look back at the vehicle. "No, it's not."

"Yes, it is. Your rear wheel is mounted on the curb, in contravention of Rule 244 of the Highway Code. So unless you move it, I may be forced to telephone the council."

The girl let out a sound somewhere between a laugh and a snort. "Wow, you sound like a right barrel of laughs. Maybe I dodged a bullet after all."

Dorothy had no idea what bullet the girl was referring to, but before she could say something suitably caustic she saw the youth turn and start down the steps, without so much as a thank-you or good-bye.

Dorothy stepped back from the door in triumph. She had no doubt that the girl had intended to ring for flat one, whose ghastly tenant made a habit of illegally subletting his second room. Dorothy had reported him to the building's landlord on three separate occasions, but so far there appeared to have been no obvious sanctions. Still, she took some satisfaction in having thwarted this particular attempt. Standards in Shelley House might have been slipping for years, but she could quite do without that disrespectful young hoodlum living across the hallway.

Dorothy glanced toward her diary on the table. She should write this interaction up now, while it was still fresh in her mind.

10:17 a.m. Impertinent pink-haired caller mistakenly enquiring about room. Educated her on Highway Code and sent her away.

But that could wait. More pressing at this moment was the abandoned pot of tea in need of resuscitation. Dorothy returned to the kitchen, accompanied by the soaring notes of Wagner's Brunhilda riding to her death in the flames.

Two

KAT

Kat opened the boot of the car and chucked her bag in, slamming the lid shut. What a waste of time that had been. She'd even texted last night to make sure the room was still available and had been reassured it was. Now she'd lost a whole morning driving here when she could have been searching for a room and job elsewhere. Kat had been wary about coming back to Chalcot in the first place; perhaps this was a sign she shouldn't be here after all these years? She yanked the driver's door open with force, grimacing as it gave a wail of protest.

"Sorry, Marge," she muttered, patting the frame. The last thing she needed was the car giving up on her today as well.

Kat climbed into the driver's seat as gently as possible, but as she was about to close the door, she heard someone shout her name. She glanced back at the building to see a white-haired man standing in the open doorway, waving in her direction.

"Hello? Are you Kat?"

She nodded but stayed where she was.

"Don't tell me you've made up your mind already?" The man gave her a crooked smile.

Was this some kind of a joke? Kat began to close the door again.

"I know it doesn't look like much from out here, but the room is lovely," he called. "You should come and take a look before you write it off completely."

He was still smiling at her hopefully. Kat opened the door and spoke slowly and loudly in case he had trouble understanding.

"Your wife told me the room has gone already."

The man frowned. "My wife?"

"Yes. She said there was no room."

He paused for a moment and Kat felt a tug of sympathy. The poor thing really was confused if he couldn't even remember his own wife. Then he grinned, his eyes crinkling.

"Oh dear, I think you may have rung the wrong buzzer! Don't worry, you're not the first."

Now it was Kat's turn to frown. "So is the room available?"

"It most certainly is. Come on in and I'll show it to you."

He stood back from the front door, holding it open for her, but Kat remained in the car. Did she really want to stay here? She could still remember the building vividly from her childhood. Whenever she'd been sent to live with her grandfather, Kat used to walk past Shelley House to get from his farm on the outskirts of the village to Chalcot Primary School. Back then, the other kids used to say that the creepy, crumbling old house was home to a wicked witch who locked children in the attic, and so Kat used to speed up whenever she passed in case the witch tried to kidnap her too.

She scanned her eyes over it now. Kat was no longer scared of child-eating witches, but there was still something eerie about Shelley House. The brickwork was faded and crumbling, the window frames warped and peeling, like something from a horror movie. Bits of the stone balustrade were missing from the roof, and the whole structure seemed to tilt ominously to one side. If this was what it looked like on the outside, God knows what state it must be inside. No wonder the rent on the room was so cheap; Kat couldn't imagine anyone willingly choosing to live here.

The man was still standing in the doorway, watching her. Above his head she could see the building name engraved into the stone. Since she'd last been here someone had vandalized it so that rather than reading SHELLEY HOUSE it now said HELL HOUSE. Kat couldn't help smiling at this, and the man grinned back at her.

"Come on, then! I've just put the kettle on."

What the heck? She'd come all this way; she might as well take a look at the place that had scared her so much as a kid. She climbed out of Marge, taking care to close the door softly.

When she reached the top of the steps, the man held out his hand. "Joseph Chambers. Pleased to meet you."

"Kat Bennett," she said, keeping her own hands in her pockets.

She followed him inside, the door slamming heavily behind them. There was no natural light in here, and it took a moment for Kat's eyes to adjust to the gloom. When they did, she saw that she was in an unremarkable entrance hall. Black-and-white checkered floor tiles hinted at the building's grander past, but now the space seemed to largely be a dumping ground for unwanted possessions. There were piles of unopened post on a shelf, and from somewhere farther up the building Kat heard the sound of drum and bass music, but there were no other signs of life. Two unmarked doors led off either side of the hall and Kat looked between them.

"I'm in number one, over here," Joseph said, pointing toward the left-hand door. "Flat two belongs to Dorothy Darling. I believe you may have had the pleasure of chatting to her already."

Kat had nothing polite to say about the old woman who'd shouted at her on the intercom, so she kept her mouth shut. Joseph chuckled.

"As I suspected. Don't worry, Dorothy's an eccentric but her bark is worse than her bite. Speaking of which . . ." He moved toward the left-hand door. As he reached it there was an explosion of yaps on the far side. "You're not allergic to dogs, are you?"

"No."

"Good." He pushed the door open and immediately a small brown-and-white Jack Russell came charging out of the flat, circling Joseph before skidding to a halt at Kat's feet. Its barks reached a new crescendo as it jumped up against her leg.

"Meet Reggie," Joseph shouted above the noise. "He'll calm down in a moment. He just gets excited when he meets new people."

Kat bent down and offered Reggie her hand. He sniffed it eagerly, his nose wet against her skin. Kat ran a hand over his head and as she did she had a flashback of another dog, his fur short and wiry like this one's, and the comforting smell of cigar smoke that always accompanied him. Reggie stopped barking as Kat scratched between his ears.

"He likes you!" Joseph clapped his hands together with glee. "Well, that's an excellent omen. He wasn't at all keen on my last lodger. Used to pee behind his wardrobe but I don't think we'll have that problem with you. Come on, Reggie, let's give Kat the grand tour."

At the sound of his name the dog trotted back into the flat. Kat swallowed as she moved toward the door, preparing herself for what was to come, but as she stepped inside her breath caught. The room she found herself in was huge, its ceiling vaulting high above their heads and a polished wood floor underfoot. The walls were in need of a repaint and there was a slightly musty smell, but light poured in through the large bay window and the biggest fireplace Kat had ever seen took up much of the far wall. Never in a million years had she imagined the inside would be so striking. Kat felt like she'd walked onto the set of a period costume drama, only the furniture was from IKEA and there was a flat-screen TV in the corner.

"Quite something, isn't it?" Joseph said.

"It's incredible."

"It used to be the home of a rich Victorian industrialist. In fact, the whole road was once made up of mansions like this, all named after famous English poets: Byron, Wordsworth, Keats, et cetera, hence the name Poet's Road. Half of the mansions got bombed during the Second World War and the rest got pulled down after and replaced with smaller, more practical houses. Somehow Shelley House survived, although it was converted into flats back in the sixties."

Kat didn't say anything as she took it all in. Her grandfather had lived in this village his whole life, which meant he must have known Poet's Road back when it was still all mansions like this. In fact, perhaps he'd even visited Shelley House? The thought made Kat's chest ache.

"If you think it's impressive now, you should have seen the place when I first moved in thirty-three years ago," Joseph continued. "It was one of the grandest buildings in the area back then and immaculately maintained. But I'm afraid various landlords have rather neglected it over the years, hence the state it's in now." He indicated a patch of damp on the wall next to them, the paint flaking off it. "Anyway, that's enough of the history lesson. Let me show you around."

Joseph set off toward the two doors at the far side of the room, Reggie scampering and sliding across the floor behind him.

"The kitchen is in here," Joseph said, pushing open the farthest door.

Kat wondered if it was going to be like something off *Downton Abbey* too, but when she peered in she saw that it was small and disappointingly ordinary.

"I think this would have once been a scullery," Joseph said. "Not palatial but it does the trick. You can make yourself at home in here, there's all the usual pots and pans. And there's an evening meal included as part of your rent."

"Oh, I don't need cooking for," Kat said quickly. That hadn't been mentioned in the advert and she had no desire to have an awkward meal with her landlord every day. She had learned at an early age it was best never to get too close to the people you lived with. Kat would never forget the seemingly sweet old lady they'd rented a room from when she was six or seven, who used to give her biscuits when she got back from school and chat with her about her day. Then one afternoon, Kat had come home to find social services waiting for her, asking all sorts of difficult questions. She and her mum had fled that night, her mum cursing Kat for "blabbing her mouth off" to their landlord. She had never made the same mistake again.

"I'll leave the food in the fridge so you can reheat it whenever suits you," Joseph said, as if reading her mind. "To be honest, you'd be doing me a favor. I've not got used to cooking for one yet, you see. It's been three years now but still . . ."

He trailed off and for a horrible moment Kat thought he was about to cry, but he blinked and looked up at her, smiling again. "It's part of the reason I have lodgers. Well, that and to help me cover the rent now I'm retired. Shall we carry on the tour?"

He showed her through the second door, which led into a small hallway. The bathroom was modest and decorated in avocado green, its wallpaper peeling off in places, but it looked clean enough. The door next to it was closed—Joseph's bedroom, she assumed—but the last one was open.

"It's not very big, but I think it's cozy," Joseph said, pausing on the threshold. "It used to be our daughter's bedroom."

The room was indeed small, but Kat liked it immediately. There was a single bed and a wardrobe, and an old-fashioned rocking chair next to a small bookcase stuffed with well-worn paperbacks. Kat glanced over the shelves: *Pride and Prejudice* . . . *Bleak House* . . . *Moby Dick* . . . all old books that she'd never read and never would. She turned back to the door and was relieved to see a lock on the inside. Joseph seemed harmless enough but you could never be too careful. Above the bed was a window and Kat walked over to see the view. She was expecting a garden or at least some greenery, but found she was looking out onto a concrete car park behind a block of modern flats.

"We used to have a communal garden, but that got sold off by an old landlord years ago," Joseph said.

Kat turned back to survey the room. It really was small, but that wasn't a problem. All her worldly possessions fit into the old rucksack in her car boot, so she hardly needed a walk-in wardrobe. And Joseph seemed nice enough—a bit chatty, maybe, but he'd soon realize she wasn't the talkative type and leave her alone. The bigger question was whether she wanted to come back to Chalcot in the first place. After all, there was a very good reason Kat had stayed away for fifteen years, and nothing about that had changed. So what if she'd found herself thinking of the village and her grandfather more and more over the past few months, the memories itching like a mosquito bite that wouldn't heal. It didn't mean she had to risk coming back here, so surely the sensible thing would be to drive far away and never return.

"So, what do you think?" Joseph was watching her. "Would you like the room?"

Kat took a deep breath. Now that she was here, she might as well stay for a few weeks. But thanks to Marge outside, she could always make a quick getaway if she needed to.

"Okay, thank you." She paused as a thought occurred to her. "Don't you want to know anything about me or get a reference?"

"Why would I want a reference?"

"Well, I dunno, I could be a psychopathic ax murderer for all you know."

Joseph let out a loud guffaw. "Oh, you don't strike me as the ax-murdering type. No, if anything I'd say you were more of the poisoning sort."

Kat couldn't help laughing at this; the guy was bonkers. But if he didn't want a reference, that suited her fine. The less he—or anyone else around here—knew about her, the better.

"Come on, then," Joseph said, moving toward the door. "You get your stuff in and I'll make us a coffee."

Three

DOROTHY

Every day, shortly after her midmorning pot of tea, Dorothy pulled on her housecoat, retrieved her handbag from the table by the front door, and conducted her inspection of Shelley House.

Over the years, she had learned that eleven o'clock was the optimal time for this pursuit as it was when the majority of her neighbors were out of the building. It was not that Dorothy wanted to hide her activities; she had nothing to be ashamed of, after all. It was simply that she hoped to minimize any unnecessary interactions with or disruption from her fellow residents.

She began, as always, in the lobby. When Dorothy had first moved into Shelley House, the lobby had been one of the building's pièces de résistance. Its walls had been decorated in a rich burgundy hue, a glass chandelier hung from the ceiling, and the tiled floor sparkled so brightly one could have eaten one's breakfast off it. These days it was quite another matter. Dorothy traversed the dark, fetid space, her lips pursed in disapproval. Alongside the usual abandoned detritus—a bag of women's shoes and a defunct vacuum cleaner—she noted the recent addition of a bicycle, propped up under a sign that read DO NOT LEAVE PERSONAL ITEMS IN COMMUNAL SPACES. Dorothy had put the sign up herself some years ago, but it had made not a jot of difference. She gave the bike a nudge with her foot. Really, it was quite a safety hazard so close to the stairs. What if someone needed to leave urgently and fell over the bike on their way down? She pulled her diary from her bag and scribbled a note.

> *11:17 a.m. Write to Alexander Properties regarding unauthorized dumping in lobby. Draw attention to ~~eight~~ nine previous missives on same subject.*

Dorothy sped up her inspection as she passed the doorway of flat one, occupied by Joseph Chambers, his rat of a dog, and, despite Dorothy's best efforts, the pink-haired girl. Dorothy had kept a particularly close eye on the young woman's comings and goings over the past twelve days, but so far all she'd managed to ascertain was that she insisted on dressing like a vagrant and did not appear to have any friends or family. This was hardly a surprise; Joseph collected waifs and strays the way other people collected Royal Doulton figurines.

Having completed her circuit of the lobby, Dorothy began to climb to the first floor, feeling every one of her seventy-seven years as her knees complained with every step. Until recently, this ascent had been quite the olfactory adventure. The Siddiq family—comprising Omar; his wife, Fatima; and his daughter, Ayesha—had been tenants in flat three for seven years. One of the family (Dorothy now deduced it was Mrs. Siddiq) was clearly quite the chef, and the most ambrosial fragrances had greeted Dorothy on her daily inspection. Then, about six months ago, she had seen Mrs. Siddiq leave Shelley House one afternoon leaning on her husband's arm, and the smells had abruptly stopped. A few weeks later, Dorothy had watched as a hearse pulled up in front of the building followed by a dark limousine, and Omar and Ayesha had climbed silently into the back of the car. To Dorothy's alarm she had felt tears well up in her eyes as the vehicles departed, and it had taken an extra pot of tea and three

Garibaldi biscuits before she had felt herself again. Since then, the first floor of Shelley House had smelled only of mildew and, more recently, the heavy, unmistakable scent of marijuana that drifted out from under the door of number four.

Dorothy stopped outside this flat now, pulled a tin of air freshener from her bag, and sprayed it liberally around the landing. From inside she could hear the heavy pulse of the god-awful music the man insisted on playing 24/7, but Dorothy knew there was no point knocking and asking him to turn it down. For the newest tenant of Shelley House was intransigent, pugnacious, and downright rude, ignoring all of Dorothy's admonishments to be more considerate of his neighbors. He had only been a resident for a few weeks and the two of them had already had multiple run-ins. Still, the one silver lining was that tenants as bad as him rarely lasted long; the landlord was bound to evict him soon.

Having thoroughly doused the area in Glade vanilla blossom, Dorothy moved upward toward the top floor. As she climbed, she stopped on each stair to check that the threadbare carpet had not come loose overnight, proving a trip hazard. Darling family legend had it that her great-great-aunt Phyllida had caught her foot on the corner of a Persian Bidjar rug and fallen to her death; thus Dorothy knew all too well the importance of strict carpet maintenance. It therefore took her several minutes to inspect each of the twenty stairs and the carpet on the final landing, which also gave her time to listen to the rather heated conversation that was emitting from flat six.

Now, Dorothy prided herself on not being nosy. That being said, as the tenant who had inhabited the building for the longest, she felt it her duty to keep an eye on the other residents to ensure their safety while dwelling in Shelley House. This was particularly pertinent in relation to Gloria Brown, occupier of flat six. Gloria had moved into the building some ten years previously with her then boyfriend, a stocky Jamaican chap with sparkling eyes. Unfortunately he had lasted less than a year, and in his wake had come a procession of miscreants, degenerates, and thugs. For if there was one skill Gloria Brown possessed—aside from looking striking in spandex—it was her terrible taste in men. The latest candidate, the slack-jawed oaf in leather, had been on the scene for seven months, and up until now the pair had seemed to be in the honeymoon phase of the relationship. However, as sure as day turns to night, Dorothy knew that the giggling and unnecessary displays of public affection would soon turn to rancor and enmity. And from the sounds coming from flat six now, it seemed that moment might be nigh.

"You're fucking crazy!"

The man's voice came bellowing from within the flat, and Dorothy winced at the profanity. So unnecessary.

"I thought you were different, but you're just like the rest of them . . . paranoid and jealous."

"Paranoid?"

This was Gloria's squeal. Really, it was hardly eavesdropping if they spoke at this volume while Dorothy was outside, was it? She moved to the fire escape door, pushing on the handle to check that it was securely shut. Dorothy had written to Mr. F. Alexander every single week since he took ownership of the building a year ago demanding that this access to the roof be sealed up once and for all. She had done the same with all previous landlords and yet nothing had ever been done. She scribbled a note.

"How is this paranoia, Barry?" Gloria's voice had reached mezzo-soprano pitch. "Tell me, what is paranoid about finding another woman's knickers in your pocket?"

"I told you, I've got no idea how they got there; must have been one of the lads having a laugh."

Dorothy snorted. That old chestnut? The man clearly had no imagination.

"It's not just the knickers. Where were you last night? You didn't get home 'til after four."

So that was who was responsible for the front door banging at four fourteen a.m., waking Dorothy. She wrote another note.

"I've had enough of this, Gloria. I don't need this shit!"

There was a loud shattering noise inside the flat, and Dorothy froze. Should she intervene? She had done so once before, several years ago, when she had been disturbed late at night by the sound of Gloria screaming. Wearing her nightdress and armed with a kitchen knife, Dorothy had marched up the stairs and threatened to call the police unless Gloria came to the door. The woman had eventually appeared and bluntly assured Dorothy she was safe. But what if it was more serious this time? What if Gloria had been hurt? There was an ominous silence from within the flat and Dorothy pressed her ear against the door, listening for any sounds of a struggle. Perhaps she should call the police now and report a—

The door swung open, catching Dorothy off-guard. She felt herself tilting forward and reached out a hand to stop from falling. It met with a thick, beefy chest.

"What the hell are you doing?"

Dorothy righted herself, feeling her cheeks flush crimson. "I was just—"

"Were you spying on us again?" Spittle sprayed from the man's mouth, hitting Dorothy in the face.

"Of course not! How dare you insinuate such a thing."

"Then why were you leaning on the door?"

His voice was low and menacing, and it occurred to Dorothy that she herself might be in peril. "I . . . I was checking that everyone had locked their doors securely. There has been a recent spate of burglaries in the area."

"What's going on, Barry?"

Gloria had appeared behind the man. Dorothy noted that she looked unharmed, although she had bags under her eyes and her hair was in need of a good brush. Her face darkened when she saw Dorothy.

"The nosy old bag from downstairs has been snooping around again," the man said.

"I was not snooping! Gloria, I wanted to check that you—"

But the woman turned away before Dorothy could finish the sentence, retreating into her flat without a word.

"Piss off and leave us alone," the man growled, and he slammed the door in Dorothy's face.

She hastened down the stairs and only when she reached the lobby did she pause to catch her breath, trying to ignore the painful sting of humiliation. This was why Dorothy avoided interactions with her neighbors, because they were a bunch of ungrateful, mean-spirited fools. Here she was, trying to look out for their safety and well-being, and all she got was insults and slanderous accusations. She reached into her handbag and retrieved her diary and pencil.

11:32 a.m. Domestic fracas in flat six. Tried to offer assistance to G.B., verbally assaulted and threatened by male inhabitant in leather jacket.

For a brief moment, Dorothy considered heading straight back to her flat for a restorative pot of tea, but no. She straightened her shoulders and thrust her diary back into her bag. There was one final task that needed to be tackled. A task Dorothy had completed every single day for the past three decades. A task she would not allow Gloria Brown and her ignoramus brute of a boyfriend to deter her from.

The post shelf.

Every morning, any correspondence that came through the letterbox of Shelley House got unceremoniously dumped on a shelf next to Dorothy's front door and largely ignored. This meant the pile of letters, flyers, and free newspapers grew constantly, like a family of licentious rabbits left unchallenged. Many years ago, Dorothy had taken it upon herself to keep the post shelf in order, and it was a job she took extremely seriously. Now she began to sift through the overflowing mountain, placing genuine post into one (small) pile and everything else onto a second (much larger) rubbish pile. There were two—no, three bills for Omar in flat three, which Dorothy knew he would collect later and hide in his briefcase before his daughter got home from school. There was also a parcel for Tomasz Wojcik in flat five from a company called Hair for Him and another parcel for Gloria Brown from Ann Summers. (Dorothy had once made the mistake of looking the quaint-sounding company up on a computer at the library and almost fainted in shock.) As usual there was no post for Dorothy herself nor for the ruffian in flat four, who had yet to receive any correspondence.

Dorothy was about to return to her flat when she heard the clatter of the letterbox. When she turned she saw a handful of brown envelopes fluttering toward the doormat. The postman must have forgotten to deliver them earlier. With a tut, she crossed the lobby and bent to retrieve them, ignoring the involuntary groan that escaped her mouth as she did. There were six envelopes in total, each one addressed to the occupier of a different flat, but there was no stamp or franking mark, which suggested they must have been delivered by hand. How peculiar.

Dorothy placed five of the envelopes on the post shelf and returned to her flat, clutching the sixth. She kept a paper knife in her table drawer, and she did not stop to sit as she sliced open the envelope and pulled out the two sheets of folded paper inside. The second one appeared to be some sort of form, so she turned her attention to the first, a typed letter.

Dorothy read the words once, then a second time, which was easier said than done when her hands were trembling. Once she had finished, her eyes flicked toward the mantelpiece, and she hastily moved through to the kitchen and located a box of matches. She lit one—it took several attempts, due to the aforementioned trembling—then held the letter away from her body and touched the match to its side. As the flame caught, she released the pages and watched as they fell into the sink. It took less than ten seconds for the letter to be consumed, the words curling and glowing until they were no more. Then Dorothy lit the stove, reached for her teapot, and vowed never to think of the letter again.

Four

KAT

There weren't many things in life that scared Kat Bennett but as she approached Chalcot High Street, her stomach was a tight knot. What if she ran into her grandfather and all hell broke loose? Or what if someone else recognized her and reported back to him? Kat might be twenty-five now and using a different name, but there was always a chance someone might see a resemblance to that scrawny, scrappy ten-year-old who had brought so much trouble. And so she held her breath as she passed the Golden Dragon takeaway and turned right onto the high street, adrenaline coursing through her veins and her feet ready to turn and sprint at any moment.

Kat had thought of this village many times over the past fifteen years, picking at the painful memories like a scab, but now that she was here, everything felt different from how she'd remembered it. Colorful bunting and baskets of flowers still hung from the shop fronts, and she recognized the old library and the Plough, the pub where her grandfather used to drink. But the majority of the shops had changed, and everything felt somehow smaller and more ordinary than in her childhood memories. The faces on the high street were unfamiliar, and no one so much as cast her a second glance as she walked down the road. All these years Kat had feared returning, as if an angry mob might carry her off to the police station the second she crossed over the bridge, yet in reality she was as anonymous here as she had been in any of the dozens of towns she'd lived.

Now that she'd overcome her fear of being recognized, Kat's next priority was to find a job. She might only be staying for a short time, but she still needed to earn money. And so she spent the next few days driving Marge around the area, trying to find work. At first it seemed like she wasn't going to have any luck; most places were fully staffed, and the few that were advertising took one look at her, with her pink hair and tattoos, and sent her away. But just as she was about to give up and leave town, Kat happened to walk past Remi's, a greasy spoon café tucked behind Winton High Street, and saw an advert taped in the window for a pot wash. The owner, a large, bearded man, grunted a few questions and offered Kat the job on the spot. It was messy, tiring work, on her feet all day with her arms deep in dirty dishwater, but it was cash in hand and she wouldn't be doing it for long.

And so it was that by her second week in Chalcot, Kat's life had settled into a quiet if dull routine. She worked ten hours a day and returned to Shelley House as the sun was starting to set. Joseph was usually out of the flat by the time she got back. In fact, Kat had hardly seen her flatmate since she'd moved in. They occasionally crossed paths in the morning before Joseph left for his daily jog with Reggie—the first time Kat had seen the seventy-five-year-old limbering up in his tiny running shorts and sweatband, she'd had to suppress a laugh—but the man seemed to sense that Kat preferred to be left alone. In fact, the main contact she had with him was through the plates of food he left for her in the fridge, always with a handwritten note on top instructing her on how best to reheat the meal. Kat had never had anyone prepare her homemade meals from scratch before—her mum's idea of cooking had been a loaf of bread and a jar of peanut butter, and sometimes not even that—and so for the first couple of days Kat had left the food untouched. But eventually a plate of delicious-looking chicken pie had gotten the better of her, and since then she'd been enjoying a home-cooked dinner every evening.

On Friday, Kat trudged up Poet's Road, her whole body aching with fatigue. She'd now worked seven shifts in a row and all she wanted was to sleep. As she climbed the steep, chipped stairs toward the front door of Shelley House, she saw a flicker of movement in the window to her right. She turned to look but all she could see were the thick net curtains. Still, she knew that Dorothy Darling was behind them now, spying on her. Kat still hadn't seen her in person, and their only interaction had been the tense exchange on the intercom the day Kat moved in, but she could often sense she was being watched as she came in and out of Shelley House. Perhaps Dorothy really was the wicked witch all Kat's classmates told tales about back at school, and right now she was plotting to pounce on Kat and lock her in the attic? Kat smiled to herself as she unlocked the front door and crossed toward flat one. Just a few steps more and she could reheat her dinner and then collapse into bed. But, as she opened the door, she was confronted by the sight of not only Joseph but four strangers, who were all staring at her with undisguised suspicion.

"Ah, Kat, perfect timing," Joseph said, rising from his chair. "We're just about to start."

Oh no, what had she walked into? Kat scanned the strange, mismatched group in front of her. Had she stumbled into an AA meeting or some kind of weird sex cult? Reggie came scrabbling over to greet her, his short tail wagging with enthusiasm, and she bent down to pat him so she could avoid eye contact with the humans in the room.

"I'm sorry I didn't get a chance to warn you, but it's been very last minute," Joseph said. "We've had a bit of bad news this week, so I called an emergency residents' meeting."

Ah, so these must be the neighbors. Kat hadn't come across anyone else who lived in the building yet, although she sometimes heard the muffled sounds of their lives: a toilet flushing overhead, music playing, or a distant argument.

"Let me introduce you to everyone," Joseph said as Kat straightened up. She opened her mouth to say she had to go and eat, but Joseph plowed on. "First off, this is Gloria Brown from flat six."

He nodded at a petite woman who looked like she was in her late thirties or early forties. She had copper-red hair and was dressed in skintight gold leggings with an immaculate face of makeup. She was tapping away on her phone with long acrylic nails and mumbled a half-hearted "Hi" in Kat's direction.

"And this is Omar and Ayesha from the flat above us," Joseph said, pointing to the pair on the sofa opposite him. Kat guessed they were father and daughter, although they were sitting as far away from each other as the couch would allow. Omar wore an expression of absolute exhaustion, while Ayesha had the look of a teenager who would rather be anywhere else but here. Kat didn't blame her.

"Nice to meet you," Omar said, giving a small nod of greeting.

"And lastly, this is Tomasz from number five."

The man Joseph was referring to was sitting in an armchair, although he was so huge it looked like it could barely support him. He must be almost seven feet tall with muscular arms the size of hams, and his head was closely shaved.

"When is this going to start?" he said in a thick Eastern European accent, not even bothering to acknowledge Kat. "I don't have all night. Princess needs her walk."

As the man spoke, Reggie let out a low growl and the hairs on the back of his neck stood on end.

"I was waiting to see if anyone else was joining us," Joseph said, and Kat noted a firmness in the man's voice she'd not heard before. Clearly he was as much a fan of Tomasz as Reggie was. "Kat, why don't you pull up a chair? This affects you too, after all."

"Actually, I'm really hungry, so I'm just going to grab some food."

"Oh, that's a shame."

Kat could hear the disappointment in Joseph's voice, but she hurried toward the kitchen. A residents' meeting was her idea of absolute hell. Besides, it wasn't like Kat was officially a resident since she was only subletting from Joseph for a few weeks, so whatever was going on had nothing to do with her. On the stove she found a saucepan with a Post-it note on top, the words *Reheat me slowly for 10 minutes* and a smiley face scribbled on it. Kat lifted the lid and was hit by the appetizing smell of lemongrass and garlic.

"Okay, well, I think we should probably go ahead and start without the other two," Kat heard Joseph say from the living room, followed by what sounded like a snort.

"As if Duchess Darling would grace us with her presence." This must be Gloria, her words thick with sarcasm. "She'd rather the building burned down than have to sit in a room with us."

"That's not fair," Joseph said gently. "Dorothy has lived here longer than any of us, so I imagine this must be deeply distressing for her too."

"Come off it, Joe. You know as well as I do she'll be celebrating the fact that you and I are being evicted."

Evicted. Kat's heart sank. She'd lost count of the number of times she'd heard that word, but it was one she'd understood and feared before she even knew her ABCs. And two weeks must be a new record, even for her. Kat took a deep breath. *You're not being evicted. This is Joseph's problem, not yours. You'll find somewhere new; you always do.*

"What about the new guy in flat four, is he not coming?" she heard Gloria ask.

"I tried knocking on his door and leaving him a note, but I've not heard anything," Joseph said.

"No surprise, that man is a nightmare." This was Omar. "Loud music all hours, rowdy parties, drug-taking. The only good thing to come out of this whole mess will be not having to live opposite him anymore."

"But even without him and Dorothy, there are still five of us here," Joseph said. "I'm sure between us we can find a way to stop this eviction nonsense happening."

"How are we meant to do that?" This was the unmistakably deep voice of Tomasz. "We are only tenants, so the landlord can do what he likes. This Section 21 form means we have to go."

There was another phrase Kat had heard more times than she cared to remember. Tomasz was right; a Section 21 "no fault" eviction notice meant they could all be thrown out even if they hadn't done anything wrong. These guys were screwed.

"So I've been doing some research since the letters came on Wednesday, and it's not necessarily as bad as we think," Joseph said. "I've looked into it and legally we can stay in our homes after our tenancy ends on the fifteenth of July. If we do, then Alexander Properties will have to go to the courts and get a possession order from a judge before we can be evicted. And we can attend the court hearing ourselves and make a defense as to why the eviction should be overturned."

"So a judge might decide we can stay?" Gloria said, and Kat heard a flicker of hope in the woman's voice.

"Absolutely. If we refuse to budge and make a strong enough case, the court could rule in our favor."

"But that's great news," Omar said.

Kat shook her head. They were seriously deluded if they thought that would work. Should she go in and tell them there was no way they could stop this eviction? But that would mean breaking her number one rule about not engaging with her neighbors. No, she should keep out of this; it wasn't her problem, after all. From the living room Kat could hear an excited bubble of chatter with Joseph's voice at the center of it. She looked down at the Post-it note with the smiley face drawn on it and sighed.

"You can try and fight this in the court but you'll never win."

Five pairs of eyes swung to look at Kat as she stepped into the living room.

"How the hell do you know?" Gloria said.

"Because a judge will only overturn a Section 21 if the landlord has made a mistake on the form, which I assume yours hasn't. If you go to court, the judge will still grant a possession order and you'll have to pay for the costs of the court action *and* pay for your own evictions. It'll cost you all a fortune."

"Are you sure about this, Kat?" Joseph said. "How do you know?"

Kat didn't reply. She wasn't going to explain to anyone about the countless times she and her mum had bailiffs turn up at the door to evict them, or how it felt to watch her few precious belongings being thrown out onto the street or growing up under the constant threat of being homeless.

"I'm sure of it" was all she said, and she turned and retreated into the kitchen.

For a few moments there was silence from the living room.

"We're doomed," Omar said, and all the positivity of a moment ago had disappeared from his voice.

"Not necessarily, Dad." This must be Ayesha. "I still reckon it's worth trying to fight this."

"But you heard Kat, love. Besides, Fergus Alexander is a pillar of the local community: he owns half the properties round here and he's even a governor at the school, for goodness' sake. The council will never side with us over him."

"Ayesha's right, we should at least try," Joseph said. "Even if we can't fight it through the courts, there are other ways we can protest. What about if we try to draw lots of public attention to our cause, maybe even get coverage in the local press? If Fergus values his reputation, perhaps we can use public pressure to get him to back down?"

"That will not work," Tomasz said, gruffly. "Landlords like him don't give a shit about public opinion, only money."

"But I can't afford another place in Chalcot," Omar said, and Kat could hear the anxiety behind his words. "We were okay when we had Fatima's salary too, but now it's just me. This place is expensive enough, but have you seen other rental prices round here?"

"I've told you, Dad, I'll get a job."

"No, Ayesha." Omar's tone was sharp. "We've talked about this before and there's no way I'm letting you get distracted from schoolwork."

"But I'm almost sixteen, so—"

"I said no!"

The teenager didn't reply, and the living room fell quiet again. Kat's food had started to bubble, and she fetched a plate from the cupboard, lifting it down carefully so it didn't make a noise and remind them all she was here.

"I went down to the council offices yesterday," Gloria said eventually. "Apparently there's a two-year waiting list for their properties. Two years!"

"You're not moving in with that boyfriend of yours?" Tomasz didn't so much say the word "boyfriend" as spit it.

"It's none of your business where I live," Gloria snapped back. "At least when we leave I won't have to put up with that stinking dog of yours."

"Princess does not stink."

"Now, come on, guys, let's stay calm," Joseph said. "We're all on the same side here."

"Princess does stink, though," Ayesha said. "I can smell her on the staircase to our flat. It's gross."

"She is not gross!" Tomasz's voice had risen. "She has bacterial problems sometimes but it is not her fault. Anyway, if you have problem with dogs, then Joseph's yappy one is worse than mine."

"Now, you leave Reggie out of this," Joseph said. "He's absolutely fine except when he's being terrorized by Princess."

Kat shook her head. What a bunch. This was yet another reason why she always steered clear of neighbors, because sooner or later it ended up in fights over some stupid thing or other. Just look at the five of them; they clearly couldn't stand one another.

"We're all getting a little distracted here," Omar said. "I thought this meeting was about the eviction letters, not people's dogs?"

"You're right, Omar," Joseph said. "Look, I don't know about the rest of you, but I want to save my home, to save all our homes. Who's going to join me in fighting this?"

There was a long silence before Kat heard the sound of chair legs scraping on the floor.

"I am not wasting my time," Tomasz said. "This is what it is, we have to accept it and move on. Now, excuse me, I have to get back to my *stinking* dog."

His heavy footsteps banged across the floor and then the door slammed shut.

"What about you, Omar? Ayesha?"

"I want to fight it, Joseph, but what can we really do?" Omar said. "Fergus Alexander has all the power and we have none."

"Mum would have wanted us to fight this," Ayesha said quietly.

"Your mother would have wanted me to do what was best for our family," Omar said, and Kat heard a wobble in his voice. "And right now that is making sure we have a roof over our heads and you focus on your exams. Now, come on, I have to cook and you need to revise."

Kat heard them walking out too, Ayesha mumbling a good-bye as she left.

"Well, it looks like it's just us, then, Gloria," Joseph said.

The woman gave a small cough. "Look, I'd love to help but I've got a lot on my plate right now. They're laying people off at work and my mum's not been well, and then there's Barry . . . I need to focus on what I'm gonna do next. I'm sorry, Joe."

"It's okay, I understand. But promise me you'll think carefully before you make any big decisions? You know my feelings on this: you deserve to be with someone who treats you well."

"I will, I promise."

Kat heard the click of Gloria's high heels across the wooden floor and the flat door closing. A moment later there was a long sigh and Joseph appeared in the kitchen doorway, his head low.

"Ah, Kat. Dinner all right?"

"Delicious, thanks."

"I assume you heard all of that?" he asked, nodding toward the living room. "I had hoped that at least one of them would want to help me, but it seems they've all given up already."

Kat fiddled with her fork, trying to hide her discomfort. She should leave the kitchen now before she said the wrong thing and made everything worse, but Joseph was blocking her exit. She waited for him to speak again, but he was deep in thought.

"It sounds like they all have their own stuff going on," Kat said eventually.

"Of course. It would just have been much easier to have an ally in the fight. I'm not very good on my own, you see; I work much better with other people around me. You know how it is."

"Not really, I'm afraid."

Joseph looked at her quizzically, and she shrugged.

"I've always believed you're better off on your own. Other people just let you down in the end."

"I'm sorry you feel that way," Joseph said gently.

"It's probably for the best, anyway. If they'd all supported you, then you might have spent the next two months battling your landlord and you'd still end up being chucked out. Now you can focus your energy on finding a new home."

Joseph's brow furrowed. "Kat Bennett, if you think my neighbors are going to stop me from fighting this eviction, then you have underestimated me. I may have preferred doing this as part of a team, but I'm not going to let one little hiccup put me off."

"Seriously?"

"Seriously. We have eight weeks until we're being thrown out, but I will fight this and I will win, not only for me but for all of them. Just you wait and see."

It was such a ridiculous statement that Kat had to laugh, and Joseph laughed too.

"You're crazy," she said.

"I am indeed. So Fergus Alexander had better watch out."

Five

DOROTHY

Dorothy had known the residents' meeting would be a disaster from the moment she caught wind of it. She was therefore not the least bit surprised as she watched through her peephole and saw the scowling faces of her neighbors when they left flat one. But really, what had they expected? That they would suddenly be able to work together like a well-oiled machine? That all their petty differences—the anti-social behavior and arguments over dogs and parking—would be forgotten in an instant as they heroically banded together to save their homes? Dorothy let out a derisive sniff. Things like that might happen in books but they did not happen in real life, and certainly not with this feckless lot.

The glacial atmosphere in Shelley House did not improve over the coming days. Omar and Ayesha, whom Dorothy had barely seen communicate since the death of Mrs. Siddiq, had now taken to leaving the house separately every morning. Dorothy noted in her diary that the girl was returning to the building later and later each evening, as if attempting to spend as little time at home as possible, while Omar looked even more harassed than usual as bills piled up for him daily. Things did not seem to be faring any better for Gloria in flat six. She and her bovine beau had now passed from the arguing-behind-closed-doors stage of the relationship to the arguing-in-public phase, and on several occasions Dorothy witnessed stand-up rows between the two of them. On Saturday, their argument became so heated that Dorothy was forced to bang on her window and politely remind them that such shows of aggression were not becoming of the residents of Shelley House, advice that was greeted with an expletive-filled tirade from the gentleman. Dorothy had not laid eyes on him since, and she hoped she never would again.

Then there was the increasingly erratic behavior of Joseph Chambers to contend with. For if Dorothy had thought that the disastrous residents' meeting might put a damper on the old fool's enthusiasm, she was sorely mistaken. On the morning after the aborted meeting, she watched Joseph march out of the building wearing a sandwich board over his body, the words **Save the Residents of Shelley House** daubed on the front and **Stop the Evictions** on the back. He did not return until late afternoon and repeated this bizarre ritual the following morning. Was this an early sign of dementia or some kind of mental health crisis? Dorothy's diary had never been as full as it was this week, as she recorded the fractious and strange behavior of her neighbors.

If all this drama were not enough, there was also the ongoing problem of the neighbor from hell in flat four. On Sunday, he held an all-night party that was so noisy that Dorothy had to bang on the door at three a.m. and threaten to call the police. Not only did that not work but on Monday she walked into her bathroom to find water streaming through a light fixture in the ceiling. She surmised that the nincompoop must have run a bath and forgotten about it, resulting in a flood. Dorothy had left several messages with the office of her landlord, but so far her pleas had remained unanswered. And so it was that on Thursday, exhausted and emotionally spent, Dorothy decided enough was enough. After breakfast and her inspection of Shelley House, she pulled on her coat, head scarf, and Wellington boots and set off to confront Fergus Alexander in person.

The journey in itself was something of an odyssey, involving catching a bus from Chalcot post office all the way to Winton, and on several occasions Dorothy almost turned back, overwhelmed as she was by the traffic and the noise and the proximity of strangers. But eventually she arrived in Winton and made her way toward the offices of Alexander Properties. Her plan was to walk in and refuse to leave until she saw Mr. Alexander himself, at which point she had a twenty-two-point list of problems to address with him. Top of the running order was the dangerous fire escape door leading onto the roof, followed by the tenant in flat four, the water damage to her bathroom, and the detritus in the lobby. Dorothy had considered adding the letter of 15 May to the list but decided against it; the less said about that nonsense, the better.

Her research told her that the Alexander Properties office was at the south end of Winton High Street, and so she marched toward it with her head held high and a look of steely determination in her eye. Nothing was going to prevent Dorothy Darling from achieving what she had set out to do today. Nothing would get in her—

"Save Shelley House! Say no to heartless evictions!"

Dorothy froze. Thirty yards ahead of her stood Joseph Chambers, wearing his absurd sandwich board and with a megaphone held to his lips, his silly little dog at his feet. So this was where the scoundrel came each day, to protest on Fergus Alexander's doorstep. For a brief second Dorothy felt a flutter of admiration at her neighbor's gumption before she pushed it aside in horror. *Nothing* that man did was admirable. Dorothy turned on her heels and began to walk away, cursing Joseph for once again ruining her plans. But she had gotten no more than five paces before she heard her name being called and the sound of footsteps following her.

"Dorothy, great to see you here."

She grimaced at the sound of her name in the man's mouth. She could sense he was near her now and she picked up her pace, but he was not to be perturbed.

"I know you must be as upset about this eviction threat as I am. We should work together; I could really do with your help."

For a moment, Dorothy was tempted to tell Joseph that he was the last person on earth she would ever help, but she stopped herself. Thirty-three years ago, she had made a vow never to utter another word to that man, and she was not going to break it now.

"Please, Dorothy." She could hear the desperation in his voice, and it made her toes curl. "I know we've had our issues over the years, but surely we can put those aside now. This is bigger than you and me; this is about our home, Ch—"

"No!" The word was out of Dorothy's mouth before she realized what she was doing. She spun around, her face contorted with rage. "You do not get to say that name, Joseph Chambers. *Never* say that name. Now leave me alone!"

Dorothy turned and began to stagger away, her vision blinded by the tears that were suddenly filling her eyes. Behind her she heard Joseph call her name again, but soon his voice was lost in the hubbub of the high street.

Six

KAT

Monday was Kat's first day off in a week and she woke after eleven, enjoying the blissful silence of an empty flat. Joseph must have left hours ago; for the past nine days he'd been protesting outside the offices of the building's landlord and Kat had barely seen him. The plates of food were still waiting for her when she got home each evening, though; she'd particularly enjoyed last night's lamb stew with a lemon tart for dessert.

Kat yawned and reached toward the small bookcase next to her bed, pulling out a book at random. *Jane Eyre* it said on the front cover. The book was obviously ancient, and when Kat opened it she saw row upon row of tiny letters. She read the first few sentences, then slammed the book shut and pushed it back onto the shelf. What was she doing? Books like this were meant for smart people, people who'd done A-levels and gone to university, not thickos like her who'd dropped out of school at sixteen. Besides, she didn't have the luxury of lying around in bed reading, even if she'd wanted to. Kat had things to do and top of the list was finding somewhere to live. Joseph might be ignoring the reality of his imminent eviction, but Kat wasn't going to make the same mistake, and she planned to spend a couple of hours at the library today looking online for a new room to rent.

The big question, and the one she'd been pondering ever since finding out about the eviction, was whether she should try to find a place in Chalcot or move somewhere else entirely. The obvious answer was to leave the village. After all, Kat had promised herself she'd only stay for a couple of weeks, and she'd already been at Joseph's for more than three weeks. Yet for some reason, whenever she thought about leaving, Kat found herself feeling unusually torn. Would it be so bad if she stayed in the area a little longer? So far no one had recognized her or linked her to the events of fifteen years ago, the job at Remi's was decent enough, and Chalcot had always been at its best in summer. Kat had memories of swimming in the river, stealing strawberries from the PYO farm, and of course the village fete, where her grandfather had won the biggest pumpkin competition three years in a row. Her stomach gave a lurch at the memory of his proud smile as he wore the winner's rosette, and she hurriedly jumped out of bed. This was why she had to keep busy, even on her day off. Too much time alone inside her own head was a dangerous thing.

Having dressed and eaten a piece of toast, Kat left Shelley House and headed to Chalcot Library. She hadn't been back there since she was a child, and it felt strange walking under the clock tower and into the old Victorian building she'd once loved so much. As with everything in Chalcot, lots about it had changed—there was now a counter selling coffee and cakes, which Kat was sure hadn't been there before—but she recognized the small Children's Room that her grandfather used to take her to whenever she came to stay. Back then Kat had still been an avid reader, and they would spend hours together browsing books, considering all the options carefully before they made their selection to take back to the farm. Kat felt another pang of painful nostalgia, and she turned away from the Children's Room to find a computer.

Thirty minutes into her search and it soon became apparent there were depressingly few properties available in Chalcot, and what there was were at least double the money she paid to Joseph. Omar had been right at the meeting the other week: rental prices in the village were outrageous. But when Kat started to look a bit farther afield in the surrounding towns, a few things came up, including an advert for a room in a six-bed house-share in Winton and a tenth-floor studio flat in Favering that were just about in Kat's limited budget. She noted the contact details down to call later.

Having exhausted the online options, Kat got up to leave the library. But as she turned toward the door, a newspaper on the nearby rack caught her eye. It was a copy of the local paper, the *Dunningshire Gazette*, and a familiar face was smiling out from the front cover. Kat lifted it up and read the headline **Local Resident Takes Up Protest Against Eviction**. Under it was an interview with Joseph about his one-man crusade to save Shelley House, and Kat felt an unfamiliar glow of affection toward the old man as she read his fighting words. He might be deluded, but there was no denying that Joseph was dedicated to his cause.

Perhaps Kat should cook dinner for *him* tonight? The thought took her by surprise. She'd never even considered cooking for a housemate before, but given all the meals Joseph had prepared for her, perhaps it would be a nice gesture. But what to make? Kat's culinary repertoire was limited to cheap and simple one-pan meals that she could cook in whatever basic facilities she had available to her. But given Joseph's well-appointed kitchen, perhaps Kat could try something a bit more adventurous tonight?

She guessed there must be a cookery book section somewhere in the library, and she set off to investigate. But as she rounded the corner of a tall set of shelves, Kat stopped in her tracks. Ahead of her was a man, his back to Kat as he browsed. He was tall and well-built, although his shoulders stooped slightly with age, and he was wearing navy dungarees and heavy workman boots, with white hair sticking out from under his tweed cap. Kat's pulse started to race and she turned to retreat, but as she did she knocked into a table, sending a pile of books tumbling to the floor. At the noise, the man startled and began to turn toward her.

I never want to see you again . . . If you ever come back to Chalcot, you'll be arrested for what you did . . . You are dead to me.

Kat closed her eyes, bracing herself for the roar of rage when her grandfather saw her, but all she heard was a shuffle of feet on the carpeted floor.

"Are you all right, miss?"

Kat opened her eyes and saw the man staring at her with a look of concern.

"What's going on over here?" A librarian had come bustling over, her voice shrill.

"It's all right, Marjorie, just a few dropped books," the man said.

Kat stared at his face lined with age, trying to find a trace of the man she'd loved so much as a child. But no, his eyes were the wrong color: her grandfather's had been blue and this man's were brown. And now that she looked closer, the chin was the wrong shape, too sharp, and the skin much less ruddy. Kat felt relief flood her body, but there was something else mixed in there too, another emotion she had not been anticipating. Disappointment. And somehow, the pain of that was even more crushing than the alternative.

For a horrible moment, Kat thought she might be about to burst into tears right here in the middle of the library. Then she turned and fled toward the door, ignoring the shouts of the librarian behind her.

Kat was out of breath by the time she got to Poet's Road. She'd been crazy to come back; what the hell had she been thinking? That man today might not have been her grandfather, but every moment she spent here she risked running into him. Besides, it wasn't just her grandfather she had to worry about. He might have been the one to banish her, but many other people had been just as furious at her, and any one of them could recognize Kat now. She had been playing a dangerous game of Russian roulette ever since she'd arrived, and enough was enough. She needed to pack her stuff into Marge, get out of Chalcot this afternoon, and never come back.

Kat let herself into Shelley House and crossed the hallway toward flat one. As she reached the door, she heard the sound of Reggie barking inside. Damn, that must mean Joseph was back already and she wouldn't be able to sneak out without seeing him. She'd have to lie and tell him there'd been a family emergency. Kat felt a twinge of regret at leaving kind old Joseph and then cursed herself for being sentimental; just look what trouble that had almost gotten her into by coming back to Chalcot in the first place. Besides, Joseph would be better off without her: she'd only end up bringing him problems, just like she had with her grandfather.

Kat unlocked the flat door and was immediately confronted by Reggie, jumping up at her leg excitedly.

"Hey, down, boy," she said, but the animal continued bouncing against her and barking. "I don't have time to play now."

Kat pulled the door closed behind her, which was easier said than done while being mobbed by the dog. She tried to push him away as she started to move toward her bedroom but then ground to a halt.

In the middle of the room, a pair of white trainers were poking out from behind the coffee table.

She dropped her bag and sprinted across the room. Reggie raced ahead of her, his barking reaching a crescendo. Kat held her breath, praying this was some kind of joke, but as she rounded the edge of the table her stomach dropped. *Joseph.*

He was lying sprawled on his back, his eyes closed. At first glance he looked like he might be having an afternoon nap, only there was a pool of dark red blood under his head, like a small crimson pillow on the polished oak floor. Kat dropped to her knees and with a shaking hand lifted his right arm and pressed her fingers to his cold wrist.

Reggie had lain down next to Joseph, his head resting on the man's chest as if trying to protect him. Where the hell was the pulse? Kat felt a wave of sickness and she reached for her mobile phone and dialed 999.

Seven

DOROTHY

The first Dorothy knew of the events in flat one was the sound of the siren. Initially, she gave little thought to its distant wail. Her grocery delivery had arrived this afternoon, and she was enjoying a particularly delicious cream eclair while she wrote a sternly worded letter to the council about a loose paving stone outside. And so it was not until the ambulance turned into Poet's Road, and its wail became so deafening that Dorothy could no longer hear *Tristan and Isolde*, that she began to take note.

She watched it approach, but it was only when it pulled to a stop in front of her window that she felt her heart rate start to quicken. It was not here for someone in Shelley House, surely? Dorothy swallowed some eclair, but her throat was dry and she gagged. The siren had stopped but the blue light was still revolving, its fluorescent rays so dazzling that she was forced to close her eyes.

The sticky sensation of hot asphalt under her bare feet.

Dorothy dropped her cake fork and it clattered onto the plate.

The shout of a man as he tried to catch up with her, the feel of his fingers grabbing her arm.

She heard footsteps running and a buzzer sounding somewhere within the building.

The pity in the paramedic's eyes.

Dorothy jumped up from the table so abruptly that her plate tilted and smashed to the floor, splattering crème pâtissière over her slippers. She ignored it as she rushed toward her front door, pressing her eye against the small glass circle. Two uniformed paramedics were standing in the hallway, their backs to her as they talked to someone. Who on earth was it? Perhaps Gloria? This would not be the first time she had ended up in a physical altercation with one of her gentlemen friends. Or maybe the man from flat four, given his obvious rampant drug usage? But when one of the paramedics stepped aside, Dorothy saw the pink-haired girl standing in the lobby, her face the color of milk. Was she ill? She was waving her hands around and then she turned and strode into flat one, the paramedics hot on her heels.

Dorothy felt the air leave her lungs.

Joseph Chambers.

The door to flat one was still open, and from this distance Dorothy could make out the paramedics standing behind a low table, looking down at something on the floor. Dorothy felt herself sway and grabbed hold of the doorframe to steady herself. She must sit down before she collapsed and needed the efforts of a paramedic herself. She shuffled across to the table, bone china crunching under her slippered feet as she dropped into her chair. Had he had a heart attack and dropped dead, right there on the floor? He had always seemed so healthy, bounding off on his ridiculous daily runs, but perhaps he had had a dickey heart all along. Or maybe it had been a stroke; a time-bomb blood clot in the arteries of his brain, so large that it wiped him out in seconds?

Dorothy's throat was parched and she reached for her teacup, her hand shaking as she lifted it to her lips and took a sip. How many times had she dreamed of this moment over the past three decades, fantasizing about the myriad ways in which Joseph might finally get his comeuppance? How many thousands of nights had she lain awake imagining the way she would feel when he was gone from her life for good? In her dreams, she had always been dancing for joy, cracking open the cooking sherry to celebrate, yet now she felt only cold and numb. It must be the shock.

A police car pulled up behind the ambulance and two officers climbed out, one of them tossing an empty burger wrapper toward the bin as he climbed the steps. It missed and landed on the pavement, but Dorothy's diary sat untouched. A few passersby stopped to gawk at the emergency vehicles, no doubt wondering what gruesome events had taken place in Hell House. Dorothy's insides coiled like a cage full of venomous snakes, but she did not rise from the table or take her eyes off the window.

Finally, after what felt like hours but her watch told her was only eighteen minutes, the front door opened again. The paramedics wheeled out a gurney covered with a white sheet, but Dorothy caught a flash of gray hair and a pair of old running trainers sticking out the bottom. For a brief moment she found herself wondering if the body would still feel warm to the touch or if it was already turning cold. She shivered and pulled her cardigan around her shoulders. The paramedics carried the gurney down the steps and loaded it carefully into the back of the ambulance, then the rear doors slammed shut and the vehicle pulled off.

Dorothy did not take her eyes off the ambulance until it disappeared from view. It was only once it had turned the corner out of Poet's Road that she realized she was not the only one watching Joseph Chambers take his final journey from Shelley House. The pink-haired girl was standing on the front step, her arms crossed over her body. Her usual scowl was gone and she looked suddenly very young, little more than a child. She stared down the empty road for a moment longer before turning and walking back into the building, allowing the front door to slam violently behind her.

Eight

KAT

It was gone five by the time the police left and Kat was finally alone. The adrenaline had long since left her body and she slumped on the sofa, completely shattered. The past few hours had been a blur, but as Kat sat back and closed her eyes, unwanted images jumped into her mind. The moment the paramedic had bent over Joseph to take his pulse, the whole room had gone silent while they waited for an answer. The wave of relief Kat had felt when the man had found a pulse, followed by the dismay when she saw the look he shared with his partner as they inspected the wound on Joseph's head. The speed with which the pair had worked to get Joseph on oxygen and onto the gurney, barely speaking as they wheeled him from the room.

Head injury . . . they had told her. *Loss of blood . . . Critical condition . . .*

And then Joseph was gone, whisked away to intensive care. Reggie had been so distraught at his master's sudden disappearance that he'd tried to bite one of the police officers and Kat had had to shut him in the kitchen while she gave her report. The officers had inspected the room, checking for signs of a break-in, and Kat had seen them photographing the blood on the edge of the coffee table and the floor, as well as the curled edge of the rug.

"It looks like he must have tripped and fallen," one of the officers had said. "Happens a lot with people his age."

Kat had bristled at the way the officer said "his age"—Joseph was hardly your typical pensioner—and she wanted to say something but Reggie was going wild in the kitchen and she knew she had to deal with him before he did himself harm. By the time she'd placated the animal with some food, the officers were packing up to leave.

"Do you know who his next of kin is?" one of them had asked, and Kat realized she knew nothing about Joseph's family except a lost wife and a daughter he'd only mentioned once.

The officer had grunted. "We'll try and trace the daughter, but in the meantime I'll put your name down," and before she could argue, they'd turned to leave.

Kat felt something move on the sofa. Reggie was sitting at the far end, looking at her with a baleful expression. He let out a pathetic little whimper.

"He'll be home soon; I'm sure of it. Joseph's a tough old guy."

The dog carried on staring and Kat felt the accusation in his eyes. Did he think it was her fault? Kat could hardly blame him; after all, she brought nothing but bad luck to anyone she allowed herself to grow fond of.

"I'm sorry, Reggie," she mumbled, but the dog just put his head on his paws, clearly unimpressed by her apology.

Kat leaned against the back of the sofa and exhaled. She felt terrible for poor Joseph, but she couldn't help feeling sorry for herself too. She'd wanted to leave Chalcot tonight, but now she had Reggie to contend with. Kat had never so much as looked after a houseplant before, let alone a pet. And what if the cops couldn't trace Joseph's daughter or she refused to take the animal? Did that mean Kat was going to be responsible for Reggie? She could hardly take him with her wherever she went next; no one would rent her a room if she had a dog in tow. No, it was impossible: she'd have to find someone else to look after him first thing tomorrow and leave straight after.

Kat reached out a tentative hand and ruffled Reggie's ears. "What am I going to do now, hey?"

As if in answer to the question, her stomach let out a loud rumble. Kat pulled herself up from the sofa and walked into the kitchen. There was no saucepan of food or friendly note waiting for her tonight, and she felt another lurch of concern for Joseph. Opening the fridge she saw a neat pile of ingredients—he'd been planning on making shepherd's pie by the looks of things—but Kat reached past them for a box of eggs. As she was cracking one into a mug, she heard the sound of the door buzzer. Who on earth was calling now? For a moment she was tempted to ignore it, but what if the police had already found Joseph's daughter and she was here to collect Reggie? Kat hurried through to the living room and checked the screen on the intercom. Sadly it wasn't a woman standing outside but a tall man with messy hair and a rucksack slung over his shoulder. Maybe Joseph had a grandson? She pressed the button.

"Hi, it's Will."

"Who?"

"Will Fletcher from the *Dunningshire Gazette*. I interviewed Joseph the other day and he's expecting me again tonight."

Shit. Not a relative coming for Reggie, then, but a journalist: much, much worse.

"He's not here."

"Do you know when he'll be back?"

Possibly never, Kat thought as she remembered Joseph's gaunt face as he lay unconscious on the floor. She shuddered. "I don't know."

"Any chance I can come in and wait? Only it's just started raining."

"Sorry, Joseph won't be back tonight."

"Damn. He texted me earlier to ask me to come round, but I must have missed him."

"Okay, bye." Kat was about to release the intercom button but stopped. "Hang on, what time did he text you?"

"About two o'clock."

"And what exactly did the message say?"

"Look, can I come in? I'm getting soaked out here."

Kat hesitated. She always worked under the assumption that any unknown male was a potential threat and to be treated with extreme caution. But this guy claimed to know Joseph, and he could have information about what had happened today. Kat pressed the release button and a moment later heard the sound of the heavy front door being pulled open. Reggie had come to stand at her feet, his ears pricked.

"You be my guard dog, okay?" she said to the animal as she opened the flat door.

The journalist, Will, was standing in the lobby, brushing the rain off his dark curly hair. He was tall and lean, dressed in jeans, a T-shirt, and a pair of battered old trainers. Kat saw what looked like a dragon tattoo curling up the inside of his right arm. He must have seen her looking at it as he smiled, showing suspiciously white teeth. Kat knew exactly his type—university-educated white men who were used to a bit of charm getting them whatever they wanted—and she didn't smile back.

"Thanks. I was drowning out there."

He took a step toward the flat, but Kat pulled the door back so that only her face was visible through the gap. Will seemed to get the message, as he stopped where he was.

"So what did Joseph's text say?"

Will pulled out his phone. "Not much. Just 'Are you free later?

Have found out something that may be relevant to my fight. Am home for the rest of the day.' And there was an emoji of a detective, so I replied with a thumbs-up emoji and said I'd be here at five thirty." Will looked up from the screen. "Has he gone out?"

Should Kat tell him what had happened? Will was a journalist, which put him firmly in the same hated category as police, teachers, and social workers. But Joseph seemed to trust him, and Reggie had slipped out the gap in the door and was sitting at Will's feet, his tail wagging. Will bent down and gave the dog a friendly pat.

"Joseph had an accident this afternoon."

He immediately straightened up. "Is he okay?"

"I don't know. I came home and found him unconscious on the floor. He's been taken to hospital; they said something about a serious head injury." As she said the words Kat realized she was shaking, and she wrapped her arms round her body.

"Oh shit. Are you okay?"

"Of course," she said, hoping her voice didn't shake too.

"Do you have any idea what happened to him?"

"The cops think he tripped on a rug and hit his head on a table."

Will raised an eyebrow. "I take it from your tone that you don't agree."

Didn't she? Kat hadn't had time to think about whether she agreed, but something did seem a bit strange. Joseph was incredibly fit for a man of seventy-five, and Kat had seen him bounding around with the agility of a person half his age. Would he really have tripped and fallen so badly?

"I'm not sure," she said slowly. "It just seems a bit weird that he'd fall for no reason. He's pretty sprightly."

"So what do you think happened?"

"I dunno. I wonder if maybe it wasn't an accident . . . Maybe someone else was involved?"

"You think someone attacked him?" Will inhaled through his teeth and Kat felt a flush of anger. Of course he didn't believe her.

"I just said maybe," she snapped, taking a step back from the door.

"Was there any sign of a break-in or a struggle?"

Was he interrogating her for a story now? Kat scowled; she'd said too much already. "I've got to go."

"I guess this'll mean the end of Joseph's fight to stop his eviction."

Oh God, Kat hadn't even thought about that. Poor Joseph; critically ill and soon to be homeless. He really was having a bad month.

"I don't suppose he told you what this discovery was?" Will said.

"No, I've got no idea."

"That's a shame." He sighed and looked around the cluttered lobby. "You know, I've been fascinated by this building ever since I was a kid. We used to make up wild stories about it when I was at school. But I'd never been inside until I interviewed Joseph last week."

Kat froze. If Will had grown up in Chalcot he'd almost certainly have gone to the local primary, the same school Kat had attended several times in her childhood, and they looked to be a similar age. Had there ever been a boy in her class called Will? Kat racked her brain, but she'd been to so many different schools that she could barely remember any of the children she met along the way. Still, that didn't mean that he wouldn't remember her, especially given what had happened. Kat stepped back into the flat.

"Bye," she said quickly, pulling the door closed.

"Hey, what's your name, by the way? I didn't catch—"

Kat clicked the door shut before he could finish his sentence. No good could come from talking to him.

Nine

DOROTHY

Dorothy had not been eavesdropping, of course. She had simply been on her way to the kitchen to return the dustpan and brush when she passed her door and happened to hear the voices in the lobby. Given the recent commotion she thought it only prudent to check who was there, and so she had placed her eye to the peephole and caught the muttered words exchanged outside flat one.

Maybe it wasn't an accident... Maybe someone else was involved?

Dorothy leaped back from the door as if she had been burned. Was the pink-haired girl suggesting Joseph had been attacked? But that was not possible. Dorothy had been here all day and would have known if some criminal had entered the building and bludgeoned her neighbor in broad daylight. The very idea was preposterous!

She abandoned the dustpan by the door and strode back to the table, reaching for her trusty diary and turning to the most recent page. There was today's date written in her neat script and under it the observations from the day.

Monday 27th May

6:43 a.m. Awoken by banging from flat four. Headache, 2 aspirin.

8:39 a.m. T.W. (5) departs with dog, placing rubbish into general waste bin. Presence of recyclable cardboard in rubbish? Speak to Tomasz re correct rubbish disposal.

8:58 a.m. J.C. (1) departs (whistling) with sandwich board, megaphone, bag, and dog.

10:20 a.m. T.W. (5) and dog return.

10:47 a.m. A.S. (3) departs with pile of books and surly expression.

11:13 a.m. Broken light switch on top landing. Write to F. Alexander re ongoing wiring issues.

11:29 a.m. Girl with pink hair (1) departs.

12:16 p.m. Black Labrador fouls on pavement near front steps. Alerted owner to presence of excrement. Excrement cleaned up.

1:15 p.m. J.C. (1) and dog return. Still whistling.

2:05 p.m. Delivery driver rings doorbell. Parcel retrieved by antisocial tenant in flat 4. Accosted him in lobby re early-morning banging. No coherent response given.

2:11 p.m. Green BMW parks illegally, blocking driveway access to number 16. Registration EB66 BGE.

2:13 p.m. Supermarket delivery arrives, 13 minutes late. Write to Sainsbury's to complain re repeated tardiness. On inspection of food delivery in kitchen, two eggs broken. Write to Sainsbury's to complain re substandard packaging.

2:25 p.m. Return to window, illegally parked vehicle gone.

2:45 p.m. A.S. (3) returns.

3:05 p.m. Girl with pink hair (1) returns.

The entries stopped at that point because the ambulance had arrived shortly after and, in her state of shock, Dorothy had failed to record the subsequent events. But making the fair assumption that Joseph Chambers had died sometime between his return to the building at one fifteen and the arrival of the ambulance at approximately three fifteen, that meant there was only a two-hour window in which the alleged attack could have taken place.

Dorothy pushed her diary aside. As much as she had fantasized over the years about Joseph being murdered at the hands of a sadistic serial killer, no one fitting that description had been in or out of the building today. Ergo, his death must have been from natural causes. She shivered again; it really was unseasonably cool this evening. Or perhaps she was coming down with a virus? She checked her watch; it was not yet six o'clock, but it might be wise to retire to bed early with a cup of Horlicks and a good book. She rose from the table, switched off the lamps in the living room, double-checked the bolt and chain on her door, and began her nocturnal routine.

Yet as she lay in bed later, Dorothy found she could not relax. It was hardly a surprise, given the drama of this afternoon. It was not every day that one watched a dead body being carted away from one's home—especially not that of one's archnemesis—and she found her mind running back and forth over the events. Had Joseph been ill in the days preceding his death? she wondered. Had he known he was dying? Had he been in pain in his final moments? Despite her long anticipation of this event, Dorothy was surprised to find that the idea of him suffering gave her little pleasure. At least she could be certain that he had died of natural causes and there was not a murderer on the loose in the neighborhood. That really *would* be something to complain to the council about.

Dorothy adjusted her pillow to get comfortable. *May this be the last evening that thoughts of Joseph Chambers ever keep me awake.* That man was gone from her life and she need never dwell on him again.

Dorothy closed her eyes. And then she opened them again and sat bolt upright as a thought occurred to her. A ghastly, menacing thought.

She was certain that no stranger had entered the building and killed Joseph Chambers this afternoon. But what if they had not needed to? What if the killer had already been in the building and had attacked Joseph during the twelve-minute interval in which Dorothy had been otherwise engaged unpacking and inspecting her groceries? She scrambled in the dark to switch on the bedside light and reached for her glasses and diary. It took a moment for her eyes to focus on the spidery letters before she reread today's entries, paying particular attention to the movements of her neighbors. Tomasz, Ayesha, and the girl with pink hair had left the building this morning but had all returned by the time the ambulance arrived. The tenant from flat four had come to the door to retrieve a parcel, but Dorothy had not witnessed any of the other residents stepping outside the front door. Which meant that, in theory at least, any one of them could have killed Joseph.

Dorothy's head spun and she took several deep breaths to try to regain some sense of calm. This was a ludicrous idea, the kind of fantastical nonsense one's brain thinks up in the middle of the night to keep one awake. No resident of Shelley House would kill Joseph Chambers, however irksome he might have been. No, she was simply getting carried away, allowing her imagination to run riot after such a disquieting day. What she needed now was a good night's sleep, and by tomorrow everything would be back to normal.

Ten

DOROTHY

At five o'clock the following morning, Dorothy was sitting at her table by the window, watching the sun rise over the rooftops of Poet's Road. She had been awake since four and was already on her second pot of tea. In front of her, on a fresh page in her notebook, she had listed the names of the residents who had been in Shelley House yesterday.

Flat one—Joseph Chambers & the girl with pink hair (illegal subtenant)
Flat two—Dorothy Darling
Flat three—Omar & Ayesha Siddiq
Flat four—Antisocial tenant
Flat five—Tomasz Wojcik
Flat six—Gloria Brown

There were eight of them in total, but if she took away the deceased and herself, that meant there were six names left. But would any of them have attacked and killed Joseph? There was no doubt the man was deeply irritating and Dorothy loathed him with a passion, but why would any of her neighbors want to harm him?

She sniffed and studied the list. There were some names on here who were clearly innocent. Gloria Brown, for example, had lived in the building for ten years and Dorothy had seen her conversing with Joseph in a friendly manner on many occasions. But then again, the woman was clearly emotionally unstable. Plus Dorothy had not seen Gloria's oafish lover in Shelley House for more than a week now, so perhaps the scoundrel had left her and Gloria had been driven to despair by the loss? Heartbreak made people do all sorts of crazy things: just look at poor Brunhilda. Could Gloria's anguish over the loss of her miscreant lover have led her to murder? It seemed unlikely, but one could never be sure. Dorothy placed an asterisk next to her name.

What about Omar and Ayesha in flat three? They seemed equally improbable, but Dorothy knew from the frosty atmosphere between them that neither was happy. Could Ayesha's grief over the loss of her mother have driven her to violence? Plus there were the bills that arrived relentlessly for Omar. The man was obviously in dire financial straits, but was his situation so bad that he might try to rob his own neighbor? Joseph was usually out all day, so perhaps Omar had thought the coast was clear to break into flat one and loot Joseph's valuables. And yet the victim returned early, surprising Omar, and in the ensuing tussle Joseph was killed. It was not beyond the realm of possibility, and Dorothy starred both their names.

She looked at her list again. Tomasz in flat five had a much clearer motive. The two men had fought over their dogs many times, the most recent brouhaha little more than a week ago and with Dorothy as a witness. It had been clear from the heated exchange that they hated each other as much as their dogs did. Had they had another disagreement yesterday, perhaps away from Shelley House in the morning, and Tomasz had become so enraged that he decided to take matters into his own murderous hands? Dorothy had always thought the man looked volatile. Perhaps yesterday he simply snapped? Yes, he was certainly worthy of an asterisk.

That only left the two nameless tenants: the neighbor from hell in flat four and the girl with pink hair. Dorothy knew very little about them given their recent addition to Shelley House, but she could immediately see that either could be guilty of the crime. After all, the man in flat four was clearly a reprobate, what with his all-night parties, flagrant drug use, and blatant disregard for his neighbors. One only had to open the newspaper to read about the heinous crimes committed by people under the influence of hallucinogens, so it was easy to imagine the man could have conducted a violent crime. And the girl from flat one? Well, just look at her. She had an air of trouble about her; Dorothy had identified it the very first time she saw her. And she was certainly well-placed as Joseph's tenant to knock him off without anyone suspecting. Dorothy thought back to the girl's pale face last night as she had talked to the paramedics and the way she had watched the ambulance depart. At the time Dorothy had assumed she was upset, but perhaps it was something far more sinister she was pondering?

Dorothy poured herself another cup of tea. So there you had it. There were six names with asterisks next to them, which meant six suspects in the death of Joseph Chambers. Six potential murderers, one of whom was sitting under the same roof as Dorothy at this very moment, celebrating their crime. Would Joseph be their only victim, or would they be emboldened and planning to strike again? And who would the next victim be? If there was a murderer on the loose in Shelley House, then Dorothy herself could be under threat, and that simply would not do.

She took a sip of tea, picked up her pencil, and began to scribble.

Eleven

KAT

At eight a.m., Kat stood in the lobby of Shelley House, sweating. She'd just taken Reggie for a long walk by the river—or rather, he'd dragged her for a long walk, clearly disgusted at her slow pace. She'd also called the hospital, which refused to give her any details about Joseph beyond the fact that he was in an induced coma, and the police, who confirmed they hadn't yet spoken to Joseph's daughter. When Kat asked the officer what she was supposed to do with Reggie in the meantime, he'd told her in no uncertain terms that the animal was her responsibility. Which now left Kat with the challenge of convincing someone else to take him in.

There was the sound of a door closing overhead and heavy footsteps on the stairs. Reggie immediately started whimpering at her feet.

"Hey, what's the matter?" Kat said, looking down at the dog, whose whole body had tensed.

A second later, she got the answer to her question. The tall bald guy who'd been at Joseph's meeting appeared at the top of the stairs and behind him was a huge dog—some kind of bull terrier by the looks of things—who started barking and straining toward Reggie. The smaller dog was cowering at Kat's feet and barking in panic as the muscular terrier got closer, its jaws open to reveal snarling teeth.

"Keep your dog back!" Kat shouted, desperately trying to pull Reggie out of the way. The last thing she needed was Joseph's dog being mauled to death while he lay in intensive care.

The man grabbed his dog by the collar. "Come on, Princess, we go," he said before opening the front door and dragging the animal out. Even when it slammed shut, Reggie was still shaking with fear. Kat bent down to soothe him.

"It's okay, buddy. The nasty dog's gone."

The poor animal looked terrified and for a moment Kat considered taking him back into the flat and spending the day with him. But no, she needed to find someone to look after Reggie so she could leave as soon as possible. Every day she stayed in Chalcot increased her risk of being recognized and word getting back to her grandfather that Kat had disobeyed him once again. And while enough time had passed that she'd probably no longer be in trouble with the police, just the thought of her grandfather's rage and a second rejection all these years later made Kat's stomach clench. She couldn't let a bit of silly sentimentality over an animal stop her getting out of here.

With a sigh, Kat started climbing the stairs toward the top floor. Of all the people in Shelley House, the woman in flat six, Gloria, had seemed to be the friendliest with Joseph at the meeting, so perhaps she'd agree to take the animal. Kat knocked on the door and held her breath as she waited for an answer.

When Gloria opened the door, Kat's heart sank. The woman looked a mess. She was wearing a ratty old dressing gown, her previously glossy red hair was pulled into a greasy ponytail, and there was mascara smudged under her eyes.

"What is it?" she snapped by way of a greeting.

"Hi, I was wondering if you could do me a favor, please? Well, Joseph a favor, really."

"What?"

"Could you look after Reggie for a little while. I've got to—"

"Where's Joe? That dog never leaves his side."

"Didn't you know?" Kat assumed everyone in the building had seen Joseph being rushed off in the ambulance. "He's in hospital. He had a fall yesterday and injured his head."

"Oh my God!" Gloria's eyes went wide. "I heard the ambulance siren but I didn't realize it was for him. Is he okay?"

"I don't know. He's in a coma and—"

"Poor Joe," Gloria interrupted, tears now running down her cheeks, spreading the mascara further. "He's always been like a father to me, especially recently."

"Yeah, he's a good guy. So that was why I was wondering if you could maybe help him out in return?"

Gloria sniffed and wiped her eyes. "I'm sorry, I'd love to, but I'm having a really bad time at the moment: I've split up with my boyfriend and my mum's sick so I can't take on a dog right now."

"It would only be for a couple of days, just until the police track down Joseph's daughter and she can take Reggie."

The woman stopped snuffling. "Yeah, good luck with that."

"Why do you say that?"

"Because Joseph and Debbie do not get on *at all*. I've lived here ten years and never seen her visit him once; I think she lives in Australia or something. So I don't think she's gonna be rushing back to take the dog."

Kat felt a tightening in her chest. With no Debbie, that meant Reggie was officially her problem. She glanced down at the animal, who had finally stopped shaking and was now lying on the floor, looking utterly dejected.

"Are you sure there's no way you could take him, even for a bit? He's really no bother."

Gloria shook her head. "Sorry, but I can't. I'm not in the right headspace, and now with the shock of Joe too."

"Okay, well, thanks for nothing."

Kat turned without saying good-bye and began to stomp down the stairs, then stopped on the first landing as she remembered something. The teenage girl at the meeting had jumped to Reggie's defense against the other dog owner. Maybe she'd be willing to help out? Joseph had said she and her dad lived in the flat above his, so Kat knocked on the door of flat three.

"Keep your paws crossed," she whispered to Reggie as they waited for a reply.

After a few moments the door opened and Kat saw the teenager peering out at them. The girl's face lit up when she saw Reggie, and she dropped to her knees to greet him. Reggie's tail started to wag enthusiastically, and Kat felt a rush of hope.

"Hi, I'm Kat. I'm staying with Joseph."

"Is he okay?" the girl said, looking up. "I saw an ambulance out the window yesterday,"

"Not really; he had a bad fall and he's in the ICU. That's why I'm here. I was wondering if you could possibly help out by looking after Reggie while Joseph's in hospital?"

"I'd love to!" The girl smiled as the dog nuzzled her. "We'll have great fun, won't we, Reggie?"

Kat exhaled in relief. "Thank you, I really appreciate that."

"Ayesha, who is it?" a voice called from within the flat. A moment later Omar appeared behind his daughter, drying his hands on a tea towel. He smiled at Kat when he saw her. "Hello. It's Kat, isn't it?"

"Yes, hi."

"Dad, I've said we can look after Reggie for a bit."

"But what about school, love?"

"It's fine, I only have a couple of exams this week, and the rest of the time I can revise from home."

Her father's expression had turned serious. "No, you can't."

"Yes, I can." Ayesha's voice was steely now too. "Joseph's in hospital and needs my help."

Omar looked at Kat. "Hospital? What happened?"

"He had a fall and hit his head badly. But I'm supposed to be moving out today, so it would be a huge help if Ayesha could look after Reggie."

"I'm so sorry, but that won't be possible. She has her exams and she can't miss school."

"Dad, it won't be for long, I'm sure. And you always said we should help our neighbors."

"No, Ayesha." His words were short and sharp.

"This is so unfair!" Ayesha stood up so that she was staring her father directly in the eye. "First you wouldn't let me fight our eviction, and now you won't let me help Joseph when he's in need. If Mum was here, she'd have let me do both."

"Yes, but sadly your mother isn't here, is she?" Omar said, his voice rising. "So you're stuck with me and I say no."

For a moment neither of them spoke, their faces inches from each other, and Kat felt the tension coursing between them like electricity. Then the girl spun on her heels and stormed out of the flat, pushing past Kat to get down the stairs.

"I hate you!" she shouted as she disappeared, and Kat heard the tremble of tears in her voice.

Omar's shoulders visibly sagged. He looked up at Kat as the front door slammed, shaking the whole building. "I'm sorry you had to see that. Things between me and Ayesha are . . . they're difficult right now."

"It's okay," said Kat, backing away.

"And I wish we could help with Reggie, but I have to go to work and Ayesha can't skip school. She's already missed so much this year, after her mother . . ." He trailed off and fell silent.

"I understand. Thanks anyway."

"Please give Joseph our best wishes," Omar said. "I hope he's all right."

Kat turned and began to make her way down the stairs, the dog trailing behind her. There was no one else she could ask, which meant she and Reggie were stuck with each other. And now she had the choice of either calling into work sick and risk losing her only source of income or leaving Reggie home alone. But in the time Kat had lived with Joseph, she'd never seen the dog left on his own for even a few minutes.

She'd reached the hallway and for a moment Kat's eyes flicked toward the door of flat two. Should she ask Dorothy Darling? She'd still not seen the woman, but as far as Kat could tell she rarely left the building, so maybe she'd be willing to help? But then Kat remembered how the woman had spoken to her the day Kat moved in and the constant flickering of the net curtain. No, the witch would probably put Reggie in her cauldron and boil him up for her lunch.

"I'm sorry, Reggie," Kat said as she unlocked the door to flat one. "I don't have any other options. I'll come back on my lunch break to take you out for a quick walk, okay?"

The dog stared up at her mournfully, and she felt a stab of guilt. Was this what it was like when you had someone else relying on you, this crushing sense of responsibility? It was not a feeling Kat was used to and definitely not one she wanted to experience again. She closed the front door and turned to leave the building, trying to ignore Reggie's whimpers behind her.

Twelve

DOROTHY

Dorothy sat by the front window watching her neighbors like a hawk. The pink-haired girl had looked particularly red-faced when she came home from walking Joseph's mongrel this morning, but was that the guilt causing her to sweat so much? Why did the delinquent from flat four look even more irate than usual? Was he panicking he'd get caught? And had the teenager from flat three found out about her father's heinous felony, and that was why she ran from the building in tears? Dorothy recorded detailed notes in her diary, using her very best penmanship. After all, what she wrote might one day be used as evidence in a court of law to convict the killer.

By ten o'clock most of the residents had left and Dorothy was free to conduct her perlustration of the property. This was all the more pressing today, given recent events, and Dorothy took extra care as she moved through Shelley House. She had read enough Agatha Christie novels to know that it was the small details that inevitably gave the killer away, and so she scrutinized every inch of the lobby in case there was anything suspicious, however small. When that threw up nothing she moved painstakingly through the upper floors, her eyes peeled for any evidence carelessly discarded by the attacker. But apart from a used tissue outside flat four and a few red hairs on the doormat outside flat six, there was nothing that gave any clues as to who might be responsible for the attack. Not for the first time, Dorothy lamented the fact that she did not have a master key with which she could gain access to the interiors of the flats as well.

Having checked that the fire escape door had not been tampered with, Dorothy began to make her way back to the lobby. But as she passed the first floor, the door to flat four suddenly flew open and the tenant staggered out, followed by a waft of marijuana smoke and a blast of music. Dorothy wrinkled her nose at the sight of his disheveled hair and unshaven face; the man was in need of an appointment with a barber, sharpish. He was holding a black rubbish bag, which he dumped on the floor, and turned to retreat into his flat.

"What do you think you are doing?" Dorothy demanded.

The man swayed slightly as he turned to look at her.

"As I have told you before, you cannot leave your refuse in the communal areas. That is what the bins outside are for."

"You throw it away if you're so bothered," the man said with a slur. He began to move back inside.

"I do not think so." Dorothy reached out an arm to stop him. The man jolted at her touch and spun round again.

"Get off me, you old hag."

"Now listen, young man, I have had quite enough of your behavior. The constant music blaring into my flat is one thing, but the rubbish is quite another. If you leave it here it could attract rats, which bring all sorts of diseases with them and could make the residents ill. Not to mention the fact that bags of refuse are a known fire hazard. Either you take this downstairs or I shall be forced to write to Mr. F. Alexander about you again."

At the mention of the landlord, the man let out a cough of a laugh. "Complain all you want," he said, then slammed the door in Dorothy's face.

"This is not the end of the matter!" Dorothy shouted through the chipped wood. "I will contact the council as well. Your antisocial behavior is not welcome here in Shelley House!"

Her words were met only with an increase in the volume of the music. Dorothy tutted and pulled out her diary to make a note. Not only would she write to Fergus Alexander about the lout, but his name was jumping right to the top of her suspect list for Joseph's attack as well. She replaced the notebook, pulled on her rubber gloves, and bent to retrieve the rubbish bag. As she did, Dorothy heard the unmistakable sound of the building's front door creaking open. She checked her watch: eleven twenty-two a.m. Who was coming in at this time of the day? Dorothy paused at the top of the stairs, awaiting whoever was about to appear, but all she heard was the sound of the front door slamming shut and a moment later Reggie's barks. It must be the pink-haired girl, but why was she back so early? She did not usually return until the evening, so this was most unusual. Suspicious even.

Dorothy's heart was in her mouth as she hurried down the stairs as fast as her knees would allow. Panting as she let herself back into her flat, she closed the door behind her and placed an eye to the peephole so as to keep watch on the lobby. It was very possible the girl might stay in there for hours, but instinct told Dorothy that would not be the case. And sure enough, after less than five minutes she saw the door to flat one open again and heard a barrage of barking from inside as a figure slipped out.

Dorothy knew at once this was not the illegal subtenant because their size and stature was completely different. This person was much taller and wearing a long black coat with the hood pulled up to cover their face, a most unlikely garment for the late-spring season, and they had a canvas bag slung over one shoulder and an umbrella in their hand. As they opened the front door, Dorothy crossed to her window in time to see the figure move down the steps. They reached the pavement and turned left, their pace slower now that they were in public. Dorothy leaned forward, her eyes trained on them as they headed down Poet's Road toward the hill. There was something about the way they walked, a slight limp in the left leg that suggested it might be an older person. They were almost at the corner now, and Dorothy's nose was touching the glass as she strained to keep the intruder in her vision. At the very last moment, as they turned left onto Fellows Road, they lifted up a hand and pulled the hood down. For the briefest of seconds Dorothy saw a flash of hair before they disappeared from view.

She slumped back into her chair, exhaling slowly. Her heart was hammering and she reached a hand up to mop the perspiration from her brow before allowing herself a small smile. After all, Dorothy had just seen the culprit behind Joseph Chambers's murder, of that much she was certain. And better still, she knew *exactly* who it was.

Thirteen

KAT

At two o'clock, Kat left the café and drove back to Shelley House. Remi had not been happy when she'd told him she had to pop out for an hour and she wouldn't get paid for the time she was absent, but right now Kat didn't care. All that mattered was that she got home and checked on Reggie.

There was no sound of barking as she let herself into Shelley House, which had to be a good sign. Perhaps he'd simply slept the five hours she'd been gone?

Kat unlocked the door to flat one and let out a gasp. The living room had been ransacked. Chairs were knocked over, Joseph's belongings lay strewn across the floor, and what looked like the torn pages of books were scattered at her feet. But worst of all, there was no sign of the dog.

"Reggie? Reggie, are you here?"

There was no answer and Kat felt a throb of panic. Not Reggie too? Joseph would never forgive her if something happened to the dog on her watch. She ran though the living room into the empty kitchen and then to the hallway. Joseph's bedroom door was open and it had definitely been closed when Kat left the flat this morning. She grabbed a heavy candlestick from the nearest table and let out her loudest, most threatening cry as she charged into the room.

"Argghhhhhh!"

Reggie was lying on Joseph's bed watching her with a startled expression. Kat dropped the candlestick and collapsed down next to him.

"Thank God you're okay!" She pressed her face into the dog's fur. "I thought something awful had happened to you too and it was all my fault."

Reggie gave her cheek a sloppy lick and she stayed pressed against his warm body for a few seconds longer, enjoying his sweet, earthy smell. She used to lie like this with her grandfather's dog, Barker, her arms round the animal's neck and her tears soaking into his soft fur. Kat's breath caught at the memory and she quickly pulled away from Reggie.

Joseph's bedroom had been trashed too: a lamp lay smashed on the floor and a carpet of feathers covered the bed from a ripped cushion. Whoever had been here, they'd really done some damage.

"What happened, Reggie?" Kat asked, giving the dog a pat.

In response, he opened his mouth and let out a long yawn. As he did, Kat saw something white on his tongue.

"What's this?" she said, reaching forward and taking the dog's jaw.

He gave her hand a lick and Kat slipped a finger inside his mouth and pulled out the object. It was a soggy, partially chewed white feather. Kat let out a groan.

"Oh my God! Did *you* make all this mess?"

She looked around the room again. None of Joseph's drawers were open, but the laundry basket was on its side on the floor, suggesting the dog might have climbed inside it to pull out the clothes. And the plug from the smashed lamp had been yanked out of the wall, as if something had tripped over the cable. Kat stood up and walked back through to the living room. Near her feet was one of the books that had been torn up and Kat bent down to survey its cover, in the middle of which she saw a row of unmistakable teeth marks.

There was a bang at the far side of the room and Kat jumped up again, her fists raised to protect herself. Standing in the open doorway of the flat was an elderly woman. She had poker-straight silver hair that reached past her waist, and the skin on her face was so pale it was almost translucent. Two dark, beady eyes were staring accusingly at Kat over a sharp, beakish nose. The woman looked like a cartoon drawing of a witch, if witches wore beige housecoats and slippers. There was only one person this could be.

"Dorothy Darling?"

"It's *Ms.* Darling to you. Does it always look like this in here?"

"No, of course not. I think Reggie's been on the rampage."

At the mention of his name the dog came scampering into the living room. When he saw a newcomer he bounded over to Dorothy, barking excitedly, and she jumped back as if he were a poisonous snake.

"Get that flea-ridden beast away from me this instant!" she shouted, waving her arms in the animal's direction.

"Reggie, come here," Kat called, and was surprised when the dog obeyed and trotted to her.

Dorothy brushed her coat as if it had been sullied and cleared her throat. "It was not the animal who did this damage. I saw an intruder leaving the flat at eleven twenty-seven this morning."

"An intruder? Are you sure?"

"Of course I am sure. What is more, I believe the person who broke in had something to do with Joseph's attack yesterday."

Kat looked at her in surprise. "Why do you say 'attack'? The police think he fell."

"You know as well as I do that is poppycock. Besides, I overheard you discussing an attack with a scruffy-looking gentleman caller last night."

"Were you eavesdropping on me?" Kat glared at her, but Dorothy waved away the accusation.

"I am certain that yesterday's attacker came from within the building, as no one else entered Shelley House all day. However, I have now come to the conclusion that they had an accomplice who returned this morning and plundered the flat. Perhaps they were looking for some incriminating piece of evidence left behind?"

Kat ran a hand through her hair. This was a *lot* to take in. Dorothy was watching her from the doorway with a strange intensity in her eyes. Joseph had said she was eccentric, but was she a crackpot conspiracy theorist too?

"I don't buy it. There's Reggie's teeth marks over half this stuff and he's got feathers in his mouth. I think he went a little crazy left on his own for so long."

Dorothy snorted. "Nonsense. The dog may have played with some of the items, assuming the ransacking was a game. He is an exceptionally stupid animal, after all."

"Reggie isn't stupid, but your theory is. Why would anyone in the building want to attack Joseph, for a start? And how do you know nobody else entered the building all day? You're not in control of who comes in, however much you might want to be."

Kat met Dorothy's eye as she said this, and she knew the old woman was also remembering their first exchange, when Dorothy had tried to mislead Kat about the vacant room.

"I keep watch on the front door for security purposes," Dorothy said, looking away. "To make sure nothing untoward happens to the residents of Shelley House."

"You mean you spy on everyone."

"I mean I remain vigilant. In the thirty-four years I have lived here, I have thwarted three separate burglary attempts. Not that anyone has ever thanked me for it."

"And you actually saw someone come into this flat, did you?"

Dorothy produced a notebook from her bag, opened it, and

squinted as she started to read. "'11:22 a.m. SH'—that stands for Shelley House—'front door bangs closed.' I was not by my window at the time so did not see who entered. But my next entry at 11:27 a.m. says, 'Figure leaves flat one wearing black winter coat with hood pulled up to conceal face. Approximately five foot nine, slight limp, carrying bag and umbrella. Exits SH and turns left toward Fellows Road.'"

Dorothy paused and looked up from the page, as if she were Hercule Poirot about to reveal the murderer.

"Not so dismissive now, are you, girl?"

Kat didn't reply as she walked across the room toward Dorothy. The woman stepped back into the hallway, looking alarmed, but Kat stopped at the entrance to the flat and studied the lock on the door.

"There's no sign that the lock was picked."

"I imagine you would know what that looks like," Dorothy said, tightly. "But I do not think this was a break-in as such. I believe she had a key."

"She? I thought you said they were hiding their face."

"I did, but that does not mean I did not see who it was. It was the limp that gave her away. That and the cheap peroxide dye."

"So who on earth was it?" Kat tried to keep the impatience from her voice, but time was ticking for her to take Reggie out and get back to work.

"It was"—Dorothy paused for dramatic effect, clearly enjoying her big moment—"Sandra Chambers."

"Who?"

"Sandra Chambers!" She glowered when Kat still looked blank. "Joseph's wife."

Oh God, the old woman was clearly losing her marbles. "I'm pretty sure Joseph's wife is dead."

Dorothy's hand flew to her chest. "But that's not possible! It was her, I know it was."

"I think she passed away three years ago."

"What are you talking about, girl? Who told you that?"

Kat stifled a sigh. "Joseph did. Well, he didn't say it in so many words, but he's clearly still grieving her loss."

"He did not *lose* her, for pity's sake! She ran off with a man from her amateur dramatics group, a dubious little Spaniard with a bad toupee. I used to see him coming and going from the flat while Joseph was out, but it took the old goat almost a year to work it out. Then one day she finally up and left—good riddance to bad blood, I say—and I have not seen her since. Until this morning, that is."

This was a surprise to Kat; Joseph had definitely made it sound like she was dead. But why would Dorothy lie about it, unless she was unwell?

"And you're sure it was Joseph's wife you saw? I mean, maybe you got confused?"

"Just because I am significantly older than you does not mean I am some doddery fool who cannot recognize her own neighbors. I am certain it was Sandra Chambers because she always had a problem with her left leg and this person had the exact same limp."

Kat thought for a moment. "If it was her, then maybe there's a simple explanation. Perhaps the police called her and she was here to collect some of Joseph's things for him in hospital?"

"Why would he need his things?" Dorothy snapped. "A dead body does not need *things*."

"But he's not dead."

At those words, the old woman's face did several things at once. Her eyes went wide with surprise while her nostrils seemed to flare in anger, and her skin flushed momentarily pink.

"He is alive?"

"Yes. I called the hospital earlier and they said he's in an induced coma."

Another strange look passed over Dorothy's face, somewhere between disappointment and relief. She paused for a moment, as if collecting herself before she spoke.

"Be that as it may, if Sandra was simply collecting his belongings, then why was she trying to hide her identity? Why the hooded winter coat in late May?"

"I don't know, perhaps she's got a cold?" Kat was getting exasperated. At her feet, Reggie was shuffling round, clearly keen to get away too. "Look, I need to take Reggie out and get back to work."

"So you are going to ignore the fact that your landlord has been brutally attacked and left for dead, and less than twenty-four hours later his erstwhile wife breaks into his flat and pillages the place?"

"For now I am, yes. But if you're so concerned about this, why don't you call the police and report her?"

"Oh, the police are no use at all," Dorothy scoffed. "I have called them out dozens of times to report problems in Shelley House, and they always treat me like a deranged old woman."

"I wonder why that is?" Kat muttered under her breath.

"I heard that, girl. I saw the way you looked at those officers when they left here last night. You dislike the police as much as I do."

It was true, Kat had never had a good relationship with the cops, but she wasn't going to admit that to Dorothy.

"You said yourself that the police think Joseph simply fell," Dorothy continued. "They will not have any interest in investigating things further unless you can present them with some evidence to the contrary. This is why you must go and visit Sandra."

"Me!" Kat said it so loudly that Reggie let out a bark of surprise. "You're the one with this loopy theory, so why don't you go and visit her?"

"Because there is no way Sandra will talk to me. We lived opposite each other for thirty years and the woman has always loathed me."

Finally Dorothy was saying something that made sense. Kat shuddered at the idea of living opposite this strange, paranoid, spying woman for that long.

"You, on the other hand, have the perfect excuse to visit her. You are Joseph's subtenant—albeit illegally—so you can tell her you are worried about him and want to find out how he is. I am sure even you can pretend to care about someone else for a few minutes."

Kat ignored the dig. "I don't have time. I have a full-time job—one that I'm supposed to be at right now—plus I'm meant to be moving and now I have Reggie to look after as well. If you want someone to investigate this, you'll have to do it yourself."

As she said the words, Kat reached for Reggie's lead by the door. She couldn't take him on a walk anymore, but she still had to let him out so he could do his business before she returned to work.

"Are you leaving this dog alone?" Dorothy said, peering down at the animal as if it had rabies.

"I don't have any other choice." Kat had googled the price of kennels and dog walkers at work this morning and almost cried when she saw what they charged. But the only other option was to take Reggie to a shelter, and that would break Joseph's heart.

"I can help."

For a moment, Kat thought she'd misheard. "What?"

"I can take the animal while you are at work."

It was such a ridiculous idea that Kat let out a snort of laughter. "But you hate him."

Dorothy did not deny the accusation. "I will, however, only assist on the condition that you visit Sandra and find out why she was at the flat this morning. I know she was involved in Joseph's attack somehow, and you need to find some concrete evidence before we can go to the dim-witted police."

"I think I'd rather take my chances with leaving Reggie alone again."

"But if you do that, then the animal may well do himself serious harm." She indicated the living room, its contents scattered everywhere.

Kat paused. On the one hand it was absurd; Dorothy clearly knew nothing about dogs, and Joseph might be furious with Kat if she left his beloved pet with her. But surely that was better than leaving him in the flat alone? Kat thought of the smashed lamp in Joseph's bedroom. Dorothy was right, Reggie might injure himself. And all Kat had to do was spend a few minutes chatting with this Sandra woman and then she could tell Dorothy she'd done her part of the deal. As ridiculous as it seemed, right now this was Kat's best—and only—option.

"How do I know you're not going to back out of this the second I've talked to Sandra?"

"Because I give you my word, and a Darling never breaks their word." Dorothy held out her hand, the skin pale and wrinkled. "You find out why Sandra was here and how she was involved in Joseph's attack, and I will look after this wretched animal while you are at work."

Kat swallowed. This was crazy.

"Okay, deal."

Fourteen

DOROTHY

Dorothy looked down at the pathetic animal, who stared back up at her with an expression of equal mistrust.

It had been a stupid, impulsive offer on her part and quite out of character. But the girl, Kat, had proven to be even more recalcitrant than Dorothy had anticipated. And so, in the heat of the moment, Dorothy had snatched at the one card she had to her advantage: the fact that the girl was clearly stuck with the mongrel against her will. And her plan had been successful, for Kat had promised to pay a visit to Sandra tomorrow morning before work. Unfortunately, Dorothy was now stuck with this mangy mutt.

Its eyes had left Dorothy and she could see it surveying her drawing room.

"Do not even think about it," she said in her most commanding voice. "You will stay by the door where you can do no damage."

The dog was still wearing its lead from the walk Kat had taken it on before she departed, and Dorothy had looped it round her door handle to ensure that it was secure. The animal now only had a small radius within which it could roam, and there was thankfully nothing in its range it could destroy.

"You will stay there and not make any noise," Dorothy said as she turned and strode toward the kitchen. It was now almost three o'clock and time for her afternoon pot of tea.

She lit the stove, placed the kettle on top, and then glanced out of the kitchen. The dog was still standing by the door, its small, silly tail pricked in the air as it looked back at her. Dorothy retreated and warmed the pot while she prepared her tea tray. She had received a fresh supply of biscuits in yesterday's supermarket delivery and she placed two pink wafers on a side plate before emptying the pot, adding loose tea and more hot water. She considered checking on the animal again but thought better of it. The less attention she gave it the better.

Once the tea was brewed, Dorothy returned to the living room. The dog was sitting on its hind legs, and it watched Dorothy intently as she crossed the room and sat down at her card table. The animal was now out of her vision but Dorothy could still sense its eyes on her as she poured milk into her teacup, followed by the tea. She raised the cup to her mouth.

"Please stop staring at me," she said aloud, not turning to look at the dog. "It is most disconcerting."

She took a sip but could still feel it watching her. It remained silent until she lifted a wafer from her plate, at which point it let out a plaintive whine.

"Absolutely not. Joseph may spoil you with human sustenance, but that will not be happening on my watch."

As she said Joseph's name, Dorothy thought back to what Kat had told her earlier. So the old rascal was not dead after all? Dorothy should have known he would cling to life like a stubborn limpet sticking to the *Titanic* as it sank. Still, "induced coma" sounded pretty serious, so perhaps he might be felled yet. Dorothy pulled her cardigan round her shoulders and took a bite of wafer. The dog let out another whimper.

"Oh, for goodness' sake!" She turned to address it directly. "You cannot sit there making noises all day. Please keep quiet and stop disturbing me."

The mutt's ears sagged and it lay down on the coir doormat, resting its head forlornly on its paws. That was more like it.

Dorothy returned to her tea and was uninterrupted for the rest of the pot. When she rose to take the tray to the kitchen, she saw that the animal had fallen asleep. Well, it had better not get too comfortable. As soon as Kat had been to visit Sandra tomorrow, Dorothy would be returning the fleabag to whence it came.

A Darling never breaks their word, Dorothy had said, and the girl had solemnly shaken her hand. Dorothy let out a snort of mirth. How naive and foolish the young.

Fifteen

KAT

Kat sat in her car, staring at the house across the road. There had been no sign of life from inside yet, and part of her hoped that Sandra would be out and she could return to Dorothy saying she'd tried and failed. Although what that meant for Reggie, Kat didn't know.

She had taken him on an extra-long walk this morning to try to cheer him up, and Reggie had seemed a little happier when she dropped him off at flat two. Dorothy, on the other hand, had seemed anything but happy to see the dog again.

Kat took a deep breath. There was no point sitting here in Marge wasting time; she might as well get this over and done with. Remi had been angry at her prolonged absence yesterday, so she couldn't risk irritating him again; she needed the paid work until the moment she left Chalcot. She climbed out of the vehicle and crossed the road toward 32 Sycamore Drive, a squat, charmless bungalow in a cul-de-sac of similarly bland properties. What a difference from Shelley House this was. Still, it was definitely the place Joseph had written in his address book, which Kat had found stuffed in a drawer of the side table where he kept his phone. Now she walked up the front path between oversized pampas grass plants and rang the doorbell.

There was barking on the other side of the frosted-glass door and the sound of a female voice calling for the animal to be quiet. A moment later the door swung open and Sandra Chambers appeared. Kat didn't know what she'd been expecting from Joseph's ex-wife, given that up until yesterday she'd believed the woman to be dead, but it probably wasn't this. The figure standing in front of her was tall and quietly glamorous, with ash-blond hair and a full face of makeup, despite the fact that it was only nine o'clock. At her feet was a small shih tzu, its long fringe held up by a cerise bow that matched Sandra's tracksuit.

"Can I help you?" Her voice was high and singsong.

"Eh, yes . . . Hi . . ."

What the hell was she going to say now? Kat had been so busy hoping that Sandra would be out that she hadn't planned what she'd actually do if the woman did answer.

"My name is Kat. I'm an acquaintance—well, a tenant—of your ex-husband, Joseph."

At the sound of his name, Sandra's face creased into an exaggerated expression of concern.

"Oh yes, I heard about his terrible accident." She lowered her voice and leaned toward Kat, blocking her view into the house with the door. "The police called my daughter in Melbourne Monday night and she rang me straightaway. I couldn't believe it! Are you the one who found him?"

Kat nodded and Sandra's mouth crumpled in sympathy. "You poor thing, that must have been horrible."

"He didn't look great."

There was a pause and Kat realized Sandra was waiting for her to explain why she was here.

"Eh, I was wondering if you had any further updates from your daughter on how he's doing?"

"No, nothing since Monday night. Debbie said the police told her it was a brain trauma and they were going to keep him in an induced coma to try and get the swelling down."

"Have you been to visit him in hospital?"

"Me?" Sandra's eyebrows shot up. "I don't know how much Joe told you, but he and I didn't part on the best of terms. He took the whole thing very badly; very badly indeed."

"So you've not seen him recently?"

Sandra glanced over her shoulder into the house before she answered. "No, I've not seen him in three years. Why are you asking me these questions?"

"Oh, well, I . . ." Kat racked her brains. "I was thinking of doing a collection among Joseph's friends, seeing if people wanted to give money to buy him a gift. So I was wondering if you might want to contribute."

"Oh, that's very sweet of you, but I don't think so. As I said, Joe and I really aren't friends anymore. Apart from correspondence over the divorce papers, we haven't had anything to do with each other for years."

"Sandy, who is it?" a male voice called from somewhere within the house.

"No one, darling," she called back. "Just a woman collecting for charity." She turned back to Kat. "That's my fiancé, Carlos. I've got to go."

"Sure, but one more thing really quickly," Kat said as Sandra started to shut the door. "Would you mind if I gave you my phone number in case you get any more updates on Joseph?"

It was a long shot and Kat waited for Sandra to slam the door in her face, but the woman let out a sigh.

"I suppose so. Let me get my phone."

She turned and disappeared inside the house, leaving the front door slightly ajar. Kat counted to five in her head and gently pushed the door open a little farther and peered inside. She was looking into a modern hallway with magnolia-colored walls and a cream carpet, a strong smell of potpourri in the air. Beyond the hall she could see a staircase and into what looked like a living room at the back of the house. Kat scanned her eyes round the hall. On the right was a table with a telephone and a vase full of lilies. Next to the vase was a framed photo showing Sandra and a short tanned man with an extraordinary head of thick black hair. Kat remembered what Dorothy had said about the bad toupee and swallowed a smile. On the left-hand wall was a coat rack, but there was no sign of a black coat with a hood. Kat heard the sound of footsteps and quickly retreated back to the doorstep. A few seconds later Sandra appeared, holding her phone.

"What's your number?" she asked, and Kat quickly reeled it off. Now that she'd done what Dorothy had asked her to, she was keen to get away.

"Thanks for your help," she said to Sandra, turning and heading toward the car.

"I hope Joseph is all right," Sandra called after her, and when Kat glanced back she saw the woman's brow crease. "He didn't deserve this; not after everything he's been through."

Sixteen

DOROTHY

Dorothy was in a predicament.

The dog was sitting at her feet, staring up at her with those pathetic brown eyes. For the past ten minutes it had been fidgeting around in its spot by the door, and more recently it had started to whine.

"What is wrong with you?" Dorothy demanded, glaring at the animal. "Are you hungry?"

Kat had dropped off some food this morning when she had deposited the dog at the door, but Dorothy had already offered a platter of the vile-smelling brown lumps and the mongrel had ignored them. It whimpered again and started scratching at the door.

Oh dear God!

Dorothy wrinkled her nose as the unsavory realization hit her. Why had she not anticipated this unfortunate consequence when she offered to take the mutt? For the hundredth time she chided herself for the impulsive proposal.

"Very well, come on, then. But you had better make it snappy."

She untied his lead and opened the door of the flat. Immediately the animal skittered under her feet and ran across the lobby toward flat one, tugging so hard on the lead that Dorothy was almost pulled over.

"Stop that at once!"

The dog let out a long, low whine.

"Absolutely not. You cannot go in there, as the girl is currently on a reconnaissance mission and Joseph is . . . indisposed."

It made another helpless sound at hearing its owner's name and continued staring at flat one.

Dorothy sighed. "Look, I know you are unhappy with this arrangement, and frankly I do not blame you. But as soon as Kat has found out what I need her to, I will be canceling the deal immediately. So rest assured, you and I will not have to put up with each other for very much longer."

She moved toward the front door and heaved it open, blinking in the bright daylight. The dog scurried outside and made its way down toward the pavement. This was an inelegant maneuver due to the animal's short legs, which meant it had to belly-flop off the edge of each step. Dorothy watched the frankly ridiculous procedure, wondering how far the lead would extend. As far as the pavement, it transpired, as the animal stopped there and looked back at her expectantly.

"Go on, do your wretched business," Dorothy called down.

The dog ignored the command.

"I am not coming out with you. You are perfectly capable of evacuating your bladder without my assistance."

Again, the dog did nothing.

"I will close my eyes if it is privacy you require."

She put a hand over her eyes and counted to ten. When she opened them again the dog had not moved. She let out a growl of frustration.

"Oh, you beastly animal! Just get on with it so I can go back into my flat."

"Are you okay?"

Dorothy jumped at a voice behind her. When she swung around she saw the teenager from flat three.

"Do you need a hand getting outside?" Ayesha said.

"I most certainly do not," Dorothy snapped.

"Are you sure? I know it can be . . . Reggie!"

The girl ran down the steps toward the animal, dropping onto her knees in front of it and ruffling its ears. The dog responded by licking her face enthusiastically, its tail wagging like a metronome set to allegro. Dorothy blanched at the thought of all those germs.

The girl looked back up at her. "I think he needs a wee."

"I am aware of that fact," Dorothy said tartly. "I am waiting for it to do its business."

"He won't do it here. Joseph's got him really well trained, Reggie won't do anything on the pavement."

"Oh, for goodness' sake! I am not taking him anywhere, so he needs to get over that pronto."

"I can take him to the park if you like, Mrs. Darling? That's where Joseph usually walks him."

"It's *Ms.* Darling. And should you not be in school?" Many years ago, Dorothy had been an English teacher, and she had never tolerated tardiness from her students.

"I don't have anything until an exam this afternoon."

Dorothy felt a wave of relief, but she kept a poker face. "As you wish, then."

The girl looked delighted and jogged back up the stairs to retrieve the lead handle. "I can let him have a quick run-around while I'm there. I'll bring him back when I'm done."

"That is most considerate of you," Dorothy conceded as the girl and the dog trotted away.

Back in the refuge of her flat, Dorothy washed her hands thoroughly before brewing herself a pot of tea. She took three bourbon biscuits from the cupboard—she deserved an extra one after that ordeal—and carried them through to her table. With any luck the teenager and the dog would be gone for long enough that she could enjoy her elevenses in peace.

But no sooner had Dorothy poured the tea and taken her first welcome bite of biscuit than a grubby white van pulled up in front of the building, its thumping bass interrupting her repose. The engine cut out and with it the music, and then the driver's door opened and a middle-aged man in sports attire climbed out. He leaned forward to retrieve something from the passenger seat, and as he did, his jogging trousers lowered and Dorothy got an unsolicited flash of graying underpants. She put the biscuit down, her appetite having vanished. The man straightened up, slammed the van door shut, and turned to face Shelley House. He squinted up at the building, casting his eyes over the three stories, then looked down at the clipboard he held in his hands.

Who on earth was this? Having finished consulting his clipboard, the man walked to the rear of the van, opened the door (*Clean me*, some cad had inscribed into the thick dirt), and pulled out an odd-looking device. It appeared to be a wheel on the end of a stick. The man began to pace along the pavement in front of the building, pushing his instrument across the ground.

Dorothy sighed again. All she wanted was a few minutes of quiet restoration, but this week had been one damn drama after another. She pulled herself up and stormed out of the flat, opening the front door of Shelley House for the second time that day.

"Who are you and what in God's name are you doing?"

The man swung to look at her and stumbled back in surprise, clutching at his chest. Dorothy crossed her arms and waited for him to either have a heart attack or regain his composure.

"Jesus, you gave me a fright there," he said, chuckling. "I thought you were a bleedin' ghost!"

Dorothy did not laugh. "You have not answered my question."

"Sorry." He bent down to retrieve his clipboard from where it had dropped on the pavement. "I'm Gary, Gary Watts. Fergus asked me to pop round and take a few measurements."

Fergus Alexander. Dorothy's pathetic excuse of a landlord. She should have guessed.

"Does that mean Mr. Alexander will finally be tackling some of the many failings in this building?" Dorothy said. "I have already written to him on a number of occasions regarding issues with the fire escape door on the third floor, the faulty light on the first-floor landing, the accumulation of detritus in the lobby, and the leak in my bathroom, to name but a few."

"Sorry, I can't help you with any of those," the man said with a shrug. "I'm just here to get some last details for the plans."

"What plans?"

"The building plans."

For goodness' sake, was the man being deliberately obtuse? "What building plans, Mr. Watts?"

He raised his eyebrows and then adopted the loud, slow voice of a person who believed they were talking to a deaf and potentially senile pensioner. "For . . . the . . . flats . . . deary."

Dorothy suppressed a sigh. "I think you have made a mistake, Mr. Watts. There are flats here already."

He scratched his stomach. "Nah, the new ones. Fergus submitted the planning application yesterday, but he wanted me to check something. You know what those suits at the council are like, any tiny error and they'll reject 'em."

Dorothy could hear the sound of blood thrumming in her ears, and she reached a hand out to steady herself on the side of the building.

"You all right?" the man called up. "Now you look like the one who's seen a ghost."

It took Dorothy a moment to form her words. "Did you say *new* flats?"

"Yeah. Twenty-four in total, if it all gets approved."

"But how will they all fit into Shelley House? It's quite crowded enough with only six."

The man squinted up at her. "It's not gonna be Shelley House anymore, love. They're tearing the whole thing down and building an eight-story block in its place."

There it was again, the dizzying rush to her head. For one horrible moment Dorothy thought she might vomit.

"Shit, I thought all you tenants knew about this?" the builder said. "Fergus told me he sent out the Section 21s weeks ago, so I assumed he told you all then."

Dorothy scanned her memory back to that wretched letter. She had burned it so it was not possible to check, but she was sure it had only said some nonsense about evictions, which Dorothy had ignored. After all, previous landlords had threatened the same thing and nothing had ever come of it. But there had been no mention of destroying Shelley House, of that much she was certain.

"Are you sure you don't need to sit down? You're looking a bit wobbly."

Dorothy was about to snap at him for patronizing her, but in truth she did feel most peculiar. She went to turn into the building and stumbled again.

"Here, let me help you."

The man jogged up the stairs and before Dorothy could stop him he had reached out and taken her arm. She recoiled, but he held it firmly and guided her into the lobby.

"Which one are you in?"

"The right one," she croaked, and he led her to her front door.

"Want me to come in and get you some water?"

"No, thank you."

Dorothy was trying to open the door but her hands were shaking so much she could barely manage it. Finally she released the latch and half stepped, half fell into her flat. As she did, her eyes landed on the mantelpiece and another wave of nausea crashed over her.

It was unclear how long Dorothy had lain on her bed; it could have been five minutes or five hours. She had no memory of Ayesha returning or what had happened to that wretched dog. All she knew was that she had closed her eyes and repeated the same words over and over in her head. *It's not gonna be Shelley House anymore, love. They're tearing the whole thing down.*

At some point she must have drifted off to sleep, because when she opened her eyes, the shadows on the ceiling told her it was well past midday. Shelley House was eerily quiet and for a moment Dorothy could not remember why she was here, lying on top of her bed fully dressed. And then it hit her again. *They're tearing the whole thing down.*

She felt something itching in her left eye and blinked it away. A second later, there was the sensation of something wet on her cheek. Dorothy raised a hand to her face and wiped it, but the water was coming faster than she could stem. She reached down to her pocket, rummaging around for a handkerchief, and that was when she felt it. Something soft and warm and unfamiliar on the bed next to her.

Dorothy jerked her head up from the pillow and opened her eyes. Though her vision was misty she saw the dog lying on the bed, staring up at her with that pathetic face. Dorothy snatched her arm back.

"Go away!" she said, but the words came out as a muffled yawp.

The dog stayed where it was, its head resting on its front paws.

"I said leave me alone!" Dorothy tried again.

The animal exhaled loudly but did not budge.

They're tearing the whole thing down.

There was a tsunami from her eyes now and Dorothy's head slumped back on the pillow, defeated. She rested her arm down on the bed again and her hand settled on the dog's body. She could feel the rise and fall of its small chest and the faint pulse of its heartbeat under her fingers. Dorothy closed her eyes, and this time she did not try to stop the tears as they fell.

Seventeen

KAT

At five o'clock, Kat left work and drove back to Chalcot. It had been a busy shift in the café, with a constant stream of customers, but as she scrubbed pile after pile of dirty dishes, she replayed the meeting with Sandra Chambers over in her mind. Whatever Dorothy might believe, there really was nothing to suggest that Joseph's ex-wife was in any way involved with what happened to him. Yes, Sandra had been a bit secretive, lowering her voice and lying to her fiancé about who Kat was, but that was hardly proof of guilt. Plus there was no obvious motive for why she might want to attack him or break into his flat, seeing as they hadn't had any contact in years, and there had been no sign of the black coat. Kat wondered again if perhaps Dorothy had gotten confused about the whole thing. It was hard to tell how old the woman was—from her bizarre appearance she could be anywhere between sixty and ninety—but it wasn't impossible that Dorothy had problems with her memory or had simply imagined seeing Sandra breaking in.

Kat climbed the front steps of Shelley House and let herself into the building. It was quiet in the darkened hallway as she trudged toward the door of flat two and knocked, bracing herself for the interrogation she was about to receive. There was no immediate response so she knocked again, louder this time. Surely Dorothy hadn't taken

Reggie out for a walk? This morning she'd made it very clear that she had no intention of leaving the flat with him, but maybe she'd changed her mind. Kat gave one final knock, then turned away.

Back in Joseph's flat, she headed to the kitchen. Without him there to cook for her, she was back to a diet of pasta, omelets, and anything she could pick up cheaply that didn't take much effort to cook. Tonight she had a lasagna ready-meal she'd gotten for half price on its sell-by date, and Kat heated it in the microwave and ate it straight from the plastic carton, standing at the kitchen counter. Perhaps Dorothy's absence meant she had finally fallen for Reggie's charms? If this was the case, then it was great news, as Kat could ask Dorothy to look after Reggie full time. She flipped open her phone and began scanning through her contacts for anyone who might be able to put her up for a few nights if she left Chalcot soon.

Kat was interrupted by the sound of the building's front door slamming shut. She crossed to the flat door and pulled it open, expecting to see Dorothy and Reggie, but the only person in the hallway was the teenager from flat three.

"Oh, hi," Ayesha said, blushing when she saw Kat. "Look, I'm sorry about yesterday. I really wanted to help with Reggie but my dad is being a total pain about my exams."

"Don't worry." Kat glanced at her watch. It was gone six now; where on earth were Dorothy and Reggie?

"I took him out for a quick walk this morning," Ayesha said. "He spent ages chasing pigeons."

"Reggie?"

"Yeah. He needed a wee and Mrs.—sorry—Ms. Darling said she wouldn't take him anywhere so I walked him to the park."

"Did Dorothy mention that she was going to take him out again this afternoon?"

"No, but I didn't see her again." Ayesha hesitated. "Actually, it was a bit weird. When I got back with Reggie, the door to the flat was open and there was no sign of her. I tried calling her name a few times but there was no answer."

"So what did you do?"

The girl looked sheepish. "Well, I needed to get to college because I had an exam. And Reggie ran into the flat and disappeared into one of the rooms, so I thought Ms. Darling was just in the loo or something. So I shut the flat door and left."

Kat felt her pulse quicken. "And you didn't see Dorothy at all?"

The girl's cheeks had gone even pinker. "Did I do the wrong thing? I assumed Ms. Darling had left the front door open so I could drop Reggie back. Is she cross with me?"

Kat didn't answer as she strode across the hallway and hammered on the door of flat two. "Dorothy, can you hear me?" she shouted through the wood. "Are you in there?"

Shit! What if something had happened to them? Kat banged even harder.

"Do you think they're okay?" Ayesha said, her voice full of panic. "Should I call an ambulance? Or a vet?"

"We need to get into the flat," Kat said, rattling the door handle as she inspected the lock. "I think I can—"

She was interrupted by the sound of a key in the front door and she spun round, holding her breath. A second later it opened and Reggie came scuttling into the lobby. His ears pricked up when he saw Kat and Ayesha.

Kat exhaled with relief, scooping him up into a cuddle. "Reggie! For a moment there I thought—"

She didn't finish her sentence as she saw Dorothy step inside. The previous occasions Kat had seen the woman, she'd been wearing the same beige housecoat and a pair of worn-looking slippers. Today, these had been replaced by an old-fashioned mac and a pair of green wellies, despite the fact that it had been a gloriously sunny day. A black head scarf, tied in a knot under her chin, covered Dorothy's silver hair. It was an incongruous outfit, somewhere between a nun and the Queen, and Kat realized she was staring. But before she could say a word, Dorothy let rip.

"The scoundrel!" she shouted so loudly that both Kat and Ayesha jumped. "The perfidious, mendacious, dastardly scoundrel!"

Kat looked at Reggie, nestled in her arms. Oh no, what had he done?

"If he thinks he can deliberately rip this place apart and I will not resist, then he has another think coming." Dorothy waved her handbag toward the door of her flat. "I swear, I will not let him lay one finger on my home."

"I'm sure he didn't do it on purpose," Kat said. "He just gets a bit bored and restless."

"What, and you think *restlessness* is an excuse for vandalism of a historic building?" Dorothy roared, two red dots forming on her cheeks. "He wants to destroy my home and you say it is all right because he is a *bit bored*. Then you are a hooligan just like him!"

"I think you need to calm down, Dorothy."

"It's Ms. Darling and I will not calm down! I have lived here for thirty-four years and that hoodlum wants to take it all away from me."

"Come on, he's only a dog."

Dorothy puckered her lips. "I am not talking about the animal, you stupid girl."

Kat glanced at Ayesha, who was looking equally confused. "But—"

"I am talking about Fergus Alexander, the conniving landlord of Shelley House. Did you know he is secretly plotting to demolish the entire building and turn it into a monstrous block of modern flats? I have just been to County Hall and seen the plans for myself. Every last brick of this place gone!"

"Oh, I see." Kat was relieved; for a moment there she'd thought Reggie had done something really bad and her chance to leave the dog with Dorothy had disappeared.

"What? Did you know already?" Dorothy said, her nostrils flaring. "Did everyone else know this is what he was planning and nobody had the common decency to tell me?"

"I had no idea," Ayesha said, and Kat saw that the teenager had gone pale.

"I didn't know either, but it's not a massive surprise, is it?" Kat said. "I mean, it explains why everyone's being evicted, for a start."

"No one is evicting me," Dorothy said, crossing her arms. "Three decades ago I made a promise to stay in Shelley House until the day I die, and if Fergus Alexander thinks otherwise then he is sorely mistaken."

Oh man, clearly Dorothy was as naive as Joseph.

"I'm afraid that's not really how it works. Once your landlord has a possession order there's nothing you can do to stop him evicting you. Besides, when he gets planning permission he can pull this place down, and you can hardly stop a bulldozer."

Dorothy scoffed, as if a bulldozer were no match for her.

"What about if he doesn't get planning permission?" Ayesha said in a quiet voice, and then looked startled when both Kat and Dorothy turned to look at her.

"What do you mean?" Dorothy snapped.

"I mean, what if there was a way we could stop the planning application going through?"

"Eh, I'm not sure it's quite that simple," Kat said. "Why would the council reject the planning application? This building's a wreck; it's amazing it hasn't collapsed years ago."

"What balderdash, all it needs is a few minor repairs and a lick of paint," Dorothy said.

"And if this Alexander guy is applying to build a load more flats, the council will look favorably on that too," Kat continued. "There's a housing shortage, after all."

"There are plenty of other places they can build new homes without tearing down perfectly good existing ones," Dorothy muttered. "The question is, how does one go about getting a planning application rejected?" She looked at Ayesha, who shrugged, so she turned her attention to Kat.

"How should I know?" Kat said. "But I imagine they only reject them if there's something wrong with the plans or the redevelopment isn't in the public interest."

"Well, this one is certainly not in the public interest," Dorothy said.

"I don't think a few tenants not wanting to be evicted counts as public interest."

"Then you need to find a way to get *more* people interested." Dorothy jabbed a finger at Kat. "The teenager is right. If hundreds of people lodge complaints, then the council will have to reject the application and then the building will be safe."

"What do you mean *I* have to find a way? This isn't even my home, I'm just Joseph's subtenant."

"An *illegal* subtenant. Do not think I have—"

"Joseph," Ayesha said, interrupting their argument. "That's how we stop the planning application going through."

"Ayesha, I'm not sure Joseph can be much help right now," Kat said, as gently as she could. "He's still in a coma."

"Having been attacked by a resident in this very building," Dorothy said, her eyes darting between Kat and Ayesha as if it might have been one of them.

"But before his accident, Joseph was protesting every day outside the Alexander Properties office," Ayesha said. "So I think we should start up his protest again."

"But—"

"Only this time, rather than only telling people about the evictions, we should be asking them to submit objections to the planning application. That's how we can stop Shelley House being destroyed." The girl looked at Kat, her eyes shining with youthful optimism.

"That's a nice idea, but I'm not sure it's very practical," Kat said. "It's hard to make strangers care about things, especially a building that's frankly falling to pieces."

"That's not true," Ayesha said. "This house has been here for more than a hundred and thirty years; it's part of the local history. We just need to get people to see it's worth fighting for."

"But who has the time for that?" Kat said. "I have a job and you're in the middle of your exams. That just leaves . . ." She turned to Dorothy, who looked aghast.

"I am not taking up some grubby pavement vigil, thank you very much."

"But we don't have to do it every day like Joseph, we could just do one big protest instead," Ayesha said. "We'd have to advertise it, put up posters and hand out flyers to let people know it's happening. Maybe we can even get the newspaper to cover it?"

"I'm still not sure it will work," Kat said. "Remember the meeting at Joseph's flat the other week, Ayesha? He couldn't even convince the residents of this building to fight against their own evictions, so what chance do you have of getting total strangers to help?"

"It has to be worth a try," the teenager said. "If we don't fight now, then it'll be too late. Fergus Alexander will get his planning permission, we'll all be evicted, and soon this building will be gone for good."

"But—"

"I know Shelley House is falling apart and people think it's an eyesore, but my mum loved this building," the girl continued, her voice wobbling. "She always said it made her feel a bit like a fairy-tale princess, living in a grand but dilapidated castle. So even if we can't stop the building being demolished, I have to at least try. For my mum, if not for anyone else."

Ayesha stopped speaking and they fell into silence. Kat waited for Dorothy to snarl something cruel, but when she glanced at the older woman she saw that she was staring at the teenager with a strange, almost pained expression on her face. Then Dorothy straightened up and turned to Kat.

"Well, come on, you heard the girl. The two of you have a protest to organize." She turned and strode past them toward her front door.

"You'll help too, won't you, Ms. Darling?" Ayesha called after her.

"If I must. But, going forward, I shall require something for the feces."

Kat wrinkled her nose and looked at Ayesha, who appeared equally horrified. "What?"

"Poo bags for Reginald," Dorothy called back. "And bring some toys when you drop him over tomorrow. The mutt keeps trying to eat my chaise longue."

Eighteen

DOROTHY

Under normal circumstances, any one of (a) leaving Chalcot, (b) being accompanied by a dog, and (c) confronting council planning officials face-to-face would have been enough to put Dorothy in bed for a week with exhaustion. But these were not normal circumstances and there was no time for any such indulgence now. Instead, less than forty-eight hours after her expedition to the council building in Winton, Dorothy once again found herself donning her dusty mackintosh and Wellington boots and standing on the threshold of Shelley House, dog lead in hand.

"Ready?" Ayesha Siddiq appeared at her shoulder, carrying a heavy-looking knapsack.

The girl had knocked on Dorothy's door the previous evening and told her that her help was required at three p.m. the following day. No further details were given. Dorothy disliked surprises almost as much as she disliked leaving her flat.

"So what are we doing?"

"We're handing these out." The girl reached into her bag and gave Dorothy a piece of paper. It was a garish blue color and had the words ***Save Shelley House*** printed across the top in a bold typed script. Underneath it were a few lines of writing, explaining that support was needed to stop the proposed redevelopment of historic Shelley

House. It also stated there was to be a public rally on Saturday, the eighth of June outside the offices of Alexander Properties. At the bottom of the page was a sketched drawing, and it was this that Dorothy found her eyes drawn to.

"Where did you find this?"

"What?"

"The drawing of Shelley House. I have never seen it before."

"Oh, I did that myself."

For possibly the first time in her seventy-seven years, Dorothy found herself lost for words. The drawing was an exquisite rendering of the exterior of her home. In simple black lines, it perfectly captured both the grandeur and the understated elegance of Shelley House. It was like a Canaletto brought to life, if Canaletto had painted slightly down-at-heel Victorian mansion houses in the English countryside.

"It is quite extraordinary," Dorothy said.

The girl gave an embarrassed cough. "Let's get going, shall we?"

They began by delivering leaflets to the houses on Poet's Road. Dorothy had been concerned she might have to converse with strangers, but thankfully they met few residents in person as they posted the flyers through letterboxes. She imagined them being collected up from doormats and discarded directly into the wastepaper bin, as she herself had done so many thousands of times. Surely no one would stop to read them? Ayesha seemed to have no such concerns, and there was an almost fanatical zeal in the way she delivered each flyer.

"It is most unusual to see a young person so passionate about a cause," Dorothy remarked as Ayesha accosted a passerby and thrust a leaflet upon him. "Your parents have obviously raised you with a social conscience."

"My mum more than my dad," Ayesha said. "Mum got involved in all sorts of local campaigns: she protested when they tried to shut

Chalcot Library and the children's center. She was a big advocate of fighting for what you believe in."

"She sounds like quite a woman."

"She was."

Obligatory small talk concluded, Dorothy carried on toward the next house. But it appeared the teenager had not finished.

"Dad used to care about things too, but since Mum died it's been like he's living on another planet."

Dorothy swallowed. "Grief can do strange things to a person."

"But I don't think it's just the grief. He's so stressed all the time, and all this eviction stuff is only making it worse."

Dorothy thought of the bills she saw arriving for Omar on an almost daily basis, the bills he always removed from the post shelf before Ayesha could see them. And could the man have Joseph's attack playing on his conscience too? Guilt over an attempted murder would not be helping his stress levels one bit.

"I am sure he must have a lot on his plate," she said carefully. "Does he know you are arranging this protest?"

"No, he'd kill me if he knew I was out here with you rather than revising. All he cares about is me getting top grades in my GCSEs so I can study law at university." The girl let out an extended sigh.

It had been a long, long time since Dorothy had conversed with a teenager, let alone discussed their problems. But the girl looked so utterly despondent that she felt she really ought to say something.

"I take it from that sigh that you are not enthralled with the idea of reading law."

"No, I'm not enthralled at all," Ayesha said, shoving a leaflet through a letterbox.

"And what, may I ask, do you wish to do?"

The girl's face lit up. "Graphic design. Like, I really loved making these leaflets, doing the illustration and all the fonts and stuff."

Dorothy looked down at the flyer she was holding and the drawing of Shelley House. "You really did this image yourself?"

"Yeah, yesterday after my maths exam."

"It is most impressive."

The girl blushed. "Thanks, I was really pleased with it too. But my dad doesn't think it's a sensible career choice. He and Mum always dreamed of me being a lawyer."

Dorothy frowned; this was uncharted territory. "I am no expert, Ayesha, but I suggest you need to speak to your father and tell him how you truly feel."

"I've tried, but he won't listen. All he does is mope around the flat, feeling sad about Mum and snapping at me. And I'm sad about Mum too, obviously, but we also need to get on with our lives."

The girl did not speak for a moment, staring at her feet.

"You know, I'd never say this to Dad, but sometimes I think the eviction might be a good thing for us, a fresh start away from all the sad memories of Mum. But then I remember how much she loved Shelley House and I feel guilty even thinking it."

Ayesha looked back up the road, and when Dorothy followed her gaze she saw she was staring at Shelley House, which rose above the surrounding buildings like a . . . what was it Ayesha had called her home? *A grand but dilapidated castle.*

"When Mum got really sick the doctors wanted to move her into a hospice, but she refused until the very end," the girl continued. "She said she wanted to stay at home, in the place she'd been so happy with her family. So I know she'd be devastated at the idea of Shelley House being pulled down and replaced by some horrible modern block of flats."

Dorothy did not speak, her attention fixed on the balustrade-topped roof of Shelley House. She felt a sudden ache in her chest so strong that she almost groaned.

"Then we shall have to make sure that does not happen," she said in a thick voice, turning from the building and snatching a handful of leaflets from Ayesha.

As she pushed one through the next letterbox, Dorothy attempted to compose herself. Why was she getting soppy over a story about a practical stranger? Yes, she and Fatima Siddiq had nodded an occasional greeting in the lobby, and yes, Dorothy had once found a pot of delicious curry outside the door of her flat when she had fallen on the icy steps and injured her knee. But she had never allowed herself the indulgence of sentimentality before, so why all these strange emotions now? It was most disconcerting.

Having covered all the houses on Poet's Road, the pair moved on to the surrounding streets. They quickly settled into a rhythm whereby Dorothy covered one side of the road and Ayesha the other, meeting up every now and then for Dorothy to restock her pile. Several times Ayesha volunteered to take Reggie, but Dorothy demurred. It turned out that a dog was a surprisingly efficient deterrent for strangers who showed any signs of talking to her. Whenever anyone got too near, Dorothy would loudly declare, "This animal is highly volatile; I will not be held responsible if he bites you," at which point most people backed off pretty sharply and Dorothy was left in peace. Remarkable.

"I think that's probably enough for today," Ayesha said when they reconvened on the corner of Oak Road.

Dorothy looked at her watch and almost did a double take. It was five thirty, which meant she had well and truly missed her afternoon pot of tea.

"Thanks so much for your help with this," Ayesha said, as they turned and began to make their way back toward Poet's Road. "I'd never have got this all done without you."

Did that mean Dorothy's services were no longer required? She gave a small cough. "And will you be needing my assistance again?"

"Oh, thanks, but don't worry. I don't want to tire you out." Ayesha must have seen the flash in Dorothy's eyes because she stammered, "Eh, I mean, I know how busy you must be, Ms. Darling."

"Not so busy that I cannot fight for my own home."

"Great! Well, in that case, shall we go out again this weekend? I have to revise tomorrow but I can take a few hours off on Sunday afternoon."

"As you wish."

They had turned into Poet's Road and were approaching Shelley House. When they got to the bottom of the steps, Ayesha paused.

"Ms. Darling?"

"Yes?"

The girl was staring at her feet again. "Thanks for talking to me about my parents. I never speak about this stuff to anyone and I don't know why it all came pouring out to you, of all people. But it was good. So yeah . . thanks."

The teenager gave an awkward smile and Dorothy was suddenly struck by an unbidden memory of her old office at the school in London and the small sofa in the corner where she used to sit and talk with any students who came to her with their problems. It had been so long since Dorothy had thought of her teaching days that the memory felt alien, as if it belonged to another person entirely.

"You are most welcome," she mumbled, starting to climb the front steps so Ayesha would not see the flush of color in her cheeks. But as she reached the top stair, the front door swung open and out lumbered Tomasz Wojcik, followed by his huge brute of a dog. The second Reggie saw the animal he started cowering. The larger dog snarled and launched toward the Jack Russell, causing him to jump sideways, almost pulling Dorothy off her feet. She grabbed hold of the handrail and tried to pull Reggie back before he was savaged.

"Get your hound away from him!" she shouted, but her voice could barely be heard over the ruckus of the dogs.

"Princess, down!" Tomasz yelled as his dog launched once again at Reggie, her jaws connecting with the smaller animal's shoulder. Reggie let out a high-pitched squeal.

"Stop him now!" Ayesha yelled, and Dorothy felt the teenager at her side, trying to help pull Reggie back. "Princess is going to kill him!"

Tomasz managed to grab hold of his dog's collar and heaved the animal back. As soon as he had, Ayesha leaped forward and scooped up Reggie.

"Your animal is a menace!" Dorothy shouted as the fear in her body was replaced by rage. "If you cannot control her, she should be put down."

"It is not Princess! This dog provokes her."

"How dare you try and blame Reginald. You and your dog are thugs, the pair of you!"

The man glared at Dorothy. "You are crazy old lady, just like that stupid old man!"

He pushed past her down the stairs, almost knocking her flying again. Dorothy raised her arm to lash out at him, but Ayesha grabbed her wrist.

"Leave it. He's not worth it."

Dorothy stepped back, but her whole body still trembled with anger. She looked down at Reggie, who was huddled in Ayesha's arms, whimpering.

"Poor Reginald," she said, reaching out and tentatively stroking his head.

"Princess terrorizes him," Ayesha said. "And that man terrorizes Joseph."

As soon as she said it, Dorothy remembered Joseph. In all the drama since finding out about the redevelopment plans she'd barely thought about his attack, but now it all came flooding back. Sandra Chambers's accomplice was still on the loose in Shelley House. And Tomasz Wojcik had just become the prime suspect.

Nineteen

KAT

Kat wasn't sure how she'd managed to get dragged into helping advertise this whole protest thing. She was usually so good at saying no, had spent her entire life perfecting the art: she'd said no to the social workers who tried to ask about her mum, no to the teachers who wanted to know if she ever went hungry, no to the sleazy men who saw her as an easy target. And yet somehow, the unlikely combination of a teenage girl and a crotchety pensioner had made Kat agree to help with their futile scheme, a fact that she found both confusing and alarming. And so here she was, standing outside the library on a muggy Wednesday afternoon, a baseball cap pulled low over her eyes, handing out leaflets to complete strangers while being criticized by Dorothy Darling.

"Do not do it like that."

"No wonder people are not taking any leaflets when you look so angry."

"Perhaps we would have more success if you cover up your tattoos?"

"Perhaps we'd have more success if you shut up," Kat snapped back at one point.

The woman ignored her but it was true that they weren't having much luck. They'd been standing on the high street for the past hour and in that time they'd barely managed to hand out thirty leaflets. Ayesha had been trying to keep their spirits up, but even the teenager was starting to look demoralized.

"Perhaps I designed the flyer badly," she said, as they watched a man take a leaflet, cast his eyes over it, and toss it into the nearest bin.

"Nonsense, the leaflets are first class," Dorothy said. "It is these imbeciles who are too selfish to stop and engage."

"What if Saturday's rally is a disaster like this?" Ayesha said, looking at Kat. "What if no one turns up and we don't get any support with objecting to the planning permission?"

Kat didn't answer. The truth was, she thought it was highly likely that nobody would turn up at the rally or bother submitting objections, but she didn't want to dishearten the teenager any more. Thankfully at that moment Reggie started barking, saving her from having to lie.

"What is wrong with him?" Dorothy asked as Reggie pulled on his lead toward a man and a young woman pushing a buggy out of the library. "Reginald, what is it?"

The dog continued his tirade, barking ferociously as he tried to get closer to the man. Kat had never seen him act like this before, snarling and baring his teeth at the two of them. The woman looked frankly alarmed and steered her pram away.

"I'm so sorry," Kat called after them as they hurried past the war memorial.

"You cannot bark at unsuspecting passersby; it is most uncivilized," Dorothy scolded the animal, who sank back on his haunches, visibly panting. She bent down and gave him a pat. "That is all right, Reginald, I am not cross with you. Here, have a treat."

Kat was about to tell Dorothy she shouldn't reward that kind of behavior when she felt her phone buzz in her pocket. She pulled it out to see a withheld number.

"Hello?"

"Is that Kat Bennett?

"Speaking."

"My name's Glenda, I'm one of the ICU nurses looking after Joseph Chambers."

Kat's stomach dropped. Was this it, the call she had been dreading for the past week? She took a few paces so she was out of earshot of Dorothy and Ayesha.

"What is it? Is he okay?"

"Well, we brought him out of the induced coma a few days ago and so far the signs are looking positive. He's been a bit groggy, obviously, but there doesn't appear to be any serious neurological damage."

Kat realized she'd been holding her breath and she released it slowly. "Oh, that's great news."

"He still has a long way to go before he can be discharged, but the doctors think he's well enough to move out of ICU and onto the general ward later today."

"That's such a relief," Kat said, and to her surprise she found herself grinning.

"The reason I'm calling is that Joseph is asking for a few bits and pieces from home: some fresh pajamas and books, that sort of thing. He was wondering if you might be able to bring them in for him tomorrow."

"Of course. Tell me what he needs."

Kat was still smiling when she hung up. *I'm just happy because this means I can leave Chalcot,* she told herself as she walked back to Dorothy and Ayesha. *It has nothing to do with Joseph; he's not my responsibility. No one is.*

"Someone looks like the cat who got the cream," Dorothy sniffed when she saw her.

"That was the hospital. Joseph is awake, and they think he's going to be okay."

"That's amazing!" said Ayesha, and before Kat could stop her, the girl threw her arms round her neck.

Kat grimaced and fought the temptation to push Ayesha away. When was the last time she'd allowed someone to hug her like this? Possibly not since her grandfather. Kat gritted her teeth until Ayesha released her.

"So the old goat has not croaked yet?" Dorothy said.

"Thankfully not. Apparently he's asking for his Brylcreem, which I reckon has to be a good sign."

Dorothy rolled her eyes. "Ugh, the vanity of that man."

"He's asked for a few other bits to be taken in, if either of you want to go and visit him tomorrow?"

"Oh, I'd love to but I have an English exam. Please say hi from me, though."

Kat looked over at Dorothy but the woman visibly shuddered.

"Why on earth would I want to go to see him?"

"I don't know, maybe because you've lived opposite each other for thirty years? And he might have more information on what happened the day he fell?"

"You are perfectly capable of asking those questions without me."

"Yes, but I thought—"

"Well, you thought wrong. Now, if we are quite finished here, I need to be getting home. Some of us have better things to do than stand around gossiping all day."

The following morning, Kat dropped Reggie at Dorothy's. The woman had stopped grumbling quite so much about looking after him, although that didn't mean she was being any politer to Kat.

"Make sure you find out what that old fool can remember about his attack," she commanded as soon as she opened her door. "He may be safe in hospital, but the rest of us are still at risk while the attacker is allowed to roam willy-nilly round Shelley House."

"Will do."

"Oh, and ask him about Sandra and see how he reacts."

Kat sighed. She'd told Dorothy about her visit to Sandra and the fact that there wasn't anything to suggest she was involved, but that had done nothing to dissuade Dorothy from her theory. In fact, yesterday she had started lecturing Kat on how she believed that Sandra and the "savage dog-owning brute" from flat five were somehow in cahoots. Kat had tuned out after the first few words; clearly her initial assessment of Dorothy as a conspiracy theorist had been correct.

Kat drove to the hospital in Winton and was there by ten. The man on reception checked on the computer and told her that Joseph had been moved to a general ward on the fourth floor. Kat wasn't sure what state she'd find him in, but when she walked onto the ward she found Joseph sitting propped up in bed, drinking orange squash and laughing away with someone sitting in the chair next to him. The only sign that Joseph had recently been in intensive care was the bandage wrapped round his head and the drip attached to his arm.

His face split into a grin when he spotted her. "There she is, the hero of the hour. My savior!"

"Stop it, Joseph," Kat chided.

The man in the chair turned to look at her, and her heart sank. It was the journalist who had called round to the flat on the night of the accident. What was *he* doing here? He was smiling at her, the same mischievous grin as when they'd first met, only this time Kat saw a small dimple in his left cheek that she'd not noticed before. She swallowed and looked away, irritated at herself for paying him any attention.

"I won't stop anything, young lady," Joseph said as she reached the end of his bed. "As I was telling Will here, you saved my life, and when I get out of here I'm going to spoil you rotten. I promise, you'll be the most pampered tenant in the whole of Dunningshire!"

Kat gave a half smile, but in truth she'd be long gone by the time Joseph was discharged. Now that she knew he was out of the woods, Kat had started hunting in earnest for somewhere new to live. Last night she'd messaged a handful of old acquaintances, and an ex-colleague in Edinburgh had replied saying Kat could crash in his spare room, which was free from this weekend. She planned to drive up there on Saturday, leaving Reggie with Dorothy after the protest. For a brief moment Kat considered telling Joseph she was going, but he was looking at her with such affection that she couldn't bring herself to break the news to him now. She'd send him a text on Sunday, once she was four hundred miles away in Scotland.

"So, I want to hear everything that's been going on," Joseph said, nodding for Kat to sit on the end of his bed. "Will's told me your interesting theory that I was attacked and that caused my injury."

Kat felt her cheeks flush with a mixture of embarrassment and anger. How could she have been so stupid as to mention that to Will? She should never have even opened the door, let alone talked to him.

"I don't think you were attacked," she said quickly, hearing the defensive edge in her voice. "You probably just tripped and fell."

"But the thing is, when the doctors told me that I'd fallen over the rug, I did think it was a bit strange," Joseph said. "I've lived in that flat for more than thirty years and never so much as stumbled before."

"Kat told me you were super sprightly and that was why she was a bit suspicious," Will said.

She glanced over to see if he was mocking her, but his face was serious.

"But the question is, who would have attacked me?" Joseph's

brow was furrowed. "I may be deluded but I don't think I have many enemies, and certainly not ones who'd try to kill me with a major head trauma."

"Can you remember anything else from before it happened?" Kat said, but Joseph shrugged.

"The police asked me the same question, but I'm afraid I can't remember a thing. I know I went into Winton and protested outside Alexander's office, and then I came home and made a cheese and pickle sandwich for lunch. But everything after that is a blank. I can't remember the fall or anything until I woke up here a few days ago. The doctors say it's not unusual with a head injury like mine."

"So you don't remember having any visitors that day or seeing anyone unusual in the building?" Will said.

"Nope. I'm sorry, I know that's no help at all."

"What about Sandra?" Kat regretted asking as soon as Joseph's head snapped to look at her. Why had she brought up Dorothy's ludicrous theory, especially in front of the journalist?

"My ex-wife? Why do you ask about her?"

"Oh, eh, I was just wondering if she'd been to see you recently."

"Goodness no, we've not seen each other for years. Sandra's with a new chap now, Carlos his name is. They're getting married, I believe, although I don't know the details."

"Why, do you think Joseph's ex-wife might have something to do with it?" Will said, and Kat could feel his eyes piercing into her.

"No, of course not."

"I'm sorry my memory is so useless," Joseph said, sinking back in the pillow with a sigh. "I hate not being able to remember what happened."

He looked so utterly forlorn that Kat had a sudden urge to cheer him up. "Reggie sends his love."

"Ah, my dear boy!" Joseph said, a smile forming on his lips again.

"I can't tell you how grateful I am that you're taking care of him, Kat. How's he doing?"

"He's all right. He got a little bit lonely the first time I left him, but other than that he's been fine."

"Goodness, yes, I didn't think about that. It's my fault, he's been spoiled rotten since the day I got him. I don't think I've left him alone once in three years. I hope he's not caused too much trouble?"

"No, not at all." Joseph would find out about the broken lamp, torn clothes, and ruined books soon enough, but it didn't need to be today. "Actually, I've had a bit of help with Reggie."

"From who? Gloria?"

"Nope."

"Ayesha, then? She's such a sweet girl."

"Ayesha has helped a bit, but the main person who's been looking after him is Dorothy."

For a horrible moment, Kat thought Joseph might be having a heart attack. His face went pale and he reached a hand up to his chest. Kat was about to shout for a nurse when Joseph spoke.

"Dorothy Darling? My neighbor?"

"Yes. I've been leaving Reggie with her while I'm at work."

"But she . . . she hates him. And me. How on earth did you convince her to take Reggie?"

"I did a favor for her and in return she offered to help me." Once again it wasn't the whole truth, but Kat wasn't about to launch into an explanation of Dorothy's batshit theory about Sandra or Kat's own part in aiding it.

"Well, I never, wonders will never cease," Joseph said, shaking his head and then wincing in pain.

"That's not all," Kat said. "Dorothy's also involved in organizing a protest outside your landlord's office on Saturday."

"What?" Joseph exploded so loudly that a nearby nurse looked over. He reassured her he was fine and turned to Kat. "Is this all some elaborate joke?"

"Nope."

Kat explained about Dorothy's run-in with the builder and what they now knew about the planning application to demolish and redevelop Shelley House. As she spoke she saw his eyes grow wider, and it occurred to her that perhaps this was too much for a man in his weakened state. When she'd finished explaining Ayesha's plan for the protest on Saturday and Dorothy's involvement in promoting it, Joseph exhaled loudly.

"If it wasn't for the almighty pain in my head I might think I was still in a coma and this was all a dream."

Kat chuckled. "Sorry, I know it's a lot to take in. But I wanted you to know that just because you're stuck in here doesn't mean the fight for Shelley House has stopped altogether. Ayesha and Dorothy are keeping it going."

"That is wonderful news." Joseph turned to Will. "I hope you'll be able to cover the protest on Saturday too. Why don't you get Kat's number now so the two of you can liaise?"

"Of course, this is a great local story for the paper." Will reached for his phone, clearly waiting for Kat, but she looked away and pretended she hadn't heard. She still wanted nothing to do with Will in case he connected her to any stories from fifteen years ago.

"I should be going," she said, standing up.

"Oh, so soon?" Joseph said.

"Sorry, I have to get to work."

"Well, thank you so much for bringing my stuff." Joseph reached out, and before Kat realized what was happening he had taken her hand in his own. "And thank you for everything you've done to help me, Kat. Not only with Reggie but the day of my accident too. If it hadn't been for you . . ."

He trailed off and Kat saw a tear glisten in his eye. He gave her hand a squeeze and Kat was suddenly reminded of how her grandfather used to hold her hands like this when she was scared as a child and how safe it had always made her feel. She snatched her arm away.

"Bye, Joseph."

"Good-bye, dear. And promise you'll come and see me after the protest on Saturday. I'll be dying to hear how it goes."

"I promise." Kat turned away from the bed as she spoke so Joseph wouldn't see the lie in her eyes.

Twenty

DOROTHY

The evening before the protest, the yob in flat four held a party that went on throughout the night, the beat of music and the boom of voices pounding above Dorothy's head. At midnight, she rose from bed and banged several times on the ceiling with her broom handle but to no avail. At three she gave up on sleep altogether and sat at her table, drinking tea and surveying her suspect list while she waited for the sun to rise.

So far, the only name that Dorothy had been able to confidently cross off was Ayesha's. Having now had several flyering excursions with the girl, Dorothy knew it was simply not possible that someone that conscientious would have violently attacked Joseph. But there remained a number of viable suspects. Dorothy was still working under the assumption that Sandra Chambers was involved, given she had been caught red-handed leaving Joseph's flat the day after the attack. In terms of her accomplice within Shelley House, the thug Tomasz Wojcik was high on the list, followed by the antisocial menace from flat four. Omar was still behaving most suspiciously, keeping his name firmly on there too, and Gloria could not be eliminated entirely from the investigation either. And as for Kat, well, she might be feigning concern for Joseph, but Dorothy had always had a nose for dodgy characters, and Kat gave off the distinctive whiff of trouble. Thus all of the residents still needed to be monitored closely.

With that in mind, at seven thirty Dorothy dressed and prepared to perform her daily inspection. This was considerably earlier than she would usually do it, but the protest meant she would be out of the house for the rest of the morning. The chances of an encounter with another resident were therefore high, yet it was either that or not do her inspection at all, and just because the building was under threat of demolition did not mean safety standards should be allowed to slip. And so at eight o'clock, Dorothy pulled on her housecoat, slipped her notebook into her handbag, and left the flat.

The lobby showed signs of last night's party, with a box of empty beer cans abandoned by the front door and a half-eaten bag of take-away chicken dumped on the post shelf, its grease leaking over the most recent delivery. Dorothy retrieved her rubber gloves and discarded the lot into the bins outside, then noted the latest offenses in her diary before continuing to the first floor. As she reached the landing, she could hear Ayesha's and Omar's voices seeping out under the door of their flat.

"I told Katie I'd go round to hers today so we could study together."

This, Dorothy knew, was a lie—a cover story concocted by Ayesha so she could attend the protest without rousing her father's suspicions.

"But I've set the whole day aside to help you revise, love."

"Sorry, Dad, I can't let Katie down, I promised I'd help her with history. I'll be back by three and we could revise together then?"

"I'm sure Katie will understand if you call her and explain. Look, I even got your favorite snacks. Now, I'll make us breakfast, and then shall we start with English literature or French?"

Dorothy paused. Despite Ayesha's best efforts, it sounded as if Omar was not buying her story. Should Dorothy step in and try to help? It was her policy never to get involved in the internal disputes of her neighbors unless their safety was at risk (see Gloria Brown), but the teenager had worked so hard to organize today. Dorothy took a deep breath and knocked on the door.

Silence fell within the flat and a few seconds later the door opened to reveal Omar's tired face. He took one look at Dorothy, who was still holding her diary and pencil, and grimaced.

"I'm so sorry, Ms. Darling, were we disturbing you? I didn't mean to be so loud."

"I have not come to complain about noise."

"Then have I mis-sorted the rubbish? Or is my car parked unsafely again?"

"No, Omar. I wish to speak to you about Ayesha's behavior."

Omar looked at Ayesha and then back to Dorothy. "Has she been causing you trouble? If so, I can only apologize, Ms. Darling. My daughter has some funny ideas at the moment, she's behaving most—"

"I am not here to complain about her behavior, quite the opposite. I have watched your daughter come and go from Shelley House and she is clearly a polite and smart young lady, so unlike the ill-mannered, feckless youth of today. You have obviously done an exemplary job in raising her and I commend you for it."

Omar looked too stunned to speak, so Dorothy pressed on.

"I was therefore hoping I might be able to borrow her for a few hours this morning. I am having terrible trouble with my knee, you see . . ." Dorothy pointed to her right leg and did an approximation of a limp. "So I was wondering if Ayesha might be willing to accompany me on my shopping trip to Winton? It will only be for a few hours and I would be most grateful for her assistance."

"Ah, I'm so sorry to hear about your knee. But the thing is, Ayesha has her—"

"Do you know, Omar, when I first fell and injured myself a few years ago, your dear wife was kind enough to leave me a container of food when I returned from hospital. So civic-minded she was, and I can see you have brought your daughter up in the same spirit."

Omar looked pained at this memory of his wife, but Dorothy's words had clearly had an effect. He hesitated and turned to Ayesha.

"Are you willing to help Ms. Darling this morning?"

"Yes, of course!" Ayesha said, perhaps a little too eagerly, for she added, "I mean, if you want."

Omar shrugged and turned back to the door while Ayesha grinned broadly at Dorothy over his shoulder.

"I suppose it's okay, then," he said.

"Thank you so much, you are both too kind. Ayesha, shall we leave at, say, nine o'clock?"

"See you then," Ayesha said, and she gave Dorothy a thumbs-up behind her father's back.

As the door closed, Dorothy heard Ayesha say, "How about we squeeze in a quick bit of revision now, Dad? I could really do with your help on the Great Depression."

Dorothy smiled to herself as she crossed the landing. If she was quick with the rest of her inspection, she might have time for a chocolate Hobnob or two before she and Ayesha left. But first, she had to confront the wretched tenant in flat four about last night's party. Steeling herself, Dorothy raised her fist and prepared to rap on the door until he answered. But as her knuckle connected with the wood, the door let out a loud creak and began to swing open. Dorothy held her breath, bracing herself for a confrontation as the door continued on its slow axis, but there was only silence from the room within. She felt a small thrill as the realization hit her: the tenant must have left his door unlocked!

Dorothy paused on the threshold, weighing her options. The sensible thing would be to pull the door closed and walk away. After all, the man in question was a suspect for an attempted murder, and any individual capable of incapacitating and almost killing Joseph Chambers would certainly think nothing of harming a defenseless lady he found trespassing in his flat. And yet . . .

Dorothy took one step forward and then another. The room she found herself in was dark, the curtains drawn against the morning sun, and it took a moment for her eyes to adjust to the gloom. When they did, she wondered if she was witnessing the aftermath of another break-in. Debris was strewn across the carpeted floor: items of discarded clothing, an electric guitar, and what looked like the bottom half of a lady's shop mannequin. The only furniture was a misshapen sofa, barely visible under scattered fast-food takeaway wrappers, and a coffee table that held empty cans and bottles, an overflowing ashtray, and a strange glass cylinder not unlike something one might find in a science laboratory. The air was thick with the smell of cigarette smoke, stale alcohol, and a base note of rotten food.

Despite her hatred of the young man, Dorothy could not help but feel a little sorry for him. After all, what kind of a lost soul chose to live in such squalid conditions as this? For a second, she considered pulling on her rubber gloves and starting to clean, but then she remembered that her presence here was technically illegal. Besides, the man could wake up any moment; every second she wasted brought her closer to danger.

Holding her breath so as not to make a noise, Dorothy began to move around the room. What she needed was concrete evidence that the slob was involved in Joseph's attack: a bag of stolen goods, perhaps, or better yet, a bloodstained item of clothing. Yet as she rooted through the rubbish, she could find nothing more sinister than an empty condom packet. He must have hidden the incriminating evidence in a different room.

Dorothy eyed the three doors leading off the living room. One of them was closed, which she assumed was the bedroom, so she crept past it to the next door and gave it a gentle nudge with her foot. The door let out a loud squeak as it moved and Dorothy winced, praying that the noise would not wake the man. Once she was confident the coast was clear, she took a step forward and was hit at once by a noxious stench. This must be the bathroom. Squeezing her nostrils shut with her fingers, Dorothy moved silently into the room. Like her own toilette downstairs, the space was small with no natural light. There was an ancient bath along one wall and the lavatory was straight in front of her, beside which was a sink and—

Dorothy froze. Lying on the edge of the sink was a hammer, its handle propped up casually against the tap. Why on earth would he need a hammer in his bathroom? From the state of the premises it was clear the man was no DIY enthusiast. Ergo, the hammer must be here for another reason, and that reason was surely a violent one. Perhaps it had been used in the attack on Joseph? In fact, perhaps the old man's DNA was still all over it now? If that was the case, Dorothy needed to confiscate the item and take it to the police immediately.

She reached into her handbag and scrambled around to find her rubber gloves. If this evidence was to stand up in court, then she could not risk contaminating it. Dorothy found that her hands were shaking as she tried to pull the darned things on. Finally, the right glove sprung into place with a satisfying snap. But at the same moment Dorothy heard another sound: a much, much more ominous one. Through the bathroom wall in what must be the man's bedroom, she heard the unmistakable thud of footsteps.

For a split second Dorothy stared at the hammer in longing, and then she turned and hastily crept back into the living room and toward the front door. With every step she was sure she would hear a roar of murderous rage as the man spotted her, but she did not dare look back as she slipped out of the flat and onto the landing. Once there, Dorothy grabbed the front door handle and pulled it to, taking care not to make a sound as the door clicked shut. Adrenaline coursing through her veins, she turned and began to hurry down the staircase. Only a few more steps and she would be back in the safety of her flat. Yet as she burst into the lobby, she ran smack bang into Gloria Brown.

"What on earth is wrong with you?" Gloria said, stepping back and taking in Dorothy's no doubt ashen face.

"N-nothing," Dorothy stammered, trying to catch her breath. "I was just . . . exercising. On the stairs. It is good for my arthritis."

Gloria frowned. "Have you been snooping again?"

"Of course I have not!"

"I suppose you saw the fire escape door was open?"

Dorothy's stomach lurched as if she were at sea. "What?"

"It was him from flat four and his mates. They woke me up at two banging about on the roof."

Dorothy felt light-headed. Had they really been up on the roof? What if one of the drunken revelers had slipped and fallen over the low balustrade to their death? She might loathe the man but she would not wish that on her worst enemy.

"You all right?"

Dorothy startled as she realized Gloria was staring at her.

"You look ill."

"I am perfectly fine," Dorothy said, clearing her throat. "Now excuse me, I have a protest to attend."

She turned and moved somewhat unsteadily toward her flat.

"Is that what those flyers I keep seeing are about," Gloria said.

"They are. We are holding a protest against the planned demolition of Shelley House."

"Demolition?"

Dorothy looked back at Gloria. "Fergus Alexander intends to pull this building down and replace it with modern flats. A fact you would be aware of if you gave two hoots about anything other than yourself and your wretched love life."

Gloria's face darkened. "You know nothing about my life, old woman."

"I know that you choose men who are far below you, both physically and intellectually, and then wonder why they inevitably break your heart. So take some advice from an 'old woman.' You would be a darn sight better off if you learned to live with yourself rather than needing some half-witted man around the whole time."

Dorothy turned and strode into her flat, ignoring the stream of profanities that followed her. As suspected, today's inspection had involved considerably more drama than she was used to. But strangely, Dorothy had found the whole thing really quite invigorating.

Twenty-One

KAT

Kat parked Marge up behind Winton station and opened the boot to retrieve the box of leaflets Ayesha had given her to bring. She also pulled out Joseph's megaphone and sandwich board, which had been sitting in the flat ever since his accident. She left her rucksack in the car, ready for the long drive up to Edinburgh this afternoon. Kat glanced down at Reggie, who was waiting by her feet.

"I'm going to leave you with Dorothy after the protest, okay?" she said to the animal, who pricked his ears at the sound of her voice. "She doesn't know she's going to be looking after you full time and she might be a bit pissed off when she realizes I've done a runner. But I know she's grown fond of you, so she'll look after you until Joseph gets out of hospital. All right?"

Reggie cocked his head to one side and gazed up at her, and Kat was surprised to feel a lump in her throat. Against her better wishes, she too had grown fond of him over the past five weeks. She looked away from the dog, trying to ignore the tug of guilt at abandoning him.

"Come on, let's go find them."

By the time Kat arrived at the Alexander Properties office, Ayesha and Dorothy were already there. Ayesha rushed over to help her carry everything while Dorothy ignored her and bent down to greet Reggie instead, pulling a dog treat from her handbag.

"Who's a handsome boy, then?" Kat heard her whisper, although she straightened up the moment she saw Kat watching. "Ah, so you're *finally* here. You should know that new information has come to light which suggests that the reprobate in flat four may have been involved in Joseph's attack."

Not another one of Dorothy's wild theories. Kat fought the urge to roll her eyes, but she must have failed, as she saw Dorothy bristle.

"I know what you think, girl: that I am some paranoid old woman imagining the misdeeds of my neighbors . . ."

This was exactly what Kat thought, but she kept her mouth shut.

"Yet I saw it with my own eyes just this morning. Right there, inside his flat: the hammer which I believe he used to brutally attack Joseph Chambers."

"Dare I ask what you were doing inside his flat? I can't imagine he invited you in for a cuppa."

"How I came to discover the evidence is none of your business. Now we just have to work out how the wayward youth is connected to Sandra Chambers, and possibly Tomasz Wojcik too."

It was so absurd that Kat couldn't help but laugh. "Dorothy, however much you may want this to be some criminal ring involving Joseph's ex-wife and half your neighbors, there's not a shred of evidence to suggest that any of them were involved. I think you need to accept that Joseph just slipped and fell."

"Rubbish! Why was Sandra creeping out of his flat the day afterward if she were not somehow involved?"

"Are you sure it was even her you saw? I mean, maybe you got confused and—"

Dorothy let out a sigh of irritation. "There you go again, treating me like some hysterical old biddy. Well, let me tell you, young lady, my mind is as sharp as a tack and I have everything recorded in here to back me up."

She dug her hand into her bag and produced a battered notebook, the same one she'd shown Kat the day after Joseph's fall.

"The answer to what happened to Joseph is in here, I know it is," Dorothy said, waving the book in the air.

Kat opened her mouth to argue but then closed it again. There was no point in trying to reason with Dorothy; she was clearly delusional and no amount of rational explanation on Kat's part was going to change her mind. Kat just needed to get through the next hour's protest, and then she was out of here and would never have to see the woman again.

"I'm going to get a cup of tea before we start, does anyone else want one?"

Dorothy scowled. "Now is not the time to be disappearing off to a tearoom."

"I meant a takeaway one."

The woman pinched her mouth as if Kat had suggested drinking Reggie's pee. "A takeaway pot of tea? What a ridiculous idea."

Kat caught Ayesha's eye and the two of them shared a bemused smile before Kat headed toward Remi's. As it was a Saturday there was a queue in the café, and it was gone ten by the time she got her drink and headed back to Alexander's offices. Would anyone else have turned up to support Ayesha? Kat was surprised to find she had butterflies circling her stomach. Why did she care what happened today? The fate of Shelley House and its residents had nothing to do with her, after all. And yet she found she was holding her breath as she rounded the corner and then exhaled when she saw a small—very small—group of people gathered outside. Still, at least it wasn't only

Dorothy and Ayesha there; Kat wasn't sure she could have faced seeing the girl's disappointment if that had been the case. As she got closer she counted four new arrivals: three of them unfamiliar but one she recognized.

"Hello again."

Will waved at Kat as she approached. He was wearing jeans and a checked shirt today, his messy curls tamed into a ponytail. Kat was struck again with the uncomfortable thought that had bugged her when she saw him in the hospital on Thursday. Will was attractive. *Too* attractive. She quickly looked away.

"Kat, this is Paul and David, they live in one of the flats opposite us on Poet's Road," said Ayesha, who was bouncing around like an excited puppy. "And this is Mrs. Bransworth, who saw one of our leaflets in Chalcot Community Library. They've all come to support us!"

Kat nodded a greeting to the new arrivals.

"We think it's such a shame they want to pull Shelley House down," said one of the men. "It adds a bit of history to the road, doesn't it?"

"It's regeneration gone mad," said Mrs. Bransworth, who looked about the same age as Dorothy and was dressed in a strange hairy coat. "And you know full well those bastards at Dunningshire Council will approve it. Your landlord is probably paying them off!"

"Would anyone like to give me a quote for the paper?" said Will, who had produced a notepad from his rucksack.

"You should speak to Ms. Darling," Ayesha said. "She's lived in Shelley House longer than anyone."

"Absolutely not." Dorothy's face was stony. "I will not lower myself by talking to the gutter press."

"Eh, I'm from the *Dunningshire Gazette*, not the *Sun*," Will said with a smile.

"You are all as bad as one another," Dorothy said. "Perjurers and rogues, the lot of you."

"Hear! Hear!" cried Mrs. Bransworth.

"What about you, Kat?" Will turned to her, and Kat felt her cheeks flush. Ugh, what was wrong with her?

"I don't talk to the press either," she mumbled, and she hurried over to join Ayesha, who was trying unsuccessfully to climb inside Joseph's sandwich board.

There was an awkward few minutes when nobody seemed quite sure what they were supposed to do, until Mrs. Bransworth grabbed the megaphone and started shouting loudly about "damn Tory councils destroying local communities." This seemed to galvanize the rest of them, and before long they were handing out leaflets to confused-looking passersby. Will had pulled out a camera and was taking photos of them all, although Kat kept her back to him so she wouldn't be featured in any. The last thing she needed was her face being splashed in the local paper for all of Chalcot to see and connect her with the girl who'd once caused such trouble.

Before long, three or four other people had joined their motley crew, including Gloria, who said she'd popped out of work on an early lunch break.

"Good of you to grace us with your presence," Dorothy sneered, to which Gloria responded with a four-letter tirade. Still, she took a pile of leaflets from Ayesha and soon her voice was added to the shouts that the small group had taken up.

"Save Shelley House!" "Down with Demolition!" "Say No to New Flats!"

Reggie was greatly enjoying himself, trotting among them all with his tail high.

"That dog is a wanton harlot," Dorothy said disapprovingly as she watched him roll onto his back and offer his tummy for a young girl to tickle. Kat laughed but then Reggie suddenly jumped to his feet and started growling, startling the child.

"Reggie, stop it," Kat said, but immediately spotted what the problem was. Tomasz from flat five was strolling past on the far side of the pavement, his dog pulling at its lead in front of him. Ayesha quickly bent down and picked up Reggie before the dogs could get into a fight.

Tomasz saw them and scowled. "What's all this?"

"We're protesting against the demolition of Shelley House," Ayesha said. "Fergus Alexander has submitted plans to have the whole place torn down."

The man made a *tsk* sound and shook his head. "I should have known. He will build dozens of flats and sell them for a fortune."

"Twenty-four flats," Dorothy said, and then looked put out that she'd willingly engaged with him.

"I work for people like him before," Tomasz said. "They care only for profit, not quality of homes or the people who live in them."

"Are you a builder?" Kat said.

Tomasz nodded. "Site manager."

"I wonder . . . Could you take a look at the plans Alexander has submitted for the application? If there's anything wrong with them, it might help you all to get the application denied."

"Okay," Tomasz said. "But don't hold your breath."

"If you're gonna stand around, you might as well help," Gloria said, and she thrust a handful of leaflets at Tomasz.

The man looked confused and Kat waited for him to storm off like he had from Joseph's meeting, but instead he shrugged and tied Princess's lead to a lamppost in front of the building.

Mrs. Bransworth had relinquished the megaphone, but the group carried on shouting slogans and handing out leaflets. Kat saw some of them being thrown into bins, but she was pleasantly surprised by the number of people who stopped to read them or put them into their pockets. Maybe this wasn't a complete waste of time after all?

"Look, it's him!" Ayesha suddenly hissed.

Kat turned to see a man standing in the doorway of the Alexander Properties offices. He must have been in his sixties and was wearing a loud checked suit and tie, his trousers held up by a pair of braces. His hands were deep in his pockets as he leaned against the doorframe, watching them all with an expression of mild amusement.

"Is that the scoundrel?" Dorothy said, coming to join Kat and Ayesha.

"I think so," Ayesha said. "He looks like the guy in the photos online."

Dorothy stared at him through narrow eyes before marching away.

"Oh no, what's she doing?" Kat muttered.

Dorothy strode over to the megaphone that Mrs. Bransworth had left on the bench, picked it up, and placed it to her mouth as she turned toward the office.

"Fergus Alexander!" she bellowed, and her voice was amplified so loudly that several people startled. "You have some nerve showing your face here today, you blaggard."

Alexander's expression remained impassive as he stared across at them.

"I am Ms. Dorothy Darling, and I have lived in Shelley House for almost thirty-five years. Over that time I have seen the building change from a desirable mansion house for respectable families to the state it is in now: neglected and decaying!"

"What the hell is she doing?" someone whispered at Kat's shoulder. She looked round to see Will standing next to her, so close she could see the dark stubble on his chin. "She's supposed to be saving Shelley House, but she's making it sound ripe for demolition."

Kat didn't reply but Will was right. Had Dorothy finally lost the plot?

"Yet despite the rot that is setting in, you are mistaken if you think you can simply pull the building down, sir. For Shelley House has stood proud for one hundred and thirty-three years, and it will take more than you and your cheap suit to destroy it now."

Kat saw a flicker of a smirk cross Alexander's lips and prayed that Dorothy hadn't seen it too.

"You think this is funny, do you?" Dorothy boomed. "Well, let me tell you something, Mr. Alexander. During its lifetime, Shelley House has beaten far greater foes than you. She stood strong against Hitler's bombs when they flattened her neighbors, all the while sheltering the families who lived inside. She has withstood storms and droughts, floods and fires. She has seen births, marriages, and deaths . . ."

Dorothy hesitated. The high street was eerily quiet; even the traffic seemed to have fallen silent for her. Ayesha, who had moved to stand next to Dorothy, raised her hand and placed it gently on the woman's arm. Dorothy glanced at her before continuing.

"Throughout it all, Shelley House has provided a home to hundreds. Not just a home but a sanctuary; a safe port against the seas of change that have wracked this country. For one hundred and thirty-three years she has protected her residents. And now, Mr. Alexander, it is our turn to protect her!"

A large cheer went up from the crowd, which had now doubled in size, and Kat whooped and clapped along with them. Who would have thought Dorothy Darling had it in her? Will had his mobile phone raised and was filming the reactions. When he saw Kat he grinned and she couldn't help grinning back.

"Did you catch all of that?"

"Sure did! That's going straight on social media."

Kat turned back to see Dorothy standing in the middle of the group of protesters, looking utterly overwhelmed as people congratulated her. The woman glanced over and caught Kat's eye. They held each other's gaze for a moment, and then Dorothy looked away.

Twenty-Two

DOROTHY

By the time the felicitations had ceased and the large crowd of onlookers had cleared, Dorothy was utterly spent. In fact, so desperate was she to get back to the quiet of her flat that when Kat offered her a lift to Shelley House, Dorothy readily accepted.

"You stay here and I'll get the car," Kat said, handing her Reggie's lead.

There was a bench nearby and Dorothy sat down with a groan of relief, allowing Reggie to jump up next to her. She had never made a speech in her life and certainly had not intended to today. But when she had seen that toad Fergus Alexander with an insufferably smug smile on his face, something quite peculiar had come over her, and before Dorothy knew it she had the megaphone in her hand. She was not even sure what she had said, but it seemed to have had some effect, as Alexander had hopped back into his office looking considerably less pleased with himself. And then there had been the reactions from everyone else. Dorothy had never known such compliments; even Gloria Brown had patted her on the back. And when Dorothy had looked at Kat she had seen an unfamiliar expression on the girl's face: surprise but something else too. Something like admiration.

Dorothy looked around her now. Most people had left, but there was still a small group outside Alexander's office. Ayesha was gathering up abandoned flyers from the floor, chatting with the strange old lady who smelled like wet goat. The young girl was grinning and Dorothy smiled too. Although she must get Ayesha back to Shelley House soon, otherwise Omar would never forgive her. And there was Gloria waving her hands around animatedly as she addressed Tomasz; at this distance it was impossible to tell if they were talking amicably or arguing. It was discombobulating seeing her neighbors outside of Shelley House. Dorothy was so used to encountering them within the walls of the building, hearing their loud noises and monitoring their antisocial behavior. Yet here, in the broad daylight of Winton High Street, they all looked somehow less threatening and more, well, normal.

The one figure missing from the scene was Joseph Chambers. As much as Dorothy hated the man, there was no doubt that he would have enjoyed today's event immensely. This was where he had staged his ridiculous one-man protest, after all. What would he have thought of her speech? Was Dorothy flattering herself to think he might have been impressed with her oratory skills? Winton General Hospital was only a few hundred meters away. Perhaps he had heard her all the way from there?

"Where's Princess?"

Tomasz's voice jolted Dorothy back to earth. She glanced over and saw the man looking around him. His awful dog had been tied to a lamppost but was now nowhere to be seen.

"Where's she gone? She was just here."

"She must be nearby," Gloria said, looking round too. In fact, everyone was turning to see where the animal was.

"She can't have run away, I tied her lead tightly!" Tomasz's voice had risen with panic. "What if she ran into busy road? What if she gets hit by a car?"

"I'm sure she won't have gone far," Ayesha said, although her face was pale.

"My baby!" Tomasz cried. "Someone must have untied her."

"Let's split up and look for her," Gloria said. "I'll head up this side of the pavement and you go the other way, okay?"

"I'll go round the back and see if she's gone toward the station," Ayesha said.

"I'll check the park," shouted the hairy-coat woman.

"I will stay here in case she comes back," said Dorothy. She had absolutely no intention of moving from this bench until Kat turned up with the car and took her home.

The others ran off in different directions, leaving Dorothy, Reggie, and the journalist, Will, who had barely looked up from his phone since the protest ended.

"This is brilliant," he said, sitting—uninvited—next to Dorothy. "I only posted the video fifteen minutes ago and already it's got hundreds of likes and shares."

"Posted what where?"

"On the *Gazette*'s social media channels. It's gone wild; see for yourself."

He passed the phone to Dorothy. It took her a moment to realize she was looking at a video of herself, megaphone raised to mouth, berating Fergus Alexander.

"I did not give my consent for this to be filmed," she said, handing the phone back to him in disgust.

"But it's great for your cause," Will said, not looking the least bit chastised. "You guys wanted people to find out about the threat to Shelley House. Well, now thousands are."

Dorothy pursed her lips. He probably had a point but it still felt improper to have a video of oneself thrust upon the interweb for every Tom, Dick, and Harry to see.

Dorothy looked down at Reggie, who had fallen asleep next to her on the bench. What a simple, carefree life he had. Nothing to worry about except what stick to chew and which fence post to urinate against. She reached down and gave the animal's neck a slow rub. Reggie twitched but did not wake up.

There was the sound of a horn and Dorothy looked up to see Kat's tin-can car pull up by the curb. She rose from the bench and began to move toward the pavement edge. As she did, Dorothy saw a green car parking up on the other side of the road, opposite Kat's. There was something about the vehicle that made Dorothy pause. She was sure she had seen it somewhere before, although she could not for the life of her remember where.

"Are you all right?" Kat shouted over, impatient as ever.

Dorothy started walking again but her eyes were on the other car. Its windows were tinted so she could not see anything of the driver apart from a faint silhouette, but it was otherwise unremarkable. In fact, there must be dozens of cars just like it in Dunningshire alone. So why was this one ringing such an alarm bell in Dorothy's mind? She paused, racking her brain.

"Do you want me to help you get in?" said Will, who had come to stand next to Dorothy.

She did not answer as her mind raced. "Oh my goodness!"

"What is it?"

Dorothy reached into her handbag and pulled out her diary, hurriedly flicking through the pages. "I am sure it is the same car."

"What car?" Kat was leaning out the window of her own. "What are you talking about, Dorothy?"

"That green car over there. It was parked most inconsiderately outside Shelley House the afternoon Joseph was attacked. I made a note of it in my diary."

Dorothy glanced back at the vehicle. The driver had not emerged from inside and its engine was still running.

"Are you sure it's the same one?" Kat said. "It looks like an ordinary BMW to me."

Dorothy finally found the page for May 27th. "What registration number does it have?"

Will moved a few steps so he could see the plate. "EB66 . . ."

"BGE," she completed, reading from the page.

There was a pause as the three of them computed what this meant.

"So whoever is in that car might have had something to do with what happened to Joseph," Kat said.

"Indeed. And now they are outside Fergus Alexander's office," Dorothy said.

"Then I think we need to find out who's driving it." Will began to stride out into the road toward the green vehicle. As he did, Dorothy heard the sound of an engine revving, and a second later the car pulled out into the road.

"They know we are on to them!" Dorothy shouted as the car began to drive away.

"Quick, get in!" Kat said, but Dorothy was already pulling open the rear passenger door.

"Come on, Reginald," she said, scooping the animal in behind her. When she sat down, she heard the sound of another door opening too.

"What do you think you're doing?" Kat said, as Will started to climb into the front passenger seat.

He looked at Kat and then at Dorothy. "Come on! I've always wanted to be in a car chase."

"Seriously?" Dorothy said. "Ugh, men are so facile."

Kat did not say anything and Dorothy could tell she was weighing up whether to throw him out.

"They are getting away," Dorothy urged, as she saw the green car disappearing down the high street.

Kat let out an audible sigh. And then, in a squeal of rubber and what smelled alarmingly like burning hair, they were off.

Twenty-Three

KAT

Unlike Will, Kat had been in a car chase before. That time, one of her mother's dodgy boyfriends had been the driver and they were the ones being chased, not the other way round. And there certainly hadn't been a seventy-seven-year-old in the back seat screeching instructions.

"Slow down! This road has a thirty-miles-per-hour speed limit."

"He has turned left, you need to indicate now."

"What is that strange smell? You really need to get this car seen by a qualified motor mechanic."

Kat bit her tongue and focused on the green car that was weaving in and out of the traffic up ahead. How had she not made the connection between Fergus Alexander and Joseph's accident before? It was so obvious: Joseph had been staging his daily protest outside the Alexander Properties office, getting bad publicity for the man, and so Alexander must have decided to take matters into his own hands. Clearly he'd sent this goon in the green BMW to pay a visit to Joseph, a visit that ended up with the old man in intensive care. Kat kicked herself for not having made the link sooner. She'd allowed herself to become distracted by Dorothy and her ridiculous theories about the attacker being Sandra or someone from within Shelley House. Once again, yet more proof of why Kat should never trust anyone's instincts but her own.

"They are heading for the bypass," Dorothy shouted. "Quick or we will lose them!"

"I thought you wanted me to slow down," Kat muttered through gritted teeth.

Next to her, Will seemed to be enjoying the whole thing a little too much, a glint in his eyes like a schoolboy on a roller coaster. What was Kat thinking letting a journalist get into her car? Still, at least she'd be gone in a few hours' time.

"Kat, pay attention, you nearly ran that woman over!" Dorothy screeched from the back seat. "Honestly, I do not know where you learned to drive but it was certainly not in any reputable driving school, that much is clear."

"Dorothy, unless you shut up I will stop this car and leave you on the pavement to walk home."

That seemed to work and for a few minutes they drove in relative peace. The green car had left Winton and they were now driving past open fields. Where were they? And more importantly, what were they going to do if and when the car stopped? The driver was someone who was capable of hospitalizing a fit man, after all. Kat had nothing at hand that could be used as a weapon aside from a megaphone and a sandwich board, so unless Dorothy was going to loudly nag them into submission, this whole plan was stupid and quite possibly dangerous.

"It looks like they're heading back toward Chalcot," Will said, as the green car turned left and started heading down a hill.

Sure enough, Kat could see a view of the village she knew well from her childhood, the river winding through it in the valley below. The green car had slowed slightly and turned without indicating into an estate of new-build houses. Kat followed.

"You need to hurry up or we shall lose them," Dorothy said, as the other vehicle accelerated up ahead.

"I'm trying," Kat said, pressing her foot down on the pedal. But rather than racing forward, the car let out a worrying clank.

"I said accelerate, not brake," Dorothy shouted.

"I didn't brake," Kat shouted back, but there was no doubt that the car was slowing. She pulled it over to the side of the road as it let out another angry groan and ground to a halt.

"We're losing them," Will said, as they all watched the green car disappear round a corner. "What happened?"

"I don't know. I think it might have been the engine." Kat watched as steam started to pour out from under the bonnet of the car. "Oh, Marge."

"Marge?" Dorothy's voice was incredulous. "Who in God's name is Marge?"

Kat didn't answer. She'd bought this car secondhand from a dodgy dealer when she turned seventeen, and even back then it had been in a poor state. Yet Kat loved Marge with all her heart. Its four wheels had been her first taste of freedom, her means of escape from bad situations and bad people, and at times her only safe place to sleep. But from the look of things now, it was very possible that Kat had just killed the car. She was meant to be driving up to Edinburgh this afternoon; how was she supposed to get there now?

"Where are we?" Dorothy said from the back seat. "I do not recognize this at all."

"It's the Upper Dean housing estate," Will said.

Kat glanced around them for the first time. They were on a road of identical semidetached houses with similar roads leading off on either side. Over the rooftops, Kat could see a large block of modern-looking flats too.

"Did this not all use to be open countryside?" Dorothy said.

"Yes, just fields and a farm, I think," Will said.

Kat looked at him. "A farm?"

"There was a small woods as well. I used to come up here blackberry picking with my mum."

"Do you know what the farm was called?"

Will thought for a moment. "Feather something?"

Kat felt a sudden tightness in her chest. *Featherdown Farm.* She looked around her again, trying to recognize something, anything from her childhood, but all evidence of her grandpa's home was gone, replaced by these grim, soulless houses. She gripped the steering wheel, willing herself not to cry.

"Who did this?" Dorothy said, and her voice was low.

"I'm pretty sure it's another Alexander Properties project," Will said. "I wasn't working at the *Gazette* when this all went up, but I remember reading about it. I think there was some local resistance to the development, but it failed."

Kat felt a flash of rage. Fergus Alexander, the man responsible for putting Joseph in hospital, was also responsible for the devastation wrought on her grandfather's farm. Had her grandpa been part of the local resistance? He had loved the farm more than anything, so Kat couldn't imagine him ever willingly selling it. The idea that his beloved home might have been snatched away from him made Kat's blood run hot.

"We cannot let him do this to Shelley House," Dorothy said from the back seat, and Kat heard the anger in her tone too. "We cannot let Alexander destroy Shelley House like he has destroyed this beautiful countryside."

Kat turned to look at her. "We need to bring the bastard down. We need to make him pay."

She expected Dorothy to scold her for swearing, but the woman nodded grimly.

"I can help too," Will said, and when Kat glanced over he was looking at her.

"We don't need your—" Kat started, but Dorothy interrupted.

"Thank you, Will. Your offer is much appreciated."

Kat looked again at the ugly houses around them. For years, whenever she thought of Featherdown Farm her memories had been tainted by that final summer: the summer she ruined everything and got sent away. But now other memories came flooding back. The afternoons spent playing in the barns, climbing trees in the woods, and taking Barker on long walks. Her grandfather and his brother had been born on Featherdown Farm and lived there their whole lives, and stays on the farm had been like a magical holiday from Kat's real life, a life of temporary housing and evictions and her chaotic, troubled mother. And even though it had all ended so badly, this place was still where she had been happiest and felt safest.

Kat took a deep breath as fury surged through her body. Fergus Alexander might have succeeded in destroying Featherdown Farm and putting Joseph in the hospital, but she wasn't going to let him harm anyone else ever again. And if that meant delaying leaving Chalcot and working with Dorothy and Will, that was what she was going to have to do.

Twenty-Four

DOROTHY

Dorothy was unsure what she had expected now that their investigation had formally begun. Perhaps that they would be staking out Fergus Alexander's office, shadowing him round town or snooping in his rubbish bins? Sadly, the reality was rather more prosaic. Will had said he would do some research into Mr. Alexander and his other properties, while Kat said she was going to do some "digging online." Dorothy had demanded to know how she could contribute, to which Kat had responded that her job was to keep an eye on things at Shelley House. Dorothy had therefore resumed her window-side vigil, which she had been rather neglecting of late.

Yet on Sunday, as she sat at her card table with diary and pencil to hand, Dorothy felt most discombobulated. Where once she could happily stay here all day, noting the comings and goings of her neighbors and their various infractions, she now found herself getting restless. Even her daily inspection provided little distraction, despite her having adjusted the time so there was a greater chance of running into other residents. The truth was, after all the activity of the past few weeks, Dorothy's life within the walls of Shelley House now seemed rather dull.

The one saving grace was Reggie. Once Kat dropped him off each morning, Dorothy had an excuse to pull on her coat and boots and take the dog out for a walk. At first they had stuck to the park and the streets surrounding Shelley House, but now Dorothy extended their arc to take in the high street and beyond. When she first moved to Chalcot, she used to go for frequent walks along the river, and she had quite forgotten the simple pleasure of wandering along the towpath, the sun on her face and the sound of birdsong in her ears. Reggie loved the river too, although he rather preferred swimming in it to walking beside it.

Yet there were only so many hours a day Dorothy could walk the dog before they both grew tired, and as soon as she returned to Shelley House the ennui set in once more. On Monday, she found she was stretching out her meals to fill time, and more than once she caught herself staring at the wall clock, counting down the minutes until Ayesha returned from school and gave her a wave through the net curtains. On Tuesday, Dorothy paid five visits to the first-floor landing in the hope of finding the door to flat four open again, but it remained firmly locked and the tenant was uncharacteristically quiet. When Kat came to collect Reggie that evening, Dorothy interrogated the girl, asking questions and lecturing her on everything from her slow progress to her unsightly tattoos: anything to keep Kat standing on the doormat for a few minutes longer. And yet still the week dragged on. By Wednesday morning, Dorothy's patience was being severely tested. Neither Kat nor Will had found anything remotely useful yet, and the clock was ticking. Once the deadline for planning objections had passed, their chances of stopping the redevelopment were all but gone. Dorothy paced her flat, accompanied by the crashing notes of *Das Rheingold*.

"This is hopeless, Reginald," she said to the dog. They had gotten back from their walk and the animal was now trying to nap on the chaise longue. "I am not Vladimir and Estragon, I cannot simply sit here and wait."

Dorothy grabbed his lead off the side table. Reggie gave a large yawn but flopped off the seat and came to join her.

"We are going for a little bus ride," Dorothy said, pulling on her boots and coat. Then a thought occurred to her and she marched to her bedroom. When she returned a few minutes later, she was sporting a lilac wool coat she had last worn for a wedding in 1987, a pair of sunglasses, and a large, floppy hat that had seen better days. The dog gave a bark of surprise at the sight of her, but Dorothy ignored him. "Come along!"

An hour later, she was back on the bench outside Alexander Properties, her eyes trained on the building's front door. Dorothy was not sure what she was looking for exactly, only that she was never going to prove Fergus Alexander was a felon by sitting in her drawing room all day. At least here there was a chance she might witness something useful: a bag of illicit cash being delivered, perhaps, or the exchange of weapons. All she needed was to see something that might incriminate the man, and Dorothy was willing to wait as long as it took until that happened.

Two hours later it had started to rain and Dorothy was rather regretting her decision not to pack either an umbrella or a picnic luncheon. There had been no activity at Alexander's office apart from a delivery driver with a parcel and a bored-looking young woman who had gone out and returned ten minutes later carrying a sandwich in a plastic wrapper. Dorothy's stomach had rumbled at the sight of it. She was also craving a cup of tea, having not had one since her breakfast pot at seven. At one point, she even considered going to a cafeteria and getting one of these takeaway drinks that everyone seemed so obsessed with, but that had struck her as a step too far. Reggie, on the other hand, was unperturbed by the rain and had been snoring on the bench next to her. Now he raised his head and let out a soft growl.

"Are you getting bored?" she asked, giving his ear a scratch. "We shall give it another half an hour and then I will buy you a bone from the butcher's."

"Think you're pretty clever, don't you?"

Dorothy startled at a voice behind her. She looked round to see the toad standing next to the bench, leering down at her.

"Not particularly," she said, looking away. She had known men like Fergus Alexander before, and she was not going to give him the satisfaction of rising to his bait.

"You know you're wasting your time, right? Your little protest last week, that sad speech you gave, and whatever *this* is . . ." He indicated Dorothy's disguise. "I'm a prominent member of the local community, Mrs. Darling. I'm a governor at two different schools and on the committee of the golf club. So believe me when I say, nothing you and your friends do will stop the council from granting me planning permission."

Dorothy crossed her arms and continued to ignore him, although her heart was beating a little faster. She could smell the man's noxious aftershave: *eau de crapaud.*

"I told that fruit fly Joseph Chambers the same thing," Alexander continued. "Shelley House will be rubble by the end of the year, and there's nothing you old fogies can do to stop me."

He turned and began to saunter toward his office, whistling loudly. How dare he speak to her like that! Dorothy might be many things, but an "old fogey" she certainly was not. And who did he think he was, comparing Joseph Chambers to a Drosophila? Before she knew what she was doing, Dorothy was on her feet and striding toward him. She was still clutching her handbag, and as she approached the man she pulled back her arm and swung the bag with full force at the back of his head.

"Agh!" He stumbled forward, grasping his skull. Reggie, who had clearly appreciated Dorothy's display of vigor, came bounding over and began snapping at the man's ankles.

"Get it off me!" Alexander yelled, still clutching his head and now hopping on one foot.

"I will do nothing of the sort. And for future reference, it is *Ms.* Darling to you."

Dorothy turned and marched away. Behind her she heard another bark from Reggie, followed by a shout of pain from Alexander. A moment later the dog rejoined her, looking extremely pleased with himself.

"Yes, you are a good boy, Reginald," she said, bending down to pet him. "Come on, let us get you that bone."

They headed off along the high street, away from Alexander's office. As they walked, Dorothy looked down at Reggie trotting next to her. Who would have thought a dog could be such an excellent sidekick? He stopped in the middle of the pavement to lick his genitals and she waited for him to finish.

"Dorothy Darling?"

She looked up and almost groaned. Standing in front of her was Sandra Chambers, an expression of confusion on her overly made-up face.

"It is you, isn't it? My goodness, what a surprise. Your outfit is . . . lovely."

Dorothy tried to look suitably haughty but it was challenging in a pair of sunglasses and a hat that kept flopping over her face.

"What are you doing in Winton? I'm not sure I've ever seen you outside the walls of Shelley House before."

"I am . . . shopping," Dorothy said, relieved that Sandra had obviously not witnessed her altercation with Fergus Alexander.

Reggie, who up until then had been quite engrossed in his own testicles, suddenly spotted Sandra and trotted over to her.

"Is that Joe's dog?" Sandra said, her penciled eyebrows rising even farther.

"It is."

"So you and he have finally made peace, have you? I never understood what happened between the two of you. I thought you got on all right, but then—"

Dorothy coughed abruptly to stop her. This conversation had gone on quite long enough. Besides, Sandra was still a suspect in Joseph's attack. Whatever Fergus Alexander's involvement, there was no denying the fact that Dorothy had seen the woman sneaking out of Joseph's flat the day after his accident. In fact, as unpleasant as this exchange was, perhaps Dorothy could use it to further her investigation. She smiled at Sandra, hoping it looked more natural than it felt.

"How is that bad leg of yours, Sandra? Still giving you problems?"

If Sandra thought the question strange, she did not give anything away. "I'll be honest, it's been causing me terrible trouble lately. I might need to see a physio again, as my hip has tightened right up."

"That is a shame. I hope it will be all right for the wedding?"

Sandra smiled. "You heard the news, did you? We're getting married in December at Oakford Park. You may remember Carlos, my . . . eh . . . friend from the Chalcot Players."

Of course Dorothy remembered the Spanish rat who had cuckolded Joseph; she had seen his horrible little toupee scampering in and out of Shelley House for months.

"Congratulations to you both. How has Joseph taken the news?"

Dorothy kept her eyes glued to Sandra's face, but clearly all the amateur dramatics had paid off, as the woman's expression did not change.

"Oh, well, I'm not sure, to be honest. He and I haven't spoken for years."

"So you have not visited Shelley House of late?"

Sandra let out a high-pitched laugh. "Of course not! Why would I want to visit that old dump?"

Dorothy paused, getting ready for her attack. "That is strange indeed, because I could have sworn I saw you there a few weeks ago. The day after Joseph's hospitalization, in fact."

Sandra's jaw visibly tensed in momentary panic, and Dorothy felt a stab of triumph. Aha, not so good an actress after all!

"I think you must've been mistaken, Dorothy. Perhaps it was someone who looked like me?"

"Oh, I do not think so. You are correct, you should probably see that physiotherapist again. Your limp looked most uncomfortable."

Two pink dots had appeared on Sandra's cheeks.

"Well, I'd better get going, I've lots to do," she mumbled. "Good afternoon, Dorothy."

"Good afternoon, Sandra," Dorothy said, and this time she did not have to fake the smile that spread across her face.

Twenty-Five

KAT

In the days that followed the protest, Kat found herself consumed with rage. With everything she did—working shifts in the café, riding the bus, walking Reggie—all she could think about was what Fergus Alexander had done both to Joseph and to her grandfather's precious home. At night she lay in bed tossing and turning as her mind played over all the things she wanted to do to that man, the ways she wanted to wreak revenge on him. But the reality was she had no idea how to actually bring him down. After all, she had no evidence that he was the one behind Joseph's attack; seeing a suspicious car outside his office was hardly incriminating evidence. What Kat needed was actual, concrete proof that Alexander had arranged to have Joseph hurt.

On Wednesday, after four nights of disrupted sleep, Kat's foul mood reached new heights. She found herself snapping at the chefs at work, slamming pots down, and snarling at anyone who tried to talk to her. Remi had already had a word with her yesterday when she'd smashed a tray of glasses by handling them carelessly, and today she felt his eyes boring into the back of her head as she leaned over the sink. At two o'clock, as she was scrubbing a greasy pan and imagining it was Fergus's face, Kat heard her boss calling her out to the front. She scowled, preparing for another telling-off, but when she emerged onto the café floor she found Will standing by the counter, watching her with those dark brown eyes of his. Kat's stomach did an unexpected somersault and her scowl deepened.

"This guy says he wants to talk to you," Remi said.

"Sorry, Joseph wouldn't give me your number but he told me you worked here," Will said. "I wanted a quick word."

"I don't pay you to chat," Remi snapped, but Kat ignored him and stepped out from behind the counter.

"What is it?" she said, pulling Will to one side, away from her boss.

"I wanted to give you an update on my research," Will said, his voice so low that Kat had to step closer to hear him. "I've been looking into the Upper Dean estate development, the one we saw on Saturday."

Kat's stomach lurched, and this time it wasn't from the proximity to Will.

"Remember I told you I thought there'd been some resistance to the development? Well, I found the article I'd originally read and I was right. The owners of Featherdown Farm had been reluctant to sell their farmland, as well as another resident who was living on a piece of land near the farm."

Kat's mouth was dry and she wished she had a glass of water. She swallowed and waited for Will to continue.

"The article I read didn't go into much detail, but I've managed to track down one of the two brothers who owned the farm."

Kat blinked slowly, allowing her eyes to close for a second. Had Will found her grandfather? A whirl of emotions tumbled inside her: delight, regret, and guilt. She opened her eyes again. "And?"

"He still lives in Chalcot, and when I called him he said he's willing to have a chat to us about what happened back then. In fact, he told me he had lots to say on the matter. I'm going to see him later and I wondered if you wanted to come too?"

Will was watching her, and Kat looked away so he wouldn't see the battle that was raging inside her. Of course she wanted to go and see if this was her grandfather, the man she had loved more than anyone in the whole world. But he had made his feelings about her very clear. Why would he feel any different about seeing her now?

"I can't. I'm busy."

"Oh . . . that's a shame. I'd got the sense on Saturday that you were interested in what had happened to the farm."

"Yeah, well, you were wrong. I'm sorry, I've got to get back to work."

Kat turned and began to walk toward the kitchen door, hoping Will couldn't see that her legs were shaking.

"If you change your mind, he lives at 17 Cressington Road, on the Willowfield estate. His name's Ted Mason."

Kat stopped in her tracks. So it wasn't her grandfather that Will had tracked down but his younger brother, her great-uncle. She didn't know whether to feel relieved or disappointed.

"I'm meeting him at six thirty," Will said behind her, but Kat didn't reply as she returned to the safety of the kitchen.

At six twenty-five, Kat was standing behind a tree on Cressington Road, watching the distant door of number 17. She wasn't going inside the house, she'd told herself repeatedly on the journey over. Although she looked very different from that scrawny ten-year-old and used a different name, it was still too risky in case Ted saw a flash of family resemblance, which no amount of pink hair dye, piercings, and tattoos could hide. Besides, what would Kat even say to him?

Although he'd had nothing to do with what happened, her great-uncle had been witness to the events and had seen firsthand Kat's banishment from Featherdown Farm. And what if her grandfather was there himself? Kat shuddered. No, she was not going into the house. But that didn't mean she wasn't intrigued to catch a glimpse of the quiet, humble man she'd known: the man who used to give her rides on his tractor and let her help him make apple pie on a Sunday morning, the air filled with the scent of cinnamon and the gentle hum of Radio 4.

Kat felt something scratch her leg and looked down to see a large, squash-faced cat batting at her ankles with its claws. A diamanté collar round its neck told her its name was Alan. Kat nudged it away with her leg, and the animal hissed and looked up at her through narrowed eyes.

"Leave me alone," Kat said, but the cat remained where it was.

A minute later, Kat heard the sound of an engine approaching and saw a red car drive past and pull up in front of number 17. Kat recognized Will's toned physique as he stepped out of the car and walked to the front door. She realized she was holding her breath as she counted down the seconds until it opened. But when it finally did, Kat couldn't see the person on the other side of the door, her view blocked by Will. Damn it. She looked around her. There was a large green wheelie bin about ten meters away, big enough that she could crouch behind it to get a better view of the door. Will was still standing on the step but he was likely to go inside at any moment, and then Kat would lose her chance to see her great-uncle's face again after all these years. She took a deep breath, ducked low, and began to run toward the bin. A second later, Kat heard a bloodcurdling wail. She looked down and saw the cat, its face full of indignation, its fur sticking out on end, and its tail under the front of her shoe.

"Shit, sorry, Alan," Kat said, lifting her foot up.

The cat let out another yowl of displeasure.

Kat turned to look at the house and swore. The cat's noise had obviously traveled across the road as two pairs of eyes were staring at her. One pair, crinkled in amusement, belonged to Will. The others belonged to her great-uncle Ted.

"Kat, you came!" Will called across the road, waving at her.

What was she supposed to do now? She could hardly pretend she'd not heard and run away. Kat began to walk slowly toward number 17, her face angled down. As she reached the front drive, her whole body tensed in case the old man recognized her.

"Ted, this is a friend of mine, Kat. She's a tenant at Shelley House, the place I was telling you about on the phone."

"Nice to meet you, Kat."

There it was, the soft, slightly gruff voice she remembered from her childhood. She kept her eyes on the gravel, not daring to look up in case he saw the pain in them.

"Well, come on in," Ted said, and Kat heard a shuffling sound as he moved into the house.

She felt Will step in after him and only then did Kat look up. She could still turn and run now, tell Will later that she had an urgent call or something. It wasn't too late to get away.

"I'll make us a brew," she heard Ted call from inside, and suddenly Kat was back there again, at the large scrubbed wooden table in the farmhouse kitchen that always smelled faintly of cigar smoke, her hands pressed against the warm Aga as Ted poured her a sugary mug of tea and let her eat the scraps of raw pastry. Kat felt almost weak at the memory, and she stepped inside and pulled the front door closed behind her.

Ted's new home was nothing like the farm, although Kat immediately recognized some of the objects in it. There was the old coat stand that used to hold Ted's and her grandfather's waterproofs, although she noted there was only a single raincoat hanging from it today. As she walked into the small living room she saw several paintings that she remembered and the old sheepskin rug that Barker used to sleep on by the fireplace.

Will was sitting on an old green sofa, one leg crossed over the other. "I'm glad you decided to come, Kat."

"Yeah, well, I was free in the end." She sat down at the opposite side of the room from him. Her throat was dry as she recognized more and more familiar objects from the old farmhouse scattered around.

"Here we go." Ted walked into the room carrying a tray holding three mugs, and Kat took her first proper look at him. Remarkably, he'd barely changed since the last time she saw him. His hair was whiter and his beard thicker, and he'd definitely lost some of his brawn now that he was no longer out farming all day, but there was no mistaking that this was the man from her childhood. He put the tray down on the coffee table, and as he did, Kat saw there was also a plate of chocolate Digestives. Those had always been her grandfather's favorite.

"Thanks so much for seeing us," Will said, reaching to take a mug.

"'S'all right, although I don't know if I'll be much help."

"We're looking into Fergus Alexander," Will said. "As I said on the phone, he's trying to redevelop Shelley House and—"

"That man is a crook," Ted interrupted. "A bully and a bloody cheat, 'scuse my French."

"Why don't we start at the beginning," Will said, putting down his mug and reaching for his notepad. "When did you first encounter Fergus Alexander?"

"Must 'ave been 2006 or 2007," Ted said. "Ever since they built the new road between Chalcot and Winton, Fergus Alexander wanted to put a housing estate on our land. Most of the area round

Chalcot is greenbelt and protected from development, you see, but Featherdown Farm wasn't."

In 2006 Kat had been seven and still a welcome visitor to the farm.

"But I take it you weren't interested in selling it to him?" Will said.

"Too bloody right. Featherdown Farm had been in our family for almost a hundred years. Wheat farming we did mainly, although my brother and I added some other crops. We had eighty hectares in total."

"So what happened?"

"To begin with, not much. Every couple of years we'd get a letter from Alexander telling us he was interested in the land, but we always threw 'em away. He wasn't even offering a lot of money and the farm was doing okay. He came to see us a couple of times, in his silly suit with that ruddy big car, but we always told 'im to bugger off."

"So why did you end up selling it to him?"

The words were out of Kat's mouth before she realized it. Ted looked at her then, as if noticing her for the first time, and Kat cringed as she waited for the penny to drop. But he just shook his head and sighed.

"The problems started six or seven years ago. At first they were small things: my tires got slashed in town and somebody broke into one of our sheds and stole some equipment. We thought it was a bit of petty crime to begin with. But then his tactics got more extreme.

"First there was the fire in the grain store. Thank goodness one of the lads saw it quickly and was able to put it out before the whole thing went up in flames, but it still caused a lot of damage. The police suspected it was arson but no one ever got charged. I knew Fergus Alexander was behind it, though."

"How?" Will said.

"Because my brother, Ian, saw 'im the very next day. He drove past the farm in that ridiculous Bentley of his, and when he saw Ian he slowed right down, gave him this big, horrible smile, and handed 'im another letter. Then he drove off without saying a word, but we got the message loud and clear. Sell me the farm or there's worse to come."

"Did you report that to the police?"

"'Course we did, but there was no evidence he was behind the fire so they said it was probably just a coincidence."

"Was there anything else?" Kat said.

Ted nodded. "Too many things to list. Wheat farming uses a lot of water so we relied heavily on our well, and one summer it dried up completely. I'd never known it to happen in all my years of farming. We eventually worked out that the water source had been dammed up a mile away, but by then the damage had been done. Next, one of our main buyers pulled out and although he never said why, we knew Fergus Alexander must have twisted his arm somehow. And then there was Polly."

"Polly?"

Ted didn't speak for a moment. "She was a wonderful dog. Lovely nature, hardworking and loyal to a T."

He paused again and Kat saw that his jaw was trembling.

"We looked for her everywhere. She wasn't the kind of dog to run off, so we thought she must have got herself locked in one of the sheds or something. We were out all night looking for her. And then in the morning I found her body in the woods, by the stream."

"I'm so sorry," Kat said quietly. She remembered how much her grandpa and Ted used to dote over Barker; Polly must have been his replacement. And then she remembered Princess's disappearance from outside Alexander's office on Saturday. Tomasz had found her in the end, chasing squirrels in the park, but was that Alexander up to his old tricks?

"Is that when you decided to sell?" Will said.

Ted sniffed and Kat saw him fighting with his emotions. "Not immediately, but we were getting pretty worn down by that point. My brother had recently had a stroke and all this stress wasn't helping one bit."

A stroke. Kat's hands gripped the arm of the chair so hard that she could feel them shaking. Ted had stopped talking and when she glanced at him she saw that he was staring at his mug, lost in thought.

"Are you okay to go on, Ted?" Will said gently.

The old man nodded. "Sorry, it's just . . . That was a hard time for us. It got so we couldn't sleep at night, wondering what Alexander was going to do next. I thought I was losing my mind. And then there was the attack."

Kat sat up in her chair. "What attack?"

"Ian had been in the Plough and they got 'im in the car park when he left. Beat him to a pulp they did: broke three of his ribs and damaged one of his eyes, then left him for dead."

"My God," Kat said, feeling the now familiar crush of fury inside her chest.

"Surely the police must have taken it seriously then?" Will said.

"They did, but it was dark and there were no CCTV cameras in the car park. Plus several witnesses claimed Ian had been drunk and lairy in the pub, trying to start fights with people, which is absolute rubbish. As I said, he'd had a stroke so he couldn't have hurt a fly, but those so-called witnesses were clearly in Alexander's pocket." Ted let out a long, slow sigh. "My brother never really recovered from that; it's like the beating stole the life from him. And without him working on the farm, I couldn't manage it myself anymore. So that's when we sold it."

He sank back in his chair, looking suddenly exhausted.

"I can't believe that bastard got away with it," Kat said, clenching her jaw. "That was arson, intimidation, and assault. That man should be in prison for what he did to m—to you and your brother."

"I know, but Fergus Alexander's got friends in high places. He was never going to get himself caught."

"But it's not fair!" Tears were burning behind Kat's eyes, and she was aware Will was watching her. She took a deep breath, trying to push down the red-hot anger that was threatening to erupt.

"Even once he got his hands on Featherdown Farm, he still weren't satisfied," Ted said, shaking his head. "There was another piece of land on the other side of the copse, where the leisure center is now, and Alexander wanted that as well. The guy who lived there didn't want to give it up and they made his life hell."

Will shuffled back through the pages of his notebook. "Was that Stanley Phelps? I read about him today."

"Yeah, that was him. Lovely chap and you couldn't have wanted for a better neighbor: kept himself to himself, maintained the land well. Then he passed away and that land got sold too."

"Do you think his death was suspicious?" Will said.

"Not as far as I know. I don't think Fergus Alexander has ever gone as far as murder."

"He's had a good go recently," Kat muttered, thinking of Joseph lying senseless on the floor, blood seeping onto the wood. Was that what her grandpa had looked like when they beat him up? Or worse? She shuddered.

"So that's about it," Ted said, looking between them both. "A sorry tale, I'm afraid."

"I'm so sorry about what happened to you and your brother," Will said. "We knew Alexander was bad news, but this is far worse than I'd ever imagined."

"You know what makes me angriest?" Ted said. "He should be in prison for what he did to my brother, but instead he's waltzing around, making money and lording it up. Just because he's some supposed pillar of the community, he can treat people like shit and nobody has ever stopped him."

"We're going to stop him now," Kat said, her voice a growl.

"Do you know of anyone else who Alexander has done this to?" Will asked Ted, but the old man shook his head.

"Not personally, aside from me and my brother and Stanley. But there must be others out there. He's done development projects all over Dunningshire, so there must be others with stories like mine to tell."

"That's how we're going to bring him down, then." Will looked at Kat. "If we can find enough people who'll testify that Fergus Alexander used illegal intimidation to get them to sell or move out of their homes, then I can put together a strong story that might be enough to stop him. But we'll need people to go on the record."

"Well, you can use anything I've told you," Ted said. "I'm not scared of that man anymore. I'm eighty-six, what's the worst he can do to me now?"

"Thank you, Ted," Will said. "I'm going to head straight back to the office now and start going through the archives. The newspaper reported your and your brother's fight against Fergus, so there must be other articles about people who tried to stand up to him over the years."

"I can help you," Kat said before she could stop herself.

Will looked at her and smiled, and for some strange reason Kat felt a flush of warmth.

"That would be brilliant, thanks. As you'll see, the archives are no small task." He turned back to Ted. "Do you mind if I quickly use your bathroom before we head off?"

"'Course. Up the stairs, first door on your left."

"Thanks."

Will walked out of the room, leaving Kat and Ted alone. She watched the old man gather the mugs up onto the tray. Part of her desperately wanted to say something, to reveal her identity as his great-niece and sob on his shoulder about what had happened. But what good would that do? Besides, it wasn't like her great-uncle had made any effort to contact her over the years. He had sided with his brother over ten-year-old Kat, so who was to say he wouldn't be furious now if he found out who she really was?

"You all right?"

Kat realized Ted was looking at her.

"Yes, fine, thanks."

"You live in Shelley House?"

Kat nodded. "But only for the past couple of months. I'm not from round here."

"I guessed as much. How're you finding Chalcot?"

Painful. Nostalgic. Confusing. "It's all right."

Ted chuckled. "I imagine it's a bit slow for you young'uns. But it's a good place to live, good community. People look out for one another round here."

Not me they didn't, Kat thought with a bitter shudder. She looked toward the door, willing Will to hurry up. This had been a bad idea; she should never have come inside.

"You know, when my brother got attacked, the whole village came together to help him," Ted said, rubbing his beard slowly. "People brought him food and gifts, sat with him when I was out on the farm. Volunteers from the library used to come every week and read to him."

He smiled at the memory, and Kat saw that his eyes were misty. Hers were too and she hastily blinked the tears away.

"Even now, they take care of him. I was down at his grave the other day and someone had left him a bunch of daffodils, his favorite."

Kat's breath caught. *Grave.* She had known this was coming, had known it since she'd walked into the house and seen only one coat hanging on the stand where there had always been two. Her grandfather and great-uncle had been inseparable their whole lives, even continuing to live together when Ian got married and his wife had moved into the farmhouse. Which meant that if her grandfather had been alive, he'd have been living here with his brother. And yet despite already knowing it in her heart, the confirmation still caused her chest to ache.

"I've got to go." Kat stood up, stumbling as she reached for her bag.

"Aren't you going with Will?"

"No. Thanks for your time." Kat started hurrying across the room toward the hall, desperate to get away.

"It was lovely meeting you," Ted called after her as Kat pushed the front door open, gasping for air.

Twenty-Six

KAT

It was only a mile walk to Shelley House along the main road, but in order to avoid Will, Kat took the longer scenic route that ran along the river instead. She knew this path well, had walked it many times as a child with her grandfather, and her whole body stung with the overload of memories.

Kat had known she would probably never see her grandfather again. And yet somewhere deep inside her, there had always been a flicker of hope that she might one day be forgiven and reunited with the man she had loved so much. Kat remembered her shock when she thought she'd seen him in the library and wanted to laugh at her own naivety. Of course she'd never see him again, never be able to make amends. And to make matters worse, Fergus Alexander had tormented him in the final months of his life. Never mind Featherdown Farm and Shelley House. More than anything else now, Kat wanted to make that man suffer for what he had done to her grandfather and great-uncle. She clenched her fists, feeling the slow burn of rage.

It was gone eight by the time she got back to Poet's Road. Dorothy would be furious with her for being late, but Kat was in no mood for a lecture tonight. She let herself into the building and banged on Dorothy's front door.

"What time do you call this?" The older woman's words emerged from the flat before she did. "When I agreed to take Reginald, this was not part of the arrangement. I usually have my dinner by—" Dorothy must have seen something in Kat's expression because she ground to a halt. "What is it?"

"Nothing." Kat reached out and waited for Dorothy to hand her Reggie's lead, but the other woman didn't move.

"You look feverish. Are you unwell?"

"No, I'm just tired and hungry."

"Well, you will not believe the day I have had. First I had a run-in with our mutual friend, Mr. Alexander. I was outside his office and—"

"Can you tell me tomorrow, Dorothy? I'm just . . . I can't tonight."

Kat saw a look of hurt flash across Dorothy's face as she handed her the lead. "Very well. Good night."

The woman turned and slammed her door closed. Kat sighed and made her way back to Joseph's flat. She didn't even have the energy to cook; all she wanted was sleep.

Six hours later, Kat woke with a start. She sat up, her senses on high alert as she scrambled in the dark for her phone: 2:47 a.m. From the living room, she could hear Reggie's frantic yelps. What was wrong with him? In all the time she'd been staying here, Kat had never once heard him bark at night.

"Reggie, shhh!" she grumbled as she climbed out of bed, tripping over her rucksack as she left the bedroom. The living room was dark with little moonlight coming through the large bay window, but Kat could make out Reggie by the front door, his tail wagging madly as he scrabbled at the floor. "What is it? Do you need a wee?"

Kat crossed to the animal and reached a hand out to try to calm him, but Reggie carried on barking.

"Be quiet, boy. You'll wake Dorothy and then we'll never hear the end of it."

He was whining now, short urgent blasts, clearly desperate to get out.

"Come on, then, but I'm not taking you all the way to the park. You'll have to pee on the pavement for once."

As soon as Kat opened the flat door, Reggie shot out and dashed into the hallway.

"For God's sake, st—"

Kat froze. The lobby light was on and at the far side she could see a tall, broad-shouldered figure standing outside flat two, his back to her. At the noise of the door, he started to turn toward Kat, a hood pulled up to conceal his face, and then—

"Ow! Shit!" The figure swore loudly as Reggie took a large, angry bite out of his ankle.

He bent forward in pain and Kat regained her senses. She charged across the lobby, one arm pulled back ready to punch the intruder before he could attack her.

"Stop! It's me!"

Kat grabbed his shoulders and used all her weight to slam him hard against Dorothy's door. The man was much bigger than her, but with the adrenaline coursing through her veins she knew she could put up a good fight. With one arm pressed against his neck, Kat yanked his hood back to see a young man, his face rigid with terror.

"I'm Vince, I live in flat four!" he gasped as Kat pressed against his windpipe.

"I've never seen you before. And why the fuck are you breaking into this flat?"

"I wasn't breaking in. I heard a noise, I came to check on her."

"What?" Kat released her arm from the man's neck. "You heard Dorothy?"

"Yes!" He wheezed, rubbing his throat. "I was going to bed and I heard a shout."

Kat shoved the man aside and pressed her ear up against the door. "Dorothy, can you hear me?" she called. "Are you okay?"

There was no answer from within the flat, but Reggie was scratching at the door with his claws, desperate to get in.

"Did you hear something too?" she said to the dog. What if Dorothy was hurt like Joseph, or worse? Kat turned to Vince. "We need to get into her flat."

"I was trying to pick the lock but I don't have a clue what to do."

"That will take too long. We need to break the door down."

Vince stepped aside as Kat moved back a few paces, took a deep breath, and then ran forward, throwing her whole weight at the door. It let out a thump but didn't budge.

"I have a hammer in my flat, we could try using that?" Vince said.

Kat was about to answer but then she heard pounding footsteps on the stairs. A moment later she saw the bald, angry head of Tomasz appear.

"What the hell are you doing?" he snarled.

"It's Dorothy, I think she's in trouble."

The man's expression immediately changed. "Stand back."

Kat and Vince moved out of the way as Tomasz crossed over to Kat's door. He turned to face Dorothy's and then ran toward it. Kat was reminded briefly of a bull charging at a matador as all six foot six of Tomasz smashed into Dorothy's door. This time there was a loud, satisfying crack as part of the wood gave way. Tomasz reached through the hole he'd created, fumbled around, and then the door swung open.

Kat pushed past him and ran into the darkened flat, feeling for the light switch. Eventually her hand connected with it and she flicked it on.

She had never been inside Dorothy's flat before, and the woman had always kept her door drawn so no one could even glimpse in. Now Kat felt as if she'd stepped into a time warp. The living room was crowded with furniture that all appeared to be antique. Everywhere Kat looked she saw faded browns and golds; the whole place was like a museum. It therefore took her a moment to spot Dorothy herself, who was lying on the floor at the far side of the room, wearing an old-fashioned white nightdress and with her silver hair fanned out around her. Her eyes were closed but as Kat ran across to her, she could see the rapid rise and fall of her chest.

"Dorothy, can you hear me?"

The woman let out another soft rasp but didn't move. Kat knelt down, not daring to touch her.

"I'll call an ambulance," she heard Vince say behind her.

"I'll get her a blanket," Tomasz called.

Dorothy didn't make a sound but winced as she tried to move her head in Kat's direction.

"Stop it, don't move," Kat said quickly, and Dorothy stilled.

Kat's hands were starting to shake with the shock, and she closed her own eyes and took several long deep breaths to calm herself. When she opened them, Dorothy's two beady eyes were staring up at her. Kat could see what looked like tears on her cheeks, and she reached out and tentatively took Dorothy's hand.

"It's okay, Dorothy," she whispered, squeezing the older woman's cool palm between her own. "You're going to be okay."

Twenty-Seven

DOROTHY

The first thing Dorothy noticed was the pain. It was like she'd been hit by an articulated truck: the left-hand side of her body ached and her throat was parched as if she had not drunk tea in a week. Next she noticed the noise: bleeps and squeaks and the murmur of strangers' voices. Where was she? Had she finally been sent to hell, and if so, why did it smell of antiseptic and Robinsons Lemon Barley Water? Steeling herself, Dorothy opened her eyes.

For a moment everything was blurred and Dorothy felt a jolt of panic. Had she gone blind? Then she blinked and the world regained focus. The ceiling above her was an unfamiliar off-white color with long unsightly strip lights, and out of the corner of her eye she could see what looked like a blue curtain. Summoning all her energy, Dorothy turned her head to one side. There was another bed and a man in a nurse's uniform—by Jove, she was in hospital!—and some kind of blood pressure machine and—

"What are *you* doing here?"

Kat, who appeared to be fast asleep in a chair beside Dorothy's bed, startled awake. She took one look at Dorothy's indignant face and gave a bark of laughter. "Good to see you too!"

"Why is that funny?"

"It's not funny," Kat said, but she was still grinning. "How are you feeling? The doctor said you'd be pretty sore when you woke up."

"That is an understatement if ever I heard one." Dorothy looked down at her left arm, which was lying limply next to her on the bed. How had she injured it and ended up here? She closed her eyes, trying to make sense of it all.

"You've not broken anything but there's going to be some bad bruising, apparently. The doctor said you're lucky that—"

"The intruder!" Dorothy shrieked, as an image flashed into her mind.

Kat leaned forward in the chair. "Do you remember what happened?"

"Yes! Some vagabond broke into my flat in the middle of the night."

Dorothy paused as the memories came flooding back. She had been woken by a thump from the drawing room, so she had grabbed the torch she kept beside her bed and gone to investigate. When she had walked into the darkened drawing room she had seen a figure standing by the fireplace picking up the picture frame, and behind them the window was wide open.

"Some crook tried to rob me. I was so cross, I remember shouting and charging at them."

Kat's eyes were wide. "What happened? Did they attack you?"

Dorothy tried to piece it all together. She had been crossing the living room, raising the torch above her head, and the person had started to turn toward the window and then—

"I think I fell."

"You fell?"

"Yes. Well, tripped, really. I remember my foot hitting something and as I started to go down I saw one of Reginald's toys lying on the floor, that ridiculous rubber chicken he likes. And I remember thinking 'wretched dog' and then I hit the floor and I do not recall a thing after that."

"And did you see who the person was?"

Dorothy concentrated, trying to picture their face, but there was nothing there.

"It was too dark. They were short and thin, though—I remember that—unattractively so. A little like your build, now I come to think of it." Dorothy looked over at Kat. "It was not you, was it?"

"Of course it wasn't me!"

"Then why are you here? And why are you wearing *that*?" Dorothy pointed at her lilac wool coat, which Kat was wearing pulled tightly around her body.

"I'm here because I was the one who found you, you ungrateful old bat. And I'm wearing your coat because it was either that or accompany you in the ambulance dressed in a Mickey Mouse T-shirt and boxer shorts."

Dorothy ignored the insult. "That still does not explain what you were doing in my flat in the middle of the night. How did you even know I had an accident?"

"Reggie."

"I beg your pardon?"

"He must have heard your shout because he woke me up with his barking. I thought he needed a pee but then I saw Vince at your door."

Dorothy frowned. "Who?"

"He's the guy from flat four. He heard your shout too and tried to get into your flat, and then Tomasz came down and smashed your door in."

Dorothy closed her eyes as she tried to process it all. The antisocial tenant from flat four had tried to help her? And that lout Tomasz? And Reggie! Dorothy felt a glow of warmth pass through her body and she turned her head so Kat would not see the tears that had unaccountably sprung to her eyes. The doctors must have given her some strong sedatives.

"Where is Reginald now?"

"I left him with Ayesha," Kat said. "The whole house was awake by the time the ambulance arrived."

No doubt her neighbors had enjoyed watching her being carted off in her nightgown. How utterly humiliating. But as she was about to ask Kat for further details, Dorothy saw a police officer walking across the ward toward her bed. He was a middle-aged man with thick facial hair, and as he got nearer, she saw a line of cappuccino foam on his mustache.

"Mrs. Darling? I'm Police Constable Elliot Reid. I was wondering if I could have a quick chat to you about what happened last night."

"It's *Ms.* Darling, but very well." Dorothy turned to Kat, who was glaring at the officer with ill-disguised contempt. "Come on, stand up and let the constable sit down."

"Oh no, I'm fine standing." The man looked at Kat and his brow creased. "Haven't we met before? You were there the night the old guy had his fall in Shelley House, weren't you?"

Kat did not answer, her arms crossed over her chest, and the officer looked back to Dorothy. "I was hoping you could talk me through what happened last night, please, ma'am."

Dorothy recounted the events as best she could, starting from the moment she was woken up to the moment she regained consciousness in the hospital. The constable took copious notes, although Dorothy saw him glance once or twice at Kat, who was listening with a scowl on her face. The girl might as well have had *I hate the police* tattooed across her forehead. When he had finished questioning Dorothy, he turned to Kat.

"And you were the one who found her, were you? Would you mind explaining your version of events?"

There was an undeniable edge of suspicion in the officer's voice, and Kat must have heard it too.

"No comment," she said.

"Oh, for goodness' sake, stop being so infantile," Dorothy snapped. "If the police are going to stand any chance of finding who broke into my flat, then they need as much information as possible."

Kat seemed to weigh this up for a moment, and Dorothy waited for another "no comment." But then the girl let out a long sigh and proceeded to give a curt explanation of what happened. As she talked, Dorothy's thoughts drifted off. How extraordinary that Reggie had known Dorothy was in trouble and raised the alarm. He really was an exceptionally smart animal. And why had Kat, Tomasz, and the antisocial tenant from flat four stepped in to help? They hated Dorothy, so she thought they would have happily left her for dead. It was all too much to comprehend.

"I told you, Fergus Alexander will be behind this."

Dorothy was startled back to the present by Kat's raised voice.

"The guy is a criminal. He's got a track record of attacking people who get in the way of his developments. You need to arrest him now for this and for what happened to Joseph."

The constable was looking at Kat as if she had two heads. "Fergus Alexander, the man who sponsors the Chalcot Summer Fete? Why on earth would he want to break into an old lady's flat in the middle of the night?"

"I told you, he's trying to intimidate Dorothy, like he did with Joseph and with countless other people. He's a violent, dangerous criminal who needs to be locked up."

The officer raised his eyebrows. "And you have evidence for all this, do you?"

"He threatened me yesterday," Dorothy said, and they both turned to look at her.

"Fergus Alexander did?" PC Reid said.

"Well, not threatened me explicitly, but he behaved in a most uncivil manner outside his office. Then I saw Sandra acting most suspiciously. I am still convinced she has something to do with it all."

"And who in God's name is Sandra?" PC Reid said, looking even more confused.

"Sandra Chambers, Joseph's vulgar ex-wife. She let herself into his flat the day after his accident and left it in a state of total disarray; she must have been looking for something quite urgently, or else trying to cover something up. I believe she is somehow connected to Fergus Alexander and was involved in Joseph's assault. And given recent events, quite possibly my attempted burglary too. I have written a comprehensive suspect list in my diary at home if you would like to see it?"

The police officer looked between them both. "Crooked landlords . . . violent ex-wives . . . this isn't bloody *Midsomer Murders*, you know?"

"Midsomer what?"

"Miss Darling, my colleagues have dusted your flat for fingerprints and we'll run them through our system, but I think the most likely explanation is an opportunistic burglar. We've had a spate of them recently, often drug addicts trying their luck. You wanna make sure your windows are properly shut, otherwise you're inviting trouble."

"My window was shut," Dorothy said forcefully. Her patience with PC Reid was wearing thin.

"I'll let you know if we come up with anything from the prints but I wouldn't hold your breath. My advice is to move somewhere safer; a run-down building like that is no place for a vulnerable older person like yourself." He stood up and reached out a hand to Dorothy, but she did not offer one back. "I'll be in touch if there's any news."

Dorothy watched PC Reid as he walked off the ward.

"The impertinent sod! 'Vulnerable older person' indeed."

"I told you not to waste your time with the cops," Kat said, spitting the last word. "And especially not that one. I could tell the second I met him at Joseph's that he was useless."

"Oh, this is all so frustrating. Where is the doctor? I wish to be discharged this instant."

"I don't think that's going to happen. They want to keep you in for a few days."

"But I am perfectly fine." Dorothy tried to push herself up and flinched as pain shot through her left arm.

"Sorry, Dorothy, doctor's orders. They said because of your age they want to monitor you before you're discharged."

"Ugh, I wish people would stop treating me like some frail old bird. And how do you know all of this anyway? What happened to doctor-patient confidentiality?"

"I told them I was your next of kin."

"You did what?"

Kat shrugged. "They said you didn't have anyone down as next of kin on your records so I said I was your granddaughter."

"How dare you!" Dorothy said, feeling herself flush. "I do not have a granddaughter, and if I did she would be a darn sight better-mannered than you."

"I'll take that as a 'Thank you so much for getting up in the middle of the night and rescuing me,' shall I?"

Dorothy snorted. "Let us call it payback for all the times you have disturbed me by slamming the front door."

She glanced at Kat, who was smiling and shaking her head, and Dorothy had to smile too. For a moment neither of them spoke.

"So what do we do now?" Dorothy said. "Time is running out and we still have no evidence to prove Alexander is a criminal and a danger to us all. Has that floppy-haired journalist been in touch with you?"

"Yeah. Will and I met yesterday with the guy who used to own Featherdown Farm."

"And?"

For a brief second, Dorothy saw Kat frown but she hid it quickly. "He had lots of stories about the awful tactics Alexander used to get his land but nothing concrete that will help us."

"And has Will found anything else?"

"No, but he's going to go through the *Gazette* archives looking for other leads."

"Well, then what are you doing here, girl? You should be helping him."

Kat did not reply, and Dorothy watched her chew her lip.

"I do not know what you have against that boy, but right now he is our best hope of finding something incriminating against Mr. Alexander. So you need to be less pigheaded and work with him."

"You're one to talk! When was the last time you worked with anybody else?"

Dorothy decided not to answer that question; it was none of Kat's business. "Will is a journalist, which means he is good at digging up dirt, plus he is offering to assist us. And given there has just been a second act of violence in Shelley House *and* we are to be evicted in a matter of weeks, right now we need all the help we can get."

Twenty-Eight

DOROTHY

If Dorothy had been expecting a quiet day to recuperate in hospital, she was sorely mistaken.

Her first uninvited visitor was Tomasz, who turned up shortly after Kat left, bearing a bunch of grapes and looking extremely ill at ease. Dorothy felt equally uncomfortable, and once they had exhausted the topics of last night's events, the Shelley House planning application, and the weather, they quite ran out of things to say. Dorothy was therefore relieved when Tomasz said he had to get to work. Yet as he was turning to depart, Gloria came sweeping onto the ward dressed in some ridiculous skintight outfit and carrying what transpired to be a box of doughnuts. At the sight of her, Tomasz suddenly seemed in considerably less of a hurry to go, and he listened intently as she waffled on about her job and flat-hunting problems. For her part, Dorothy tuned out and focused on the doughnuts, which were really quite delicious. If only someone in here knew how to make a decent cup of tea to go with them, as opposed to the pathetic excuse of a hot beverage they had served Dorothy earlier. Really, how were patients supposed to get better without the fortifying aid of a properly brewed tea?

By the time Dorothy had finished her second doughnut, Gloria had swept out again, leaving Tomasz staring forlornly after her.

"For goodness' sake, why do you not ask the woman out for dinner?" Dorothy asked, at which point the man blushed bright pink and scurried off.

And yet that was far from the end of Dorothy's visitations. At six o'clock, as she was explaining the difference between tea steeping and stewing to a young nurse, Ayesha appeared, full of apologies at having not come sooner. Now that her GCSEs were over, the girl had a summer job working in a small local law firm, stuffing envelopes and other equally mundane tasks. The job had been secured for her by her father, who hoped it might give Ayesha an insight into the fascinating world of law. Unfortunately, and rather predictably, the opposite was true.

"It's so boring," she lamented as she flopped into the chair next to Dorothy's bed. "I'm spending eight hours a day sitting at a desk in a silent office, counting down the minutes until five o'clock. Today the most exciting thing to happen was when I accidentally misfiled a letter and Sharon from accounts told me off."

"It does sound rather uninspiring," Dorothy said. "Have you told your father how much you dislike it?"

"Nah, he's got enough on his plate and he'll only tell me I've got to stick it out. I just hope I can get through the next six weeks without going mad and killing Sharon with a stapler."

Dorothy promptly changed the subject to Reggie, at which point the girl became decidedly more animated. They chatted for another twenty minutes before Ayesha sighed and said she had to head home.

"Just keep the stapler away from Sharon," Dorothy said, and felt a flush of pride when Ayesha laughed.

"Who's Sharon?" Omar was standing at the end of the bed holding a bunch of cellophane-wrapped flowers and looking between Dorothy and his daughter. At the sight of him, Ayesha stopped laughing and her face clouded.

"I've got to go," she said, standing up and pulling her rucksack over her shoulder. "Bye, Ms. Darling."

"Bye, love, see you at home," Omar called after her, but Ayesha did not acknowledge him. The man's whole body sagged. He turned back to Dorothy and gave her a small, awkward smile. "These are for you. I wanted to pop by and say how sorry I was to hear about your break-in."

Dorothy accepted the flowers graciously and offered Omar a seat. He seemed a little confused by this invitation and Dorothy could hardly blame him; the two of them had barely communicated over the seven years they had been neighbors, aside from the occasions when Dorothy had been forced to complain about something. He sat down nonetheless, perching on the edge of the seat.

Dorothy cleared her throat. "Omar, there is something I have been meaning to say to you. Something I should have said a while ago."

She saw the man sit up, clearly expecting the worst.

"What is it, Ms. Darling?"

"Please, call me Dorothy. I wanted to say how sorry I am about the death of your wife. Although I did not know her well, she always struck me as a kind and compassionate woman. Her loss must be very hard for you."

Dorothy watched the man blink in surprise.

"Thank you, Ms. . . . Dorothy. It has been very hard. Fatima was the light in our lives, and without her everything seems so much darker."

Dorothy swallowed. She knew that feeling, the pain at that sudden loss of light. After all, she had lived in darkness for many years. "How are you and Ayesha coping?"

Omar let out a long sigh. "I'm afraid to say, I don't really know about Ayesha. We used to be so close but now she's shut herself off from me. We barely speak and when we do it's only to argue over silly things. It seems that without Fatima, we don't know how to be a family anymore."

"That must be very difficult."

"I'm her father, I'm supposed to protect Ayesha, but I'm failing her. All she wants is to stay in Shelley House, and soon we'll be evicted and another precious link to her mother will be lost."

Dorothy paused. Now that she had offered her long-overdue condolences, should she end the conversation and move on to lighter things? After all, Omar and Ayesha's family life was of no consequence to her. She looked at Omar, his head hung low as he stared at his lap.

"Omar, please forgive me for giving unsolicited advice, but it seems to me that perhaps you and Ayesha need to be more honest with each other."

"What do you mean? I never lie to my daughter."

"Perhaps not deliberately, but there are many things you keep from her. Like all the credit card bills that come through the front door, for example."

The man blushed. "Well . . . those are . . . it's all under control now, she doesn't need to worry about that."

"A moment ago you said that you want to protect Ayesha, which is of course very natural; what parent does not wish to protect their child from pain?" Something caught in Dorothy's throat and she took a sip of water from the glass beside her bed. "But Ayesha is sixteen now, a young woman, and a smart and thoughtful one at that. I think if you stopped trying to protect her quite so much and were more honest with her, you might find that your relationship becomes considerably easier."

Omar ran a hand through his hair and did not respond. Oh dear, Dorothy had clearly said too much. After all, what right did she of all people have to lecture anyone about raising a teenage daughter?

"Is Ayesha keeping secrets from me too?" Omar said. "Does she have problems I don't know about?"

"It is not my place to tell you about your daughter. All I know is that she wants to talk if you are willing to listen."

"Okay. Thank you, Dorothy." He stood up to leave. "By the way, I hope you don't mind but this morning I took the liberty of tidying the post shelf. I know it's a job you usually do but I didn't want it to get too chaotic in your absence."

Dorothy was shocked; she had not realized anyone knew she was the one who sorted the post.

"If you like, I can ask Tomasz to fix your broken door too?" Omar continued. "Also maybe I'll do a quick walk around the building tomorrow, just to check everything is in order. I noticed earlier the light is flickering on the landing again, so I'll take a look at that."

Dorothy felt her eyes sting for the second time today and she pretended to study the cannula in her arm. What a kind man Omar was. As soon as she got home, she would be crossing his name off her suspect list once and for all.

"Thank you," she managed with a cough.

"Not at all. And thank you for being there for Ayesha, too. It's good to know she has a friend in her corner."

Dorothy waited for the sound of Omar's shoes squeaking on the floor as he walked away. Once she was sure he was gone, she closed her eyes and let the unfamiliar word roll round her head.

Friend.

Twenty-Nine

KAT

If Will had been surprised to receive Kat's call earlier, he didn't show it as he greeted her at the front door of the *Dunningshire Gazette* office. Kat waited for him to ask why she'd run off yesterday, but instead he showed her into the newsroom, which was a small, run-down office space filled with computers, empty coffee cups, and bored-looking employees.

"The archives are back here," he said, leading her to a door off the rear of the room, next to what looked like a kitchen.

Kat was expecting to find more computers or perhaps one of those microfilm readers she'd seen on TV, but the reality was a windowless room with floor-to-ceiling shelving units lining the walls. Stacked along every shelf were dozens of box folders, each marked with a different date.

"What are these?" Kat said, looking round at the hundreds of brown boxes.

"The archives. Each box contains old copies of the *Gazette* from a certain time period, usually across six months. They theoretically stretch right back to the start of the paper in the 1920s, although some have obviously gone missing over the years."

"But don't you have all the stories available on some kind of database we can search?"

Will chuckled. "I'm afraid we're not the *Times*, we don't have the budget to digitize all of this lot."

"So you're saying that if we want to find old stories about Fergus Alexander we have to physically go through every copy of the *Gazette* published for the past twenty years?"

"Forty years, actually. As far as I can tell, he started out in the property business in 1984."

"But that'll be like looking for a needle in a haystack! How many copies will we have to go through?"

"By my rough estimation, about twenty-two hundred."

Kat let out a groan and Will laughed again.

"Let's get on with it, then, shall we?" He began pulling box files off the shelf and carrying them over to the small table in the middle of the room. "I only managed to get through 1984 to 1987 last night, so we're kicking off in 1988 today."

To begin with they worked in silence, both bent over the table as they leafed through faded old copies of the *Gazette*. Every now and then, Will would point out a silly headline about a sheep holding up traffic on Favering High Street or acrimony over the judging of the best-kept-village competition, and after a while Kat joined in too, competing to find the most ridiculous story. After two hours they'd only gotten to the end of 1990 and hadn't come across a single story mentioning Fergus Alexander. They had, however, found a couple of references to Poet's Road, which they'd put on one side to photocopy.

At two, Will popped out and returned with sandwiches for them both, which they ate at the table as they pushed on into 1991.

"Look, here's an article about the centenary of Shelley House," Kat said, as she flicked through a paper. "It looks like they organized a party to celebrate it. I'll put it aside for Dorothy and Joseph to read."

"It's mad to think they've both been living in Shelley House since before I was born," Will said, shaking his head.

"When were you born?"

"In 1997. I was runner-up in the *Gazette*'s Cutest Baby Competition later that year, so you can have a good laugh at my expense when we get to that issue."

So Will was two years older than her? That meant they wouldn't have been in the same year at school. In fact, Will would have left Chalcot Primary altogether by the summer everything happened with Kat. She felt her shoulders relax a little with the realization that he might not have even heard about the incident.

"What about you?" Will asked.

"Was I ever the winner of the *Gazette*'s Cutest Baby Competition?"

"No! I mean when were you born?"

"In 1999."

"And where are you from?"

"Near Manchester."

It wasn't the truth, but the honest answer—that she'd moved around so much in her early life that she wasn't "from" anywhere—was too complicated to explain.

"So what brings you to Chalcot? Apart from the excellent cultural opportunities, cutting-edge restaurant scene, and handsome, eligible bachelors, of course."

Kat arched an eyebrow at the last comment and then regretted it when Will grinned. Whatever happened, she must *not* flirt with this man.

"None of the above. I just put a pin in a map and it landed here."

Now it was Will's eyebrows that shot up. "Seriously?"

"Seriously." That was a lie too, but the truth—that Chalcot had haunted her dreams for so long that she'd felt pulled back to this village, like a moth drawn to a flame—was not something she was going to admit to anyone. Especially now that she knew she was too late anyway and her grandfather was already gone.

"That's so cool," Will said, oblivious to the emotions swirling inside Kat. "So do you move round lots, then?"

"Eh, yeah, I guess. If I spend too long in one place I get itchy feet."

"I'm the opposite, a proper homebody." Will put the paper he was reading on the pile to be photocopied and took a new issue. "Apart from when I went to uni, I've lived within five miles of Chalcot my whole life."

"Wow!" Kat heard the incredulity in her voice. "Why?"

Will chuckled at her surprise. "Well, it's a beautiful place to live, my family are still here and lots of my friends too. Every now and then I consider moving somewhere else for a bit, but my heart is never in it. My mum always says a home isn't about bricks and mortar but the people in it, and I guess my people have always been here in Chalcot. I can't imagine anywhere else feeling like home."

Had anywhere ever felt like home to Kat? Certainly not anywhere she'd ever lived with her mum; there had been so many different places that she couldn't remember more than vague details about any of them, and her mum had never been someone to make a place feel "homey." Kat had moved out on her own as soon as she turned sixteen, and since then there had been a series of bedsits and flat-shares and sofas, most of which she preferred to forget. An image of a wooden table and an open fire jumped into her mind but Kat hastily pushed it away. Who said you needed somewhere to feel like home anyway? Wasn't it better to be free, living a life of variety and new opportunities, rather than stagnating in one place?

"I'd go crazy if I stayed here too long," Kat said, picking up another paper.

"Yeah, I get that, especially if you're used to big cities. But at the end of it, I find I always want to come back to the comfort of the place I've known since I was born. That makes me sound pathetic, doesn't it?"

"No, not pathetic. I just . . ." *I just don't understand because nowhere has ever felt like comfort to me,* Kat wanted to say. Another memory of Featherdown Farm appeared unbidden in her mind: Barker snoring in an armchair and the sizzle of frying bacon.

"Don't get me wrong, I'm not saying Chalcot's some perfect idyll," Will said. "It has its problems, like anywhere, and it can get a bit claustrophobic when everyone's known you since you were the four-year-old who wet himself on Santa's knee at the church Christmas fair."

"You didn't?" Kat said in mock horror.

"I did. And if you come across any mention of it in one of these papers, I'd ask you to please burn the copy straightaway."

"Are you kidding? I'd make a hundred copies and paste them up all over the office," Kat said, and Will roared with laughter.

"So do you reckon you'll be staying in Chalcot for long?" he said when he'd composed himself.

"I doubt it. I'd planned to leave weeks ago, but then Joseph had his accident, so I've had to stay and look after Reggie."

"Oh, right. So you'll be leaving once Joseph's out of hospital?"

"I will."

Kat glanced up as she said this and found that Will was looking at her across the table. For a moment they held each other's gaze and Kat felt a throb of longing in her chest. She quickly blinked and looked back at the newspaper in her hands. What was she doing? Allowing anything to happen with Will would be a *very* bad idea. Even if she wasn't leaving Chalcot soon, he wasn't simply some random guy in a bar. For one, he was a journalist, which made him even less trustworthy than a normal person. Plus there was the fact that he could still easily work out who Kat really was, and then the secret she had worked so hard to keep buried would be out. No, however much she might be attracted to Will, it was simply not worth the risk for a quick bit of fun.

"Before you leave town, do you fancy going out for a—"

"We'll be here all week if we carry on this slowly," Kat interrupted, keeping her eyes fixed on the page in front of her. There was another headline referencing the Shelley House centenary, and she dropped it on the photocopy pile without bothering to read it. "Fergus Alexander didn't seem to be up to much back in the nineties, so I think we should start looking in more recent copies instead."

Will paused, and Kat wondered if he was going to say something else, but then he stood up and turned to a shelf. "Sure thing."

He began to pull down boxes and Kat exhaled. Crisis averted.

Thirty

DOROTHY

Despite the noises on the ward, Dorothy surprised herself by sleeping better that night than she had done in months. So much so that when the doctor visited on their morning rounds and told Dorothy she had to stay in for another day, she was secretly delighted. Of course, she made a great pretense of complaining and demanding to be discharged, but when the doctor left she settled back on her pillow with the last doughnut and a copy of *Good Housekeeping* that a nurse had lent her. Many years ago, Dorothy had been an avid reader of women's magazines, and it was fascinating to see how much they had changed. Gone were the crochet patterns and articles on how to keep your husband happy; now it was all "upcycling" and something called "tray bakes." Dorothy was enjoying it immensely until a movement at the other side of the ward caught her eye.

Joseph Chambers, dressed in ridiculous striped pajamas, was being pushed in a wheelchair toward her bed. What was *he* doing here? Dorothy quickly dropped the magazine and shut her eyes, feigning sleep. She heard the wheelchair pull up next to the bed, the porter bid good-bye, and then silence. Dorothy kept her eyes shut, praying that Joseph would lose interest and leave. But when she snuck a glance five minutes later he was still there, happily working his way through her bunch of grapes.

"Stop it! Those are mine."

Joseph looked up and grinned. "Oh, so you are awake. How are you feeling?"

"Tired. Unwanted guests keep disturbing me." She glared pointedly at him but he was too busy choosing a grape to notice.

"Well, you're a celebrity these days, aren't you? I saw that video of you berating Fergus Alexander on the *Gazette* website, and very impressive it was too. You should have gone into politics, Dorothy."

Was he mocking her? Dorothy glared at him.

"Don't be embarrassed, I think it's wonderful. I'm only sorry I haven't been able to fight alongside you." He picked a suitable grape from the bunch and popped it in his mouth. "And I hear I owe you thanks for helping with Reggie, too."

"He is a mangy, flea-ridden, flatulent mongrel without even the most rudimentary training."

"Are you talking about the dog or me?"

"Oh, just leave me alone."

Joseph did not move and Dorothy felt a flash of rage. How dare he corner her when she had no means of escaping! Plus she must look awful, dressed in her nightie and with a huge bruise flowering across her cheek from when she fell. Dorothy ran a hand over her hair, wishing Kat had had the foresight to pack her a comb.

"So I'm guessing you're not in here as an excuse to see me?" Joseph said, giving Dorothy an impertinent wink. She rolled her eyes so high it hurt.

"Certainly not. If you must know, I tripped whilst trying to restrain an intruder who broke into my home."

That wiped the smile off the wretched man's face. "My God, Dorothy! Are you okay?"

"Of course I am. It takes more than a fall to put *me* out of action."

If he caught the intended barb, he ignored it. "What happened? Was it a burglar?"

"If it was, I jolly well put a stop to them before they could steal anything."

Joseph was looking at her with a strange expression. Was that admiration? Dorothy narrowed her eyes; that was the last thing she wanted from him.

"Hang on a second. Kat told me her theory that Fergus Alexander might be behind my accident. Do you think he was involved in this too?"

"I think it is highly plausible. After all, you and I have both publicly tried to stop him. And on Wednesday, he threatened me in broad daylight."

"Did he? What did you say?"

"Nothing. I allowed my handbag to do the talking."

Dorothy had not intended this as a joke, but Joseph threw his head back and began to laugh so loudly that several people stopped to listen.

"Stop it!" Dorothy hissed, but the man continued to guffaw.

"Oh, Dorothy," he said, wiping his eyes. "I've missed you."

Dorothy bristled. What was he talking about? They had not spoken for more than thirty years. Clearly the man was either on strong painkillers or he had finally gone doolally.

"This is not a laughing matter," she scolded, fanning herself with the magazine. "Someone may have tried to kill us both, or at least silence us. I do not find that the least bit amusing."

"Sorry, you're right." Joseph ran a hand down his face in a comic gesture of turning his expression serious again.

"Besides, I do not think I would be quite so jovial if my ex-wife were breaking into my flat the day after someone attacked me."

Dorothy watched Joseph as she said this and saw his face turn serious, for real this time. "What?"

"Did Kat not tell you?"

"No, she didn't. What happened?"

"The morning after you were taken to hospital, I saw Sandra creeping out of your flat whilst trying to disguise herself in a most unusual manner. And when Kat returned, she discovered your flat in the utmost disarray. Clearly, Sandra was on the hunt for something and had been *very* keen to find it."

Joseph had gone pale. "Are you sure it was her?"

His tone was so somber that Dorothy found she did not have the heart to goad him. "Quite sure, I am afraid."

Joseph looked lost in thought for a moment.

"It occurred to me . . ." Dorothy paused. Did she really want to share her theory with Joseph Chambers, the man she had sworn to hate? But perhaps he might have some pertinent information he could share. "It occurred to me that perhaps Sandra may be involved in everything that has been going on at Shelley House. That she may have some connection to Fergus Alexander, your attack, and my recent intrusion."

"You think Sandra could have tried to have me killed? But why would she do that?"

"I do not know, that is why I am asking you."

"I've got it!" Joseph said abruptly. Despite herself, Dorothy leaned forward with interest. "Perhaps Sandra still holds a long-standing grudge over my inability to put the toilet seat down and now she's extracting her evil revenge?"

Dorothy sank back with a growl of frustration. "Why do you always have to make a joke out of everything?"

"I'm sorry, Dorothy," he said, chuckling. "It's a nice idea, but I'm afraid the only thing Sandra is capable of murdering is a Gilbert and Sullivan aria."

Why had she ever thought she could have a serious conversation with this maddening man? "It is not only me who thinks this. Kat has also been doing some—"

"What have I been doing?"

Dorothy looked up in surprise. Kat was standing at the end of her bed, awkwardly holding a large duffel bag in her arms. She looked tired, like she had not slept in days.

"Ah, hello, dear. Dorothy and I have been chatting about you," Joseph said.

"Dorothy complaining about me again?" Kat said, but she was smiling in a manner that suggested she was not being serious. "How are you both feeling?"

"Oh, I'm fit as a fiddle," Joseph said, flexing his arm muscles in the most absurd manner.

"Never better," Dorothy said, not to be outdone. "What have you got in that bag?"

Kat did not reply as she reached for the blue curtain that divided the beds on the ward and began to pull it round them.

"What are you doing?" Dorothy said, alarmed to be enclosed in a small space with these two.

Kat waited until the curtain was drawn, blocking the rest of the ward from view. "I've brought you both a surprise."

She put the bag on the end of the bed and unzipped it. A moment later a small brown-and-white head popped out.

"Reggie!" Joseph gasped.

The dog took one look at the old man and let out a yelp of delight. Kat coughed to cover up the noise as the animal bounded off the bed onto Joseph's lap. It immediately started covering his face in excited licks.

"Oh, I've missed you, boy," Joseph said, burying his face in Reggie's fur. When he pulled back, his cheeks were wet with tears. "I don't know what to say, Kat. Thank you."

Dorothy shook her head in dismay. What a sentimental old fool he was, crying like a child over a silly animal. Dorothy would never be so stupid as to—

"Oh!"

She recoiled as Reggie jumped off Joseph's lap onto the bed and came trotting over to her, planting a wet nose on her cheek.

"Silly mutt," Dorothy said as she gave the dog a scratch behind the ears. He rolled onto his back, revealing his pink tummy, and she gave that a scratch too. When she looked up, Joseph and Kat were smiling at her. Dorothy pulled her hand away and cleared her throat. "You are not allowed to bring animals into hospital. It is a clear health and safety infraction."

"I think our secret's safe," Kat said as Reggie curled up on the edge of the bed between Dorothy and Joseph. "Besides, he was missing you both."

"Any further developments with the investigation?" Dorothy said, keen to move the conversation on.

"I spent yesterday going through the *Gazette* archives with Will," Kat said, and Dorothy saw a slight pink in her cheeks as she said the boy's name. Aha! So *that* was why she had been so reluctant about getting his help; Kat was attracted to the scruffy, long-haired young man. Well, there really was no accounting for taste.

"And have you discovered anything useful?"

"We haven't gone through them all, but we've found a few articles about Fergus Alexander and some mentions of resistance to his developments. Will is seeing if he can trace any of the relevant people today." Kat reached into the bag Reggie had emerged from and pulled out a plastic folder full of sheets of printed paper. "I've got all the articles we've found so far, plus some old pieces about Shelley House and Poet's Road that I thought you two might be interested in. I've not read them all yet but you can take a look."

Kat handed the small pile to Dorothy, and she began sorting through the pages, scanning the headlines on each. **Fergus Alexander Sponsors College Scholarship** . . . **Protest over New Faversham Housing Development** . . . **Local Businessman Honored with Gong for Services to Community** . . . Dorothy turned to the next sheet and then stopped, her breath catching in her throat.

"I wish I could help you and Will, but the doctors say I'm still too weak to be discharged," Joseph was saying to Kat.

"Don't worry, we've got it under control. We're meeting again on Sunday afternoon to go through the rest."

Dorothy started to tremble as she stared at the piece of paper in her hands. She knew what it was without having to read a single word. Which was just as well, as the letters were swimming in front of her eyes, a sea of moving black squiggles and lines. But the photo was clear as the day it had been taken.

"Dorothy, are you okay?"

This was Kat's voice, although it sounded distant, as if she were underwater. Dorothy's throat felt dry and she wondered if she was about to be sick. Joseph had stopped talking and she could sense they were both staring at her, but she could not take her eyes off the photo. Off that face.

"Dorothy? What is it?"

She felt a wave of violent nausea and closed her eyes. As soon as she did it all came flooding back. The sound of footsteps on the stairs. The ambulance siren below. The feel of the hot breeze whipping her skin.

"Dorothy, what's the matter?"

Joseph's voice. She screwed her eyes shut even tighter, as if the simple act of willing it would make them leave. How could she be sitting here talking to this man as if they were two ordinary people passing the time of day?

"Go away." The words sounded strange in her throat.

"What's wrong?" Kat's voice this time. "Should I call a doctor?"

"Go away!" Dorothy said again, louder. She was aware of a bleeping sound. Was that the ambulance?

"I think we should leave her alone," she heard Joseph say above the siren.

"But what's happening to her? Her heart rate monitor is going crazy."

"Is everything all right here?" Another voice, unfamiliar.

"I don't know, she was looking at some old articles and then—"

"Leave me alone!" Dorothy screamed the words and this sound was familiar. She had screamed these words before, back then.

"Can I have some help over here? We need to get something to calm her down."

"Dorothy, are you okay?"

"Come on, we should leave."

"Is she having a heart attack?"

Dorothy felt something wet against her hand, the hot breath of an animal, and she pulled her arm away and yelped with pain. There was the sound of footsteps around the bed, a clamor of voices, questions, but she did not open her eyes. Pain seared through her, poker-hot, but she did not know if it was her body or the memories causing it. Someone tried to take her hand and Dorothy lashed out, pushing them away. And then she felt another pain, a sharp scratch on her arm, and heard a voice say, "It's okay, Ms. Darling. You can have a little sleep now." Dorothy tried to shout at them to go away but then she felt a heaviness settle over her body like a blanket, a momentary fall, and everything went dark.

Thirty-One

DOROTHY

Despite her repeated demands and protestations, it was another forty-eight hours before the doctors discharged Dorothy. She was given a large box of painkillers but was refused the one thing she really wanted: the magic medicine that blocked out the memories that plagued her waking hours, sending her into a glorious, dreamless sleep. Instead, Dorothy was handed a referral letter for something called CBT, which she immediately threw in the bin.

The hospital had arranged a taxi service to take her home, and so at two thirty she was dressed and waiting for a porter to wheel her downstairs when she saw Kat walking across the ward. Dorothy had not seen the girl since the incident on Friday. Apparently she had tried to come again yesterday, as had Joseph, but Dorothy had given the nurses strict instructions that she did not want any visitors, so they had both been turned away. Now the girl looked uncharacteristically diffident as she stopped in front of the bed. Dorothy held her breath, waiting for her to bring up the newspaper article, but instead Kat lifted her bag from the floor.

"What are you doing?" Dorothy snapped, reaching to grab it back.

"I've come to take you home."

"There is no need; the hospital has arranged transportation."

"I've told them to cancel it."

"But you no longer have a car."

"Do you want me to push you down in a wheelchair or will you walk?"

"I can walk. I am not an invalid."

Damn, Dorothy had hoped to minimize her movement today. With a deep breath she stood up, holding on to the edge of the bed to ensure that she was steady. She felt Kat's hawk eyes on her as she turned and began to make her way toward the exit.

"Bye, Ms. D, take care," a nurse called after her, but Dorothy was concentrating on not falling over and did not have a chance to say thank you.

"Are you sure you don't want a hand?" Kat said when they reached the lift, but Dorothy brushed her off.

They rode down to the ground floor in silence and Dorothy hobbled out into the busy hospital lobby, her whole body aching.

"It's not far now. Will's waiting for us outside," Kat said, pointing her toward the exit.

"Will?"

"I told him you were leaving hospital today and he said he'd give you a lift back to Shelley House."

Dorothy bit her lip. Why were they helping her? Was it out of pity for poor old *vulnerable* Dorothy? Or because they wanted to trap her in the car and interrogate her? Either way, Dorothy did not like it one bit.

It was only a hundred-meter walk to Will's vehicle, yet it felt like a marathon. All around her, traffic roared and pedestrians bustled past, one of them nearly knocking her over.

"Hey, watch it, you prick!" Kat shouted at him.

When they finally reached the car, Will was waiting for them with the rear passenger door open.

"Hi, Dorothy," he said, but she ignored him as she lowered herself into the seat. Reggie was waiting for her and he gave a bark of greeting, but Dorothy did not have the energy to pet him.

Kat got into the front passenger seat and Will turned on the engine. Loud music blasted inside the car and Dorothy cringed. He quickly flicked it off and they set off in silence.

It was only a twenty-minute drive from the hospital to Shelley House, but Dorothy felt every second. She could sense the questions hanging in the air, the whats and whys and hows mixed with suspicion and contempt. Had they worked it out? Of course they must have, and if they had not, then Joseph would surely have told them by now. Dorothy wondered how he had spun the story, what falsities he had told about his own part in the miserable tale. Did Kat hate her? Not that Dorothy cared one iota what the girl thought.

Finally they turned into Poet's Road and Will pulled the car up outside Shelley House. It looked foreboding today, the air oppressive and gray clouds hanging in the humid sky above. A storm was on its way.

"Let me help you," Kat said, opening the rear passenger door.

Dorothy shook her hand off and started to pull herself out of the car, then let out an involuntary moan as pain shot through her left arm. Kat leaned forward and gently took hold of Dorothy's shoulder to lever her out. This time Dorothy did not push her away, although as soon as she was standing she grabbed her bag and began to move toward the front steps.

"Please shout if you need anything, Dorothy. And I'll see you later, Kat," Will called after them, but Dorothy did not look back.

Kat unlocked the front door and Dorothy moved into the lobby, inhaling the familiar musty scent. Thank goodness she was home. She had already located her key during the car journey and she slid it into the lock of flat two, trying to ignore the shaking of her hand. Eventually the door clicked open.

"Do you want me to—" Kat started, but Dorothy had already stepped inside and pulled the door closed behind her, leaving Kat standing on the other side.

With a sigh of relief, she dropped her bag and slipped off her shoes. Then, with some trepidation, Dorothy looked up to take in the drawing room. She had been unsure what she was going to find in here, whether there would be any sign of her struggle on Wednesday night, but the room appeared to be exactly as it always was, if a little dusty after seventy-two hours without a clean. Dorothy shuffled across to the mantelpiece. The picture frame she had seen the intruder pick up was still there, and Dorothy lifted it and studied the photo inside. A fifteen-year-old girl stared back, grinning. She had mousy brown hair tied into two neat plaits that hung on either side of her long, thin face. Brown eyes and a small nose, decorated with freckles. Slightly crooked front teeth that would soon need to be remedied by braces. A badge on her blazer proudly showing her place at secondary school.

Dorothy heard a sound and realized it was a whimper escaping from her own mouth. She turned and limped toward her chair by the window, carrying the frame with her. She sat down clumsily, not bothering to suppress the yelp of pain now that there was nobody to witness it. She looked at the picture again, at that beautiful, angelic face. *Charlotte.*

A noise made Dorothy start. It took a moment for her to realize what it was. A soft, inquiring knock at her door.

"Dorothy, can you hear me?"

Dorothy studied the girl in the frame. There was laughter in her eyes, a twinkle as if the photographer had made a joke and she was starting to giggle. What funny thing had they said to make her so happy? It was a question Dorothy had asked herself many thousands of times over the past thirty-three years.

"Please let me in. I just want to check that you're okay."

There was pity in Kat's voice, and Dorothy scowled. The last thing she wanted was pity. That emotion was reserved for those who deserved it, those who had earned it, and Dorothy had earned nothing but condemnation and misery.

"Dorothy?"

She tutted and stood up. Her progress across the room was slow, her whole body protesting at the movement. When Dorothy reached the door she released the latch, then turned and started back to the table. Behind her she heard the door creak open and the scrabble of small feet on the oak floor as Reggie rushed over. Dorothy lowered herself back into her chair but did not turn round to look at the young woman who had stepped into the room. She heard Kat cross to the table and could sense her standing behind the chair.

"I have let you in and you can see I am perfectly well, so now you can leave again." She hoped Kat could not hear the tremor in her voice.

"I'm so sorry about showing you that article, Dorothy. Neither Will nor I read beyond the headline so we had no idea it was about you. Joseph said—"

Dorothy winced at that name. "What did he tell you?"

"Only the vaguest details."

"Which are?"

"Just what the article said, really. That there was some kind of accident in Shelley House. That a girl—your daughter—died. I'm so sorry."

An accident. So he had not told her the whole story, not even half of it. Trying to protect himself, as ever.

"I can't begin to imagine what it must have been like," Kat said. "To lose a child must be the—"

"Stop it." Dorothy could not bear it, this sympathy and kindness. She needed Kat to be like she always was, vicious and angry. "He did not tell you the whole story."

"What do you mean?" Kat's tone was soft and patronizing, like she was talking to a child. "Obviously you don't have to tell me. I don't want to make you relive it again."

Dorothy almost laughed at this. As if she had not relived it every single day for the past thirty-three years. Although she had never said it out loud, that much was true; she had never told a soul what really happened that summer day. Only one other person knew the truth, and it appeared he still wanted to keep it a secret.

Dorothy looked at the photo again, at Charlotte's beautiful, innocent face. She would have been forty-eight now. A grown woman, with a career and maybe even a family of her own. Except instead she was frozen in time, a fifteen-year-old schoolgirl forevermore. All because of something Dorothy did. Something Dorothy had hidden from the world all these years.

"I really am sorry I gave you that article and stirred up painful memories," Kat said behind her.

This time Dorothy did laugh, a horrible sound.

"I shall tell you," she said, putting the frame face down on the table so Charlotte did not have to witness what was about to occur. "I shall tell you so that you never have to feel sorry for me again. But you must swear you will not tell another soul."

"Of course."

And so Dorothy took a deep breath and started to talk.

Thirty-Two

It was 1991, the year Shelley House turned one hundred, and Dorothy's first full summer living there. They had moved eleven months previously when Phillip got a job as the manager of Barclays Bank in Winton, leaving their old flat in West London to start a new life in the countryside. At first, Dorothy, a Londoner since birth, had struggled with the slower pace of village life. She missed the excitement of the cosmopolitan city: her job of twenty years as an English teacher in a large secondary school, the restaurants and the galleries, not to mention her friends. But Phillip loved his new job, a promotion that brought them considerably more money, and Charlotte had settled in quickly, adoring her new home and enjoying the freedoms that came with rural living: playing in the woods or down by the river with her friends, only returning home each evening when she got hungry. And so Dorothy had vowed to try to be satisfied with her new life as a middle-aged bank manager's wife in a small, sleepy village.

To that end, she had thrown herself into making their new flat a perfect family home. Their initial plan had been to buy a house in one of the new housing estates that were popping up all over the area, but on their first exploratory visit, Dorothy had seen Shelley House and it had been love at first sight. In a village of cottages and boring 1960s terraces, the eccentric old Victorian mansion had felt sophisticated and historic, like a small slice of urbane living in the countryside. Phillip had been unconvinced, his fiscal conservatism telling him it was better to buy rather than rent, but when Charlotte had seen the building and announced she loved it too, he had been forced to concede. Once they moved in, Dorothy had enthusiastically set about redecorating the flat to restore it to its former glory, reading up at the library on how to repair cornicing, painting the walls in elegant tones, and replacing their modern furniture with period chairs and ornaments she picked up at markets and antique fairs. Dorothy also made every effort to befriend the other residents of Shelley House, a mixture of middle-class families and retired couples, several of whom had lived in the building for decades.

It was as part of this effort to impress her neighbors that Dorothy suggested they celebrate the centenary of Shelley House with a soiree in the communal garden for the residents of Poet's Road. She had an image in her head of neat crustless sandwiches and scones, games for the children and Pimm's for the adults: an archetypal English country garden party. The others had readily agreed, a date had been picked for a Saturday in mid-August, and Dorothy had volunteered to organize the whole event herself. Now that the flat redecoration was complete, she was pining for the bustle of her old London life again, and so organizing a party was exactly what she needed to keep herself busy and in good spirits.

A week or so after the decision was made, there was a knock on her front door while Dorothy was cooking supper. She assumed it was one of the children from the building calling for Charlotte and was therefore surprised to see Joseph Chambers standing on the doormat. Joseph had moved into flat one a few months previously with his wife, Sandra, a rather brassy woman with a loud, shrill voice, and a teenage daughter about the same age as Charlotte. Dorothy had rather taken against Sandra after she had knocked on the door of flat one to welcome her new neighbor with a lasagna, only for the woman to take the food but barely utter a word of thanks. To make matters worse, she had never returned the dish, which had been one of Dorothy's favorites. After that, Dorothy made little effort to engage with the new family, although Charlotte got on well with the daughter, Deborah, and the girls regularly spent time together outside of school.

Dorothy was therefore somewhat taken aback to find herself face-to-face with the husband, Joseph, who had a dark mustache and a nervous smile on his lips. She was even more surprised when he told her he wanted to offer his services for the centenary celebration, as long as it did not involve baking, which he confessed to be terrible at. Dorothy had laughed and asked him if he could source some tables they could use to serve the food on. A few days later, Joseph had knocked on the door again and told her he had found not only tables they could borrow but also thirty folding chairs and some picnic rugs for the children to sit on. Dorothy had been delighted and recruited him as her right-hand man on the spot.

Over the coming weeks, the two of them spoke almost every evening when Joseph returned from work. Given the proximity of their flats, it was easy for them to walk across the lobby any time they needed to discuss cutlery provisions or the musical playlist. Before long, they were sharing little tidbits of their lives with each other too. Joseph confided that Debbie had been struggling with their move to Chalcot, blaming her parents for uprooting her from their previous home, and had started misbehaving and playing up at school. In turn, Dorothy admitted how much she missed her old life too: not only her job and her friends but her independence and sense of self. She had not even admitted this to Phillip, who was so engrossed in his new position that he barely had time for her these days. Joseph, on the other hand, was an excellent listener, and Dorothy soon found that she looked forward to their conversations as the highlight of her day.

The week of the centenary party finally arrived and excitement gripped Shelley House. Mrs. Renoir from flat four had borrowed a fish kettle and was steaming a whole salmon to be served as the centerpiece of the buffet, and Mr. Gregory from flat six had put together a musical ensemble from the children of Poet's Road to perform for the gathered guests. Dorothy's doorbell rang near constantly with a stream of residents dropping off food and alcoholic drinks for the festivities, which now filled Dorothy's kitchen and many of the surfaces in the drawing room too.

The day before the party, Joseph took the afternoon off work and he and Dorothy spent it hanging bunting and balloons around the garden, their arms tanning in the hot August sun. They finished at five o'clock, surveying their work with pride, and then headed to Joseph's flat for a final review of the running order for the next day. Joseph made a jug of Pimm's, and although Dorothy rarely drank she accepted a chilled, refreshing glass as they sat side by side on the sofa, running through the final arrangements.

After a while they finished the list, but rather than get up and leave, Dorothy allowed her glass to be refilled. Sandra was out visiting her mother, and Debbie and Charlotte were off playing somewhere together, as they had been all summer holidays, and Joseph's flat was cool and quiet. So quiet, in fact, that Dorothy found herself slipping off her shoes and leaning back into the sofa, her eyes closing as she appreciated this moment of calm amid the frenetic chaos of the party planning.

When she opened her eyes, Dorothy glanced at Joseph and saw he was looking at her, that gentle smile on his lips. She had caught him watching her once or twice before, but whenever she glanced up he had looked away, embarrassed. Dorothy had not thought much of it; after all, Joseph was a married man and younger than her. But still, she could not pretend that she was not flattered by his attention.

Joseph was a handsome chap and a gentleman too, always holding the door open for her and offering to carry anything heavy. But more than that, he paid attention to her. Unlike Phillip, who barely noticed Dorothy these days unless she was serving him a plate of food, Joseph listened to her when she talked and laughed at her jokes. Around him, she did not feel like a frumpy, suburban, forty-four-year-old housewife but an educated, entertaining woman.

Dorothy flicked her eyes to Joseph again and realized he was still watching her. This time she did not look away, and in that instant she felt something between them shift. Neither of them had physically moved, yet suddenly Dorothy became aware how close they were to each other, so close she could see the soft, downy hair on Joseph's cheeks. What would it feel like to reach out and touch his face, to run her hand over that smooth skin? Just the thought sent a shiver through Dorothy. She and Phillip rarely touched each other anymore and certainly not in that way. It had taken them many years to conceive Charlotte, and once she was born it was like they both gave up, relieved never to have to do that again. But now Dorothy felt her body start to stir. Joseph was still watching her, his eyes heavy, his lips slightly parted. It would be so easy for Dorothy to lean forward, no more than a few feet, and brush her lips against his. Would they be soft? Would he kiss her gently, tentative and shy? Or would he be passionate, slipping his tongue into her mouth and running his hands through her loose hair? Would he take her by the hand and lead her through to the bedroom, or would he pull her down onto the floor right here so she felt the cool polished wood against her skin? Dorothy's breath caught and she saw a flash of something in Joseph's face, as if he too were imagining the same thing. For a moment everything else stopped and all Dorothy was aware of was her own rapid breathing and Joseph's face, so close to her own. So close she could almost—

A scream pierced the silence and Dorothy and Joseph jolted apart.

Above them they heard the hammering of footsteps coming down the stairs.

"Was that Charlotte?" Dorothy said, at the same moment Joseph whispered, "Debbie."

They jumped up from the sofa and crossed toward the door. Joseph got there first, pulling it open, and they stepped out into the lobby. Seconds later Debbie came staggering down the stairs and almost knocked into them both.

"What is it, child?" Dorothy said, but Debbie had fallen into her father's arms with a wild look in her eyes, a look that made Dorothy's blood run cold.

"It's Charlotte," the teenager sobbed.

Before she knew what she was doing, Dorothy was running toward the stairs and climbing them two, three at a time. She could hear voices behind her, Joseph calling for her to stop and Debbie's muffled sobs, but Dorothy paid them no attention. The first-floor landing was empty, so she continued on up. The girls sometimes played with the Gregory children in number six, but when Dorothy got to the third floor she saw that the door to their flat was shut. There was, however, one door open, sunlight pouring through it into the dark hallway.

The fire escape.

Within seconds, Dorothy was outside and climbing the metal steps that led up to the flat section of roof. She'd only been up here once before, when they had first viewed the flat and the landlord had taken them on a tour of the building. A "communal terrace" he had rather grandly called the flat roof, although in reality it was an empty area with a two-foot-high balustrade around the edges. Dorothy had told Charlotte not to go up there and had not thought about it since.

As she reached the top of the steps and emerged onto the roof, the first thing Dorothy noticed was the music. A soft beat and an unfamiliar melody were playing somewhere in the background. And then there was the pain on the soles of her feet. Under the glare of the August sun, the asphalt on the roof had become red hot, and when she glanced down, Dorothy realized she still had bare feet. She quickly jumped back onto the top step, jolting against Joseph, who had come up after her. Dorothy looked up, scanning her eyes around the flat roof for Charlotte, but the girl was nowhere to be seen.

"Where is she?" Dorothy heard herself say. "Where's Charlotte?"

The only response was a strangled wail from Debbie.

And that was when Dorothy saw it, over on the south side of the roof. Two half-empty glasses sat next to a bottle of Malibu on the rim of the balustrade, alongside the small pink portable stereo they had given Charlotte for Christmas. Dorothy started to move forward again, ignoring the viscous heat under her feet as she ran across the roof. Joseph was with her this time, his hand reaching out and grabbing her arm as if to try to stop her.

"Leave me alone!" Dorothy roared as she wriggled her elbow free, dodging from Joseph's grasp as she reached the far side.

She grabbed the balustrade and leaned over the edge, looking down into Shelley House's communal garden, fifty feet below. There were the balloons and the bunting that she and Joseph had so carefully hung only hours ago. There were the tables they had laid out, waiting for all the food and drink to cover them tomorrow, and the picnic rugs artfully arranged around the garden. And there, in the middle of the parched lawn, was the body of a girl lying on her back on the grass, as if she were bathing in the sun.

Thirty-Three

KAT

Dorothy was staring out the window, but her eyes were unfocused. Kat waited for her to continue, but the woman said nothing, the words appearing to have abandoned her. The room was still, the only movement the small, rhythmic motions that Dorothy's right hand made as she stroked Reggie, who was asleep on her lap. After several minutes, Kat gently cleared her throat.

"Dorothy."

The old woman startled and her eyes swung sharply to Kat, as if she'd forgotten there was anyone else in the room.

"Would you like me to make you a cup of tea?"

Dorothy looked like she was going to say no but then gave a small nod. Kat stood up and moved through to the kitchen. Like the living room, this was a relic from the past; nothing seemed to have been updated in decades, from the beige Formica cupboards and old-fashioned orange wall tiles to the stained linoleum on the floor. Kat located an ancient kettle, lit the frankly terrifying gas stove with a match, and waited while the water slowly boiled. She couldn't get her head around the fact that Dorothy had once had a teenage daughter and a husband. But where was he now? Had he died as well?

On the sideboard, Kat found a teapot, a teacup, and a saucer, but it took a proper rummage through the cupboards before she found more cups, none of which appeared to have been used in years. There was no sign of teabags anywhere, only a tin of what must be loose tea. Kat had no idea what to do with it, so she threw a couple of spoonfuls in the pot and covered it in boiling water. When she opened the fridge it was barely cold and the only items inside were half a tin of dog food, a shriveled cucumber, and some days-old milk that smelled like sweet corn. Kat poured it away and then carried the teapot and cups back through to the living room.

Dorothy appeared to have collected herself over the past few minutes, and she wrinkled her nose as she watched Kat pour the tea, yet she still didn't speak. Kat sat down on the edge of the sofa and looked into her own cup to see bits of loose tea floating on top of the water. Clearly she'd gotten something very wrong in the process. She put it down, waiting for Dorothy to say something caustic, yet for several minutes there was only silence. Kat was beginning to wonder if Dorothy had fallen asleep when the woman finally spoke.

"The girls had stolen a bottle of Malibu that someone had donated for the party. Debbie claimed it was Charlotte's idea to take it, although I had never seen my daughter show any interest in alcohol before. They had drunk half the bottle between them, listening to music and dancing on the roof. Then Charlotte apparently felt nauseated and leaned over the edge to be sick. That is when she lost her balance and fell."

"Oh my God."

Dorothy didn't react, her eyes fixed on the teacup on the table in front of her.

"I'm so sorry, Dorothy. I hadn't realized you had a family," Kat said to fill the silence. It felt strange saying that word out loud, and Dorothy clearly didn't like it either as she winced.

"I do not have a family," she said, gruffly. "My daughter is dead and my husband left me four months later. He blamed me for what happened and one morning he departed for work and never returned."

"What? Why did he blame you?"

Dorothy looked at Kat as if she'd asked if the earth was flat. "Because I should never have let Charlotte get drunk up on the roof, of course."

"But from what you described, you had no idea she was up there drinking. Phillip must have realized you couldn't have stopped something you didn't even know was happening?"

Dorothy shook her head. "After we came home from the hospital he could not even look at me. He banished me from the bedroom and barely spoke a word, and then one day he simply left. He has continued to pay the rent on this flat ever since, but I have not heard from him since the day he walked out."

"Bloody hell! I'm sorry, but your ex sounds like an arsehole. What kind of person treats a grieving mother like that?"

Dorothy just shrugged. "I do not blame him for any of it."

"Please tell me you don't blame yourself too?"

"Of course I do. My daughter got drunk and fell off the roof while she was supposed to be under my supervision. Her death was entirely my fault."

"But she was fifteen, Dorothy. By that age I was skiving school, running away from home, and going to illegal raves. You can't have been expected to be supervising Charlotte every minute of the day."

"She was my child," Dorothy said slowly. "I was responsible for her safety and yet instead of looking out for her, I was sitting in another man's flat, behaving like a harlot. She would never have died if I had not been flirting with Joseph Chambers."

"Come on, it wasn't like the two of you were having some drug-fueled orgy. You were having a drink and discussing a garden party, for God's sake."

Dorothy put her hand up to stop Kat. "You may be trying to make me feel better, but you are wasting your breath. I knew that roof was dangerous the second I saw it, but I did not tell the landlord to block off the door. I was so fixated on impressing my neighbors that I neglected my own daughter all summer. And I was so obsessed with my own pleasure that I sat fantasizing about infidelity while my daughter lay dying in the back garden less than thirty meters away."

"But that doesn't make you culpable for her death, Dorothy. Believe me, I know a thing or two about negligent mothers, and from what you've described you do not fit that description. Charlotte had a horrible, cruel accident, but it was an *accident*, not your fault."

Dorothy didn't reply, her lips pursed in a determined line. Kat's mind was reeling. No wonder the woman appeared so bitter and hostile all the time. She'd spent all these years punishing herself for something that wasn't her fault, the guilt eating away at her like a maggot in a rotting apple.

"Can I ask a question?"

Dorothy gave a small nod.

"Why have you stayed here? Why didn't you move out and get a fresh start somewhere new, away from all the painful memories in Shelley House?"

"Charlotte did not get a fresh start, so why should I?" Dorothy didn't look at Kat as she spoke. "I should have been watching out for my daughter's safety, but I did not, and she died. So I made a vow to stay in the home she loved and make sure that nothing like that ever happens again."

A chill ran through Kat's body as she realized what Dorothy was saying. All those hours the woman spent sitting by the front window, watching her neighbors come and go. The angry complaints, the bossy laminated signs about rubbish, and the daily snooping round the building when she thought nobody was looking. Everyone thought that Dorothy was simply a nosy neighbor spying on them, but the truth was something different entirely. She was making sure they were safe.

"Shelley House and its residents aren't your responsibility," Kat said as gently as she could. "It's time you forgave yourself so you can move on with your life."

"What the hell do you know?" There was a hardness in the woman's voice that had been absent for the past hour. "You are not a mother. You have no idea what it is like to see your own child lying in a coffin or grieve alongside a husband who hates you. So do not dare tell me that I need to 'move on.'"

"You're right, I don't know what it's like to be a mother or lose a child. But I do know what it's like to have made a terrible mistake and blame yourself for it. That's why I'm—"

"I want you to leave."

There she was, the prickly Dorothy with her guard slammed down. Kat knew there was little point trying to reason with her anymore. "Okay, but would you like me to check that your windows are securely shut before I go? After the break-in you must be feeling a bit—"

"I do not need anything from you, girl."

Kat sighed. "I was just offering to help."

"Well, I do not need your help, I am perfectly fine on my own. You can go, and take the mutt with you." She wriggled her legs and Reggie let out a disgruntled yelp as he was evicted from her lap.

"Dorothy, are you sure I can't—"

"I said leave me alone!"

Thirty-Four

KAT

Kat had arranged to meet Will at the *Gazette* offices at five to go through more of the archives, and she spent the whole bus ride there running Dorothy's story over in her mind. She still couldn't get her head around the fact that Dorothy had spent all these years blaming herself for her daughter's death. The self-imposed isolation, the daily inspections, the complaining: it was all Dorothy's way of atoning for a crime she hadn't committed. What made it even more tragic was that Dorothy had clearly once been a social, lively person: one who made friends with her neighbors and organized garden parties, for God's sake. And now look at her, so angry and bitter at the world, having deliberately cut herself off from all human contact. Plus there was her hatred for Joseph, a man she had obviously once been attracted to. *What if Charlotte hadn't fallen and died that day?* Kat found herself wondering as the bus entered Winton. Would Dorothy and Joseph be together now, a happy couple of more than thirty years? It was a strange thought and unbearably sad.

When Kat arrived at the *Gazette* offices, Will greeted her at the door with his usual lopsided smile. He was dressed in jeans and a shirt, the sleeves rolled up to show the tattoo running up his forearm.

"How's Dorothy?" he asked as they made their way through the newsroom. As it was a Sunday there was no one else there, and the office felt strangely quiet without the background hum of voices chatting and phones ringing.

"Not good."

"Did she tell you any more about her daughter's death?"

"Not really." It was a lie but Kat had made Dorothy a promise.

"I had another look through the 1991 papers to see if there were any other articles about the accident," Will said, as he pushed opened the door to the archive. "The only thing I found was this funeral notice."

He handed Kat a photocopied page that was sitting on the table, a small box of text circled in red pen.

> The funeral of Charlotte Darling to take place at 1 p.m. on Friday 30 August at Winton Crematorium. Family only. No flowers please.

Kat pictured Dorothy sitting straight-backed during the service, her husband silent and distant beside her, with no friends or anyone else there to support her. It was a heartbreaking image and she pushed the page aside.

"Shall we crack on with this, then?" She sat down and opened the nearest archive box. She might not be able to heal Dorothy's pain, but the least she could do was help save her and Charlotte's home.

"I've managed to trace two of the people mentioned in the articles we found," Will said as he sat down opposite Kat and picked up a pile of newspapers. "One of them refused to talk to me, but the other one had plenty to say about Fergus Alexander and his tactics."

"And are they happy for you to write about their experiences in the paper?"

"They are, as long as I keep them anonymous. But I think I need a few more people to go on the record before I can publish the article.

The more stories I can get, the better our chances of getting the police to take it seriously. We need to prove that what Fergus did at Featherdown Farm wasn't a one-off but part of a long history of illegal harassment."

At the mention of her grandfather's home, Kat gave an involuntary frown. Will must have noticed because he paused for a moment before he spoke again.

"You have some kind of connection to Featherdown Farm, don't you?"

"No," Kat said, but she knew the wobble in her voice gave her lie away. She sighed. "Well, yes, I do, but only distantly. It was my grandfather's farm."

Will's mouth fell open. "Hang on, but that must mean Ted is your great-uncle. But why—"

"Why didn't he recognize me? Because we've not seen each other for fifteen years."

"Shit! When did you last see your grandfather?"

"That was fifteen years ago too."

"Why didn't you say something?" Will was staring at her in disbelief. "It must have been awful sitting there and hearing what happened to your grandfather and the farm. I'm so sorry, Kat."

She shrugged, hoping she looked nonchalant as opposed to someone who might cry at a virtual stranger's kind words. "It's fine."

"I had no idea you were from Chalcot. Did you grow up here?"

Kat swallowed. The more she told Will, the greater the chance he'd work out who she really was. But from the way he was staring at her with those piercing blue eyes, Kat knew she couldn't fob him off with a lie. A part truth would have to do.

"I spent a bit of time here as a kid. I used to stay with my grandfather in the school holidays and sometimes in term too. But my mum and I moved away when I was ten and I've not been back since."

"And is that why you came back here, to try and find your grandfather again?"

Kat thought before she answered. "Maybe. I don't know, I've just felt myself drawn to this place recently, like perhaps there was unfinished business or a reason I needed to come back."

Will let out a low whistle. "Well, that explains why you're so determined to destroy Fergus Alexander. I didn't really understand why you were getting so involved, but the guy totally screwed over your grandfather and great-uncle too. You must hate him."

Kat let out a sharp laugh. "That's an understatement. Ever since I heard Ted's story, all I've been able to think about is getting revenge. But it's not *just* about Featherdown Farm. I hate Fergus Alexander for what he's doing to Shelley House too. Joseph, Ayesha, Dorothy . . ." Kat thought of the poor woman earlier, her face contorted with grief. "They're good people, much better than me, and they don't deserve to be yet another victim of that bastard's greed."

Will was still watching her and she saw a smile dance over his lips. "I don't think you're such a bad person, Kat. Quite the opposite, actually."

She felt herself blush and looked away. "If I'm going to get my revenge, we have a lot of reading to do."

They worked intently for the next few hours, poring over box after box of old issues, and as they got into the 2000s, more and more stories about Fergus Alexander started to pop up. At eight o'clock they ordered in takeaway from the Golden Dragon in Chalcot, and perhaps it was the cold beers they drank with the food, or the fact that Kat was feeling more relaxed around Will now that he knew about her grandfather, but she found herself sharing little bits of her life with him. He was a good listener, asking sensitive questions, and before Kat knew it she was talking to him about things that she'd never discussed with anyone before.

"I can't imagine what it must have been like growing up under the constant threat of eviction," Will said, after Kat had told him a little of her unsettled childhood. "I've always taken for granted that my home was secure and couldn't be taken away from me."

"Yeah, well, you're lucky," Kat said, hoping she didn't sound too bitter. "There's thousands of people out there right now living in fear they're going to be made homeless at the sudden whim of their landlord, even though they've not done anything wrong. These Section 21 no-fault evictions are utterly evil."

"I had no idea," Will said, shaking his head. "And so what did you do about school if you were moving around so much?"

"My mum would enroll me in a local school wherever we went, but my education was pretty disrupted, as you can imagine. I actually loved school when I was little, especially English." An image flashed into Kat's mind of a head teacher's office and a metal bin, and she took a long swig of beer. "But I used to play up a lot too, wind up the teachers and get in trouble, and by the time I got to secondary school I had so many holes in my learning that I basically gave up. I left school the day I finished my GCSEs."

"I'm sorry, Kat. That's so shit."

"It is what it is."

"Have you ever considered going back to school? If you enjoyed English, then you could study for your A-level now."

"I think my school days are over, sadly. Besides, I'm not sure any college would let me in with my track record."

"What about Dorothy? Didn't the newspaper article say she used to be an English teacher?"

It was such an absurd idea that Kat laughed. "You want Dorothy to teach me? Oh my God, we'd kill each other within five minutes!"

Will chuckled. "Fair point. She's an absolute dragon, isn't she?"

"You know, I used to think that but she's not so bad, really."

"At the protest she spent a good five minutes complaining about my poor posture and scruffy clothes; it was like being lectured by a combination of my old science teacher and Queen Victoria. No wonder she's got no friends!"

Will laughed again but stopped when he saw Kat's face.

"Sorry, that was a bit insensitive of me," he mumbled.

"No, it's okay. It's just I don't think Dorothy was always like this. I think before Charlotte died she was a completely different person."

"Yeah, I can imagine the grief of losing a child could change you forever."

"It's not just that." Kat paused, wondering how much more she should say. Will was watching her, his face open and patient. Would it be so bad if, just for once, she trusted someone? She took a deep breath. "The thing is, Dorothy blames herself for what happened. She was—well, she was otherwise occupied when Charlotte fell, and she's never forgiven herself for not stopping it."

"But the newspaper report said the death was an accident?"

"I know, but Dorothy still thinks she would have been able to save Charlotte if she'd not been . . . distracted. And things haven't been helped by the fact that her husband blamed her too and then left her."

"Oh my God, what an arsehole!"

"That's exactly what I said. But I think Dorothy has basically been punishing herself ever since. It's like she's deliberately pushing people away because she doesn't think she deserves any happiness."

"Wow, poor woman," Will said, shaking his head.

"I know. And it's yet another reason why we have to stop Fergus Alexander. I'm not sure Dorothy will ever forgive herself if she loses Charlotte's home on top of everything else."

"Well, I'll start calling these new names first thing tomorrow and see if any of them will talk," Will said, pointing to the growing pile of photocopied pages between them. "With any luck I might be able to file a story in time for the next issue."

"That would be amazing," Kat said, and for the first time in weeks she felt a glow of positivity.

She looked up at Will and saw that he was watching her across the table. There was something in his expression, an intensity that made Kat's whole body suddenly tense with desire. She'd spent the past few weeks desperately fighting her attraction to Will, but now, alone together in this small, quiet room, she felt an almost physical pull toward him. All she wanted to do was swipe the papers onto the floor and climb across the table to reach him. She swallowed, trying to calm the heat that was rising within her. But Will was still watching her, that slight smile on his lips and the small dimple in his—

Before Kat knew what was happening, they were both on their feet. In one swift movement Will had leaned across the table, his lips and hands finding hers. Kat let out a moan of pleasure and sank forward into him, and in that instant everything else—Fergus Alexander, Dorothy Darling, her grandfather—was gone.

Thirty-Five

DOROTHY

In the days after her confession to Kat, Dorothy felt like she was wading through treacle. Her body ached far more than it had done in hospital, and the bruising from her fall had emerged in large, furious patches all over the left-hand side of her body. She had given up on any attempt to keep the flat clean, and even a simple task like walking to the kitchen was a Herculean effort that left her exhausted afterward. Yet when she climbed into bed each night and closed her eyes, all Dorothy could see was Charlotte's body on the grass.

Why had she told Kat the truth? She had guarded this secret for thirty-three years, not telling a soul what had really happened that day: not the police who interviewed her while she sat slumped on the floor, nor her own husband when he rushed back from work. *I had popped into the kitchen* she had told them, because even in her state of shock she could not bring herself to admit what she had done, what she had been thinking of doing. *I was making a pot of tea when I heard Debbie's scream and ran to the lobby.* There was one brief moment a few days later, as she and Phillip drove in bewildered silence back from the undertakers, when Dorothy had opened her mouth to tell him the truth. *It is even worse than you thought,* she had almost said. *I was not making tea. I was in Joseph Chambers's flat, about to kiss him.* But Dorothy had not gotten past "It" when Phillip had leaned forward and switched the radio on, Bryan Adams drowning out her confession.

And so she had never spoken of it again, until two days ago when she had blurted the whole sorry tale out to Kat. Perhaps it was those pills they gave her in hospital, the ones to help her relax and sleep; perhaps they had relaxed her tongue too? Although Dorothy knew she could not really blame those. No, the reason she had told Kat was the look in the girl's eyes when she had collected her from hospital. The look that said "poor old Dorothy, with her tragically dead daughter. She needs sympathy and kindness." But Dorothy did not need sympathy and kindness now, just as she had not needed it back then. Not when her neighbors had rung her doorbell bearing casseroles and cakes, asking what they could do to help. Nor when people stopped her on the way to the shops to say what a lovely bright young girl her daughter had been, and how she and Phillip did not deserve this tragic loss. *But I did deserve it,* Dorothy wanted to scream. *It was all because of me.*

But of course she could not say that without admitting the truth, so instead she had pushed their sympathy and kindness away. She refused to take the flowers and pot roasts that were left on her doorstep; refused to make eye contact with her neighbors when they tried to talk to her in the lobby; shouted at them when they got too close. And it had worked: the sympathy and the kindness stopped until eventually her neighbors ignored her altogether, Phillip ran away, and Dorothy was left alone with her guilt and pain. Just as she deserved to be.

On Tuesday morning, Dorothy ate breakfast at the table in front of her window. There had been so much turmoil in her own life of late that it seemed strange to watch the rest of the world carry on as normal. There were Tomasz and Gloria chatting as they left the building together; they both looked toward Dorothy's window and she was glad of the net curtain to hide her shame. There was Ayesha, dashing off to her summer job, and Omar, inspecting the paving stones outside the house. And there were Kat and Reggie, bounding up the front steps and into Shelley House.

Dorothy had been avoiding Kat since their conversation and therefore by proxy the dog too, who was spending his days with Omar and Ayesha. Now she waited to hear the animal scampering back to flat one but instead heard a knock on her door.

"Dorothy, are you in there?"

She groaned. The only reason Dorothy had told Kat the truth was to make the girl loathe her and leave her alone for good, yet it appeared not to have worked. Why did Kat not realize that Dorothy had no desire to hear whatever modern mumbo jumbo she wanted to spout about "moving on" or "forgiving herself"? And what could a girl her age possibly know about losing a loved one or the utter agony of knowing it was your own fault?

Kat knocked again and Dorothy reached to turn up *Tannhäuser* when she heard Kat's raised voice outside the door. "Dorothy, it's important. It's about the Shelley House redevelopment."

Dorothy stopped. With everything that had been going on she had barely thought about that wretched Fergus Alexander, but now it hit her again. There was less than a month until the end of her tenancy, when she was supposed to move out and let that hoodlum destroy Shelley House. The building where her beloved daughter had lived so happily and died so tragically. The building—and its residents—which three decades ago Dorothy had sworn to keep safe. She stood up, crossed to the front door, and pulled it open.

Reggie came charging in first, jumping up at her so excitedly that Dorothy had to grab the wall so she did not topple over. She hobbled back to her chair and allowed the dog to leap onto her lap and cover her face in his little wet kisses. Only once he had finished did Dorothy address Kat.

"Well, what is so important?"

"Will and I have finished going through the archives. Altogether, we've found records of thirteen different developments where the *Gazette* reported there was some kind of resistance to what Alexander was doing."

"And?"

"Will has been trying to trace people who were involved in these redevelopments, either the original landowners, tenants, or local residents who were unhappy with what went on. He's managed to speak to several of them already and it's explosive, Dorothy. Harassment, threats, intimidation: you name it, Fergus Alexander seems to have done it."

There was an energy in Kat that Dorothy had never seen before; the girl was so excited she was almost dancing from foot to foot.

"I do not know why you are looking so pleased about this," Dorothy said, frowning. "It hardly seems like something to celebrate."

"Most of these people never pursued it with the police because they either had no proof or were too scared of Alexander and his goons. But now a couple of them have agreed to go on the record. Will wants to speak to a few more, but he's hoping to have his article in next week's issue. This is it, Dorothy. This is how we bring the bastard down."

Kat's mouth split into a smile then, broad and dazzling. Dorothy realized she had rarely seen her smile before and it was quite beautiful.

"Well, thank you for informing me," she said, looking away. "You may go now."

Kat hesitated and Dorothy could sense her wanting to say something. Then she heard an audible sigh.

"Fine. Come on, Reggie."

The animal did not move from his spot on Dorothy's lap. She was about to manually remove him when a flash of movement outside the window caught her eye. A police car had pulled up in front of Shelley House and two officers were climbing out. One of them Dorothy recognized as the officer who had spoken to her in hospital, while the other was a slightly older woman with dark hair and glasses.

"What do you think they want?" Kat said as they walked toward the front steps.

"Goodness only knows. That man made it clear on Thursday that he had little inclination to find whoever broke into my flat, so I assume they are simply here to inform me their inquiries have failed and to remind me how old and vulnerable I apparently am."

"You want me to tell them to bugger off?"

"You may as well let them in to see what they have to say. But do not offer them any refreshments."

Kat snorted and crossed to the door, pressing the button to allow them in. Reggie barked excitedly at the sight of new people, something which seemed to disarm PC Reid, who was clearly not a dog person. Yet another character flaw.

"Good morning, Mrs. Darling," the female officer said as she stepped inside.

"It's *Ms.* Darling," Kat interjected, just as Dorothy was opening her mouth to say the same.

"My apologies. I'm Inspector Linda Hudson and I believe you've met PC Elliot Reid already."

Dorothy nodded at them in a way she hoped was suitably supercilious. They both stood awkwardly next to her table, clearly waiting to be invited to sit, but Dorothy said nothing.

"I'm sorry about the delay in coming to see you; we had some staff shortages over the weekend," Inspector Hudson continued. "But we've come to give you an update on our investigation."

Dorothy stifled a sigh. This was the moment when they announced they had not found a thing.

"As I think Elliot explained to you at the hospital, we found some fingerprints at your property that we believe belong to the intruder. We ran those prints through our database to see if there were any matches with our records."

"Yes, and he also explained how unlikely it was to find a match," Dorothy said, resisting the temptation to roll her eyes. Really, the last thing she wanted was to be making small talk with police.

"That's right. But in this instance, I'm pleased to tell you there was a match."

Dorothy paused. "You know who broke in?"

"Well, we don't know for sure, of course. My colleagues are currently on their way to the individual's last known address to try and speak to them. But we also wanted to check in with you, in case the person is an acquaintance of yours and their prints may have been in your house legitimately."

"That is highly unlikely," Dorothy said. "For one, I do not associate with anyone who might have a criminal record. And secondly, up until this week I have not had any visitors in my home for more than thirty years."

If this surprised Inspector Hudson she hid it well.

"We have a photo of the suspect, Ms. Darling, and we were wondering if you could take a look and see if you recognize them."

"Of course." Suddenly this had all gotten a lot more interesting. Dorothy looked at Kat and could see that the girl was thinking the same thing; if this was the man who had broken into her flat, perhaps he was also Joseph's attacker and the driver of the green car?

PC Reid made a great show of pulling a piece of paper out of his pocket, given this was clearly his one big moment in the visit. He handed it to Dorothy, who unfolded the page to look at the culprit.

It was not a man but a woman who looked to be in her sixties, if not older. She had lank gray hair that hung round her sunken cheeks, and her dark eyes stared vacantly at the camera, as if she were mindlessly watching a TV program rather than having her mug shot taken in a police station. Dorothy was not sure she had ever seen such a tragic-looking individual, and it was hard to imagine her having the strength to open the window, let alone attack and almost kill Joseph Chambers.

"Do you know this woman?" Inspector Hudson asked.

"I certainly do not, and I am offended you think I might."

She went to hand the sheet back to PC Reid, but Kat held out her hand.

"Can I take a look?"

"Of course, but prepare yourself for the worst. She is an unappealing specimen."

Kat took the page from Dorothy and looked down at it. As she did, the color drained from her face as if she had seen a ghost. Inspector Hudson must have spotted the reaction too because her own face perked up.

"Do you recognize this woman?"

"Eh . . ."

Dorothy had never heard Kat lost for words before. Goodness, what was wrong with her? "Kat?"

She looked up like a startled rabbit in the headlights. "Sorry. For a second I thought she looked like someone I used to know, but it's not her. Different eye color." She smiled and gave a small laugh but it was entirely unconvincing.

"So what is the plan of action now?" Dorothy said, directing Inspector Hudson's attention off Kat and back onto herself.

"Well, as I said, my colleagues are going to try and track this woman down and discover her whereabouts on the night of your break-in. As soon as we have any more information I'll be in touch again."

"Very well, then," Dorothy said, but her eyes were still on Kat's ashen face. "Thank you for coming to see me. I look forward to hearing more anon."

Inspector Hudson and PC Reid turned to leave. Dorothy pulled herself up to open the door, but Kat was already on the move.

"I'll show them out."

"Thank you."

Dorothy needed to get the poor girl a glass of water; she looked positively feverish. She stood up and began to shuffle toward the kitchen. Behind her she heard the two police officers saying good-bye and a moment later the front door slam shut.

"I am fetching you a drink," Dorothy called out, but there was no answer. When she looked back toward the front door she saw that Kat had gone too, leaving Reggie behind.

Thirty-Six

DOROTHY

For the rest of the day, Dorothy and Reggie sat by the window waiting for a sighting of Kat. Dorothy knew nothing of her neighbor's past, but it did not entirely surprise her that Kat knew some unsavory characters. Still, her reaction to the photo had been most dramatic.

Kat usually collected Reggie at six o'clock, but the time came and went. By seven, when there was still no sign of her, Dorothy left her flat and crossed the lobby, the dog at her heels. She knocked on the door and waited, unsurprised when there was no reply.

"Kat, are you in there?" she called, pressing her face close to the door. "It is me. Dorothy Darling,"

Still no answer.

"I suspect you are in there and ignoring me. I shall try knocking once more before I depart."

Dorothy waited another minute but still nothing. Oh well, she had tried but the girl clearly did not want to be disturbed. She turned to retreat to flat two but Reggie let out a high-pitched whine of protest. When she looked down at him, he was staring up at her with his large, accusatory eyes.

"It is no use, Reginald. If she does not wish to speak to me I cannot force her. That girl is stubborn to the core."

The dog gave another whimper but Dorothy moved past him

across the lobby. It was just as well, really. What if Kat had answered the door and invited her in? Dorothy had not stepped foot in flat one since that fateful day, and she had no intention of doing so now. Besides, Kat clearly wanted to be left alone, and Dorothy of all people knew to respect that. She reached her own door and began to push it open, ignoring Reggie's protestations behind her. But as she was about to step inside, an image floated into Dorothy's mind.

It was from the night that the intruder—that woman—had broken into her flat. Between the moment Dorothy had started falling, seen Reggie's damned toy at her feet, and blacked out and the moment she awoke staring up at the hospital ceiling, she could recall one other brief incident. It was a feeling, more than a memory: a sensation of a hand holding hers in the dark, gentle but firm, and a low reassuring voice telling her she was going to be all right. In hospital, when she had first remembered this, Dorothy had thought it had been a dream of her mother, pulled out of the depths of her subconscious. But now she realized it had not been her mother's voice at all. It had been Kat's.

"I know you are in there, young lady. Open up at once!"

Dorothy crossed back to the door of flat one and banged heavily on it.

"You cannot hide from me forever. I shall stay here all night if I need to."

Still no answer, but Reggie was finding this most exciting and was scrabbling against the door with his claws.

"Reginald is hungry and I have no food for him. If you do not open the door the poor animal will suffer."

At the sound of his name Reggie let out a loud howl.

"Do not make me fetch Tomasz to break this door down!"

"All right, all right. Keep your hair on, I'm coming."

Dorothy heard a lock being drawn on the other side of the door. She looked down at Reggie in satisfaction.

"Excellent work, my little friend." She winked at him and then composed her face as the door opened.

Although Dorothy was not one to judge, Kat looked utterly gruesome. She was wearing what appeared to be a pair of men's underpants and a scruffy T-shirt, and from the state of her hair it seemed she had been asleep. Her expression, however, was very much awake, and mutinous.

Reggie gave Kat's leg a cursory sniff before scampering into the flat. As soon as he was inside, the girl began to close the door again, but Dorothy stuck her foot out to stop it.

"What are you doing, Dorothy?"

"Who was that woman?"

"I have no idea."

"Do not give me that nonsense. You know exactly who she is."

"I said, I don't know." Kat's voice had risen ominously. "She's probably some crack addict hoping to rob you for her next score. But I'm sure the police will arrest her and you'll get justice, if that's what you're worried about."

"I do not give two hoots about justice," Dorothy said. "Right now, all I am worried about is you."

The words were out of Dorothy's mouth before she realized what she had said. There was a moment of stunned silence as the two women looked at each other. Then Kat turned and disappeared into the flat.

Dorothy cursed herself. Why had she said that and scared Kat off? She started moving back across the lobby when she heard the girl call after her.

"I don't have a teapot and the tea's in a bag, so you better not bloody complain."

Dorothy turned around and stepped up to the open door of Joseph Chambers's flat.

She had seen it once in recent months, the day Sandra broke in and Dorothy had come to tell Kat. That time, the flat had been in disarray and Dorothy had paid attention to little except the mess. Now, however, the flat looked tidy and distressingly familiar. The high ceilings—the cornicing in here had always been nicer than Dorothy's—and the grand fireplace. Some of the furniture had been updated, but there was the same rug in the exact spot where Dorothy and Joseph had sat side by side, staring into each other's eyes. Dorothy felt a wave of vertiginous nausea.

"Come in, then," Kat said, disappearing into the kitchen at the back.

Dorothy remained on the threshold, her pulse pounding. What would Charlotte think if she knew her mother was breaking her word and about to enter Joseph Chambers's flat again? *But this is for Kat*, she told herself. *She helped you and now you must help her in return.* After another moment of hesitation, Dorothy took a deep breath and stepped inside.

If she had been expecting a thunderbolt to strike her down or some other divine intervention, she was sorely disappointed. In fact, nothing extraordinary happened at all as she walked slowly round the room. There were several modern sofas and two armchairs, and a large dresser against the wall holding mementos of Joseph's life. Dorothy walked over and ran her finger along the dresser, inspecting it. There were specks of dust clinging to her skin but it was not totally unacceptable.

"You can sit down," Kat said, reentering the room. She was carrying two mugs—*mugs*—of tea.

Dorothy perched on the edge of an armchair and tried not to blanch as she was handed a mug, its contents an insipid, dishwater color. She took a suspicious sip and was surprised when it did not taste completely revolting. She placed the mug down on the coffee table—no coasters—and waited for Kat to speak.

"The woman's name is Sylvia Mason. She's my mum."

Dorothy said nothing. The thought had crossed her mind but she had dismissed it as being ridiculous. That woman looked far too old to be Kat's mother.

"I had no idea she was in this area; the last I heard she was living near Liverpool. And I'm sorry, I should have told the police. I just panicked."

"No need to apologize, that is quite understandable given the circumstances. When did you last see her?"

"Six years ago. I've changed my name and completely cut her out of my life, which is why it was such a shock to see that photo."

"Like a ghost from the past," Dorothy said, then regretted the ill-judged expression, given the woman really had looked like a ghost. She took a sip of tea and waited for Kat to speak again.

"The irony is, I thought she was clean now. Although I don't speak to her I hear the occasional report from people, old acquaintances of hers, and the last I heard she was trying to sort her life out. I should have known that would never last." Kat said this last part with the weariness of someone who really should have known better.

"Has your mother always been an addict?"

She shrugged. "I suppose so, although it wasn't quite so bad when I was little. I mean, she'd always drunk way too much, and she was chaotic and made terrible life choices, especially when it came to men. But she didn't properly get into drugs until I was about nine."

Nine. Dorothy pictured Charlotte at that age, with her plaits and missing teeth, still playing with dolls. "Did you have anyone else in your life? Any stable adults?"

Kat exhaled. "I did once. My grandfather was around when I was younger and I used to stay with him whenever mum went AWOL or couldn't look after me. But when I was ten, I . . ." The girl paused and Dorothy could see her fighting with a memory. "I did something bad and it caused a lot of fuss, so he said he didn't want to see me anymore. And after that there was no one else, just me and Mum."

"I am so sorry, Kat."

"It is what it is."

"It must have been a very unhappy childhood."

Kat thought for a moment. "The worst part was how unpredictable it was. Like, there were periods where she'd promise me she really wanted to stop: she'd get sober, move us to a new city to get away from the 'bad influences' as she called them, find us somewhere to live and me a new school. But it never lasted more than six months. And every time she relapsed, everything got a little bit worse."

"Is that why you stopped contact with her?"

"Yeah, that and other reasons." Kat paused, staring at the mug she was cradling in her hands. "When I was nineteen I was living in London, sleeping on random people's couches and floors. Back then I had this crazy idea of trying to rent somewhere myself, like a proper home." Kat let out a snort at this, as if laughing at her former self for having the audacity to dream. "Anyway, I'd been saving for months to get enough for a deposit, because you need to put down the first six weeks' rent to get a place. And then one night my mum turned up on my doorstep in tears. I hadn't heard from her for ages but she told me she'd had enough of the drugs and was desperate to get clean once and for all. She said her doctor had found her this treatment center in Devon that could take her on a rehab program, but that she needed three thousand pounds to pay for it today or she'd lose the place. Obviously I didn't have that much, but I gave her every penny I'd saved for my flat deposit."

Kat took a swig of her tea before she continued.

"Of course, it was all a lie. Two days later I was walking down Camden High Street and saw her slumped against a wall, high as a kite. That was the moment I made the decision that I couldn't carry on letting her do this to me. That for my own sake, I needed to cut her out of my life. I left London that day and I haven't seen her since."

Dorothy's heart sank. Poor, poor Kat. She could not begin to imagine how difficult it must have been to cut one's own mother out of one's life. "I can see why it was such a terrible shock to see her photo after all these years."

"Yeah. And she looked so rough as well. I mean, she's always looked old for her age, thanks to all the drugs she's taken, but she looked ill. You saw her; it's a wonder she's still alive, let alone able to break into people's houses."

"About that. If the police do find her and arrest her, I am happy to drop the charges. I do not want to be the one responsible for sending your own flesh and blood to prison."

"They can chuck her in and throw away the key as far as I'm concerned. That woman is dead to me."

Kat said the words with such force that Dorothy almost recoiled. No wonder the girl was always so angry, if she carried this much rage at her mother twisted inside her.

"I wouldn't be surprised if she was behind Joseph's attack too," Kat said, picking at a loose thread on the arm of the sofa. "Knowing her, she's probably burgled half the flats in this area to fund her habit."

"Well, if that is true, let us hope the police apprehend her soon."

"Cheers to that," Kat said, raising her mug in a mock toast.

Reggie, who had been curled up next to Kat, raised his head and yawned.

"I suppose I should feed him," Kat said, and Dorothy took that as her signal to leave.

She pushed herself up from the armchair and Kat led her to the front door. When she opened it, Dorothy stepped out into the lobby but paused there. She wanted to say something to the girl, something about how sorry she was for what Kat had been through and how much she admired her bravery. But Kat was staring at her feet, clearly desperate to get rid of Dorothy now that she had shared her miserable tale, so she did not say anything and began to move toward her own door.

"Dorothy?"

She turned back to face Kat, who was looking at her now.

"Yes?"

"Thank you."

Thirty-Seven

KAT

Kat had a shift in the café the following morning. She wanted nothing more than to lie in bed all day but she forced herself to get up at seven a.m. and take Reggie for a walk. As her feet found their rhythm on the river footpath, Kat's mind drifted back to her conversation with Dorothy yesterday. She'd never told anyone about her mum before because she never let anyone close enough to have those kinds of conversations with. But if a bored colleague or random stranger ever did ask her about her family, Kat always said she'd never known her father, which was true, and that her mother was dead, which might as well have been true. So why had she decided to tell the truth last night, and to Dorothy Darling of all people? Perhaps it was only the shock of seeing that photo. Or maybe it was because Dorothy herself knew the pain of losing someone you loved and the shame of living with such an enormous secret, and she had let Kat see that shame. Whatever it was, Kat was surprised to realize that she didn't completely regret the decision this morning. In fact, in some strange way she felt a little lighter, as if the words spoken out loud had carried some weight away with them.

After her walk she showered and dressed, then dropped Reggie round to Dorothy's. They didn't stop to talk beyond a morning greeting, but Kat felt a question in Dorothy's eyes as she handed Reggie over, and she gave the woman a small reassuring nod in reply.

The first half of the shift was busy, but things quieted down around two. Kat was loading clean cutlery into a holder when the front door opened and a familiar figure walked in.

"Dorothy?"

The older woman had her rain hood on, despite it being twenty-four degrees outside, and Reggie on a lead. She stared around the café as if she'd never been in one before.

"Are you okay?" Kat said, walking over to her. "Is something wrong?"

Dorothy shifted from foot to foot, looking deeply uncomfortable.

"Can I get you a drink or something to eat?"

"I am not staying," Dorothy said, eyeing the nearest table with alarm. "I just need to tell you something. I have had a call from Inspector Hudson."

"Let's go outside," Kat said, grabbing her arm. The last thing she needed was Dorothy blabbing about her mum in front of everyone in the café. She led Dorothy across the road to a nearby bench. "What is it?"

Even as she said the words, Kat knew the answer. The police must have found and charged her mother. She'd been expecting this since the moment she saw the photo yesterday; her mum always was terrible at hiding her tracks. But still, the idea of her locked in a police cell was still a sucker punch, even all these years later.

"They located your mother this morning and brought her in for questioning," Dorothy said.

"Right. Well, thanks for telling me."

"That is not all," Dorothy said, and Kat found she was holding her breath, despite herself. What other crimes had her mother committed?

"Your mother admitted breaking into my flat, but she claimed that it was not with the intent to burgle."

Kat laughed so loudly that she saw Dorothy startle. "Right, of course it wasn't. What was her excuse this time, that she was the tooth fairy lost on the job?"

"No. She said she was looking for you."

Kat froze.

"That's bullshit," she spat, hearing the anger in her own voice. "She doesn't know I live here, nobody does. That's part of the reason I move so often, so she can't trace me. And even if she had, why break into *your* flat in the middle of the night rather than ring my doorbell like a normal person? Someone at the police station must have worked out we were related and told my mum, and she was using it as an excuse as to why she was robbing you. I can't believe the cops fell for it!"

Dorothy waited for her to finish. "I do not know the exact details of what happened. All I know is what Inspector Hudson said, which is that your mother claimed she was trying to get into your flat but entered the wrong one by accident."

"That's so like her, trying to weasel her way out of her own actions." Kat's whole body was shaking with fury. Screw her mum for making her feel like this yet again.

"I am sorry," Dorothy said gently. "I did not want to upset you. I just thought you should know."

"I'm not upset." Kat exhaled slowly. "Where is she now?"

"At Winton police station, I believe, although it sounded as if they will release her soon. I am not going to press charges given nothing was stolen."

"What? But you ended up in hospital because of that bloody woman's actions!"

"I tripped and fell over a dog toy, Kat. That was hardly your mother's fault."

"But still, she broke into your flat!" Kat felt like her blood was boiling. God, she really needed to be alone before she punched something or someone.

"The reason I came to tell you this was not to agitate you. I thought that maybe you might want to see your mother."

Kat looked at Dorothy in horror. "Are you kidding me? I told you yesterday, I want nothing to do with her."

"I know you did. But I was thinking about it all night and I wondered if it might be helpful for you to see her. All this rage you carry inside cannot be good for you. Maybe it would be helpful to talk to her?"

Kat let out a sharp laugh. "You can talk, Ms. Secret Dead Daughter. What do you know about talking?"

Dorothy didn't reply and even in the midst of her anger Kat knew she'd gone too far. "I'm sorry, Dorothy. I didn't mean that."

"You do not need to apologize. You were correct when you said that I am I stuck in my past and cannot move forward with my life, but it seems to me that you are the same, young lady. You are understandably haunted by your mother's poor decisions and the profound impact they had on your childhood. But what kind of life is it to constantly relocate every few months, never trusting anyone? I know I am the last person to offer advice on this but I think seeing your mum, talking to her, might help you."

"If I saw her I'd want to hit her, not talk."

"Well, maybe that is what you need to do, then." Dorothy looked down at Reggie, who was trying to eat Kat's shoelace. "I should be getting Little Lord Fauntleroy home, he needs his lunch."

She stood up, but Kat stayed sitting.

"I really did not mean to agitate you, Kat. I simply wanted to give you the chance, that is all. I shall see you later."

Kat watched Dorothy walk away, Reggie at her side. This was

exactly why she never told people about her mum, because they always stuck their noses in and made everything worse. Kat had hoped Dorothy might be different, but she was just like all those damn social workers, teachers, and do-gooders when Kat was a kid. *Your mum wants to see you. She says she's changed. You should give her a second/third/hundredth chance.*

Kat stood up and stormed back into the café, slamming the door so hard behind her that a customer spilled water over themselves. She returned to the cutlery, but with each knife she dropped into the holder, she found herself cursing Dorothy. Kat's first instincts about the woman had been right all along: she was an interfering old witch. How dare she lecture Kat about forgiveness when she'd spent decades hating Joseph so much? Kat shoved a handful of knives into the holder and began on the spoons.

"If you carry on like this we'll have no customers left."

Remi was glaring at her across the counter.

"What?"

"You look like you want to kill someone and you're throwing those spoons in there like missiles."

"I'm fine."

"No, you're not, you're distracted and angry and your energy is bringing the whole place down. Go home."

"I don't need to—"

"This is an order, not a request. Go home and come back tomorrow in a better mood, otherwise your job goes to someone else."

Kat glowered at him, then chucked the last spoons in and went to fetch her bag. Outside the café, she turned to walk home but then changed direction. The last thing she wanted was to go back to Shelley House and face Dorothy.

She headed off into town, not paying any particular attention where she was going. She needed to be outside, breathing fresh air, surrounded by anonymous strangers. She turned left onto the high street and walked past the Alexander Properties office. The door was closed but through it she could see the receptionist at the front desk. For a moment, Kat considered storming in, demanding to see Fergus Alexander, and smacking the man in the face. That would make her feel a *lot* better. She took a deep breath and carried on past. Why did she care anyway? Joseph should be out of the hospital any day now, and the second he was, Kat planned to leave and move somewhere else, far away from this stupid area and all its painful memories.

Kat reached a corner and looked up to cross the road, then ground to a halt. Without her realizing it, her feet had carried her to the police station. Was her mum still there? She'd probably been released ages ago. But still, Kat found herself sitting down on a wall across the road from the building. Dorothy had been wrong; Kat had absolutely no desire to talk to her mother ever again. But maybe it would be useful to see her this once, from a distance, just to remind herself what a walking time bomb the woman was. Kat had a sweatshirt in her rucksack and she put it on and pulled the hood up to shield her face, then sat back and watched the police station door.

For the next half hour, she saw a slow stream of people enter and leave the building, but none of them were her mother. After an hour, Kat's bottom was beginning to go numb. What had she been thinking? This was a complete waste of time.

She was about to stand up and leave when she saw her. It was the walk Kat recognized first: the small, tentative steps her mother took, like a nervous bird. She was wearing an oversized cardigan and blue leggings that showed her skinny legs, and her hair was pulled up into a ponytail. Kat couldn't see her face as her mother walked down the ramp outside the police station, but she could visualize the woman's expression, chewing her lip as she racked her brain as to where she was going to get the next hit. The woman glanced in her direction and Kat pulled her hood farther forward, stood up, and began to make her way away from the police station. But she'd only made it a few steps when she heard a raspy voice calling out.

"Leanne?"

Thirty-Eight

KAT

Kat froze as if her feet had been stapled to the floor. If she started running now she'd easily be able to get away; her mum couldn't jog more than a few paces without collapsing in a heap. Yet for some reason Kat's feet wouldn't move. She could hear her mum call her name again and her voice sounded nearer. This was it, Kat's last chance to get away. The train station was round the corner so she could run there now, jump on a train, and get hundreds of miles away from this place, Dorothy, and her mother.

"Leanne?"

Kat turned around.

The first thing that struck her was how different Sylvia looked from the photo Kat had seen yesterday. Her cheeks, which had been so sunken in the police mug shot, were fuller now, and her skin a more natural pink color as opposed to a pallid gray. But it was her eyes that looked most different: bright and alert as opposed to the blank stare of an addict. These eyes were staring at Kat now, full of hope.

"How are you, Ley-Ley?"

Kat's breath caught at hearing her childhood nickname. But she wasn't Ley-Ley anymore, hadn't even been Leanne for six years. That person was gone.

"Why did you break into Dorothy's flat?" Kat's voice sounded hard in her own ears.

"I wasn't trying to rob her, I swear. I was looking for you."

"That's bullshit. Don't lie to me."

"I'm not, honestly. I'd seen you go into that house before with a little dog and then I saw the dog at the window so I assumed that flat was yours. And I knew if I rang the doorbell or tried to talk to you in the street, you'd tell me to piss off, so I was gonna put a letter through the front door for you."

"And what happened? You forgot what a letterbox looked like?"

"When I came to deliver it I saw that the window was ajar—the same window I'd seen your dog in—so I thought I'd climb in and leave the letter for you. I thought you might be more likely to read it that way, not throw it straight in the bin. I know it sounds mad but it was the only way I could think to make contact with you."

Sylvia reached into her handbag and pulled out a slightly crushed envelope, as if this were proof of her innocence.

"I don't believe you. Dorothy saw you holding a picture frame, about to nick it."

"Nah, I wasn't! I put the letter down and then I saw the photo of a girl and I wondered who it was. For a second I thought maybe you had a kid—that I was a grandma—but I realized the girl was too old. And then the next thing I knew, the old woman was behind me yelling and then she tripped and I freaked out, grabbed the letter, and ran."

Kat crossed her arms. "I still don't believe you."

"How is the old woman? I was worried she might be hurt."

"She's okay, no thanks to you."

"Please, will you tell her I'm sorry? I feel awful about what happened."

"How did you find out where I lived? Nobody knows I'm here, I've even changed my name."

"I know you have. But then Billy Walsh—remember him? He knew I was looking for you and sent me a video of an old woman kicking off about some housing redevelopment, and I recognized you the second I saw you. You may have changed your hair, but your face is exactly the same as when you were a kid. And you had that expression on you, like your nana Betty."

Kat didn't respond to this. She'd never met her grandmother, who died before she was born, but she'd seen photos of Ian's wife and the woman had looked like a bulldog.

"Anyway, the article said the protest was about Shelley House in Chalcot, which I remembered from when I was a kid, so as soon as I could I came down here to have a look. I must have sat up the road for about eight hours before I saw you walk in."

"So you decided to break in in the middle of the night rather than ring the doorbell?"

"Look, I know it was a dumb thing to do. But I saw that the window was easy to pop open, and all I was gonna do was leave the letter and go. I thought you could read it and decide whether you wanted to see me or not."

"Well, I can tell you now, I don't want to see you. So you can piss off back to whichever crack den you came from."

The words had intended to hurt, but Sylvia gave a small, sad smile. "That's fair enough. I thought that might be your answer, which is why I wanted to give you the letter rather than ring your doorbell."

"Yeah, well, next time you want to send someone a letter I suggest you use Royal Mail like everyone else."

This had been a terrible idea; Kat should never have come here, never have opened herself up to her mum's bullshit and lies again. She turned and began to walk away.

"What are you doing back in Chalcot?"

Kat could hear her mother's footsteps behind her.

"Is this something to do with your grandpa?"

She ground to a halt and swung round to face her mum. "He's dead. Did you know that? Your own father is *dead.*"

Sylvia sighed. "I know, Leanne. I'm so sorry."

"And the farm got stolen from him, did you know that too?" Kat realized she was shouting but she didn't care. "He got beaten up so badly that they sold the farm and then he died."

"I know. The whole thing was awful."

Kat was about to shout again but paused. "Who told you about it?"

"He did."

"What?" Kat felt sick as she realized what her mum was saying. "You saw Grandpa before he died?"

There was a twitch in her mother's eye, something Kat remembered from when she was a child. A twitch that gave away when her mother was nervous. "Yeah, I reconnected with him a few years ago. I was with him when he died."

Kat felt the words like a series of punches. "But I thought . . ." She trailed off, unable to formulate the sentence.

"You thought he'd disowned me."

"He disowned both of us! Back when I was ten, you told me he never wanted to see either of us ever again because of what I did. I've stayed away from Chalcot, from him, for all these years because *you* told me I had to!"

Sylvia didn't say anything for a moment, staring at Kat with eyes full of pain. When she spoke, her voice was so faint it was almost a whisper. "I'm so sorry, Leanne. I'm so sorry for everything I did back then."

"What do you mean? What did you do?"

"I lied to you, sweetheart." She paused, as if unwilling to say the words, then took a deep breath. "Your grandfather didn't disown you. It was me who broke contact, not the other way round."

Kat frowned, trying to process what her mum was saying. "That's not true, you're misremembering it, Mum. I started the fire at the school and then Grandpa sent for you to take me away and said I was never allowed to go near him or Chalcot ever again. I swear, I can remember it as if it were yesterday."

Even as she said the words, Kat could see it all playing out in her mind, the images crystal clear. The teacher who'd thrown her out of the classroom for disrupting yet another lesson. The headmistress who'd shouted at her and then left Kat in her office while she went to deal with something else. Kat's rage at the teacher and the headmistress and her mum, all adults who were supposed to look after her but made her life worse. The box of matches poking out of the woman's handbag and the metal bin filled with paper. The feeling of satisfaction as she dropped the lit match in and watched the pages catch. The flames suddenly leaping from the bin to engulf the curtains, the blinding smoke, Kat choking so hard she could barely breathe. The alarm and the sirens and the firefighters who rescued her. The shocked expressions of the pupils and teachers lined up in the playground, the police and her grandpa's face, so full of sorrow and confusion. And then her mother's sudden arrival that night, the muffled shouts from behind the closed kitchen door, and Kat being stuffed into the back seat of her mum's car and driven away from the farm, so upset she didn't even turn around to get a last glimpse of it.

Sylvia was staring at her feet when she started speaking.

"You're right, that is what I told you. But . . . it's not what really happened. Your grandfather didn't disown you because of the fire."

"What?" The word was a gasp.

"That was just the excuse I gave you so you'd accept that we couldn't see him again. I know it sounds cruel but I was desperate and I knew that if I told you the truth, you'd go rushing back and I'd lose you for good. So I made up that—"

"Hang on, what about the letter?" Kat interrupted, falling over her words in her haste to get them out. "You showed it to me. The one where Grandpa said I was dead to him; how the whole village was furious at me for damaging the school and if I ever came back to Chalcot I'd be taken straight to the police station and arrested for arson. I remember reading it and—"

Kat stopped when she saw her mother's crestfallen face.

"You made that up too?"

"I'm so sorry, Leanne."

Kat's head was spinning and she closed her eyes for a moment as she tried to make sense of it all. "But why would you make all that stuff up? Why did you want to stop me seeing him?"

Rather than reply, Sylvia turned and walked several paces back to the wall Kat had been sitting on earlier. She leaned against it, resting her hands together as if in prayer, and only then did she speak.

"I don't know how much you remember, but that spring—the spring before you turned ten—I was not in a good place. I was living with this guy, Ritchie, who—"

"I remember that scumbag," Kat spat.

"Yeah, he was bad news. He was the one who introduced me to heroin, and once I'd started that, things went downhill pretty quickly. That's when your grandpa stepped in and took you to stay with him at the farm."

"None of this explains why you lied to me and stopped me ever seeing him again."

"I'm trying, Leanne. Your grandpa had been worrying about you for a long time, and he'd made several threats that if I didn't sort my act out, then he'd apply to the courts for guardianship of you. He'd never followed through with it but that year, when I met Ritchie, everything changed. He got a solicitor and was going to make an application to the courts saying I was unfit to take care of you and he should be granted custody."

Her grandfather had wanted custody of her? He'd never mentioned anything about that to Kat, she was sure of it. But that would have meant . . .

"I could have gone to live with him permanently?"

"That's what he wanted. To keep you at the farm, away from me."

Kat was too shocked to speak. Throughout her childhood that was all she'd ever dreamed of: to be able to stay in the safety of Featherdown Farm under the watchful eye of her grandfather and great-uncle. No more living with the constant threat of eviction and homelessness, no more having to worry that she'd come home from school to find her mum missing, or worse.

"So what happened?" Her voice was a croak.

"What you have to understand is that I was scared. I knew that your grandpa had a really strong case and I was terrified of losing you. My life was chaotic and difficult but you were the only good thing in it. And so when I found out what he was planning, I panicked."

"I asked, what happened?"

Sylvia let out a long sigh, staring at her feet. "As soon as I heard, I came to collect you from the farm. Your grandpa and I had a blazing row, but he didn't have temporary custody yet so he couldn't physically stop me from taking you. So I put you in the car and drove us far, far away from Chalcot and Ritchie and anything that linked me to the past. I wanted a fresh start, just you and me, where none of them could ever find us."

Kat remembered it now, the small damp cottage they'd gone to stay at in Scotland. Her mum had told her they were in hiding so the police wouldn't find Kat and arrest her for starting the fire, and for weeks she'd barely dared step outside, cowering in the corner while her mum lay in bed, sick with withdrawal. After that they'd gone to Spain for a bit, then back to the UK and a cold, miserable winter in various bedsits and moldy flats in the northeast. Never in one place for more than a few months at a time. And no more holidays at Featherdown Farm.

"Why couldn't you have just told me the truth? Why did you have to make me think we left because of the fire?"

Sylvia glanced up, her expression bleak. "I'm so sorry. I didn't even know about the fire when I picked you up; your grandpa never told me about it. But then you mentioned it in the car and asked if that was why you had to leave Chalcot, and I jumped on it as a reason for why we couldn't go back. I knew at the time it was a shitty thing to do, but I was desperate. I hoped that if you thought your grandfather was mad at you, it might somehow make the separation easier and you wouldn't keep asking to go back there, like you usually did."

Kat didn't say anything as she processed her mother's words. For fifteen long, painful years she'd thought it was her fault, that she'd made her grandfather so angry that he had never wanted to see her again. But the opposite was true. He'd wanted to keep her, to give her a permanent, safe, loving home at Featherdown Farm. And her mother had stolen it all away from her.

"And what about the whole police thing? Did they really have a warrant out for my arrest?"

"No, I made that up too," Sylvia said, her cheeks flushed red with the shame. "I'm so sorry, Leanne. I was so scared of losing you."

"Fuck," Kat said, lifting her hands up to rub her face. "All this time I blamed myself, Mum. Fifteen years of guilt and self-hatred thinking I'd driven my own grandfather away. Do you have any idea what that feels like?"

"I have no excuses for my behavior." Sylvia looked even smaller now, hunched over on the low wall. "I was an addict—I am an addict—and I messed up your childhood. But believe me, I do know what it's like to live with guilt and self-hatred."

Kat exhaled slowly. There were so many things she wanted to scream and shout at her mother, but she suddenly found she was exhausted.

"I know this will be no consolation to you, but I'm sober now," her mother said when Kat didn't speak. "I have been since before your grandpa died. I've got my own place in Birmingham: nothing fancy, just a little studio, but I've been there for two years now and I've got a job cleaning offices."

"Hooray for you," Kat said, but the sarcasm fell flat. All she wanted was to go back to Shelley House and curl up in bed like she had done when she was a child and it all got to be too much.

"I'm not asking for you to forgive me; I'd never ask that. All I'm asking is that you read this letter." Sylvia was still holding the envelope, and she thrust it toward her. "No child should have to grow up like you did, and no stupid letter is ever going to make up for what I took away from you. But I wanted to—needed to—write it all down and tell you what really happened. I was a bad mother, Leanne, I lied to you and failed you, and I will never, ever forgive myself for that."

Kat opened her mouth to argue, but as she did she thought of Dorothy. That woman had twisted and tormented herself with guilt for thirty-odd years, become a self-imposed prisoner of her own self-loathing. Kat looked at her mother, so small and fragile, and any remaining anger deflated from her body.

"Addiction is a sickness, Mum. You were ill. You don't need to punish yourself anymore, you just need to focus on staying well."

Sylvia blinked and Kat saw tears in her eyes.

"Thank you," she said, her voice quivering. She held the letter out again, her hand shaking too. Kat stared at it for a moment then reached out and took it.

"Good-bye, Mum. Take care."

"You too. Be happy."

This time when Kat walked away, Sylvia didn't follow.

Thirty-Nine

DOROTHY

Dorothy watched Kat as she walked along the pavement toward Shelley House, her face angled down so that her features were hidden. Dorothy had spent the whole morning sitting by the window, anxiously awaiting this return. She had no idea if she had done the right thing in alerting Kat to her mother's presence at the police station. She had hoped that it might allow the girl some answers or catharsis even, but there was an equal chance it might have caused nothing but further pain and anger. Dorothy therefore found she was holding her breath as Kat climbed the front steps, her face still concealed by her pink hair. Dorothy rose and limped to her front door, pulling it open as her neighbor stepped into the lobby.

Kat turned her head at the noise, revealing cheeks stained with tears. *Oh no.* Dorothy had clearly done the wrong thing after all.

"I am so sorry, Kat."

The girl said nothing as she wiped her sweatshirt sleeve across her eyes.

"I shall leave you alone. I only wanted to check—"

"I don't suppose you fancy a cuppa, do you?"

Dorothy was so surprised that she did not know how to respond, so she turned and hurried into her kitchen, leaving the front door open for Kat to follow. This was the first time she had made a pot of tea for another person in decades, and she located a lace doily in a bottom drawer, which she laid on a plate. If she had known she would be entertaining, then she would have ordered in some good biscuits, but custard creams would have to do. When Dorothy carried the tea tray out a few minutes later, she found Kat sitting on the sofa, Reggie curled up next to her. Neither of them spoke as Dorothy put down the tray and poured tea through the strainer before passing a cup and saucer to Kat. The girl also took a biscuit, which she ate silently.

"I went to the police station," she finally said as she fed the last bit of biscuit to Reggie.

"Did you see your mother?"

"I did."

"Did you speak to her?"

"I did."

"Did you punch her in the face?"

This elicited a minuscule smile. "I did not."

Kat took another biscuit from the plate and took a bite, chewing it slowly. Dorothy waited for her to speak again.

"She said sorry for breaking into your flat and scaring you. It seems she really was trying to get to me."

"And did she not consider using the front door as per custom?"

"She said I wouldn't have spoken to her if she'd rung the doorbell, which, in fairness, is true. She said she wanted to leave me this." Kat reached into her bag and pulled out a rather sad-looking envelope.

"I see. And will you read it?"

Kat gave a noncommittal shrug.

"Did you mother hint at what the letter might say?"

"Not really. Although she did tell me some things . . ." Kat hesitated, the first time Dorothy had ever seen her lost for words. Then she took a deep breath. "When I was a kid I used to stay with my grandpa in Chalcot. He owned Featherdown Farm and I loved it there with him and my great-uncle; I think it was the only place I've ever felt truly happy. Then when I was ten, my mum told me that my grandpa had disowned me because of my bad behavior and he never wanted to see me again; that if I ever came back to Chalcot he'd have me arrested for what I'd done. But today, she told me that was a lie. He never disowned me, quite the opposite. He wanted me to live with him permanently, and my mum took me away to stop that from happening."

Dorothy had never heard anything quite like it, and she had to restrain herself from saying something indelicate. What kind of a mother would do something so monstrous to her own child?

"I just don't know what to do with this information," Kat said, playing with the frayed cuff of her sleeve. "Part of me is relieved to know my grandpa didn't hate me and send me away like I'd always thought. But I'm also so bloody angry at my mum for stealing my chance of a stable childhood; for stealing my chance to have a proper relationship with my grandfather. The things I went through living with her—the drugs and the shitty boyfriends and evictions—and I could have escaped it all."

Kat looked down at her teacup and Dorothy could tell she was fighting back tears.

"I am so sorry. That was a truly terrible thing your mother did to you."

"I keep thinking, *What if?* What if I'd grown up right here, rather than moving every few months with my mum? What if I'd been able to stay in school? What if—"

"My dear, that way madness lies."

Kat glanced up at her. "What do you mean?"

"I mean, thirty-three years ago my perfect future was snatched away from me, like your mother's lie snatched yours away from you. And ever since, I have allowed myself to be tormented by *what-ifs*.

What if I had complained about the dangerous roof and had the fire door sealed up? What if I had kept a closer eye on my daughter, rather than flirting with Joseph? What if I had been a better mother? I have become so consumed with these *what-ifs* and the life that was stolen from me, I stopped living the life I still have."

Dorothy indicated the room around her: the faded old furniture and peeling wallpaper that had not been changed since the day Charlotte died.

"You've been grieving," Kat said.

"Yes, and you have been grieving too. You have spent many years believing you drove your own grandfather away."

"Thanks to my bloody mother," Kat muttered.

"I am sure your mother must have had her reasons, however misguided. But perhaps you should not waste your energy being angry at her, Kat. After all, today she has given you a gift."

"What, this letter?" She waved the crumpled envelope she was still clutching.

"No. She has released you from a painful lie that has defined your whole life. Now you are free to live the life you want. The life you deserve."

"As are you," Kat said, but Dorothy brushed her away.

"Did you come back to Chalcot in the hope of being reunited with your grandfather?"

Kat exhaled so loudly that Reggie woke with surprise. "I'm not sure why I came back, to be honest. I've spent my whole life staying away because I believed that was what he wanted and that I'd get in trouble if I returned. But recently, I kept thinking about this village and him. I guess a small part of me hoped he might still be alive and I might be able to apologize and make peace."

"I am sorry you did not get the chance to do that, or to say goodbye to the man you loved. But at least now you know you had nothing to apologize for. You have been punishing yourself all these years for a crime you did not commit."

In response Kat raised an eyebrow at Dorothy, the meaning of her expression clear as day.

"This conversation is about you, girl, not me," Dorothy said, looking away.

Kat gave a half smile. "Well, either way, it's too late now. My grandpa is gone and so is his farm, destroyed by Fergus Alexander. I'm too late."

Aha, so *that* was why Kat was so determined to bring down their landlord. Dorothy had wondered why she had suddenly become so focused on proving Alexander's crimes.

"You may not have had the reconciliation you hoped for, but I would say it is not too late. We can still fight and get some justice for what Fergus Alexander did to your grandfather."

"I suppose." Kat ran a hand over her pale face.

"You require another cup of tea," Dorothy said, pushing herself up from her chair.

"I'm fine."

"Nonsense. Let me make a fresh pot and we can discuss our next move. I will not sit around idly while we wait for Will's article to be published. And we have still not worked out who attacked Joseph either. I have been reassessing my suspect list, if you would like to see it?"

"Sure. And a couple more of those biscuits wouldn't go amiss either, please. I'm starving."

"Of course, your ladyship." She gave a mock curtsy and was rewarded with a small laugh from Kat.

Dorothy picked up the tray and carried it through to the kitchen. She had been so quick to judge Kat when she had first moved in, but beneath the tattoos and ridiculous hair was a sensitive and kind girl, one who had been treated abominably by the very person who was meant to protect her. Just the thought of that wretched woman made Dorothy's blood boil. To think she could have lied to her own daughter, despite the obvious distress it would cause the child, and then allow that lie to ferment into adulthood, doing untold damage. Why, Dorothy had a good mind to track down Sylvia Mason and give that woman a piece of her mind.

"Here you go," Dorothy said, as she carried the tray back through. "Tea and biscuits, although I have run out of custard creams so I am afraid plain old digestives will have to—"

Dorothy stopped short when she saw Kat's face. The girl was still sitting on the sofa, the most recent copy of the *Dunningshire Gazette* open on her knee. Dorothy had retrieved it from the post shelf when she returned from her visit to Kat's place of work this afternoon but had not yet looked at it. Kat had, however, and it appeared that whatever she had read had caused her some distress.

"Whatever is the matter?" Dorothy placed the tray down on the table. "You look terrible."

"I . . . I . . ." Kat stuttered.

"What is it? Is there something about your mother? Or that rat Fergus Alexander?"

Kat did not reply, but her lips were trembling as she stared up at Dorothy.

"Come along, it cannot be that bad." Dorothy reached down to retrieve the paper from Kat's lap, but the girl grabbed it as if to prevent her. "What are you doing?"

Kat continued to hold on to it. "Please, Dorothy. Don't read it."

"Why ever not?"

Dorothy tugged harder and the newspaper released from Kat's hand. Really, what strange behavior. Dorothy sat back down in her chair and looked at the page Kat had been reading. There was an article about a charity Zumbathon in Favering, whatever that was, and the upcoming Chalcot Summer Fete, but surely neither of these would have alarmed Kat so much? Dorothy scanned to the next page. There were several articles here, but her eyes fell on a familiar photograph. It was a black-and-white image of Shelley House, the same one the newspaper had used in its previous report about Joseph's one-man campaign. Above it was a headline. **Redevelopment Threat Brings Back Painful Memories for Residents.**

"I had no idea Will was going to write this," Kat said, but Dorothy did not look at her as she read on.

> Property developer Fergus Alexander has set his sights on a historic mansion block in Chalcot for redevelopment into luxury flats, evicting its residents in the process. But Shelley House in Poet's Road holds other tragedies in its past, tragedies that have been brought back to the surface by recent events. In the summer of 1991, residents were devastated by the death of Charlotte Darling, a fifteen-year-old who died in an accident in the building. Her mother, Dorothy Darling, seventy-seven, still lives in Shelley House, and has spent the past three decades plagued by guilt at not being able to prevent her daughter's death. Now, Ms. Darling, along with other residents, is determined to stop the redevelopment plans and save the striking Victorian building that was once Charlotte's home.
>
> The redevelopment plans for Shelley House are currently . . .

Dorothy stopped reading, the newspaper dropping from her lap. She looked over at Kat, the girl who only moments ago she had been consoling.

"How could you?" Her voice was a rasp.

"I'm so sorry. I told Will this in confidence, I had no idea he'd write an article about it."

"You promised you would keep it a secret."

"I know. I only told Will because I was worried about you and—"

"Everyone knows." Dorothy gasped as the realization hit her. Ayesha. Omar. Gloria. The whole of Chalcot and beyond would read this and know about Charlotte's death and Dorothy's guilt. Her insides twisted at the thought and she bent forward in pain.

"It's really not as big a deal as you think," Kat said, although the panic in her tone suggested otherwise. "People will just feel sorry for you when they hear about Charlotte and—"

"Do not dare say my daughter's name!" Her voice was no longer a rasp but a roar.

"I'm sorry, I just—"

"I cannot believe I was stupid enough to trust you of all people with my secret."

Dorothy saw Kat bristle at her words, but all she wanted was to hurt the girl the way Kat had hurt and humiliated her.

"The first time I saw you I knew you were trouble. Joseph may have been fooled by you, but I knew you were rotten from day one."

Kat's eyes flashed dangerously and Dorothy saw that she was gripping her hands together.

"No wonder your grandfather wanted nothing to do with you, when all you bring is pain and destruction to those around you."

"Stop it, Dorothy. Please."

But Dorothy could not stop, drunk now on the rage that flowed through her veins at the girl who had laid her guilt bare for the world to see. "I bet you were behind Joseph's attack as well, were you not? You and your crack-addled, good-for-nothing mother who—"

Dorothy did not get to finish her sentence as Kat leaped to her feet, sending the tea tray flying. Its contents came crashing onto the floor and Dorothy saw them shatter into pieces.

"Don't you lecture me about bad mothers," the girl said, her whole body visibly shaking. "Whatever failings my mother may have, at least she managed to keep me alive."

Dorothy swayed as if she had been physically hit, and she saw regret flash across Kat's face.

"I'm sor—" Kat started, but Dorothy was on her feet now too.

"How dare you bring Charlotte into this. Leave now!"

"With pleasure!" Kat reached for her bag and Dorothy heard china crunching underfoot.

"I never want to see you again," Dorothy shouted as the girl pushed past her toward the door. "Get out of Chalcot and never come back!"

"I hope they bulldoze this place with you inside it," Kat said, and Dorothy could hear a choke of tears in her voice. A second later her flat door swung open and Kat was gone.

The flat was silent now, the only sound Dorothy's own panting breaths. She looked down at the article on the coffee table, damp from the spilled tea, and let out a low moan. Kat was right, she had as good as killed her own daughter, and there was her culpability in print for everyone to see. Turning from the paper, Dorothy started to move across the room and then felt a searing pain in her foot. A shard of her beloved teapot, the one that Phillip and Charlotte had given her for Christmas, had pierced through the sole of her stockinged foot. Dorothy whimpered but continued to walk, hobbling every time she put pressure on it. When she reached the farthest door she looked back and saw a trail of blood across the oak floor. But there was no time for that now. Dorothy left the drawing room and limped past the bathroom and her own bedroom, feeling light-headed from the pain. When she reached the last door, she pushed it open and staggered in.

Like the rest of the house, Charlotte's bedroom had remained unchanged all these years. The same posters of Nirvana and R.E.M. decorated the walls, the same clothes hung in the wardrobe, and on the dressing table was the same silver hairbrush with which Dorothy used to brush Charlotte's long brown hair every morning until she was old enough to do it herself. Each item meticulously dusted every week but left exactly where Charlotte had put them on that last morning.

Dorothy dragged her bleeding foot across the carpet until she reached the bed. It had Charlotte's favorite duvet set on, the one with faded pink flowers. Charlotte's teddy bear sat on the pillow waiting for her, and Dorothy moved it now as she lowered herself onto the bed, trying not to groan as her foot knocked against the side. When Charlotte first died and Phillip pushed her away, Dorothy had spent a lot of time on this bed, had slept in it for weeks on end, leaving her husband to stew with resentment in their bedroom. When he left she had moved back to the principal bedroom and she had not lain down on this bed since. Now Dorothy put her head on Charlotte's pillow, clutched the teddy to her chest, and closed her eyes, waiting for sleep to come.

Forty

KAT

Kat stormed around the flat, slamming doors and banging cupboards. How could Will have betrayed her like this? To think she'd been naive enough to open herself up to him, to tell him things from her own life she'd never told another soul, and all along he was simply pumping her for gossip to put in his articles. She remembered kissing him in the archive and hurled a cushion across the living room.

And then there was Dorothy. Kat had never seen hatred in a person's eyes like she had with Dorothy just now, and who could blame her? She'd told Kat her deepest, darkest secret and Kat had broken her trust. There was no way Dorothy would ever forgive her for what she'd done. *Get out of Chalcot and never come back!* Kat shuddered as she remembered Dorothy's words, the very same ones she'd been told her grandfather had said fifteen years ago.

There was a knock on the door and Kat rushed to answer it, praying it was Dorothy. But when she pulled it open, the person standing in the lobby was Will.

"Hey!" He gave her his lopsided grin, which disappeared when he saw Kat's face. "What's the matter? Did I get the wrong time?"

Kat looked across the lobby toward flat one; the last thing she needed was Dorothy seeing her with Will. She pulled him inside and slammed the door shut.

"How could you?" The words came out as a half shout, half sob.

"What?" Will looked genuinely perplexed.

"The article you wrote about Dorothy. How could you do that to her? To me?"

"I don't understand. I thought writing about her story would help gain public sympathy for what's happening here. I thought you'd be pleased!"

"Are you kidding me?" Kat turned and paced across the room so she didn't have to look at his stupid, handsome face. "I told you that in confidence, Will. You weren't meant to write it in the sodding paper."

"But why not? Everything in that article was already public knowledge; Charlotte's death has been written about before."

"Not for thirty-three years it hasn't. And even then, the article only said Charlotte had died but not that Dorothy blamed herself. Now you've brought it all up again so everyone will be gossiping about it. Didn't you think about how Dorothy might feel?"

"But I didn't say anything bad about her."

Kat spun back round. "You talked about her feeling guilty, you moron. That guilt has been eating away at her for three decades, and now this is going to make it one thousand times worse."

"I know you're pissed off but you can't blame all of this on me." His tone had turned defensive. "You never told me Dorothy's story was a secret. And you said you wanted to help save Shelley House for her, so that was exactly was I was trying to do too."

Kat slumped on the sofa. She wanted to scream at Will, but he was right, she couldn't blame him entirely. She was the one who'd been stupid enough to think she could trust another person. The one who had let her guard down and allowed someone to get close. After all the years of her mother's lies and false promises, why did Kat ever think she could rely on someone else without getting hurt?

"Can I do anything to help fix this?" Will said, perching down next to her. "Should I go and talk to Dorothy now, apologize to her?"

"No!" Kat jumped up again. "Stay away from Dorothy. She hates us, and you'll only make things worse."

"She'll calm down eventually. And until then, we can carry on trying to save her home."

"Dorothy has spent thirty-three years trying to atone for Charlotte's death, and you and I just put it in print for the whole town to see. I don't think she'll ever forgive me for this."

"I'm sorry, Kat. I honestly thought I was helping the cause."

"Yeah, well, you definitely haven't." Kat walked to the door and yanked it open. "You should go now."

"Seriously? Kat, I said I'm sorry."

"I don't want to see you anymore, Will."

"But I thought we were going to grab a drink and talk about the article. I spoke to another old tenant of Alexander's today who's given me some—"

"I don't give a shit about that. Now leave me alone."

Will looked baffled as he walked past her and stepped out into the lobby. He turned round to speak to her again, but Kat slammed the door in his face. She'd hoped it would make her feel better, but if anything she felt worse. Kat remembered Dorothy's hurt expression, the rage in her eyes, and the furious words that had spewed from her mouth. *No wonder your grandfather wanted nothing to do with you, when all you bring is pain and destruction to those around you.*

Kat felt the sting of tears, and she angrily wiped them away. Then she turned and marched to the bedroom to start packing.

Forty-One

SIX MONTHS LATER

DOROTHY

Dorothy was woken at six thirty by the redundant clanking of the ancient pipes. She lay in bed for several minutes, willing herself to return to her dream. In it, not only was Charlotte alive but a grown woman, with laughter lines around her eyes and hints of gray at her roots. She had been sitting on a bus reading, and although Dorothy had not been able to converse with her, she had drunk in the sight of her beautiful daughter. But alas, as soon as Dorothy was awake the cold started to seep into her bones and any chance of returning to the dream was gone.

She rose from bed, wincing at the numerous aches in her body, then felt her way in darkness to the bathroom. The electricity had been cut off and there had been no hot water for more than a week, so Dorothy ran icy water into the sink and splashed it over her body, trying not to yelp at the cold. She was unable to make tea or boil an egg now that there was no power, so she fetched herself a glass of water and carried it through to the card table by the window.

As she drank, Dorothy observed the morning activity outside. The white vans arrived a little before eight, parking in front of Shelley House and disgorging their passengers onto the frosty pavement.

There were four builders today, and they grunted greetings to one another as they finished cigarettes and unloaded equipment. They had first appeared ten days ago, nodding uncomfortable hellos to Dorothy as they let themselves into the building. So far all they seemed to have done was remove items from the other flats: Dorothy had watched kitchen sinks, lighting fixtures, and a wardrobe door with an exam timetable still taped to it being unceremoniously dumped in a skip.

An almighty crash from upstairs signaled that it was eight o'clock and the start of the builders' working day. Dorothy rose to dress, which involved pulling a skirt and sweaters on over thermals, as well as a hat, fingerless gloves, and her pearls. Once ready she changed the beds, swept the oak floors, and dusted the pictures and ornaments on the mantelpiece, accompanied by Wagner's *Parsifal* on the CD player, turned up high to block out the noise of sledgehammers overhead.

At ten o'clock, she had just sat down to imbibe a glass of water when she heard a commotion farther up Poet's Road. For a moment, Dorothy thought she might have misheard among the din of the builders, but when she looked outside she saw a small brown-and-white dog running up the pavement toward Shelley House, yapping excitedly. Dorothy smiled but did not get up from her seat. Instead, her eyes moved behind the dog to the figure who was following it up the steps.

A few moments later she heard the click of her front door opening and Reggie came bounding in.

"Hello, you good boy," Dorothy said, as the animal leaped up onto her lap and began licking her face. She closed her eyes and allowed him to cover her in kisses. "Yes, I missed you too, Reginald."

When she opened her eyes, Joseph Chambers was in the doorway, watching her.

"Do not stand there like a lemon," Dorothy snapped, and Joseph gave a mock salute and moved toward the kitchen.

She turned her attention back to Reggie, tickling under his chin. Joseph had started bringing the dog to visit her back in October. Before then he had still been living in Shelley House and Dorothy had seen the animal most days. But after Fergus Alexander's planning application was approved and the possession orders arrived, Joseph and the other residents had decided the fight was up and he had moved to a bungalow in a retirement community in Little Whitham. Dorothy had refused to speak to the old man for weeks, such was her disgust at his betrayal, but he had kept turning up on Poet's Road with Reggie and eventually she had relented. Now Joseph brought the dog over twice a week, on a Monday and a Thursday. To start with he had dropped the animal off on the doorstep and gone for a walk, returning an hour later to collect Reggie. But as autumn turned to winter and the weather had become more inclement, Dorothy had felt obliged to invite Joseph in. On the first few occasions he had sat in silence on the sofa, both of them focusing their attention on Reggie. Then one day, Joseph turned up with a carrier bag and disappeared into the kitchen, returning with two ham sandwiches.

"I get hungry" was all he had said as he sat down on the sofa to eat. Dorothy had stared at her sandwich in horror until Reggie had jumped up on the table and eaten it.

The next time Joseph came, he brought two bacon sandwiches, serving them up on plates. Dorothy had vowed not to eat a morsel of anything Joseph Chambers made, but it had smelled so good and she was so hungry that she ended up devouring the whole thing as soon as he left. On his next visit he presented her with some sort of savory filled bun and they had eaten them in silence. And so the frost had begun to thaw.

Today it was bowls of homemade chicken soup, which Joseph poured from a thermos flask and carried through on a tray.

"I was thinking I could pop to the garden center after lunch and get you a small tree," he said as he sat down at the card table next to her. "I can help you decorate it, if you like?"

Dorothy sniffed. "I told you, I do not celebrate Christmas. And certainly not this year."

"You should at least have a small one. I can lend you some baubles if you don't have any."

She did have decorations, a whole box of them stored away somewhere. Phillip used to bring them out every year to great fanfare, and the three of them would decorate the flat together. The year they moved into Shelley House, they had bought a six-foot-tall plastic tree, which Phillip erected in the window, where Dorothy now sat. It had been the only Christmas they had celebrated here as a family. By the following December, both Charlotte and Phillip were gone. The tree and decorations had sat in a cupboard ever since.

"What are you going to do on Christmas Day?" Joseph said.

Dorothy swallowed a spoonful of soup, grateful for its nourishing warmth. She had not had a hot meal since Joseph was last here four days ago.

"I will do the same as I do every other day of the year. Although at least I shall get a break from this infernal racket." She nodded toward the ceiling, through which the insistent buzz of an electric drill could be heard.

"You know you're very welcome to spend it with me?" Joseph said it quietly, almost like an apology. "They put on a lunch in the residents' center with all the works and then everyone sings carols after the Queen's speech, apparently. It's meant to be fun."

Dorothy grimaced and Joseph chuckled.

"Fair enough, I suppose it doesn't sound *that* much fun. But I could cook a turkey at my place. I make a mean roast potato, if I do say so myself."

"I have never seen the point of turkey. Horrible dry bird."

"And you know they're not going to send the bailiffs in on Christmas Day. You'd be safe to leave this place for one day."

"I hate carols too. Awful, dirgelike things, and no one can ever sing in tune."

"Speaking of which, have they sent you an eviction date yet?"

"This soup is surprisingly pleasant. Did you put thyme in it?"

"You can't change the subject every time I bring this up, Dorothy. The bulldozers are approaching, quite literally. They must have sent you an eviction order by now."

"And there are leeks in here too, I think."

"Dorothy—"

"Stop it, Joseph."

From upstairs there was a loud bang as a sledgehammer connected with something and Dorothy's table rattled precariously. She watched the ripples on the surface of her soup until they settled.

"I'm just worried about you," Joseph said softly. "You've already ignored one possession order. The next step will be sending you an eviction date, and when that day comes the bailiffs will turn up, whether you like it or not. You can't put your head in the sand forever."

"Perhaps they have decided to spare flat two?" Dorothy did not look at Joseph as she said this, but she could tell he was shaking his head.

"Oh, Dorothy," was all he said.

For dessert, Joseph produced two slices of apple pie; homemade, Dorothy noted with approval.

"So, did anything interesting happen over the weekend?" he asked as he dolloped a generous spoon of cream on each portion of pie.

This was a conversation they had every time Joseph visited, and

Dorothy reached for her diary and flicked it open, scanning the most recent entries.

"The couple from number 18 had another argument on Saturday."

"Oh dear, not again."

"She accused him of being a poorly endowed excuse for a man who wouldn't know how to entertain a woman if his life depended on it."

"She actually said that?"

"Well, no, I am paraphrasing; the expressions she used were far more vulgar."

Joseph chuckled. "Divorce must be on the cards for them, surely?"

"And yesterday the man from number 27 reversed his van into the car belonging to the family at 24. There was no obvious damage but I made sure he reported it to them anyway."

"Quite right. And what's this?"

The diary had fallen open on a well-worn page. Dorothy snapped it shut. "Nothing."

Joseph gave a soft sigh. "Dorothy, we've been over this a dozen times. None of our neighbors were responsible for my injury, so you can stop obsessing over your suspect list."

"I am not obsessing over anything, thank you very much."

"After everything we've all been through, you can't seriously still believe that Gloria might have attacked me?"

"Just because a woman has a pretty face and brought me doughnuts in hospital does not mean she is innocent. Have you never heard of a femme fatale?"

"Well, I know it wasn't Tomasz. I told you he and I have become friends now; we've even been to the pub a few times. I'm pretty sure he wouldn't be buying me pints if he'd tried to knock me off."

"You see, this is your problem, you are far too trusting," Dorothy said with a tut. "Have you ever considered that he might be befriending you for exactly this reason, so you do not suspect him of his crime? And I told you my theory that he was the post thief."

"Oh dear, not this again. Do—"

She raised her hand to silence him. This was a discussion they had had several times before and she knew they would never agree. At the end of the summer, before the possession orders arrived, Dorothy had worked out that someone was stealing their post. She only made the discovery thanks to her assiduous management of the post shelf, which meant she knew exactly what arrived for each resident every day. Then one afternoon she overheard Gloria complaining that an Amazon parcel had not been delivered, even though Dorothy knew full well it had as she had given said package a good inspection that very morning. A few days later, Ayesha told Dorothy that her exam results had not arrived when they were supposed to, and over the coming days every other resident in the building began to grumble about missing post too. Every resident except one . . .

"Tomasz is still very much a suspect," Dorothy said, folding her arms across her chest.

"Well, please tell me you've at least crossed Sandra's name off?" Joseph said, and then his eyebrows shot up when Dorothy did not respond. "I've told you a hundred times, my ex-wife did not try to kill me!"

"Out of everyone on the list, she is the one we have most evidence against. After all, she ransacked your flat; I saw it with my own eyes."

"She didn't ransack my flat, that was Reggie."

"But why was she even there the day after you were attacked? And why did she sneak in and out so as not to be seen? What was she hiding?"

"Oh, Dorothy," Joseph said, shaking his head. "What if I could promise you with one hundred percent certainty that it wasn't her?"

"You know full well you cannot do that. You said yourself that you have not seen or spoken to her in years. So how—" Dorothy stopped when she saw a strange expression cross Joseph's face. "What? Why are you looking at me like that?"

He did not answer but his cheeks had turned a shade of salmon pink.

"What is it? What do you know?" Dorothy demanded.

"I . . . eh . . ."

"Joseph Chambers, either you tell me the truth now or I shall throw you out of my flat and never speak to you again."

He must have realized she was not joking as he let out a sigh. "If I tell you, will you promise not to get cross with me?"

"I will promise nothing of the sort."

Dorothy saw the Adam's apple in Joseph's throat bob as he swallowed.

"Sandra didn't come to my flat to ransack it. She came to retrieve her umbrella."

Dorothy let out a snort. "Seriously, Joseph, if you want to cover up for that woman's criminal behavior, then you should make up a better story than that. An umbrella indeed!"

"It's not a cover story, I promise. The day before my fall, Sandra and I had met up. It was raining and I'd forgotten my coat so she lent me her umbrella. And then after she heard I was in hospital, she came to the flat to get it back."

Dorothy's eyes narrowed. "But you told me you had not seen or spoken to her for years, and Sandra told me the exact same thing. Why did you both lie to me? Were the two of you . . ." Dorothy stopped, unable to finish the sentence.

"Oh, God no, it's nothing like that," Joseph said quickly. "Sandra had been . . . well, she'd been helping me with something. But her fiancé is a jealous man and she didn't want him finding out we were in contact, so she made me promise not to tell a soul and I had to respect that. That was why she snuck in and out of my flat, because she didn't want anyone knowing she was here in case word got back to Carlos."

There was something in Joseph's tone that told Dorothy he was telling the truth. Yet still, it did not entirely add up.

"Why were you in touch with her in the first place? That woman cuckolded you and then left you brokenhearted. What could she possibly be helping you with?"

Joseph chewed his lip and did not reply. Dorothy had never seen him look so uncertain. What on earth could he be about to confess?

"I had cancer, Dorothy."

The word hit her like a bullet in the chest. She stared at Joseph, waiting for him to crack his silly smile and tell her it was a joke.

"It was in my prostate. I started having symptoms eighteen months ago and was diagnosed just before last Christmas."

"But are you . . . is it . . ." Dorothy found she could not formulate the required words.

"I'm okay. I was extremely lucky that it was caught early and responded well to treatment. But when I was diagnosed, I contacted Sandra and asked her to tell Debbie. Although my daughter and I have not spoken for many years, I felt she should know what was going on."

Dorothy watched Joseph as he spoke. *Cancer.* But he was always so sprightly, like a darn jack-in-the-box. How was this possible?

"After that Sandra and I met up a couple of times for coffee, the last of which was the day before my attack. She's been very supportive of me, so I know she wouldn't have tried to hurt me."

Dorothy watched Joseph as he spoke. Was he telling her the truth or was this yet another cover story to protect Sandra? And why had he not been honest with her in the first place? Dorothy opened her mouth to scold him but then thought of what he had just told her. She closed her mouth again, suddenly unable to summon the energy to be cross with him.

"Do not ever lie to me again" was all she said.

Joseph nodded, and she saw a flicker of what might have been relief in his eyes. They returned to eating their apple pie.

After lunch, Dorothy played with Reggie while Joseph washed up.

"I'll take your bins out before I head off," he called through from the kitchen.

Dorothy was about to tell him she was perfectly capable of doing it herself, but she let it slide. The man clearly liked to feel useful. He collected the wastepaper basket from the drawing room and carried it through to the kitchen. Reggie had fallen asleep at Dorothy's feet, and she watched the dog's chest rise and fall as he snored. It was calming to watch, and with the warmth of a good meal inside her, Dorothy found her eyes getting heavy. Maybe she could have a little doze while the builders were on their lunch break? Just a quick—

"Dorothy, what's this?"

Her eyes jerked open. Joseph was standing in front of her, holding a brown envelope in his hands.

"How should I know? Junk mail, I assume."

"No, it's addressed to you. Look." He placed the envelope down on the table in front of her. "You need to open it."

"If it is an electricity bill, I am not paying it. I have not had power for a week, the builders must have cut a cable."

"Please, Dorothy. Just read the letter."

She sighed but the man had his hands on his hips and was clearly not going to relent. She reached for her letter knife and slid it through the envelope, pulling out the papers inside.

"See, what did I tell you? Junk mail," she said, casting it aside.

"This is not junk mail." Joseph snatched the letter up.

"Excuse me, that is private!"

Joseph's eyes scanned the first few lines and she saw his pupils dilate. "Dorothy, it's your eviction notice."

Of course it was. She had known it the second the envelope had dropped through the letter box, and she had stuffed it to the bottom of the bin.

"When did this arrive? The letter is dated December sixth, that's ten days ago."

"It must have got caught up with some takeaway flyers."

Joseph carried on reading to the end and then looked up at her again.

"Your eviction date is this Thursday, the nineteenth."

"The nineteenth of December?" The date rang like an alarm bell in Dorothy's mind.

"Yes. It says here that all your belongings need to be out of the property by midday so the bailiffs can take over the property. What are you going to do with all your stuff?"

Dorothy did not reply. The nineteenth was only three days away. There was much she needed to do before then.

"You need to start packing. I still have some of the boxes from my move; I'll bring them over this afternoon."

"There is no need."

"You also have to speak to the council and ask to be put on the emergency housing list. If you leave it much longer they'll say you made yourself deliberately homeless and they won't help you. I can take you down to the offices now."

"I said there is no need."

"What do you mean there's no need? You have less than seventy-two hours to pack everything up and find somewhere to live. You need a plan."

"I have a plan."

He let out an audible sigh of frustration. "Throwing legal documents in the bin isn't a plan, Dorothy. We need to get you down to the council offices now."

His voice sounded so desperate that she could not help but smile. "I appreciate your help, I really do. But I am not leaving the flat to go to the council. I am not leaving the flat to go anywhere."

"But—"

"Joseph, I have lived here for thirty-four years. It is my family home, the place where my daughter died, and it is the place where I intend to die too. So the only way I am leaving is when they carry me out in a coffin, and not a moment sooner."

Forty-Two

KAT

"Oi, turn that bloody music down. I said, turn it down, or I'll call the cops!"

Kat turned the music up. The neighbor banging on her wall—a shaven-headed man named Chaz—was a petty drug dealer, and Kat knew there was no chance of him calling the police. Besides, it was five thirty p.m. on a Monday, so she was hardly keeping anyone awake.

She got up from her bed and went to make a cup of coffee. To accomplish this, all Kat had to do was take four short strides across her room until she was in what the letting agent had ambitiously called a "kitchenette" but was in reality a small fridge in the corner with a one-ring hob resting on top. There was no sink, so to get water she had to go to the shared bathroom down the hall, which was often occupied by one of Chaz's customers using his wares. It was hardly ideal, but however unsavory this place was, it was an improvement on the last one, a bedsit she'd rented back in June. On the first night there, Kat had been woken at four a.m. by a strange rustling sound and she'd flicked on the light to discover a plague of cockroaches marching across her bedroom wall. She'd screamed so loudly that one of her neighbors actually *had* called the police.

Kat drank her coffee, changed out of her work uniform into jeans and a sweater, then locked and padlocked the door. Her room was on the top floor of the building, which meant that to get to the exit she had to walk down four flights of stairs and run the gauntlet of her neighbors. These included Creepy Ken on the third floor, who walked around in his dressing gown and stared too much; Strange Sue on the second floor, who kept five snakes in large tanks even though pets were forbidden; and Shane the Chef on the ground floor, who was always setting off the smoke alarm with his late-night drunken cooking sessions. They made the residents of Shelley House look like angels, but thankfully none of them were around as Kat hurried down today, and she made it out onto the pavement without any run-ins.

It was a short walk to the bus stop, where she hopped on a number 88 and began to make her way into Central London. It was mid-December and decorations sparkled in windows as the bus crawled along. Kat had never been a fan of Christmas, having been disappointed too many times as a kid, so she'd agreed to work a double shift at the pub. But last week, she'd received a text from her mum inviting her over for Christmas lunch. Kat still hadn't replied to the message, unsure what she wanted to do. She had finally read her mother's letter three months ago, having carried the envelope around with her since the day she'd been given it outside the police station. A week after she'd read it, Kat had sent a text to the mobile number her mum had included in the letter, and since then they'd been exchanging messages every couple of days. It was never anything groundbreaking; they usually just commented on something they'd watched on TV or what they were having for dinner. Once or twice her mum had suggested they meet up for a coffee, but Kat had always found an excuse. But this invitation for Christmas felt different, more significant, and it had thrown Kat more than she cared to admit. She wished she had someone she could talk it through with, but of course there was no one. After the disaster of Shelley House, Kat had learned her lesson, and she'd not made more than a casual acquaintance with anyone since.

It was almost seven by the time the bus pulled up at her stop and Kat jumped off, pulling her coat around her against the chill air. The lights were on in the building ahead of her and she walked quickly up the front steps and into the foyer. The security guard grunted a greeting as Kat passed and walked down the long corridor, the only sound her feet squeaking on the floor until she reached the door for room 16 and stopped.

The first time Kat had come here, back in September, she'd not made it up the front steps before she changed her mind and ran away. The second time she'd gotten as far as this door and had stood with her hand on the knob, dumbstruck with fear, until she'd heard other people coming up the corridor behind her and had turned and fled. When she eventually got into the room on her third visit, she had sat mutely in the back row, and when someone had tried to talk to her she'd ignored them until they left her alone. But today Kat opened the door and walked inside without so much as a grimace. She sat down in the middle of the room, nodded a silent hello to the man in the seat next to her, switched off her phone, and looked to the front.

"Right, if everyone's here," called the clear, calm voice of Vanessa, the woman standing in front of them all. "As you know, tonight is our last session before the Christmas break, so I thought we'd get through everything as quickly as we can and go to the pub for an end-of-term drink. What do you think?"

A murmur of approval passed through the room. Kat smiled, although of course she had no intention of going.

"Okay, well, in that case let's crack on. We were talking last week about the male characters in *Jane Eyre* and the differences in the characterization of Rochester and St. John. Today I'd like us to have a think about Jane herself and her relationship with Bessie. Who'd like to share their thoughts first?"

The two hours passed in a blur, as they always did. By the end of each A-level English class, Kat's hand ached from all the notes she'd scribbled and her head was full of ideas. She packed her bag up slowly to allow the others to file out, and when Vanessa passed her desk and said, "You coming to the pub, Kat?" she nodded and said she'd catch them up. Once everyone had gone, Kat slipped out of the building and turned right, in the opposite direction. She reread her copy of *Jane Eyre* on the bus home, referencing things they'd discussed in class and making notes in the margin, and it wasn't until she was back in her cramped room that she pulled out her mobile phone and switched it on. Immediately a message appeared on the screen.

> Hi Kat, Joseph Chambers here. I hope you're well. Dorothy is being evicted on Thursday. She's refusing to leave the house and I'm worried about her. Please give me a call if you get this.

Dorothy. Kat had tried hard not to think about her old neighbor over the past six months; had tried not to think about anything that had happened in Chalcot. But the odd memory had jumped up and caught her at unsuspecting moments: when someone in an old film on TV had poured tea from a china teapot or when an obnoxious customer in the pub had called her "girl." And every time, Kat felt the same rush of emotions: anger, guilt, and regret. But if there was one thing she was good at it was burying unwanted feelings, and so Kat had turned her music up louder, walked a little faster, and told herself it was history.

She reread Joseph's message. So Fergus Alexander must have gotten his way and Shelley House was being demolished, with Dorothy Darling as the last man standing. It was hardly a surprise; she'd always been stubborn as hell. But still, Kat couldn't imagine it was very pleasant there right now with everyone else gone. What did Dorothy do all day if she didn't have her neighbors to watch over? Did she still do her morning inspection of the house? And now the bailiffs were coming. Well, good luck to them; Kat wouldn't want to be the poor sod trying to tell Dorothy she had to leave her home. Would she be alone when they came on Thursday? Joseph was obviously in some form of contact with her, but the other residents must all be long gone by now. Kat imagined the bailiff's van arriving outside Shelley House and Dorothy being frog-marched out of her home, with no one to witness it except the pigeons. For a moment she wondered if she should be volunteering to go back there, but she quickly pushed the idea aside. The last person Dorothy would want to see right now was Kat, the Judas who had betrayed her so badly and doomed her to this eviction. No, the best thing Kat could do was stay well out of the way. She glanced at Joseph's text again and pressed delete.

Forty-Three

DOROTHY

On Thursday, Dorothy slept in late, not waking until past eight. It was another bitterly cold morning but she took her time getting ready. She found her old cocktail dress at the back of the wardrobe, a dark purple number with puffball sleeves she'd bought on the King's Road sometime in the eighties, and she brushed the cobwebs off and pulled it on over her thermals. In the bathroom, she stood in front of the small mirror and applied powder and an old pink lipstick. It was a little crumbly as it went on, but she still wanted to make an effort, today of all days.

It was gone nine by the time Dorothy sat down at the window. There were no builders today; they must have been given the day off especially. She had grown strangely fond of the men who crashed and thumped around her in the building; it was nice having some company in Shelley House after weeks of being here alone. Once she had drunk her glass of water, Dorothy put the *Die Walküre* CD on—she had been using Charlotte's old battery-powered portable stereo since the power went off—fetched her box of photos from the cabinet, and sat down on the sofa with them.

In the early days after Charlotte's death, Dorothy had looked at these photos incessantly, tormenting herself with the memories. However, over the years she had become concerned that too much handling would damage the old prints, and so now she only allowed herself to get them out on special occasions. There was Charlotte's first Christmas, her newborn daughter wearing a dress decorated with stars that Dorothy had sewn herself. There was Charlotte's first day of school, standing proudly on the front step of their old flat in London, and the holiday in France where she tried her first escargot. Dorothy smiled as she flicked through the faded images. Some of these were almost fifty years old, yet each conjured up a memory so strong Dorothy could almost smell the sea air or taste the chocolate cake.

After a couple of hours of browsing, she came to the photo she was looking for, taken on Charlotte's fifteenth birthday. They had only moved into Shelley House a few months previously, and Charlotte had invited some of her new classmates for a sleepover. Dorothy had driven them all to Blockbuster Video where they had cajoled her into letting them rent a VHS of *Dirty Dancing*, and back at home they had watched it curled up on the sofa with plates of party food balanced on their knees. This was the photo Dorothy had taken, her teenage daughter giggling with her new friends as Patrick Swayze cavorted with a young Jennifer Grey. How grown-up Charlotte had suddenly seemed. *What comes next?* Dorothy remembered thinking. *What will my little girl be like at sixteen and eighteen and twenty-one?* And yet she had never gotten to find out.

Dorothy slipped the photo back into the box along with the others. It would do no good to become maudlin; today was a day of celebration, after all. Dorothy checked her watch. It was eleven thirty, time to get started on luncheon. She had received a supermarket delivery yesterday with the ingredients for all of Charlotte's favorites: cheese and cucumber, egg mayonnaise and ham and mustard sandwiches—all with the crusts cut off—sausage rolls, Hula Hoops, Party Rings, and Jammy Dodgers. Dorothy found her paper doilies and arranged the food on plates, which she laid out on the card table. Finally, she retrieved the bottle of champagne and carried it through to the living room with a glass. As the carriage clock on the mantelpiece struck twelve, Dorothy popped the cork, filled her glass, and raised it in the air.

"Happy birthday, darling Charlotte!"

She said the words out loud to the empty room and took a sip of the champagne. It would have been much nicer if the fridge were working and it had been chilled, but this was a tradition Dorothy was never going to let go. Phillip had brought a bottle of champagne to the hospital the afternoon Charlotte was born and they had celebrated her birthday with a glass ever since. Dorothy smiled as she remembered how they had allowed Charlotte a taste on her fifteenth birthday, and how she had winced and spat it out. She would like it now, though, Dorothy was sure of that. Her daughter would have grown up to have sophisticated tastes.

Dorothy took another sip and picked up a sandwich. She lifted it to take a bite but stopped, mouth open. She had not been paying attention to the activity on Poet's Road this morning, having been too distracted with the photos and preparing Charlotte's birthday meal, but now she stared out the window in disbelief. Was she hallucinating? Dorothy closed her eyes and took a deep breath before opening them again, but the scene in front of her remained unchanged.

A group of people had gathered on the pavement, milling around talking to one another. Many of them were unfamiliar, but several Dorothy recognized immediately. There was Gloria, dressed up in a bright red coat and a Santa hat, holding hands with Tomasz, who looked like all his Christmases had come at once. Omar and Ayesha were there too, chatting with the young couple from Poet's Road who had come to the rally. Dorothy surveyed the other faces. Now that she looked closer, she realized they were not strangers at all. She recognized the two women who had lived in flat four a decade ago, whose screaming baby had kept Dorothy awake for months, and the man who had lived in flat six before Gloria and who Dorothy had constantly argued with about his cat bringing in mice. What were they all doing here?

A familiar face caught Dorothy's eye. Joseph was standing in the midst of the group, chatting with the woman in the Afghan coat, but when he saw Dorothy staring, he broke off and started to walk up the front steps, Reggie at his heels. Dorothy realized she was still holding her sandwich, and she put it down and hurried to the door. She pulled it open as Joseph stepped into the lobby.

"Afternoon, Dorothy, you look nice. Sorry if we're disturbing your lunch."

"What in God's name is going on out there?"

"They've come for your eviction."

Dorothy's stomach dropped. Was this some kind of sick joke? She knew she had not been a popular neighbor, quite the opposite, but had all these people really come to gawk at her being evicted—an impromptu street party to celebrate her demise? She felt a mixture of shame and fury flood her body.

"Well, if they are expecting some kind of entertainment at my expense, then they are wasting their time. I am not going anywhere, so you can tell them all to—"

"It's not what you think," Joseph interrupted. "They're not here to celebrate your eviction. They're here to help."

"What?"

"After I left you on Monday, I texted a few people to tell them what was happening. Gloria suggested that we come down here today and offer you some support. I expected a handful of people but it seems word has spread, and there are more on their way too."

Dorothy was too shocked to answer. Joseph saw her expression and laughed.

"Don't look so surprised, Dorothy. You've given your life to Shelley House and the people who live here. It's about time we gave something back to you."

Behind Joseph, the front door had opened and she saw Ayesha, Omar, Gloria, and Tomasz step into the lobby. Their expressions were all anxious as they looked at Dorothy.

"You really all came to support me?" she said, not even trying to hide the surprise in her voice.

"Of course we have," Gloria said. "I wanna give that Fergus bastard a piece of my mind."

"We could not let you go through this alone," Tomasz said.

"It's what Fatima would have wanted," Omar said, and Ayesha reached out and squeezed her father's arm.

Dorothy swallowed, willing herself not to burst into tears in front of them all. Joseph must have sensed her emotion as he stepped back from the door.

"We'll head outside again and leave you in peace. We just wanted to say hello."

"Thank you," Dorothy said, her voice a croak. She watched her neighbors start to leave, and then a thought occurred to her.

"Wait, stop!" They all turned back. "This might sound strange, given what is about to occur, but today is Charlotte's birthday. I always celebrate with a special luncheon of her favorite foods. I was wondering if you would care to join me?"

Ayesha smiled at her. "We'd love to, thank you."

Dorothy ushered them all inside and closed her door. It felt strange having so many people in her flat, but not in a bad way. She asked Joseph to move some chairs while she went into the kitchen to find more plates and glasses. Back in the drawing room, she poured everyone a glass of the warm champagne.

"We should toast," Tomasz said.

"Quite right. To Shelley House!" Omar said, raising his glass.

"And to good neighbors, even if it took us a while to work it out," Ayesha said, and they all laughed.

"To you, Dorothy, and everything you've done for us over the years," Gloria added, smiling at her.

"And to Charlotte." Joseph looked at Dorothy as he said this, and she saw he had tears in his eyes. She raised her glass and chinked it against his.

"To Charlotte."

Over the next hour, the gathering in Dorothy's flat became something of a party. There was so much food they invited the others out on the pavement inside too, and soon the flat became quite crowded. Someone must have been to the shops, as there were bottles of wine and beer being handed around, and the CD was changed so that there were pop tunes rather than Wagner. Joseph and Tomasz moved Dorothy's furniture aside to create more space, and soon an impromptu dance floor popped up in the middle of the room. Dorothy demurred invitations to dance but watched the scene with satisfaction, especially when she saw Omar and Ayesha dancing joyously together and Tomasz throwing Gloria into the air with gay abandon. Reggie was having a whale of a time too, sauntering round the room being fed party food by everyone.

But the biggest delight were the surprise guests. Dorothy was amazed when an elegant woman in her forties came over and introduced herself as Alison Gregory, who had been only a small girl living in flat six when Dorothy had first moved into Shelley House. She was equally astounded that the boisterous boy doing knee slides across the polished floor was the very same baby who had kept her awake ten years ago. Even Will the journalist was there, looking somewhat less sheepish than when she had last seen him in the summer, and he had apologized profusely for the article.

There was only one person missing, although her absence was hardly a surprise. Still, despite the harsh words that had passed between them, Dorothy could not help wishing Kat were here too. She had thought of the girl many times over the past six months, and each time her anger had subsided a little, so that now all Dorothy felt was remorse at the sickeningly cruel things she had said to Kat. Where was she now, Dorothy wondered. Had she reunited with her mother? And most importantly, was she happy? Dorothy wished there was a way of finding out, but both Joseph and Will had confirmed that she had cut all contact with them too. It appeared Kat had disappeared once more and was determined not to be found.

"This is quite a party," Ayesha said, collapsing down into the chair next to Dorothy, her face flushed.

"It is indeed. And I am so pleased to see you and your father are getting on better."

"Yeah, it's good. This might sound weird but things started improving as soon as we moved out of Shelley House. Dad's even accepted that I don't want to do law at uni. I think we both needed a fresh start, away from all the sad memories of Mum in this place." The teenager winced as she realized what she'd said. "Sorry, I didn't mean . . . I know you have lots of sad memories here too."

"It's all right, my dear." Dorothy reached over and patted her hand. "I am glad you have both had a new beginning. Your mother would be pleased too, I am sure."

"I think a fresh start will suit you too. I know it'll be strange at first, but I think you'll be happy somewhere new. And I'll still come and visit, I promise."

"Thank you." Dorothy smiled, although there would be no fresh start for her. Of that much she was sure.

"Ayesha, you dance?" Tomasz was striding over to the table and offering her his hand.

"I will, but first there's something I need to tell you." The girl's cheeks had gone even pinker. "Tomasz, I'm so sorry, but I was the one who set Princess free that day at the rally."

The man's eyes flashed and Dorothy prepared herself for the roar of wrath she suspected was to come.

"I know it was a terrible thing to do and I've felt awful about it ever since," Ayesha added quickly. "I was so cross about the way Princess kept scaring Reggie and about how aggressive you were to everyone. But as soon as I'd done it I realized what a mistake I'd made. I'm sorry, it was such a stupid thing to do."

Tomasz did not say anything for a moment, and both Dorothy and Ayesha watched him for a reaction. Then his shoulders sagged. "It is okay, Ayesha. I forgive you."

"You do?"

"I know Princess and I could be difficult neighbors. I am taking her to obedience classes now, and she is doing great. And I am trying hard with myself too. I have a good teacher."

Tomasz looked over at Gloria as he said this, and Dorothy saw his face soften.

"Well, in that case, I'd love a dance!" Ayesha said, jumping up.

Dorothy watched them go with a smile and then looked around the crowded room. To think that she had lived among these people for thirty-four years, watching over their lives without any interaction aside from complaining, and now here they all were: for Shelley House and for her. Dorothy's eyes fell on the framed picture of Charlotte on the mantelpiece, her daughter beaming out at the room. *Do you like your birthday party?* Dorothy thought, although she already knew the answer. Charlotte would have thoroughly approved, especially of the dancing. Would she approve of what Dorothy planned to do later, though? That one was less clear. Dorothy shivered despite the warmth of the crowded room, and turned her attention back to the dancing.

Forty-Four

KAT

Kat lay in her narrow single bed, staring at a patch of mold above her head. Fifty miles away, Dorothy would be waking up for the final time in Shelley House. Had she managed to pack her belongings up in time? That flat was full to the rafters with a lifetime's worth of furniture and ornaments; what the hell was Dorothy going to do with it all? And had she found a new home? The idea of her living anywhere but flat two, Shelley House, was utterly unsettling.

At nine, Kat grew so restless that she pulled on her trainers and set off for Parliament Hill. Ever since looking after Reggie, she had got into the habit of taking a long walk every morning, a chance for some fresh air and to clear her head. She wasn't working today, so after this she planned to spend the morning in the library getting ahead on her reading for next term, like Vanessa had suggested. Kat smiled to herself. Look at her, the teacher's pet! If only Dorothy could see her now.

At the thought of her old neighbor, the smile disappeared from Kat's face. The woman might be a battle-ax but Kat had seen behind her tough exterior, seen the pain in Dorothy's eyes when she talked about Charlotte. Leaving Shelley House today meant abandoning her daughter's home, the one thing she'd sworn she'd never do. Poor Dorothy, her heart must be breaking.

Kat stopped walking so abruptly that a man bumped into her. He swore but Kat ignored him as she looked at her watch. It was almost ten, and she knew from experience that bailiffs usually came in the afternoon. That gave Kat only a few hours to travel across London on the Underground, catch a train to Winton, and then a bus to get back to Chalcot. That wasn't enough time, was it? But she knew better than anyone how awful an eviction could be. So however much Dorothy might hate her right now, Kat couldn't let her go through this alone. She turned and started to sprint.

The tubes were crowded with Christmas shoppers, the train was delayed, and the bus on diversion, so it was gone twelve thirty by the time Kat made it to Chalcot. Was she too late and Dorothy had already been thrown out? She got off at the bus stop outside the post office and set off at a run toward Shelley House. She usually went down the hill and through the estate, but today she was in such a hurry that she decided to cut through the graveyard instead to save time. It was a cold day and there was still frost on the gravel path, and Kat dug her chin into her coat, wishing she'd put on something warmer. She jogged round the side of the old church and headed toward the small gate at the back that led out onto Fellows Road. But as she was approaching it, something caught Kat's eye. A gravestone to her right-hand side, newer than many of the others, with a bunch of bright yellow daffodils lying in front of it.

Kat paused. She needed to rush if she was going to make it to Dorothy's in time, and besides, that grave could belong to anyone. Lots of people loved daffodils. But still, she found herself veering right and walking over toward the flowers. The grave had a smart gray stone, and as Kat got closer she could see the epitaph carved into its surface.

IAN PATRICK MASON, 1939–2020

Husband, brother, father, and grandfather.

He loved Chalcot and was loved by it in return.

Kat stood in front of her grandfather's grave fighting the urge to turn and run from this place and the conflicting emotions that were battling inside her. All these years she'd spent hiding from this village and this man, thinking he didn't want to see her, and all along she could have been here with him. What would her life have been like if she'd had her grandfather in it? If she'd been able to help him in his fight to save the farm and when he got sick? The feeling of regret was so strong that Kat had to clench her fists to stop herself from crying out.

She took a long, deep breath. What had Dorothy said to her? *I have become so consumed with these* what-ifs *and the life that was stolen from me, I stopped living the life I still have.* Kat could not let that happen to her. With one final look at the gravestone, she turned and walked away.

By the time she got to Poet's Road, Kat was feeling no calmer. How many times had she walked along here as a child on her way from Featherdown Farm to the school? She could still clearly remember the fear she had felt as she passed Shelley House, hoping that the witch inside wouldn't jump out and snatch her. But there had been no witch after all, only a lonely, grief-stricken woman keeping watch over her neighbors. A woman who was about to be evicted.

There was no sign of the bailiff's truck and the road was suspiciously calm. But as Kat got nearer, she heard what sounded like music coming from the direction of Shelley House. Strangely, it wasn't the usual shouty opera that Dorothy played or the thumping bass that used to come from flat four. Instead, it was "Last Christmas" by Wham! Who on earth was listening to that? Kat had assumed that everyone else had moved away, but perhaps one of the other residents was still there. She walked farther, keeping to the far side of Poet's Road so she could make a swift exit if she needed to. As she came parallel with the house, she almost dropped her bag in surprise.

Dorothy's front window was wide open, despite the December

cold, and through it Kat could hear not only music but the sound of voices, laughing and chatting. What's more, the net curtains that were kept permanently closed had been pulled back and Kat could see what looked like dozens of people inside the flat. It appeared that Dorothy was having some sort of party.

Kat watched for a few minutes, taking in the scene of merriment in front of her. She could distinctly make out the back of Dorothy's head sitting in front of the window, her signature silver hair nodding along to the music. Behind her, Kat could see Ayesha and Tomasz dancing together, and Joseph and Gloria too. Kat's heart lifted at the sight of her old landlord spinning Gloria around. The last time she'd seen Joseph he'd still been recovering in hospital, but now he was clearly fit and well again. Above the music, Kat heard the unmistakable bark of Reggie and she smiled to herself. She'd missed that dog more than she cared to admit.

Kat paused for a moment longer, drinking in the view of her old neighbors one last time. It hadn't occurred to her that they would all come today to support Dorothy. No one had ever done anything like that for Kat and her mum the numerous times they'd been evicted. But the fact they were all here in Dorothy's hour of need . . . Kat felt an unfamiliar lump in the back of her throat, and she turned and began to make her way down Poet's Road, away from Shelley House.

"Kat!"

She startled at her name being called. When she glanced round, she saw Will jogging down the front steps of Shelley House. He looked exactly as she remembered him, the same dark hair and big eyes, although his usual grin had been replaced by a look of nerves. Kat's stomach somersaulted and she had to quickly remind herself that this was the man who had betrayed her and Dorothy so badly back in the summer. She carried on walking away.

"Hey, wait! Kat, stop!" He jogged to catch up with her. "I was hoping you'd come today. Does this mean you got my message?"

"No." Kat had no idea what message he was referring to; she'd blocked his number the day she left Chalcot.

"If you've come to support Dorothy, then you should go in; I'm sure she'd love to see you."

Kat let out a snort that she hoped conveyed how ridiculous that statement was.

"Today is Charlotte's birthday," Will continued. "Dorothy's having a party to celebrate."

Kat faltered. My God: her daughter's birthday on the same day she was getting evicted. The poor woman. But Dorothy had people with her, people she would actually want to be there.

"How is she?" Kat asked, despite herself.

"Still refusing to leave Shelley House. She says she has a plan, although she won't elaborate on what it is."

That didn't sound good. Maybe Kat should try to talk to her? Then she remembered the angry words she and Dorothy had screamed at each other back in June, and Dorothy's insistence that she never wanted to see Kat again.

"Will you come in?" Will said.

"I need to get back to London."

Beside her, she heard him sigh.

"Look, Kat, I know I messed up back in the summer and I'm really sorry. It was an honest mistake, I swear. I was trying to help Dorothy and Shelley House."

"Yeah, well, given she's being evicted today, I think we can safely say your plan failed." The vitriol in Kat's voice was stronger than she had intended. "I take it you didn't publish your newspaper article about Fergus Alexander?"

"I did, and the police said they'd investigate, but it wasn't enough to save Shelley House, I'm afraid."

"It's not me you have to apologize to," Kat said, glancing back at the window of flat two.

"I already apologized to Dorothy and she's forgiven me."

She had? This was a surprise. Kat couldn't imagine the old woman ever forgiving Will for what he'd done. Or maybe it was only Kat she was still angry with, given that she'd been the one to betray Dorothy's trust.

"Look, you can stay mad at me if you want, but—"

"I'm not mad at you, Will. I just want to move on from it all."

"Well, if you're not mad at me, why haven't you replied to any of my messages?"

"I blocked your number."

"Ah, right." Will looked slightly crestfallen. "So I take it you didn't see my message about the green car?"

Kat stopped in her tracks. "What message?"

"I finally traced the owner. It's taken me months but I managed to find the name and address the car is registered to. I messaged you about it yesterday."

"So who is the owner? Have you tracked them down yet?"

Will shook his head. "I've not had a chance. All I have so far is a name—Amy Edwards—and an address in a village the other side of Winton."

"But you realize this person could be the answer to who attacked Joseph?"

"I know, that's why I texted you," Will said, a hint of frustration in his voice. He glanced down at his watch. "We could go now? My car's here and it's only a twenty-minute drive."

Kat swallowed. She'd come back here to support Dorothy during the eviction, but her help wasn't needed after all. So surely she should get on a bus to the station and head straight back to London, away from Chalcot and all the trouble it had caused her. What happened to Shelley House was not her problem anymore. And then she remembered the gravestone she'd stood in front of earlier and the words engraved on it.

Kat looked up at Will. "Fine, let's go."

They didn't talk much on the drive over to Winton. Will had switched the radio on, filling the car with Christmas songs, but the rhythmic tapping of his hand on the steering wheel suggested he was as nervous about this as she was. Kat knew that finding the driver of the green car wasn't going to suddenly save Dorothy's home, but after all these months of trying to identify the attacker, she was desperate to finally get an answer to the question of what happened to Joseph that day.

As they reached the outskirts of the town, Will suddenly turned the radio off, cutting Mariah Carey off mid-warble.

"I really am sorry for the newspaper article about Dorothy."

"It's fine, you don't need to apologize again," Kat said.

"No, I do. I had the best intentions but I realize I betrayed your trust."

"As long as Dorothy's forgiven you, that's all that matters. She's the one it affected, after all."

Kat leaned forward to switch the radio back on, but Will reached out and put his hand on hers to stop her. Kat felt a jolt of electricity at his touch and drew her hand back sharply.

"There's something else I want to say too," Will said. "I realize this really isn't the time or the place, seeing as we're driving to confront a potentially violent attacker, but seeing as you've blocked my number I've got to grab the moment while I can."

"Will–"

"No. Let me say this, please. I know we didn't get to know each other for very long, but I really enjoyed hanging out with you over the summer. I'm not going to lie, half the reason I took such an interest in the whole Shelley House story was because it meant I got to spend time with you."

What was he talking about? Will had only spent time with her so he could get the inside story on Shelley House, not the other way round.

"And I know you've left Chalcot now and probably want nothing more to do with this small, sleepy village and its boring inhabitants—"

"Chalcot is hardly boring," Kat interrupted. "Attempted murders, break-ins, countryside car chases . . . that's hardly sleepy-village stuff."

Will grinned across at her and Kat's stomach twisted again, not entirely unpleasantly. "Fair point, I'll rephrase that. I know you probably want nothing more to do with this dangerous village and its violent inhabitants. But I wanted to say that I would like to have more to do with you, if you want. I know I'm a self-professed country mouse, but I am capable of getting on a train and coming up to London. So if you'd like to ever meet up for a drink or a housing protest, then I'd be very much up for that."

Kat looked out of the window as they drove up Winton High Street so Will wouldn't see the confusion in her eyes. *He betrayed you*, she told herself. *You learned many years ago not to rely on other people, and look what happened when you trusted someone. Don't let—*

She stopped, thinking back to the scene she'd just witnessed at Shelley House. Dorothy Darling, a virtual recluse who had shut other people out of her life for thirty years, had been throwing a party for her neighbors, people who until a few months ago she had hated and had been hated by in return. If Dorothy could change, who was to say that Kat couldn't too?

"Okay."

Kat didn't look at Will as she said this, but she could tell he was smiling.

"Great. Does that mean you'll unblock my number now?"

Kat smiled too. "I suppose so, as long as—"

She stopped mid-sentence. Surely it couldn't be?

"As long as what? Come on, you can't leave me hanging."

"I don't believe it," Kat muttered, turning her head to make sure she really had seen what she thought she had. But there was no mistaking it.

"What is it?" Will said, glancing back to try and see.

"I think I may have found our missing puzzle piece," Kat said, turning to look at him. "But we're going to have to hurry."

Forty-Five

DOROTHY

By two o'clock there was still no sign of the bailiffs, and Dorothy was beginning to wonder if she had gotten the wrong day. Not that she minded the mistake, given the party around her was still in full swing. More alcohol had miraculously appeared, as much of it seemingly spilled on Dorothy's floor as consumed, and the guests were now having a Christmas sing-along accompanied by Reggie's exuberant howls. As they launched into a rowdy rendition of "Good King Wenceslas," Dorothy rose from the table and made her way through the crowds to the kitchen to fetch a glass of water. As she entered, she found Gloria and Tomasz engaged in a passionate embrace. They pulled apart when Dorothy entered, their expressions like a pair of guilty teenagers.

"Look what Tomasz gave me!" Gloria held out her left hand and Dorothy saw a small, sparkling diamond on her fourth finger.

"Is this what I think it is?" Dorothy's question was answered by the silly grins plastered on their faces.

"I was planning to propose on Christmas Eve but we were dancing and I got a little carried away," Tomasz said, blushing.

"It's so romantic," Gloria gushed. "Shelley House is where we met, after all."

"My sincerest congratulations to the pair of you," Dorothy said, smiling at them both.

"I go call my mother to tell her the good news," Tomasz said.

He kissed his fiancée and strode out of the kitchen, leaving Gloria staring dreamily after him. Dorothy gave a polite and then not-so-polite cough before the woman snapped out of it and moved aside to allow her access to the sink.

"We're going to get married next summer in Chalcot Church," Gloria said as Dorothy reached for a glass. "You'll be guest of honor, of course."

"Thank you, but there is no need for that." Dorothy would not be attending any wedding, but it was a generous invitation nonetheless.

"No, I'm serious. Me and Tomasz would never have gotten together if it wasn't for you."

"I am sure that is not the case."

"It is! You won't remember this, but back in the summer you and I had a fight and you told me I always choose men below me. You said I should learn to live with myself rather than always needing some useless man around."

Had Dorothy really said that? How presumptuous of her.

"Well, you clearly did not listen to my advice," she said, pointing at the ring on Gloria's finger and smiling in a manner she hoped conveyed that she was jesting.

"But I did. Up until then I'd been so sad about Barry leaving and desperate to get him back. But your words struck a chord with me. That day I decided to stop moping over him and start prioritizing loving myself instead. And as soon as I made that decision, Tomasz walked into my life."

"Gloria, dear, he hardly walked into your life. He had been living opposite you for two years."

"Yeah, but if it hadn't been for you telling me I deserved better, I'd have kept going for scumbags like Barry. But after our argument, I told myself I wasn't going to go running into another relationship with the next leather-jacket-wearing dickhead that chatted me up. And that's when I realized that actually there had been a good, kind man living under my nose the whole time. And he's a Sagittarius."

"Well, I am very pleased you have met your match," Dorothy said. "I may have had my reservations about Tomasz in the past, but it turns out he is very different from all those other 'leather-jacket-wearing dickheads,' as you so eloquently put it."

"Haven't you met your match too?" Gloria said with a wink.

It took Dorothy a moment to realize who she was talking about. "Do not talk such utter nonsense."

"It's never too late for love, Dorothy. What star sign are you anyway?"

"I do not have the faintest idea."

"Ohh, let me guess. Aquarius? When's your birthday."

"April twenty-fifth."

"A Taurus!" Gloria laughed. "Of course you are. And Joe's a Virgo, so that's perfect."

"Did I hear my name?" Joseph had appeared in the kitchen door.

"Dorothy and I were chatting about astrology," Gloria said, and Joseph's eyebrows shot up.

"I have absolutely no idea what she has been talking about. Complete poppycock," Dorothy said, to which the other two laughed.

From the drawing room there was the sound of breaking glass and Joseph winced.

"Sorry, Dorothy, I'm afraid things have got a little out of hand. I hope we haven't ruined your celebration for Charlotte?"

"Ruined? Not at all, this is the perfect birthday party. She would have loved it; she always enjoyed Christmas carols and insisted we sing them on her birthday."

Joseph smiled as Dorothy said this, but there was a sadness in his eyes that she had not seen before. Perhaps he was remembering Christmases from his own past?

"You never did tell me what happened between you and Deborah?" As soon as she said his daughter's name, Dorothy saw Joseph draw breath. "I am sorry, you do not have to tell me if you do not wish to."

"No, it's okay," Joseph said.

Gloria excused herself and exited the room, leaving Dorothy and Joseph alone.

"Debbie's and my relationship was always pretty strained," Joseph said. "I think I told you that she never really forgave me for uprooting us and moving her to Chalcot, and her behavior had become a bit wild. And after Charlotte's death . . ." He glanced up at Dorothy as he said this, but she nodded for him to continue. "I handled it all really badly, to be honest. She was distraught about what had happened, obviously, and I should have been more of a support to her. But I think I was angry at her too, even blamed her a little for what happened."

"Oh, but it was not Deborah's fault," Dorothy said quickly. "She was only a child herself."

"I know that now, of course. But at the time it was all such a shock, and I felt like Debbie had somehow led Charlotte astray with the alcohol. Even though I never explicitly told Debbie how I felt, I imagine she could sense what I was thinking. And I'm not sure our relationship ever really recovered from that. She went away to university and then moved to Australia, and that's been that."

His face fell as he said this, and Dorothy saw what looked like a tear in his eye. The poor man. All these years she had spent hating him and all along he had been grieving his own loss too.

"I am so sorry for you," she said quietly. "It must be very hard."

"Well, not as hard as it's been for you," Joseph said, wiping a hand across his eyes. "At least Debbie is still alive, and we're connected on Facebook so I see what she and the kids are up to."

"You have grandchildren?"

He nodded but there it was again, that melancholic smile. "Two boys, fourteen and eleven. I've never met them but Sandra tells me they're wonderful."

"Oh, Joseph," Dorothy said, for there really were no other words.

"It's okay, I don't need sympathy," he said, blinking away the sadness.

"Perhaps you should call your daughter on Christmas Day this year?" Dorothy said, and then regretted it when Joseph frowned. Had she said the wrong thing? Unsolicited advice was always a bad idea, and what did she know about relationships with adult daughters?

"Do you know what? Maybe I will." Joseph looked up at her. "Thank you, Dorothy."

There was something about the way he said her name that made Dorothy's skin tingle. She wanted to look away but Joseph's gaze was holding her own like a magnet, as it had done all those years ago.

"They're here!"

A shout from the drawing room cut above the music, jolting Dorothy from her reverie. A moment later the song switched off abruptly and the whole flat was plunged into silence. Joseph's expression had changed, and Dorothy now saw her own fear reflected back at her. They stared at each other for a moment longer, and then Joseph turned and marched out of the kitchen.

"Right, everyone, let's go!"

His voice rang out through the silence. Immediately, Dorothy heard footsteps moving in the other room.

"What is going on?" she said, following him through to the drawing room. The partygoers were already pulling on their coats, hats, and scarves, the jubilant atmosphere replaced by grim faces.

"You do not have to leave so soon," Dorothy said, looking round at them all. "Just because the bailiffs are here does not mean the party has to end."

Omar, who was standing nearby, glanced at Dorothy as she said this and gave her a small smile. Oh God, there it was again. *Pity.*

The door to the flat was open and the guests started to leave. Not one of them stopped to say thank you or good-bye to Dorothy; they clearly could not wait to get away now that the bailiffs were here. Dorothy watched Gloria and Tomasz file out without even looking at her and felt her heart sink. So much for thinking these people were her friends. Although she could hardly blame them for going. Why would they want to hang around to witness what was about to happen?

Joseph was the last to leave. When he got to the door he paused and looked back at Dorothy.

"Are you coming?" His eyes pleaded even if his words did not.

"You know the answer to that."

"You've put up an incredible fight, Dorothy. You could walk out of this house today with your head held high, knowing you did everything you could to stay here."

"But where would I go? This is my home."

"You'd find somewhere else, I could help you look. Or you could always . . ." Joseph trailed off and when Dorothy looked at him he was staring at the floor.

"I could always what?"

It was a moment before he lifted his eyes to hers again. "You could come and live with me."

Dorothy did not reply, the statement hanging in the air between them.

"I fell in love with you the day I first saw you, Dorothy Darling. Those weeks we spent together planning the party were some of the happiest of my life. And I know . . ." He faltered and she saw him swallow. "I know that you blame me too for what happened, but my feelings for you have never changed. I have loved you for thirty-three years. And I think, on some level, you have loved me too."

Dorothy opened her mouth to speak but Joseph carried on.

"You've been punishing yourself for something that was not your fault, or mine or Debbie's or anyone's. It's time to let go of that guilt and move on. We're not so old, Dorothy, and it's not too late to give ourselves a happy ending. Please, leave with me now."

For a moment she allowed those words to settle in her chest, feeling the warmth of their glow. Then she glanced over at the mantelpiece.

"I am sorry, Joseph, but there is something else I must do. I made a promise when Charlotte died and I have to keep it."

Dorothy waited for him to do something else, to beg her to reconsider or to grab her by the hand and pull her out of Shelley House. But instead he just watched her for a moment longer, his eyes full. Then he turned without saying a word and stepped out of the flat.

The room, which had felt so hot and crowded a moment ago, was now cold and empty. Dorothy looked around at the empty glasses and discarded plates of food, the only evidence of what had occurred. Silence hung in the air, heavy and oppressive. She moved over to the CD player and removed the Christmas carols disc someone had put in, replacing it with the CD she had been listening to earlier. As Wagner's *Die Walküre* filled the air, Dorothy took a fortifying breath and walked toward the window.

The net curtains had been pulled back and the window opened

by a guest earlier so she had a clear view of Poet's Road. An anonymous-looking blue transit van had parked up by the far pavement and two burly men and a woman were standing in front of it. The woman, dressed in a shapeless black coat and unflattering shoes, was holding a clipboard and studying whatever was on it. The men, who looked as if they had a combined IQ of less than eighty, were staring at Shelley House and the crowd of people who had spilled out of it onto the pavement. Dorothy's old neighbors were all loitering around, clearly saying their good-byes to one another before they departed. Joseph walked down the front steps of Shelley House to join them, his head turned toward the bailiffs across the road. Dorothy looked back to them too and saw the woman, who she assumed was in charge, say something to the meat-headed men. The three of them turned and began to walk purposefully across the road toward Shelley House.

"Now!" Joseph shouted.

As he did, the group in front of Shelley House began to move too. Dorothy watched them part, expecting to see them turn and hurry away. But instead, she saw that they were starting to form a line in front of the building. In fact it was two—no three—lines, one in front of the other, each made up of a dozen or so people standing next to one another in formation. Once everyone was in place, Dorothy saw Joseph raise one arm in the air, and immediately each individual reached out and took the hand of the person next to them. Dorothy watched in utter confusion. What in God's name were they doing? And then the reality hit her and she let out a gasp.

Her neighbors were forming a human shield in front of the building. They were protecting Shelley House, and they were protecting her.

Forty-Six

DOROTHY

Dorothy watched the scene unfold in wonder. The bailiffs looked utterly unimpressed by what had just occurred and continued to stride across the road toward the human barricade. Joseph was standing in the middle of the first row, and when the female bailiff reached him she started to speak. Dorothy tried to make out what was being said but the woman's voice was low and only a few words drifted over. *Court official . . . Eviction notice . . . Mrs. Darling must vacate the premises.*

"*Ms.* Darling does not wish to vacate the premises," Joseph said, and Dorothy could hear his voice loud and clear.

The woman carried on mumbling. *Trying to be reasonable . . . only doing our jobs . . . police if required.*

"By all means call the police," Joseph said, and Dorothy saw him pull his shoulders back. "But they'll have to arrest all of us before they can get to Ms. Darling."

The woman consulted with her two goons and then retreated and pulled out a mobile phone. She must be calling the police! Dorothy leaned out the window.

"Joseph. Joseph!"

He glanced back from his position in the front row and grinned cheerfully at her before returning his attention to the road.

"What are you doing, man? You will all be arrested."

Joseph chose this moment to pretend he could not hear her. Goodness, he was infuriating.

"Gloria! Tomasz!"

No response.

"Oh, for pity's sake, not you two as well. I know you can all hear me and I will not have you getting yourselves incarcerated on my account."

No one so much as glanced at her.

"Omar, surely you can see sense? Do you really want Ayesha to get a criminal record that will seriously hamper her future opportunities?"

Finally, Ayesha looked over her shoulder at Dorothy.

"It's okay, Ms. Darling. We're being elephants."

"What?" Dorothy was shouting now but they must all be drunk.

"It was Dad's idea. He said that mother elephants form a protective ring around their calves to protect them from their predators. So we're protecting you from your predators too." Ayesha grinned at her father as she said this, and Dorothy could see pride in the girl's eyes.

"This is the most ridiculous thing I have ever heard! I am not some pathetic elephant calf who needs protecting. I am Dorothy Darling and I am perfectly capable of defending myself, thank you very much. Now clear off, the lot of you, or I shall call the police myself."

But Dorothy's words fell on deaf ears, as not one person moved. Across the road, the bailiff had finished her phone call and the three of them had climbed back into the van, clearly awaiting backup. Dorothy stepped away from the window and began to pace her flat. What was she supposed to do now? She had a well-laid plan. It had been in place since the day she found out about the planning application for Shelley House; the day she had lain on top of her bed, fully dressed, and sobbed for the first time in thirty years. But that carefully curated plan did not involve either a declaration of love from her old nemesis or forty-odd neighbors forming a human barrier across her house and risking imprisonment in the process. It was really most inconvenient.

From outside there was the noise of a car pulling up in front of the building. Was that the police already? Dorothy was running out of time; she needed to get a move on. Her handbag, which she had packed several days ago in preparation, was sitting on the table amid the detritus of the party. Dorothy crossed to retrieve it and as she did, she glanced outside.

It was not a police car that had parked up in front of Shelley House but a dark green BMW. *That* green BMW. Dorothy felt anger rise in her chest. That bloody Fergus Alexander must have sent his henchman to help the bailiffs, the same henchman who had been here the day Joseph was attacked and then sped away from them at the protest. Well, if he thought he was going to lay one finger on any of Dorothy's neighbors, he had another think coming. She grabbed her handbag, a weapon she had already used once this year, and prepared to march outside. But then the front passenger door of the BMW opened wide, and so did Dorothy's mouth.

A head of faded-pink hair was emerging from the vehicle, talking to whoever was sitting in the driver's seat. What in God's name was *she* doing here? Dorothy squinted as she tried to piece it all together. Did this mean Kat was somehow connected to the driver of the green car and Joseph's potential attacker? Or was *she* the attacker herself? But if so, who had been driving the green car the day that Kat, Dorothy, and Will had chased it across the Dunningshire countryside? Oh, this was all most vexing, and not at all what Dorothy should be focusing on right now. But still, she found she could not tear her eyes away from the vehicle as its remaining doors opened.

An unfamiliar woman was the next to climb out from the

passenger's door. She was in her late forties and wearing a ghastly Christmas jumper with unfortunately positioned baubles on her chest. She moved around to the rear door to help another passenger out. It was clearly an elderly person, as both the Christmas-jumper woman and Kat reached into the back seat to assist them. It appeared to be an elderly man, his head as bald as a baby's, and he seemed to be having great trouble in standing. When he finally straightened himself, he lifted his head and stared straight at Shelley House. For a second their eyes met through the window and Dorothy almost cried out in shock.

Phillip.

Forty-Seven

DOROTHY

The last time she had seen her ex-husband had been the morning he had left for work, briefcase in hand, and never returned. He did not leave a note and had never sent any correspondence. Eight years after his departure, Dorothy had received divorce papers from a solicitor in London, which she had signed and duly returned, but aside from that there had been no communication. Yet here he was, on her eviction day, being assisted from the vehicle toward the building.

"Hey, you can't go in there!" The bailiff was out of her van and marching back across the road. "No one is allowed on the property, orders of the owner."

Immediately, the lines in front of Shelley House stretched out to engulf Kat, Phillip, and the woman, sweeping them inside their protective ring.

"You are now illegally trespassing on private property," the bailiff shouted as the trio began to walk up the steps.

Dorothy saw Phillip flinch; he had always hated confrontation. Still, he continued his climb, leaning heavily on the women on either side of him. After a moment they disappeared from view at the front door. Dorothy reached a hand up to smooth down her hair and realized it was shaking wildly.

There was a faint knock on the door and a moment later it opened.

Kat was the first to step into the flat, leaving the other two in the lobby.

"Hello, Dorothy."

The girl looked well, or at least better than she had six months ago. She had put on a little weight, which suited her, and there was more color in her cheeks. But her expression was uncharacteristically timid.

"Would you care to explain what is going on?" Dorothy knew it was hardly a friendly greeting, but now was not the time for pleasantries.

"I've brought someone to see you."

"I am not really in a position for visitors right now, as you can see." Dorothy indicated the bailiffs hovering at the other side of the road like vultures.

"Please, Dorothy. Phillip has something he wants to say to you."

Dorothy sighed. What could that man possibly have to say to her after thirty-three years, and today of all days? Although knowing Phillip, he probably had not even realized it was Charlotte's birthday. Plus the clock was ticking; the police might be here any minute and her neighbors outside would only be able to hold them off for so long.

"I do not—"

"Please, Dorothy." The girl's expression had changed from nervous to pleading. "It will only take a minute and I really think you should hear what he has to say."

Dorothy sighed. She might as well acquiesce and get this over and done with rather than waste more time arguing. She nodded and Kat stepped aside to help Phillip in. He was stooped as he crossed the room, concentrating on his slow steps, and as he lowered himself onto the sofa a small groan escaped his lips. Only then did he look up at her.

"Hello, Dotty."

She tried not to balk at hearing the pet name he had always called her, a name she had not heard for many years.

"We'll give you some privacy," Kat said, starting to move toward the door.

The other woman looked at Phillip. "Is that all right, Dad? I'll be out in the car if you need me."

Dad. Dorothy felt the word like a dagger.

Kat and the woman left, closing the door behind them, and the flat fell into a deathly silence. Over the years, Dorothy had imagined many times what she would say if she ever met her ex-husband again. She had pictured shouting and recriminations, curses and threats. But in all these imaginings, never once had she considered that her first words would be . . .

"By God, you are an old man."

Phillip gave a half smile. "You're no spring chicken yourself."

"And you have another daughter." She tried to keep her voice light, to not hint at the tempest of emotions beneath the surface.

"Stepdaughter," Phillip corrected. "Her name's Amy. I've been living with her and her family since my wife passed away."

So he had remarried and had grandchildren too? The dagger twisted further, leaving Dorothy almost breathless.

"How are you, Dotty? Still kicking about this old place, I see."

"I do not have time for small talk, Phillip. I do not know if Kat told you but I am being evicted today."

"I heard. I'm sorry you—"

"Spare me the false sympathies. Are you here to explain why I saw your car parked outside at the exact time Joseph Chambers was attacked? Or why you fled from us on the day of our protest in Winton?"

"Kat asked me the same question earlier and I had nothing to do with Joseph's attack, I swear. Why on earth would I? I always liked the man."

Dorothy swallowed. Clearly Phillip had never worked out what had passed between her and Joseph that day. "Then why were you here? What is your connection to all of this?"

Phillip sighed. "One thing at a time, please. Let's start with Winton. I'd gone into town to buy some new fishing tackle from Petersons, but it was busy and I couldn't find anywhere to park. I'd pulled into a space and I was trying to work out if I was allowed to park there or if it was permit only. You know what it's like in Winton these days, the council will slap a fine on you for—"

"You are waffling, Phillip."

He grimaced. "Sorry. So I was trying to park but then I looked up and saw you standing on the opposite pavement glaring at me. And I'll admit it, I panicked. It had been so long since I'd seen you and you looked so angry, I couldn't face a fight after all this time. So I drove away. I'm sorry, Dotty, it was cowardly of me."

Dorothy's only response was a snort of disdain.

"Kat told me that you'd chased me but I had no idea. My eyesight's been letting me down a bit lately and my reflexes aren't what they once were. In fact, Amy won't let me drive her car anymore; she says I'm not safe."

"So you were not visiting our landlord's office that day?"

"Absolutely not."

"Then what about the twenty-seventh of May? I keep a record of activity on Poet's Road and am certain I have never seen your registration plate here before. How do you explain your suspicious appearance here at the exact moment Joseph was attacked?"

Phillip looked down at his lap, and it was a moment before he spoke.

"I read a piece in the *Dunningshire Gazette* about Joseph and the evictions from Shelley House. As soon as I read that Fergus Alexander was involved, I knew that meant he was going to rip the place down. And so I wanted to come and visit it one last time."

"What balderdash! You never even liked Shelley House; I had to cajole you to live here. Do you really expect me to believe you came to pay your respects to the building? You are a liar, Phillip."

"I didn't come here to pay my respects to Shelley House. I came to pay my respects to Charlotte."

It was the first time he had said their daughter's name, and Dorothy gripped the edge of the table to suppress the sob that was threatening to burst from her mouth.

"She loved living here," Phillip continued, looking around the room slowly. "That was why I carried on paying the rent all these years, because I wanted to keep the place where she had been so happy. And that's why I came that day. I wanted to see our family home one last time before it disappeared altogether."

Tears sprang to Dorothy's eyes and she found herself momentarily lost for words.

Phillip was watching her. "Today is Charlotte's birthday, you know."

"Of course I know. She was my daughter too."

"Sorry, Dotty, I didn't mean . . . I just couldn't believe it when Kat told me you were being thrown out today of all days."

"Yes, well, there is never an ideal time to be evicted from one's home."

"Kat told me you blame yourself for what happened." Phillip must have seen her body stiffen because he started to stutter. "I didn't mean . . . I didn't mean to upset you. I'm sorry, I was just so shocked when she told me."

"What I do and feel is absolutely none of your business. In fact, I would like you to leave now." Dorothy pointed to her door, but Phillip seemed to have sagged further into the sofa.

"I'm sorry, Dotty. I'm making everything so much worse, just like I did back then."

Dorothy paused. Phillip was staring at his hands, and it was a moment before he spoke again.

"I'm so bad at all this: talking about my emotions. Amy is always telling me I need to get better at saying what I'm feeling, but I'm not made for it. I'm not sure you are either."

He looked at Dorothy for agreement, but she looked away. She was not going to give him the pleasure of admitting he was correct.

"I think that was part of our problem," Phillip continued. "Neither of us told each other how we felt, we just kept it locked up inside."

"I think you made your feelings perfectly clear."

"What do you mean?"

"I mean, you never tried to hide how much you hated me. How much you blamed me for Charlotte's death."

When she glanced back, Phillip was staring at her, his mouth slightly agape. "I didn't hate you."

"There you go, lying again. You shut me out of our bedroom for months."

"No, *you* moved into Charlotte's bedroom. That was your choice."

"You stopped speaking to me."

"I was grieving. Every time I tried to talk to you I thought I might burst into tears."

"You could not even look at me, Phillip."

"That's because every time I looked at you I saw how much pain you were in, and it killed me. I was your husband, I was supposed to support you, but I didn't have the first clue how to help. And that guilt ate me up."

"And then you left me. Four months after our daughter died you went to work one morning and never came home. No explanation, no note, nothing. You can try and rewrite history now, but I was there, Phillip. I saw the rage in your eyes, your hatred for me and my part in Charlotte's death. To pretend anything else is an insult to our daughter's memory."

When Phillip spoke again, his voice was low. "What part did you have in Charlotte's death, Dotty?"

"I should have saved her."

"But you couldn't. Remember what the coroner's report said? She died on impact. There was no way she could have been saved."

"I should have stopped her going up on the roof."

"She and Debbie were up on the roof that whole summer; I'd seen her up there myself. She wasn't doing anything she'd not done many times before."

"But still—"

"Charlotte's death was a horrible accident. But it was just that, an accident."

Dorothy sighed. It was time she told him the truth, made him realize how culpable she really was.

"That afternoon, while Charlotte was drinking on the roof, I was with Joseph Chambers."

"I know, you two were planning that party together."

"Yes, but it was more than that. I was in love with him."

The words were out of Dorothy's mouth before she realized what she was saying, and she almost laughed with relief. Joseph had been absolutely right; of course she had been in love with him. How had she never realized that before?

She saw Phillip swallow as he took in the news.

"Were you having an affair?"

"No, not yet. But when Charlotte fell, I was imagining just that.

Fantasizing about another man and another life. When I should have been watching out for my daughter."

Dorothy waited for it—the roar of rage, maybe even the violence that she knew she had always deserved. But instead, Phillip gave her a small, sad smile.

"Nothing that happened was your fault, Dorothy. I didn't blame you then and I don't blame you now."

Dorothy felt her shoulders deflate. Now that the truth had been spoken out loud she had hoped for some form of retribution, but Phillip was offering her something else entirely. Something unexpected.

She glanced outside the window. Her neighbors were still standing hand in hand, joined to protect her. Kat and Joseph were talking to Phillip's stepdaughter, but Joseph must have sensed Dorothy's gaze because he turned and caught her eye. He gave her an "Are you okay?" look and she nodded back.

"I'm sorry I left," Phillip said from behind her. "It all got too much: my grief, your grief, the guilt at not being able to help you. I felt like I was drowning. But rather than sit down and talk to you about it, I took the coward's way out and ran. But I have always regretted leaving you like I did."

Dorothy took a deep breath. Phillip had given her something today, and it appeared there was something she could give him in return.

"It is all right, Phillip, I forgive you. As you said, neither of us knew how to talk back then."

"I had no idea you blamed yourself for what happened. I wish I'd known so I could have reassured you it was not your fault."

"Truthfully, I am not sure I would have believed you, even if you had. But thank you for saying it now."

In the distance, Dorothy could hear the wail of a siren.

"I think that might be for me," she said, turning to the window once more.

"We should get going," Phillip said, and Dorothy could hear the fear in his voice. "I'm not getting arrested, not with my sciatica. Will you help me up?"

Dorothy did not answer. Her eyes moved from the bailiffs to Joseph, who was standing resolutely in front of Shelley House, his stature tall and proud. There was no fear in that man, only compassion and kindness, and perhaps a little false bravado. Dorothy remembered his words of a few moments ago, that gentle offer of a future together. For a moment she allowed herself to imagine what it might be like: the companionship not only of Joseph but of Reggie too, the walks and talks and home-cooked meals by a gas fire. It was a blissful image.

"Dorothy?" Phillip's voice again, more frantic this time.

She turned from the window, stood up, and helped Phillip from the sofa. He was surprisingly heavy for one so frail, but once he was on his feet she stepped back. "Will you be all right getting outside or shall I call in your daughter?"

"I'll be okay." He was already moving toward the door with surprising speed for someone who had required the help of two grown women on arrival.

Dorothy glanced back out the window. Her neighbors were still standing in their lines, hands linked like chain mail. Dorothy wished she had time to stay and watch them, this extraordinary gesture of solidarity from the people she had lived among for so long. But the clock really was ticking.

"Are you not taking any of this stuff with you?" Phillip had turned to face her from the door. "If you leave it, then God knows what will happen to it all."

Dorothy looked around the room at the lifetime's worth of possessions that were crowded into it. "There is no need. Where I am going, I will not need any of this."

Phillip shrugged. "Well, come on, we'd better leave."

Dorothy picked up her handbag, surprised at its weight until she remembered what was in it. Hoisting it over her arm, she crossed to the door. Once there she paused, taking one final look around her beloved home. Charlotte's home. Then she stepped out into the lobby.

Phillip had crossed the floor and was at the front door. "Well done, Dotty," he said when he saw her. "If you leave without making a fuss, then I'm sure you won't be in trouble."

"I hope you are right." She paused by the post shelf. "Actually, there is something I have forgotten. You go ahead and I will be right behind you."

Dorothy stayed where she was, waiting until Phillip had shuffled out of the building and the front door had slammed shut behind him. Only then did she move.

Forty-Eight

KAT

From her position in between Joseph and Tomasz on the pavement, Kat watched Dorothy's window, but all she'd been able to see was the back of the woman's head. What was taking them so long?

Kat knew it had been a risky strategy bringing Phillip here today. But once she had established who he was and why he'd been at Poet's Road back in the summer, she'd begged him to come and talk to Dorothy. Her hope was that he might be able to finally convince Dorothy that Charlotte's death wasn't her fault, and in doing so help her to walk away from Shelley House with some sense of peace. But given the old woman's stubbornness, it was very possible Phillip's visit would have the opposite effect entirely.

Kat looked around for Will but there was still no sign of him either. He had left her at Phillip and Amy's house and then rushed back to Winton to investigate what Kat had seen on their drive. She'd messaged him to say she was bringing Phillip to Shelley House and that he should meet her here but hadn't heard back from him. Would he manage to get here in time? Kat felt a twist of anxiety.

"Oh good lord, it's him."

Joseph's voice caused Kat to spin back round. A familiar figure was walking down the road toward them, a self-satisfied smile on his face. Kat felt anger ignite in her like a fire.

"Try and keep calm," she heard Joseph mutter next to her, although from the man's viselike grip on Kat's hand, she could tell he was anything but.

"You've got some nerve showing your face here today," he said, as Fergus Alexander drew near.

"I'm only coming to check the job's done properly."

"You mean you've come to gloat over a seventy-seven-year-old woman being thrown out of her home?"

"It didn't have to end like this. Mrs. Darling has been given plenty of opportunities to leave on her own terms."

"*Ms.* Darling doesn't want to leave," Joseph said. "And she doesn't want you to destroy Shelley House. None of us do."

Fergus's eyes glanced up at the building behind them. "Come on now, this place should have been torn down years ago. It's a health hazard."

"It is only a health hazard because you've let it fall into such disrepair," Joseph said, but Alexander snorted.

"This building's problems started long before I took it over. Spending money on repairing it would've been like using a plaster to fix a leaky dam. Pointless."

Kat opened her mouth to argue, but at that moment she heard a door creak behind her. When she swung round, she saw Phillip walking out onto the top step of Shelley House. Immediately, Kat dropped Joseph's and Tomasz's hands, ducked under the lines of people behind her, and ran up the steps to meet him.

"Is Dorothy okay?" she asked as soon as she reached Phillip.

"I think so. We finally cleared the air."

"Where is she now?"

"She's coming, she's right behind me."

Phillip began to move down the steps toward the pavement but Kat stayed where she was, her eyes trained on the closed door.

"Right, folks, the party's over!" Fergus Alexander boomed. "You're all breaking the law by obstructing a public highway. The police are on their way, so unless you move you'll be arrested."

Kat didn't turn around but from the silence behind her she could tell that nobody had moved. Good on them; she'd never have had her old neighbors down as such rebels. But where was Dorothy? If she was right behind Phillip then she should be out by now. Kat pushed open the front door, ignoring the shouts of Alexander and the bailiffs behind her. She put her head into the lobby but Dorothy wasn't there. The door to her flat was open, however, and Kat stepped inside Shelley House and crossed toward flat two, inhaling the familiar scent of dust and damp. It made her feel almost nostalgic.

"Dorothy, are you here?"

She poked her head round the flat door. It was unrecognizable from the last time Kat had been here. The furniture had been moved aside and there were empty plates, glasses, and bottles littering every surface, but there was no sign of the occupier.

"Dorothy?" Kat shouted again, her words echoing round the space. If she wasn't in the flat, where was she? She'd definitely not left Shelley House, of that much Kat was sure.

She stepped back into the lobby, and as she did she felt a cold draft blow across her face. That was weird; the front door was shut, so where was it coming from? She looked around her, confused, until she felt it again. And then Kat's eyes swung toward the staircase.

Within seconds she was racing up the stairs, taking them two at a time. Dorothy wouldn't, surely? But where else could she be? Kat sped up as she raced past Omar's front door toward the top landing. When she got there, her worst fear was confirmed: the fire escape door to the roof was wide open. Kat charged outside, her feet banging on the metal steps. She was out of breath as she reached the top of the stairs and swung round onto the flat roof of the building.

Dorothy was standing at the far side, looking down over the low balustrade onto what must be the back of Shelley House. She was wearing a purple dress and her long silver hair was loose and blowing in the wind. Other than that, she was completely motionless.

"Dorothy?"

The woman didn't reply. Kat took a few tentative steps forward. She could see that Dorothy was holding something in her hands, although from this angle Kat couldn't tell what it was.

"Dorothy?"

"Go away."

The knot in Kat's stomach tightened. Should she run at Dorothy and rugby tackle her to the floor, hoping that her yells would be loud enough to alert those below that she needed help? Or was it better to try to chat with Dorothy, distract her until she could be talked away from the edge? She took a deep breath.

"Dorothy, I think I may have worked out who was behind Joseph's attack."

The woman didn't move, and Kat took another couple of steps closer. Soon she would be near enough to grab her if she needed to.

"Did you hear me, Dorothy? I think I've worked it out. And what's more, I'm pretty sure we can bring Fergus Alexander down in the process. Earlier on I saw—"

"This is not about Fergus Alexander," Dorothy interrupted, her voice low.

"What do you mean?"

"Even if he is stopped, another developer will step in and pull Shelley House down. I will never be able to save her."

Kat opened her mouth to argue but stopped herself. Now was not the time for false promises.

"Maybe Shelley House will be demolished, Dorothy. But in the end, it's only a building. Will once told me that a home isn't made by bricks and mortar but by the people in it, and I've come to realize that's true."

For a moment Dorothy didn't say anything, and Kat wondered if her words were sinking in.

"Please," she said, hardly daring to breathe. "Let's go downstairs, walk away from Shelley House and—"

Kat never got to finish her sentence, because in one sudden movement Dorothy Darling had stepped up onto the balustrade and thrown her arms wide open to the sky.

Forty-Nine

DOROTHY

She rose into the air and for a moment seemed to float above Shelley House, suspended on the cool December breeze. Then a gust of wind took hold and in an instant she was whipped away, tumbling and twirling through the sky like a dancer.

On the roof of Shelley House, Dorothy watched as Charlotte's ashes scattered, a million tiny motes illuminated against the bright winter sky, before dissipating in the blink of an eye. Dorothy looked down into the small ornamental box she was holding, the one that had rested next to the picture frame on her mantelpiece for thirty-three years. There were still half the ashes left and for a moment she was tempted to shove them back into her handbag, to keep the last vestiges of her daughter as she had done all these years. But she held out the box and shook it gently so that the remaining ashes fell out. The wind caught them immediately and in a flash Charlotte was gone.

Dorothy closed her eyes, allowing the wind to catch her too, blowing her skirt and hair around her in a frenzy. She had imagined this moment many times over the years; imagined how it would feel to fly. All it would take was the smallest step forward and she would be free at last.

A gust of wind blew, stronger this time, and Dorothy wobbled. She glanced down at the patch of concrete below where the garden of

Shelley House had once been. How long would it take to reach it? Two seconds, maybe three? The paramedics had told her that Charlotte would have died on impact, that she would have felt no pain at all. How Dorothy had longed for that ever since; to feel no pain at all.

"Dorothy."

Kat's voice behind her was soft and tentative.

"Listen. Can you hear that?"

Dorothy closed her eyes again, hearing only the wind whistling in her ears. But wait, there was something else too, a distant sound carrying on the breeze. Was that Ayesha's voice she could hear, and Joseph's too? Were they singing? Dorothy could not make out the words but she smiled as she allowed the melody to wrap around her, the harmony of her neighbors' voices like a nursery lullaby, sending her to sleep. For sleep was what she wanted now. A dreamless sleep from which she would never have to wake.

"Save Shelley House! Save Shelley House!"

Dorothy opened her eyes. It was not a lullaby but a chant. No, a war cry. And was that a siren she could hear too, its piercing wail growing as it approached?

Her knee sagged and in an instant she felt Kat's hand grip her arm. Dorothy looked up into the sky once more, but there was no sign of Charlotte.

The siren was loud now, and the chants of Dorothy's neighbors had grown louder too, and more defiant. She felt them in her body, their rhythm like a heartbeat. A vital, living heartbeat.

Dorothy took a long breath and stepped down from the balustrade onto the roof below. Once both her feet were on the floor she turned to look at Kat, whose face was ashen. For a moment they stared at each other and then Kat did something utterly unexpected. She opened her arms and pulled Dorothy into a wordless embrace.

Dorothy was not sure the last time she had been held, and she allowed herself to soften into Kat's small body, feeling the weight of her arms around her back. They remained like this for a few seconds, until the air was pierced with a sudden sharp cry.

As one, they turned and hurried to the other side of the roof so they could look down onto the street below. A police car had pulled up outside Shelley House. Dorothy's neighbors were still standing in three lines, their hands linked tightly together, although from up here they looked small and rather vulnerable. In the middle of the front row Dorothy could see a head of white hair. *Joseph.*

She turned and began to rush toward the stairs.

"What do we do now?" Kat called as she followed.

"I do not have the faintest idea," Dorothy said, for it was the truth. This had not been part of her plan.

"I should warn you, Fergus Alexander is here," Kat said as they reached the first floor.

"Of course he is, the toad." Well, if he had come all the way hoping to see her sobbing and defeated, he would be waiting a very long time.

They had reached the lobby and Dorothy faltered by the main door.

"Are you okay?" Kat said, coming to stand next to her.

Was she? Dorothy glanced into her flat, feeling an almost physical pull toward it. She could see her card table by the window, where she had sat and watched her neighbors come and go. Now those same neighbors were outside, about to be arrested in order to protect her.

"One moment."

Dorothy strode into the flat and across the room to the mantelpiece, picking up Charlotte's framed picture and sliding it into her handbag. She retrieved her box of photos from the table and returned to Kat.

"Shall I help you with those?" Kat asked, and Dorothy handed her the box to carry. "Are you ready now?"

Dorothy took a deep breath, resisting the temptation to look back into her home one last time. "I am."

She threw open the front door of Shelley House rather harder than intended and it slammed against the wall, causing a colossal bang. Immediately, forty-odd heads swung round to locate the source of the noise. Dorothy's eyes sought Joseph, who was watching her with a serious expression on his face. Standing behind him was Fergus Alexander, an oily smile illuminating his grotesque visage. Beyond them, two officers were climbing out of their vehicle. As they turned to face Shelley House, Dorothy saw that it was Inspector Hudson and PC Reid. Another red car had pulled up too, and from it Dorothy saw Will emerge. Quite an audience for her departure.

"You can walk straight past Fergus, you don't have to deal with him," Kat whispered into Dorothy's ear.

She nodded and began to descend the first step, but as she did her knee wobbled again and she felt herself pitch sideways. Immediately Kat's hand reached out and snatched hers. Dorothy gripped it back and they continued together, hand in hand. As she reached the final step, the lines of her neighbors began to part like the Red Sea to allow Dorothy and Kat to walk through. Up ahead she saw Joseph, Omar, Ayesha, Gloria, and Tomasz all watching as she approached. Reggie, who had been standing at Joseph's feet, gave a bark and ran to greet her.

"Dorothy," Joseph said as she reached them. "I'm so—"

"Finally saw sense, did you?" This was Fergus Alexander's ingratiating voice. "You could have saved us all a lot of bother if you'd done this months ago."

Dorothy opened her mouth to reply but felt Kat's hand gripping her own. Fergus smirked when she did not respond.

"Shall we go?" Joseph said, his eyes still fixed on Dorothy.

She nodded, although where she was going to go, she had absolutely no idea.

"Officers, I'm so sorry you've had a wasted journey," Fergus said, his voice booming as he addressed the police. "Mrs. Darling has finally vacated the property so your assistance won't be required after all. Unless you'd like to help me start demolishing Shelley House?" He chuckled loudly at his own joke.

"Don't rise to it," Kat hissed at Dorothy as they walked past him.

"Actually, it's not Ms. Darling we're here to see," Inspector Hudson said. "Am I correct in thinking you're Fergus Alexander?"

"That's me," Alexander said. "Fergus Alexander, MBE of Alexander Properties, landlord and property developer. I'm the owner of Shelley House, although it won't be called that for much longer."

Dorothy paused and turned back to see Inspector Hudson consulting her notebook.

"Mr. Alexander, we have just been presented with evidence to suggest that you have been harassing the tenants of Shelley House. This is an offense under Section 1 of the 1977 Protection from Eviction Act."

"I think you must be mistaken," Fergus said. "I've got a court order for possession of this property. This eviction is entirely legal."

"Sir, according to the evidence we have heard, an agent acting on your behalf has consistently interfered with the peace of the occupiers of Shelley House over the course of several months."

"What?" His face was reddening. "I have no idea what you're talking about."

Dorothy had no idea what they were talking about either. What agent?

"Don't lie," Will said, stepping forward from where he'd been standing by his car. "And it's a strategy you've used many times before, isn't it? Along with verbal harassment, threats, and physical violence."

"This is slander!" The man's skin was now almost purple. "You have no evidence, it's all rumors stirred up by my competitors. It's an unfortunate consequence of being so successful."

"It's not rumors," PC Reid said.

"Yes, it is. Tell me what evidence you have this instance or I'm calling my solicitor."

"They have me."

Dorothy did not know where those words had come from, and clearly neither did the others around her as they began looking about in confusion. Only Will and the police officers seemed to know who had spoken, as they had turned toward Will's car. A figure was climbing out of the front passenger seat, wearing a brown leather jacket and a baseball cap pulled down to conceal their face. Only when they were standing did they remove their hat, at which point Dorothy let out a gasp.

"Hi, Dad," said the antisocial tenant from flat four.

Fifty

DOROTHY

"Vincent, what the hell are you doing?" said Fergus, who was now looking rather more egg-white pale than beetroot red. Reggie seemed to be equally shocked at the new arrival, as he had started barking wildly.

"Mr. Alexander, your son was brought to see us at the police station earlier and made some very serious allegations," Inspector Hudson said. "He has claimed that you moved him into flat four of Shelley House with the deliberate intention of causing disruption to the tenants in order to drive them out of the property. Among other things, he told us that you made him hold noisy late-night gatherings to keep the tenants awake, steal residents' post, and deliberately cause a flood to leak into the flat below."

My God, all that thumping noise had been on purpose? And the leaking bathroom! Dorothy felt a flash of anger, but she held her tongue.

"This is rubbish," Fergus said. "I have no idea why he's making up these lies, but none of it's true. And can someone shut that damn dog up, it's giving me a headache!"

"Calm down, Reggie," Joseph said to the animal, whose barks dropped to a low growl.

"Come on, Dad, there's no point denying it," Vince said, and his tone was one of sadness. "You've had me doing the same scam for years now in different properties."

"Vincent, why are you trying to destroy us with these malicious stories? This is your business too, your livelihood. What is wrong with you?"

Vince ran a hand through his greasy hair and let out a long sigh. "I've told you before, I'm tired of making people's lives a misery just so we can make a few extra quid on their rent. Do you have any idea how tough it is being the neighbor from hell the whole time? For once, I'd like to live somewhere where my neighbors don't hate me."

"I've never asked you to make anyone's lives a misery, you lying little shit," Fergus hissed. He turned to Inspector Hudson. "Madam, who are you going to believe here? My son, an unemployed, drug-smoking wastrel, or me, an upstanding member of the community and long-term benefactor of the Dunningshire Police Benevolent Fund?"

If this was meant to impress Inspector Hudson, it appeared to have the opposite effect. "Mr. Alexander, I am arresting you—"

"What? You're not serious?"

"On suspicion of harassment. You do not have to say anything but it may harm your defense if you do not mention when questioned something you later rely on in court."

"I want my solicitor!" Fergus shouted, but PC Reid had already stepped forward and taken the man firmly by the elbow.

"Anything you do say may be given in evidence," the inspector finished, at which point she grabbed Fergus's other arm.

The man looked like he was going to struggle but then thought better of it and allowed himself to be led toward the police car. He didn't so much as glance at his son as he walked past, and Dorothy saw the young man's head fall. No one spoke as they watched him being helped into the back seat.

"Vince, we'll be in touch soon about further details on your father's business operations," Inspector Hudson said as she climbed into the driver's seat. "I strongly advise you make yourself available when we need you."

They all watched in silence as the police car drove away. Only when it had disappeared round the corner did Dorothy turn to Will.

"How on earth did you discover that Vince was related to Fergus Alexander?"

"It wasn't me, it was Kat who worked it out," Will said, and Dorothy heard admiration in his voice.

"I spotted them outside Alexander's office when we drove past earlier," Kat said. "They were having some kind of argument and the second I saw them together I noticed the similarity."

Vince frowned at this, as if offended by the physical comparison to his father.

"While Kat was with Phillip, I tracked down Vince and he confessed straightaway and agreed to come and talk to the police with me," Will said.

"It was a bit of a relief, to be honest." Vince gave a shrug. "I'm tired of being the baddie all the time, it's exhausting."

"You're not a baddie, Vince," Joseph said, rather too magnanimously in Dorothy's opinion. "After all, you played a significant part in rescuing Dorothy after her fall."

Reggie, who had been emitting a low growl throughout the conversation, suddenly let out a loud bark and lunged toward Vince's ankles in an attempt to bite them.

"Reggie, stop it!" Joseph scolded.

Dorothy was about to reprimand the animal too when a thought occurred to her and she drew breath.

"Oh my goodness, Reginald, you are right!"

She turned to Vince, who was nervously backing away from the dog. "You are the culprit behind Joseph's attack, are you not? That is why Reginald is so upset, because he witnessed you knocking Joseph out."

The boy started shaking his head wildly. "No, that wasn't me, I swear!"

"You are lying. Why else would Joseph's dog be so disturbed at the sight of you?"

"I dunno, but I promise it wasn't me. I've done some bad things at my dad's request, but I've never hurt anyone."

"I still do not believe you. Reginald never behaves like this with anyone e—" Dorothy stopped. What she was about to say was not strictly true. She had seen Reggie be aggressive in an unprovoked manner like this several times before: at a couple walking past when she had been flyering outside the library and at a man on a dog walk down by the river. And each time, the recipients of Reggie's attention had had one thing in common with Vince.

Dorothy turned to her old neighbors, who were all watching her with confusion writ across their faces.

"Gloria, when we were talking earlier, how did you describe the kind of men that you are attracted to?"

Gloria's cheeks flushed. "Dorothy, I'm not sure now's the time to be discussing my sex life."

"You told me you went for 'leather-jacket-wearing dickheads,' am I correct?"

"I don't wear a leather jacket," Tomasz said, looking hurt.

"I know you don't, love, which was my point." Gloria put a placatory hand on his arm. "The guys I went for before you were all the same type: little men with big egos who treated me like shit. But you're different, you're kind and gentle and lovely, nothing like my exes."

Tomasz smiled at this and leaned forward to give Gloria a sloppy kiss, to which she eagerly responded. Dorothy looked away.

"I'm sorry, but what does this have to do with anything?" Omar said.

In response, Dorothy slipped a hand into her bag and reached for her trusty diary. She opened it with a flourish and flicked through until she found an appropriate page.

"Wednesday 15th May, 11:32 a.m. Domestic fracas in flat six. Tried to offer assistance to G.B., verbally assaulted and threatened by male inhabitant in leather jacket." She turned to another page. "Saturday 18th May, 7:18 p.m. Argument between G.B. and her leather-jacket-wearing paramour on front steps. Knocked on window to politely ask them to keep the noise down. Sworn at in response." Dorothy looked up from her page at the assembled crowd. "I could continue, there are many other such entries."

For a moment there was a stunned silence, which Dorothy hoped was one of admiration as opposed to concern.

"Oh my God, it was Barry!" Gloria squealed, filling in the blanks for anyone who had not yet worked it out. "Barry attacked Joe!"

"I believe he did. And dear Reginald has been trying to alert us to the fact ever since by barking at men in leather jackets. Have you not, you good boy?" Dorothy said, addressing the dog directly.

"I can't believe it," Gloria wailed, slumping on the edge of the pavement and putting her head in her hands.

"I can go kill him if you like?" Tomasz said, leaning down and putting a protective arm around her.

"No, babe, that's all right. But I love you for offering."

Dorothy looked at Joseph, who appeared utterly dazed.

"Do you have any memory of an altercation with Barry that day?" she asked him, but Joseph shook his head.

"Not a thing, I'm afraid. Although we had argued several times in the past, so it's entirely possible. I was not a fan of Barry's and had made my feelings about him clear to Gloria."

"Yeah, he always thought you were trying to turn me against him, which in fairness, you were," Gloria said from her position on the ground. "But that's still no excuse for what he did to you."

"What was he even doing in Shelley House?" Dorothy asked, leafing through her diary. "I have no record of him being in the property since Saturday 18th May, nine days prior to Joseph's attack."

Gloria looked suddenly sheepish. "Yeah, well, we'd broken up but then I bumped into him in the pub and one thing led to another, as it sometimes does . . ." She glanced at Tomasz and blushed. "Anyway, the next day I realized what a mistake I'd made and split up with him for good. He was in a terrible temper when he left that afternoon. He must have seen Joseph on his way down and taken his rage out on him."

"You must report all of this to the police," Dorothy said. "I will give them my diary too, which should provide them with the evidence they need to charge Barry."

"I will. And I'm so sorry, Joe."

Joseph patted her shoulder. "Don't be silly, it's not your fault."

"I owe you all an apology too," Vince said, and when Dorothy looked at him he was staring at her. "I'm so sorry for all the trouble me and Dad caused everyone, especially you, Ms. Darling. I know this will be no consolation but I always hated making you all unhappy. None of you deserved it."

"At least your father has been apprehended now and he won't be able to do this to anyone else," Joseph said. "It sounds like far too many people have been hurt by his scams."

At these words, Dorothy remembered Kat's grandfather.

"Vince, did you have anything to do with your father's purchase of Featherdown Farm a few years ago?"

The young man shook his head. "Not personally, but I remember him doing that deal. He really wanted that land and so I think he got Bob on the case."

"Bob?"

"I always stayed away from that side of things, but Dad used to get Bob involved whenever he needed a bit of extra muscle."

Kat had turned rather pale and she was uncharacteristically quiet. The poor girl, she really had had quite the day after everything up on the roof as well.

"Please, will you tell the police everything you know about what happened with Featherdown Farm and this Bob gentleman," Dorothy said to Vince. "It is imperative that the criminals pay for what they did there as well."

Vince nodded. "I will. And I'm sorry again."

He looked up at Dorothy but she would not catch his eye, so he turned and began to walk away. Still, she could not help feeling a tiny bit sorry for the boy. He may have been a delinquent neighbor from hell with appalling domestic cleaning skills, but nobody deserved Fergus Alexander as a father.

Now that the drama had ended, the crowd started to ebb away. The bailiffs had skedaddled as soon as the police left, and many of Dorothy's old neighbors had headed off too. She looked around at those who still remained. Gloria had risen from the pavement and Tomasz had his arm wrapped around her. Omar and Ayesha were standing together, the teenager leaning on her father's shoulder. Kat and Joseph were both still looking rather shocked at what had transpired. Only Reggie seemed unfazed by the events of the past few hours, happily licking his genitals.

"Are you all right, Kat?" Dorothy asked her old neighbor.

Kat ran a hand through her hair. "Yeah. It's all a bit of a shock to have everything confirmed, isn't it? But I'm glad that man is going to finally pay for what he did to my grandpa, and to you." She sighed, suddenly looking much younger than her twenty-five years. Will, who had moved to stand beside her, reached out and put a hand on Kat's back. Dorothy expected her to shake it off angrily, but to her surprise the girl looked up at him with a small smile.

"What's going to happen to Shelley House now?" Ayesha said, vocalizing the question that had been nagging in the back of Dorothy's brain.

"If Fergus is charged for all his crimes, that'll surely be an end to the redevelopment plans," Omar said.

Kat looked back at Dorothy. "He's right, you know. Shelley House may well be safe now. You might be able to stay in your home after all."

Dorothy was aware they were all looking at her as the implications of this began to sink in. She did not say anything as she turned to face her beloved Shelley House. The red bricks were faded now, the once ornately embossed white masonry crumbled and gray. It was a very different façade from the one Dorothy had stood in front of more than three decades ago and pledged to make her home. And yet, despite its decaying appearance, the building still stood proud and strong: not unlike Dorothy herself. And whatever happened next, she was confident they would both be all right.

She turned to Joseph. He was watching her with a nervous smile on his lips, the same smile he had worn thirty-three years ago when he had knocked on her door and declared himself to be a terrible baker. At his feet, Reggie was watching Dorothy expectantly, his little tail high in the air.

"Do you have a teapot?" she asked Joseph.

"I do. And English breakfast tea, of course, and an excellent selection of biscuits. Plus the entire Wagner back catalog."

Dorothy sniffed. "What about a garden?"

"Yes. It's small but I'm planning on starting a vegetable patch."

"And a—"

She stopped herself. *A home is not made by bricks and mortar but by the people in it.*

"Very well, then, I suppose it will do." Dorothy handed her diary to Kat, for she would not be needing it any longer, and took Joseph's proffered arm. "Let us go home."

Epilogue

From her armchair by the window, Dorothy took in the vista in front of her. The daffodils were out in full force, their garish yellow heads nodding and bowing in the May breeze like a gaggle of gossiping housewives. Outside number 14, Hilary Armitage was on her hands and knees weeding her flower beds, while next door at number 15, Vikram Singh was pruning his rambling rose. The two of them were highly competitive over their gardens. Just last week, Dorothy and Joseph had been returning from a recital in the residents' center when they witnessed an altercation in which Mr. Singh accused Mrs. Armitage of cutting back his magnolia tree while he had been on holiday in Benidorm. The whole thing had gotten quite heated, to the extent that Joseph had had to step in to calm the pair down, much to Dorothy's amusement. Armitage and Singh had been exchanging passive-aggressive greetings and murderous glares ever since.

A bark from farther up the cul-de-sac caught Dorothy's attention, and she turned to see Reggie scampering along the pavement on his squat little legs, followed closely by Princess. Joseph and Tomasz were ambling behind them, an incongruous sight given Tomasz was twice the size of Joseph in every direction. The young man came over most Saturday afternoons while Gloria was at work, and he and Joseph took their dogs out together on a long walk. Dorothy had no idea what they conversed about; she had once asked Joseph, who had simply tapped the side of his nose and said "boys' stuff" in an infuriating manner.

The two of them had reached number 7 and Dorothy waved good-bye as Tomasz climbed into his van with Princess and drove off. A moment later, she heard the front door click open and Reggie's soft bark of greeting as he ran in. As ever, he jumped onto her lap and covered her in wet licks as if he had not seen Dorothy for two months, as opposed to just two hours.

"Reginald, you smell," Dorothy said once he had completed his reunion routine.

"I think he rolled in fox poo," Joseph said as he entered the room. Dorothy wrinkled her nose and pushed the dog gently to the floor.

"How is Tomasz?"

"Good. He and Gloria have their twelve-week scan on Monday."

"How exciting. I wonder if it will be a girl or a boy?"

The couple had made their pregnancy announcement last Friday, when the former residents of Shelley House were gathered for Ayesha's seventeenth-birthday celebrations. The room had erupted into cheers, and Dorothy had found herself so swept up in the jubilations that she had quite forgotten to make any observations about their as-yet-unmarried status. In retrospect, she was glad she had not said anything. After all, that sort of thing did not matter so much these days. Just look at her and Joseph.

"What did I miss while I was out?" Joseph had come to stand beside her, looking out the window.

"The Great Garden War has reached DEFCON 2," Dorothy said, nodding toward Mr. Singh, who was scowling at Mrs. Armitage over the fence. "I would not be surprised if he were out there beheading her precious camellias tonight."

"I bumped into the warden earlier, and he told me that Mrs.

Armitage has complained about Mr. Singh's leylandii overshadowing her property."

"Really?" Dorothy shook her head in disbelief. "Honestly, people can get worked up over the silliest little things."

Joseph did not reply, and when she glanced at him he was looking at her with a wry smile on his lips.

"What are you insinuating with that smirk, Joseph Chambers?"

"Nothing, my dear. Nothing at all." He chuckled as he bent to place a kiss on the top of her head. Dorothy pretended to brush him away, but she could not help smiling.

"I'll go and check on dinner," Joseph said, straightening up. "What time are Kat and Will arriving?"

"Her last message said they were visiting her great-uncle Ted this afternoon and so should be with us around seven o'clock, although that girl is always late. Are you doing dauphinoise potatoes with the stew?"

"Of course. And the apple pie you love," Joseph said, and Dorothy nodded her approval.

He headed to the kitchen and Dorothy stood up to retrieve the good china from the dresser. This was only the second time Kat had been to see them since Dorothy had moved here, five months ago. The girl was so busy with her college studies and bar job that she had not had a day off in weeks, but they kept in touch with regular telephone calls. She and Will were apparently seeing quite a bit of each other, which Dorothy thoroughly approved of, and Kat was also in contact with her mother, which Dorothy approved of considerably less. Still, she had to accept that she could not protect Kat from the vagaries of her mother, however much she might want to. Kat was a grown woman and she had to be allowed to take risks and make her own mistakes. And whatever happened, Dorothy and Joseph would be here for her when they were needed.

Dorothy laid the table for four and then sat back down by the window. The sun had almost set, and Mr. Singh and Mrs. Armitage had retreated into their respective bungalows. The only sounds Dorothy could hear were Joseph's melodic whistling floating in from the kitchen along with the gentle snores of Reggie at her feet. The air was rich with the delicious smell of boeuf bourguignon, and Dorothy felt a deep peace settle in her chest. Perhaps she could have a quick nap before Kat and Will arrived, just so she was on her most sparkling form for their guests? She took a deep breath and allowed her eyelids to drift closed.

The bang of a front door jolted Dorothy awake. She opened her eyes to see Mrs. Armitage emerging from the house opposite, staggering under the weight of a large refuse sack. She paused by her gate, glancing up and down the pavement to check that there were no passersby. Then, when she was confident the coast was clear, the woman walked into the front garden of number 15, lifted the lid of Mr. Singh's wheelie bin, and dumped the bag inside.

Dorothy gasped. Had Mrs. Armitage just deliberately and wantonly broken Fieldhouse Retirement Community rule 37b by using someone else's refuse facilities without permission? Or was it even more sinister than that? After all, the obvious weight of that sack suggested it was not simply your average household waste. Was there something suspicious in the bag, and if so, was Mrs. Armitage trying to implicate Mr. Singh for a crime he had not committed?

"Would you like a glass of sherry, my love?" Joseph's voice called through from the kitchen.

But Dorothy did not answer, for she was otherwise occupied trying to locate a new notebook and pencil.

Acknowledgments

People often talk about a "difficult" second book or album, but for me it was this, my third novel, that has proven the most challenging (and rewarding) so far. I would therefore like to give my eternal love and gratitude to the following amazing individuals, who have all helped nurture this from the initial idea to the book you now hold in your hands.

Firstly, as always, to my fabulous agent, Hayley Steed. Some agents are great editorially and others are kick-ass dealmakers, but I'm extremely lucky that Hayley is both. Thank you for always pushing me to make my ideas as good as possible, for your patience and hard work on my behalf, and for your endless support. Thanks as well to the wonderful Elinor Davies for being such an utter joy to work with, and the wider team at Madeleine Milburn for everything you've done for me and my books.

To my fantastic editor, Kerry Donovan, for giving me the opportunity to write more stories and for encouraging me to grow as a writer. I feel so lucky that I get to carry on working with you and the dream team at Berkley, especially the legends that are Tara O'Connor, Chelsea Pascoe, Jessica Plummer, Hillary Tacuri, Mary Baker, Christine Legon, and Liz Gluck. I wish I didn't live three thousand miles away so I could give you all hugs! And thank you to the uber talented Lila Selle for this gorgeous cover.

In the UK, thank you to Sarah Bauer for your endless creativity and sense of fun, and to Melissa Cox for taking on this book with so much enthusiasm. Thank you as well to the wonderful Bonnier family: Ellie Pilcher, Beth Whitelaw, Natalie Perman, Vincent Kelleher and the whole sales team, plus the genius Jenny Richards for her excellent cover design once again. You all live considerably closer so I will happily hug any of you anytime.

To all the brilliant book cheerleaders out there: the booksellers, librarians, book reviewers, bloggers, and bookstagrammers who work tirelessly to champion us authors and our work. I'll never get to thank you all personally, but please know that I am so grateful every time I see one of your posts or read one of your pieces. You are all rock stars.

To my writer friends around the world who have offered me so much help, encouragement, and (more than once) a shoulder to cry on. To the Berkletes, for keeping me sane and always making me laugh. And to my Faber Academy gang, for all the brainstorming, workshopping, and writing Zooms. And to all the fantastic authors who have championed my books by reading them and saying such lovely, generous things about them. I won't name you all as I'm terrified I'll forget someone, but if you flick to the front of this book you'll see lots of them listed there. Thank you all so much!

To Marcus Sedgwick, Wibke Brueggemann, Tamzin Cuming, and Geoff Mamdani: four writers who I spent an incredible week with at a retreat in France when my confidence in this book was at its lowest. Thank you for all the inspiration and encouragement you gave me that week, and for helping me to fall in love with this story again. Marcus, I will miss you and that magical place you created, but I feel privileged to have known you even for a short time.

Finally, to my amazing friends and family. Sorry I moaned so much while writing this one, but thank you for your continued faith in me. I am so proud of this finished story, and it would never have happened without your love and support.

Nosy Neighbors

FREYA SAMPSON

READERS GUIDE

Discussion Questions

1. If you could choose to live next door to any one of the characters in the book, who would it be, and why?

2. What do you think most appealed to Kat about renting a room from Joseph?

3. What did you think about Dorothy's isolation at the start of the book, her habit of jotting down infractions, and how that balance changed throughout the book?

4. In your opinion, which one of the residents of Shelley House showed the most character growth over the course of *Nosy Neighbors*?

5. What do Kat's and Dorothy's different ages bring to their friendship?

6. After reading *Nosy Neighbors,* has your opinion of the motives of busybody neighbors changed at all?

7. Have you seen evidence of gentrification where you live? What is the biggest negative impact in your area?

8. One of the main themes of *Nosy Neighbors* is how individuals within a community can pull together and make a big difference. Did you have a favorite emotional moment in the storyline?

9. After finishing *Nosy Neighbors*, what advice do you think either Kat or Dorothy would give to someone punishing themselves for a past mistake?

10. Did you have a favorite romantic pairing in *Nosy Neighbors*?

KEEP READING FOR A PREVIEW OF

The Lost Ticket

APRIL 2022

"This is the 88 to Parliament Hill Fields."

The electronic announcement rang round the bus as Libby heaved her two rucksacks on board. There was a queue of passengers behind her, and she heard an impatient tut as she rummaged in her handbag to find her wallet. Finally she located it and tapped her card to pay, but not before she heard someone mutter, "Bloody tourist." Libby hurriedly scooped up her bags and began to maneuver toward the one free seat on the lower deck, but she'd gone only a few paces when a teenage boy pushed past, almost knocking her into the lap of an elderly woman, and threw himself into the vacant seat.

Libby gave the boy her best death stare, then turned and climbed the narrow stairs toward the front of the upper deck, clinging to the handrail so she didn't fall as the bus swerved out of Vauxhall Station. When she reached the top, she was relieved to see that the nearest seats in the first row were available, and she dumped her bags on the floor and sat down.

The bus edged its way through the London traffic, and Libby looked out of the front window. Everyone seemed in such a hurry: crowds of pedestrians streaming along the pavement, car horns honking like angry geese, a cyclist gesturing and swearing at a taxi driver. As the bus drove onto Vauxhall Bridge, Libby turned right to get a view along the River Thames. She recognized the Tate Britain art gallery, and behind it the London Eye, its glass pods glistening in the late April sunshine. Simon had taken Libby on it once as a birthday treat, three or four years ago. They'd drunk prosecco as the wheel had rotated them high above the city, and afterward they'd bought hot dogs and walked along the South Bank, hand in hand. It had been one of their rare day trips to London, and Libby remembered feeling so lucky to be there with Simon. And yet—

"Oh my goodness, it's you!"

A voice to Libby's left made her jump, and she swung around to see an elderly man sitting across the aisle, wearing a burgundy velvet jacket that had seen better days. His face broke into a grin when he saw her.

"It really is you, isn't it?"

Oh god. She'd been in London only ten minutes and already she'd picked up a weirdo.

"I'm sorry. I think you've mistaken me for someone else," Libby said, and she turned away from him.

"Oh . . . oh, I am sorry."

Libby pulled her phone out of her handbag. Usually, if a stranger tried to make unwanted conversation, she'd ring someone for a chat instead. But who on earth could she call now? Certainly not her parents, and all her friends these days were Simon's friends too, the wives and girlfriends of his mates, and they were the last people she wanted to speak to. Libby slid her phone back into her bag.

"I'm sorry I disturbed you," the man continued, his voice shaky. "I get a little confused sometimes."

There was something in his tone that made Libby turn back around. He was staring at his lap, looking so utterly dejected that she had a sudden urge to make him feel better.

"Don't worry. Strangers are always mistaking me for someone else. It's my face, I think. I look very average."

"Average?" His head snapped up. "You don't look average. With that marvelous red hair, you look like Botticelli's Venus."

Libby ran a hand though her long, thick curls. Her hair had been called many things over the years—ginger nut, Weasley, carrot top—but never compared to a Renaissance painting, and she couldn't help but smile.

"Sorry. You must think I'm very strange," the man said. "I don't usually accost young women on the bus and tell them I like their hair, I promise."

"It's fine. I needed a compliment today, so thank you."

"Bad day?"

"You could say that."

"I'm happy to listen if that would help?" He ran a hand over his own hair, which was bright white and stuck out at all sorts of unruly angles from his head. "People often tell me their problems, especially on the night bus. Once they've had a few drinks, complete strangers confess all sorts. You wouldn't believe the things I've heard on here."

For a brief second, Libby considered pouring her miserable story out to this stranger, but where to even begin? "That's a kind offer but I'm okay, thanks."

The man nodded and turned to look out of his window, and Libby returned to hers. The bus wound its way behind Tate Britain and along toward Parliament Square. It was busy this morning, crowds of tourists queueing to get into Westminster Abbey, a small huddle of protesters with placards outside the Houses of Parliament being monitored by some bored-looking police officers. Libby checked her phone; it was two fifteen, and according to Google Maps she should be at her sister's house around three.

The thought made Libby shudder. When she'd turned up at her parents' house late last night, still numb with shock, she had assumed they'd let her stay with them for a few days while she worked out what to do. But this morning, over a strained breakfast at which her father could barely look at her, Libby's mum had announced that she'd called Rebecca, who had offered Libby her spare bedroom. This had struck Libby as odd, given the two of them weren't exactly close, but when she'd tried to argue, her mum had brushed her protests aside. And so here she was a few hours later, on an unfamiliar bus in an unfamiliar city, with her life packed into two ancient bags.

"Excuse me." The old man from across the aisle was looking at her again.

"Yes?"

"I'm sorry to be nosy, but I couldn't help noticing that. Are you an artist?"

Libby looked to where he was pointing and saw an old, battered sketch pad stuffed in a side pocket of her backpack. She hadn't even realized it was there; that showed how long it was since she'd used this bag.

"I'm afraid not. That's from years ago when I was at school."

"Did you draw back then?"

"I did, but I haven't done anything artistic in a long time."

"And why is that?"

Libby opened her mouth to answer and then stopped. Why was she about to tell her life story to a complete stranger? The old man was right; there was clearly something about him that made people spill their secrets.

"I haven't had time" was all she said.

"Nonsense, there's always time to draw. You could sketch me now if you like?"

"Thanks, but I think my drawing days are long gone."

The bus pulled up outside Downing Street and more passengers boarded, their voices a jumble of languages under Libby's feet.

"It's never too late to start drawing again, you know," the man said. "Did you study art at school?"

"Yes, and I wanted to go to art college but . . ." There she went again, about to spill out her guts to him. "I did medicine at university instead."

"Medicine? Lordy, you don't strike me as the doctoring sort. No, I wouldn't trust you with my dickey hips for one minute."

Libby looked up in surprise, but the man winked at her.

"I'm only joking. I'm sure you're a wonderful doctor."

"Actually, you're right. I'm not the doctoring sort. I hated medical school and left before I could do damage to anyone's dickey hips."

The man chuckled and Libby smiled despite herself.

"So, what do you do now, then, if not medicine or drawing?"

She didn't reply, unsure what to say. Up until twenty-four hours ago Libby had worked for Simon, doing the accounts and admin for his gardening firm. But now who the hell knew?

The bus was approaching Trafalgar Square and Libby saw the four majestic lions sitting as defiant sentries, accompanied by a flock of fat pigeons. In the middle, Nelson's Column rose tall above the crowds of tourists and buskers, the admiral on top watching over London like a disapproving parent. Behind him stood the grand pillars and domed roof of the National Gallery. At the sight of it, Libby felt a memory stir. She'd been to the gallery once, on a school trip. Most of her classmates had got bored quickly and complained they wanted to go to Madame Tussauds instead, but Libby had been in awe of the huge building with its ornate ceilings and room after room of extraordinary paintings. But that had been back when she still held out hope of going to art school, before her parents put their foot down about her doing a "proper" degree so she could get a "real" job.

Libby looked at the old man and saw he was lost in thought too, his eyes misty as he stared out the window. He must have sensed her looking at him, as he shook his head as if waking himself from a dream.

"You know, someone once told me you didn't need to go to art school to learn how to draw. She said all you needed was to spend time here, at the National Gallery, and it was like studying under the greatest artists in the world."

"Really?"

"She used to practice sketching on the bus too. She said it was the perfect place to learn life drawing because there's always a choice of interesting models."

"I think I'd find it impossible—far too bumpy."

The man turned to look at Libby. "Have you ever been to the National Gallery?"

"Once, when I was a teenager. I've always meant to go back."

"Well, in that case, why don't we go now? We can start your art education right away!" He reached to the pole behind his seat and hit the stop button with force.

"I'm sorry. I can't," Libby said, and she saw his shoulders sag.

"Of course, silly me."

"I have somewhere I need to be. Plus, I've got these beasts." She indicated her two bags.

"I'm sorry. I don't know what's got into me. I'm behaving very strangely today."

"Not at all. And I will go another time, I promise."

But the man had stopped listening to her, staring back toward the gallery. The bus pulled up at a stop, letting out a low moan as its doors opened. He was still looking out the window.

"You know, I think I'll get off here," he said, pulling himself up into a standing position. "There's a painting I'd like to go and see."

Libby watched as he shuffled out from his seat, clinging to the pole for support. He looked as though he might topple over at any moment.

"Do you need a hand on the stairs?"

"No, thank you. I'll be fine." The man looked down at her. "My name is Frank, by the way."

"It was nice to meet you, Frank. I'm Libby."

"Libby." He smiled as he repeated her name. "Why don't you give drawing on the bus a go? I have a feeling it might suit you." And with that he turned and made his way slowly down the stairs.

Photo by David Levenson

Freya Sampson is the *USA Today* bestselling author of *The Last Chance Library* and *The Lost Ticket*. She studied history at Cambridge University and worked in television as an executive producer, making documentaries about everything from the British royal family to neighbors from hell. She lives in London with her husband, children, and cats. *Nosy Neighbors* is her third novel.

VISIT FREYA SAMPSON ONLINE

Freya-Sampson.com

FreyaSampsonAuthor